The Caretaker's Daughter

Gabrielle Goldsby

Yellow Rose Books

Nederland, Texas

ISBN 1-932300-18-X

First Printing 2004

9 8 7 6 5 4 3 2 1

Cover design by Donna Pawlowski

Published by:

Yellow Rose Books
PMB 210, 8691 9th Avenue
Port Arthur, Texas 77642-8025

Find us on the World Wide Web at
http://www.regalcrest.biz

Printed in the United States of America

For my mother, who gladly spent her last dollar to purchase whatever book I desired. And for my father, who never blinked once when I brought her home for dinner.

Prelude

"BRONTË. BRONTË? WHERE are you, girl?"

"I shall be there in a moment, John." Brontë quickly handed the remaining linens to one of her servants. Picking up her skirts, she ran down the hall and up the stairs to her husband's room.

"What took you so long?"

"Forgive me, John. I was inspecting the linens with Beatrice." Brontë tried in vain to catch her breath as she approached her husband. "May I help you with something?" Her practiced eye sought and found the crop that John used to reach objects just out of his reach. With some relief she noted that it was safely on the bed and could not be used as a weapon this time.

"More likely you were doing her job. You should have made it known sooner that you aspired to be a maid, Brontë. I could simply have hired you as a servant, and made some more advantageous marriage."

Lady Baptiste approached her husband cautiously, aware of his volatile temper. "Did you need something, John?"

"Yes, I need you to help me with this." John gestured angrily at the wooden spokes of his bath chair. "It is stuck in the curtain again." Brontë quickly approached and bent to free the wheel.

John made her pay for her momentary lapse in concentration. He leaned over and slapped her across the face, knocking her to her knees.

"Next time, get here faster, girl," he said.

Brontë had ceased to be surprised by her husband's propensity for sudden cruel acts. Blinking back her tears, she quickly freed his chair and backed away, stopping just out of striking distance.

"Will there be anything else, John?"

John didn't bother to answer; he just waved his hand, much as he would with any of his servants, and dismissed her.

Brontë, glad for the reprieve, picked up her skirts and exited the room hastily. Halfway down the long corridor, she leaned against the wall and allowed hot, angry tears to race down her cheeks.

Chapter
One

WHEN BRONTË FIRST agreed to marry John Patrick Baptiste, she had no idea that her life would end up as it had. She had, of course, suffered no misconceptions about why he had asked her to marry him. As the last living member of his family, John needed an heir, and her mother had produced four strong boys for her father. Her friends and family had seen the marriage as a step up in social status. They had no way of knowing that she would soon become little more than a well-dressed servant in her own home.

Brontë did not mind hard work, for she was not by nature a lazy person. However, whenever he got the chance, John seemed to delight in hurting her. Although the physical bruises did not last long, the fact that her own husband hated her so much for no apparent reason plagued Brontë's nights. Sometimes it almost seemed to her that John blamed her for the injury that caused him to rely on others for his mobility.

John's hatred had not been apparent during their short courtship. Though he was every bit the spoiled gentleman even then, he had been nothing but polite and courteous. Brontë's mother had told her that she should count herself lucky to be marrying someone as well bred as the Lord of Markby.

The Lord wanted heirs, and her father needed money to help him out of a bad business venture. So Brontë had married John with the knowledge that she would be saving her family the embarrassment of having to sell the family estate and assets to pay off the debt. There were advantages to be gained by both families.

GLOOM WEIGHTED THE dark gray skies on the day of the wedding. To Brontë it seemed as if the world were in mourning for her, but she pushed the morose thought firmly from her mind. She accepted the nervous primping from her mother and older female relatives, wondering all the while if she should at least attempt to appear happy. After trying to paste a smile on a face that felt as foreign as her new home, she decided that perhaps a little nervousness would be more acceptable then a pained smile threatening to fail.

"You look beautiful, my sweet." Brontë's mother kissed her lightly on the forehead.

"Mother, I ..." Troubled green eyes begged for a reprieve.

Brontë's mother's face looked compassionate for a split second before it hardened into determination.

"You will learn to love him, Brontë." It was said with so much confidence that Brontë almost believed her. Almost.

Brontë's father led her down the red carpet toward John. Even as Brontë noticed how beautifully the area was decorated, she wondered how the world could go on while hers seemed to be ending.

Finally, she reached John, and her father gave her hand to him. John raised the gossamer white wedding veil and looked at her face. Putting his hand on her chin in what could have been interpreted as a loving gesture, he tilted her face so that he could look into moist green eyes. His handsome brow furrowed; cool blue eyes grazed her delicate blond eyebrows and small pale features as if appraising a prize horse or hunting dog. With a nearly imperceptible nod, John turned to the priest and nodded again.

"We are gathered here today to join ..."

Brontë stared down at the vivid green grass beneath her feet, then looked up at the dark skies. A small drop of water hit her forehead, then another. Brontë wondered if the skies were weeping for her. Behind the priest, in the thick forest surrounding Markby Estates, a movement caught her eye. She watched for a few seconds, but whatever it was, it seemed to have gone. Brontë consciously made an effort to return her attention to the words spoken by the priest.

"...love, honor, and obey, so help you, God?"

"I will."

Brontë wondered at her ability to say the words without them sticking in her throat. She had said them with so much confidence that one could almost believe her a girl in love. Almost.

Brontë drifted through the rest of the day and evening without much thought to her surroundings. John, the dutiful husband, kept a hand on his new wife's person at all times. With each movement of the clock's hands, the walls seemed to creep ever closer. The chill of her mother's lips as she bid her daughter farewell felt as final as last rites.

The wedding night was much as Brontë's mother had explained. Painful, but for the most part uneventful. Brontë stared up at the vaulted ceilings and wondered about the fabulous artisans who had carved the intricate patterns in the dark wood. She had just started to make up a whimsical tale in her head about a family of wood carvers when John grunted loudly and lay heavily down upon her. She felt annoyed that her little tale had been interrupted so soon after she had begun to weave it. Mother had said it would only be a minute or two, but she didn't think John had lasted much past fifteen seconds.

John groaned again and rolled off of her. Brontë got up from the bed and looked at her husband, still breathing heavily with an arm thrown across his closed eyes. Moments later, he heaved himself out of bed and had disappeared through the door that separated the two rooms without so much as a goodnight.

That was it? Brontë thought, as she got out of bed, grateful for the water basin and cloth always left in her room. John apparently had no such longing for cleanliness. The sound of his low fragmented snores could be heard even before she had finished washing herself.

Brontë stood for a moment, staring perplexed into the gently swirling water. She had heard rumors that John had a mistress living not far from the estate. Brontë had always considered such wanton women prey to their own desires; now, though, she wondered if there might be some other reason for them to willingly enter into such a degrading situation. *What kind of woman would wish for that all of the time?* Deciding she would never understand it, she finally returned to bed, and despite the fact that John's snores seemed to increase in volume, was soon fast asleep.

The following morning Brontë was dressed and exploring the large home before John had even awakened. She had been studying the portraits that graced the walls of the estate when she began to feel the disquiet of the secretly observed.

"Pardon me, m'lady."

Brontë turned to find one of the servants standing directly behind her. "Yes?" she snapped, unable to hide her annoyance and discomfort at being caught unaware.

"Lord John asked me to inform you that you should not expect him for tea."

"Did he say when he would return?"

"No, m'lady, but he left with Lord Humphries and Lord Smythe. They took the hounds and I am told they usually do not return until near dark."

"Well, thank you." Brontë shook her head, the solemn-faced young servant's name completely escaped her.

"Thomas, m'lady." With a curt bow, Thomas took his leave.

Brontë was ecstatic to be able to explore her new home without interruption. Walking along the great corridors, she studied the pictures of the men and women of John's family; she hoped fervently that her children took more after her own. She stopped in front of one particular portrait and stared at what might have been a man clothed in a diamond tiara and pale blue ball gown. Leaning closer to the portrait, Brontë read from the plaque beneath it.

"Emmaline Margarite Baptiste."

Brontë stared in awe at the woman she assumed to be John's great-grandmother. She giggled and turned away from the portrait of the rigidly poised, pinch-faced woman.

"Now I understand why John wants all boys."

Brontë reached the end of the great hall and looked curiously at a set of large double doors. Turning the knob, she opened the door and poked her head into the room. Her gasp of delight echoed as she looked at what could only be described as an avid reader's paradise. Brontë walked into the middle of the cavernous room and turned in a circle, mouth agape as she took in the thousands of books that lined the walls of the Markby library.

"My safe haven," she said aloud.

Hurrying to a narrow set of stairs, Brontë practically skipped up them to get to the small walkway that traversed the entire library. She tentatively pushed against a tall ladder that allowed one to get to the top level of books. The ladder moved easily on its tracks, as if it had been lately oiled, though the library had that musty odor that comes to forgotten or abandoned rooms.

Brontë moved along the walkway, trailing her fingers along the spines of the dusty bound volumes, unsure where she wanted to begin. She paused at a volume that had not been pushed back into its proper place.

"*A Compilation Of Greek Myths* by Sir Brice Norton Boyd," she read aloud. Intrigued, Brontë pulled the volume from the shelf. She noted the lack of dust on the book, while the spines of its neighbors were so covered that it was nearly impossible to read the titles embossed in gold.

Opening the book, Brontë gasped with delight at the colored sketches that graced the gilded pages. She traced the strong lines of Pegasus with her fingertips as she read about how Zeus created the winged creature. Closing the book, Brontë took her find back down to the main level of the library. She opened a window, hoping to ease some of the stuffiness in the room, and settled into a large comfortable leather chair located in a corner.

She was well into a story about Poseidon when the sound of shouting reached her. Brontë put the book down and hurried to look out the open window. Twenty or so hunting hounds were yapping excitedly around three mounted huntsmen. One of the horsemen was lying over the back of his horse, his body limp. Not recognizing the other two men, Brontë realized that the unmoving form had to be John Baptiste.

Brontë picked up her skirts and ran as fast as she could down the long corridor, down the stairs, and out the open front door.

Shocked servants stood rooted in their places as the two men tried to remove John from his horse. Brontë's throat closed in horror as John's body fell boneless to the ground. The two men, Brontë, and the terrified servants all stared in horrified fascination at the unmoving Lord of Markby now lying supine on the grass. Only the hounds, still barking madly, seemed to comprehend the pressing nature of the situation.

Brontë barely noticed when another rider appeared out of nowhere, jumping agilely from a handsome horse. The stranger went quickly over to John and touched his neck, apparently searching for a pulse. Long dark hair secured by a piece of leather fell past broad shoulders and down the strong back, curved down toward the fallen Lord. As if suddenly becoming aware of the chaos, the tall, dark-haired stranger let out a shrill whistle that quieted the dogs almost instantly, then turned shocking blue eyes on the gaggle of stupefied people.

"You there, Thomas, get those dogs into their pen." The voice was deep, authoritative, and demanded immediate obedience.

"You there, help us get the Lord into the house."

The two noblemen reacted as if they had been doused with cold water. They woodenly took up positions on either side of the unconscious man.

"Milady, if you would tell us where we should take Lord Baptiste, we will bring him inside." Brontë ran ahead as the two gentlemen, the stranger, and one of the servants brought John into the house. Noting the length of the staircase, Brontë determined that taking John to his own room would be out of the question. She could already hear the four laboring under the weight of her husband's sturdy six-foot frame. Brontë instead led them to a small room that served as the quarters for servants of visitors to the estate.

John was finally settled on the bed, and Brontë approached to survey his injuries. She had first assumed that John had taken a spill from his horse, but from the amount of blood that coated his stomach and trousers, this was not the case.

"He's been shot!" Brontë said. "What happened?" She tore open John's hunting jacket, unable to stifle a shocked gasp as she surveyed the damage. "How did this happen?"

One of the gentlemen stepped forward and identified himself as Lord Humphries. "We had not even set loose the hounds, milady, when out of nowhere a shot was fired. We all scattered and took cover." His skin darkened and his worried brown eyes looked away from Brontë. "We hid for over an hour. We had no idea where Lord Baptiste was. We had assumed that he had hidden as we had." A thin, graceful hand traced a meticulously groomed mustache. "We found him behind a tree. He looked as you see him now; he had obviously been thrown from his horse after being shot."

"So neither of you is responsible for this?" Brontë looked down at her husband's bloodied chest.

Lord Humphries shook his head from side to side vigorously. "We had not even drawn our rifles to hunt as of yet. We were still taking our positions."

"I beg your pardon, milady, should we not send for the sheriff and Doctor Quimby?" The stranger politely stepped forward, hat doffed. Brontë blinked in surprise as she realized that the person she had, in her haste to get John into the house, assumed was a man, was in fact a woman. A very tall, broad-shouldered one wearing trousers, but a woman nonetheless.

Brontë nodded and turned back to John as the woman left the room, presumably to get the doctor and the sheriff. Brontë fought down the acrid bile that rose in her throat as she cleaned the dried blood around John's wound. She silently prayed that he would live, that the doctor would come quickly, and be able to help him.

It was, however, the sheriff who arrived first. He collected all three hunting rifles, inspected them carefully and announced, "Why, none of these rifles have been fired recently." He seemed more than a little surprised by his discovery.

The tall dark-haired woman returned with the doctor within minutes of the sheriff's arrival. The doctor emptied the room as he rolled his sleeves up and put on what looked to be a butcher's apron. After assuring Brontë that he would let her know if John's condition worsened, Doctor Quimby shut the door, leaving Brontë with the odd group of strangers.

The next two hours were spent in virtual silence, each of them wondering what went on behind the closed door. The sheriff eyed the two men with suspicion while the two Lords eyed the strange woman's attire with disgust, and no one except the tall woman even looked twice at the quiet blonde.

Brontë, for what it was worth, prayed that John would survive. While it was true that she did not love him, she did not wish him harmed.

Realizing at last that she had neglected to introduce herself to the woman who had helped bring John into the house, Brontë approached the stranger who seemed almost to have disappeared into the darkened corner. Somber blue eyes glinted for a moment, then once again dimmed behind half-closed lids.

"Please forgive me. I have been so worried about Lord Baptiste that I did not think to thank you for your help—I do not even know your name."

"My name is Addison Le Claire, milady." Brontë was quite surprised when instead of a curtsey she received a bow. She was not sure that she liked the way this Addison Le Claire looked at her. The voice sounded polite and respectful; the eyes, however, were distant at best.

The rotund sheriff cleared his throat and approached the two women. Addison's body tensed as the sheriff effectively blocked her access to the door. Blue eyes narrowed and the tall body straightened from its relaxed position. She glared at the sheriff as he pulled a watch out of his vest pocket and checked the time, as if bored.

Brontë felt a chill as she saw Addison's posture change. "I think I am going to sit down and wait for the doctor," she said, hoping that the sheriff would follow suit.

The sheriff, who had not been blessed with Brontë's quick mind, had decided it was time to put this creature in her place. He coughed a few times under Addison's unwavering gaze. Brontë thought Addison looked amused, though the emotion did not quite reach her eyes. "I believe you informed us that your name was Addison Le Claire?"

"Yes, that is what I informed Lady Baptiste."

"What, exactly, is your business here at Markby Estates?"

"I live here," Addison said.

The sheriff's first and third chins quivered as he guffawed. His rodent-like eyes regarded Addison's well-worn but clean attire with contempt.

"You live here, you say?" He cast amused looks about the room before returning his attention back to Addison.

"Yes," she said, now glaring at the sheriff as he, in his amusement, stepped even closer to her, his stomach protruding so far out that if he were to take a deep breath, he would no doubt come into contact with her. With a profound certainty, Brontë felt that the sheriff had waddled his way into a great deal of danger. Ever the peacemaker, Brontë attempted to give the sheriff time to escape those flashing blue eyes.

"May I ask what your duties are, Miss Le Claire?" Brontë inquired before the sheriff could get himself in any more trouble. She experienced a moment of anxiety in which she feared her question would not be answered.

"I am the caretaker's...the caretaker's daughter. I help him with the horses, game, and the livestock, as well as anything that needs to be fixed here in the house or on the grounds."

"And where is your father now?" the sheriff asked, still

unaware of his precarious situation.

"He...he was not feeling well this morning."

"Not feeling well? I would think you people come from hardier stock than that." Brontë winced as the sheriff laughed at a joke only he seemed to understand. Addison went on as if she had not been interrupted.

"I told him that I would check the gardens and the fences on my own. I was on my way to check the fence on the west side of the property when I heard the cries for help."

Addison never raised her voice or made any perceptible move or threat toward the dim-witted man in front of her. He must have sensed the peril anyway because he finally backed away from the cornered woman, who smirked and relaxed against the wall.

"So, you are the caretaker's daughter?"

"That is what I said."

"You and your father must have at least one hunting rifle, then?" From the sheriff's tone it was obvious that he intended to get the information from Addison whether she liked it or not.

"Yes, we do."

"Well, speak up, woman. Where is it?"

"It is in my cottage."

"Do you not carry it with you?"

"Why should I? I was not hunting."

"Yes, well. I will want to see that gun. Just so we can rule it out as being the one that fired the shot that kil—injured Lord Baptiste."

"Of course." Addison and the sheriff stared at each other for a moment before he turned on his heel and stalked back to the chair.

"You should be taking care of babies, not taking wages from hardworking men." The words dropped from his lips like stones, sending new waves of tension radiating throughout the room. Brontë fought the urge to laugh. Everyone's eyes went to the sheriff, who seemed unaware or uncaring that he had voiced the thought.

Addison straightened from the wall, blue eyes glinting. Brontë racked her brain for something to say that would defuse the situation. She looked for help from the other two men, but they were watching Addison nervously. The sheriff, still unaware of the tension in the air, blew hot air onto the face of his pocket watch before cleaning it on the front of his vest.

Several things happened at once: Addison took two steps toward the sheriff, Brontë leaped from her seat, the two gentlemen each took a nervous step back, the sheriff's eyes bugged out, and the doctor opened the door to the room where he had just finished operating on Lord Baptiste.

"Lady Baptiste, you may see him now. He has yet to regain consciousness, but I am afraid that I have done all that I can for him. I will return tomorrow to check on his condition."

The doctor approached the sheriff as Brontë entered the room to see her husband of one day. Several blankets covered John's nude, six-foot frame, making him look much smaller than usual.

He almost looks asleep. She brushed the hair back from his forehead and wondered if she would ever get to know her husband. Deep in the recesses of her mind, a tiny voice questioned whether she wanted to get to know him. *What kind of person has people trying to kill him?*

Brontë frowned, feeling she was betraying John by her thoughts, but she could not shake them off. No, it was true she did not love John, but he was her husband, and she would give him her loyalty for as long as he breathed.

With that determined, Brontë returned to the front room to question the doctor about the seriousness of John's injuries.

The doctor was already writing explicit care instructions. "I do not mind telling you that I am worried about him. He was extremely lucky. The bullet passed straight through his side and out his back, managing to miss all vital organs. I am more worried about the swelling around his neck. He could have been injured further after he had already been shot. I have seen injuries like his from people thrown from their horses, and they usually do not recover completely."

Brontë blanched at Doctor Quimby's dire proclamation. She looked up just in time to see Lord Smythe's pasty complexion pale even further; they shared the memory of John's body falling to the ground, Smythe's hands grasping uselessly at air. Brontë chose to ignore Lord Smythe's reaction. Bringing up such things at this point would help no one.

"Well, then I suppose we should leave the Lady to see to her husband," the sheriff said. Strolling over to Brontë, he gallantly bent over her hand and kissed it. Brontë forced herself not to wipe her hand on her dress. "I shall meet you at the caretaker's cottage, Miss Le Claire. I will, of course, need to see all the rifles that you may have access to." He turned and swept out of the room with the heated stare of Addison Le Claire burning into his shoulder blades.

Brontë shuddered. Addison Le Claire was not someone to be taken lightly, yet the sheriff seemed to want to go out of his way to irritate her.

Addison straightened from her position leaning against the wall and cleared her throat. "If I am no longer needed here, milady, I will see to the Lord's hounds and horse."

"No, I think that should be all, Miss Le Claire."

"Very well then, milady. Good night." With a curt nod to the others in the room, Addison moved toward the door.

Brontë forced herself to remain still as the tall woman brushed past. There was something very disconcerting about her. Although Addison was probably no more than a few years older than she, she just seemed to be much more knowledgeable. *It is as if she knows a secret.* Brontë colored at the direction her thoughts had taken.

"Would you mind if we saw Lord Baptiste before we left?" Smythe asked, speaking his first words of the evening.

"Of course not," Brontë said, stepping aside to allow them to enter. The doctor had just finished gathering all of his tools, and, after further assurance that he would be by the next day, he was out the door. Brontë sank into an overstuffed chair and closed her eyes.

Both men returned from their visit with John looking pale and drawn. It was obvious to Brontë that they were thinking about how close they had come to being in the same position.

They tried to make polite conversation, but it was apparent to Brontë that both men wanted nothing more than to escape to the safety of their respective homes. When the door closed behind them, it echoed with finality throughout the house. Brontë stared after them for a moment before she entered the room and sat next to John's bed, trying to figure out how she would handle the situation.

"You will not panic," she told herself, though her ears strained for the cautious steps of a servant, the scuttle of a mouse, or any sound that would disprove her feeling that the house had joined her in some kind of macabre deathwatch. "There is nothing here to be afraid of," She told herself. After a few moments, the muscles in the back of her neck began to relax. Brontë allowed her mind to drift. She closed her eyes, intending only to rest them, but she must have fallen asleep.

"Pardon me, milady, I did not wish to wake you." Disapproving brown eyes scraped Brontë and settled on John. "I was told this morning what had befallen poor Lord Baptiste. Is there anything I can do for him, milady?" The servant's voice had a humble but oily quality. She wondered if she was just being silly. There was something about this man that she did not like.

"Thank you, Wesley. I believe that the Lord is as comfortable as can be expected. Am I needed for anything?"

"Oh, no, milady, nothing that I cannot handle. Cook is in need of a signature on the receipt for the food. I will be happy to do that for you since I know you are very busy."

Brontë watched as the man backed out of the door with a humble smile plastered across his face. She frowned; *Perhaps things are done differently at Markby.* Just as Wesley turned to go, she saw what could only be described as contempt on his face. Brontë caught him before he entered the kitchen.

"Wesley? Has Lord Baptiste allowed you to sign Cook's receipts in the past?"

"Well, no, milady, but I had assumed..."

"Then why would you think that I would want you to sign for them now?" Brontë studied Wesley with interest, hoping she had been mistaken about his intent.

Wesley opened and closed his mouth, his hand fluttering to his chest. "Well, Lady Baptiste, surely a Lady of your stature does not need to be bothered with such issues, especially with the Lord being so sick." The oily tone had crept back into his voice as he commented on the man's obviously serious injuries.

"Nevertheless, as Lady of Markby I will be handling all of my husband's affairs for the time being."

Brontë turned away from the servant to retrieve the list with John's care instructions.

"But, surely, milady does not wish to..."

"Enough, Wesley!" *How dare he question my authority?* She was the Lady of Markby, and he would damn well mind his manners or he would be out on his ear. "I will let it pass this time; however, I will not have my decisions questioned by you. Furthermore, if I need your assistance in a matter, I will seek you out and request it. Is there anything you do not understand, Wesley? I shall gladly write it down for you, if you feel there is need."

"No, milady. I mean, yes, milady." Wesley gave a stiff, slight bow and turned to walk away.

"One moment please, Wesley. Please take this list to Cook and ask her to make sure that we have everything on it delivered by this afternoon."

"Yes, milady," Wesley said curtly. "Will there be anything else, milady?"

"Yes, now that you mention it, there is. Please have all of the receipts for the last month delivered to me in Lord Baptiste's office."

Looking as though he were close to arguing, Wesley uttered a strained "Milady" and exited the room as quickly as he could.

A low chuckle followed his exit, and Brontë whirled to find Addison standing in the open door with a large trunk at her feet. The smile on her lips seemed strained and did not reach her eyes. Brontë wondered if Addison Le Claire ever really allowed herself to smile.

Chapter
Two

"IF I MAY say so, milady, you handled that very well. I believe old Wesley has been allowed to do as he wishes inside this house for so long that he believes that he is the Lady of Markby."

"He would not have lasted ten minutes in my mother's home," Brontë stated before she could catch herself. She realized that she probably should not be talking to one servant about another. It was odd, but she didn't think of this self-confident woman as a servant. Not that she believed in mistreating any servants. In fact, the sharpest she had ever had to speak to anyone had been to Wesley tonight.

The tall woman gave Brontë another half smile and pointed down at the trunk in front of her. "These were delivered early this morning. With everything that has happened, I thought you might sleep late. I asked that they be left at the door and told them I would make sure that you received them."

"Oh, wonderful! I wondered when the rest of my belongings would arrive. I will find a few of the other servants and we can get them moved." Brontë had already started for the east wing of the house when Addison called out to her.

"Milady, if you will just tell me where you want them, I can move them myself."

"But surely they are too heavy for..."

Addison had already hoisted the larger of the trunks onto her shoulder and was waiting for instruction.

"Are you sure you will not need help?" Brontë turned and led the dark-haired woman to the stairs.

"I have lifted things heavier than this trunk all my life," Addison said as she easily traversed the stairs.

"So much for the whole 'lifting heavy objects will stunt your growth' theory."

A surprised chuckle from behind caused Brontë to peer over her shoulder, as she realized the tall servant had overheard her murmured comment. *So, she does indeed have a smile, and a beautiful one, at that.*

Addison considered the events of the last few days, and the Lady's responses to them. Perhaps she had been wrong about this one. Maybe she could trust her. Addison studied the small form in front of her curiously. *No, I cannot. She is like the rest of them.* Addison vowed to stay away from her. She only remained at Markby to find information. After she found what she needed, she would leave this hellish place and never look back.

Addison followed Brontë into what she assumed was the suite in which the Lady slept. Moving with a slight hesitation, as though feeling odd in this room, Addison placed the trunk on the floor and turned to retrace her steps.

"Oh, Miss Le Claire, would you be so kind as to leave the trunk marked books in the library?"

Addison turned and looked as if she wanted to refuse the request. "Yes, milady," she said, and all but ran from the room. Brontë looked after her, confused. *What was that all about? It is not as though I asked her to do something difficult.*

Brontë went downstairs, and, after checking on John, went in search of Addison. She found her glaring down at the remaining trunks, back tensed and balled fists shoved deep into her pockets. Brontë watched as Addison lifted a trunk, shook it gently, then set it back down. She repeated the process twice more before she hoisted the largest of the three to her shoulder and then turned so quickly that she almost ran into Brontë.

Addison waited, her expression unreadable, as Brontë stood with a confused frown on her face. *What is wrong with the servants here? How dare she shake my belongings?*

So there they both stood, staring at each other, both angry, and both inexplicably hurt by the other's volatile stance.

"I will just put this in the library, milady." Addison walked past Brontë, careful not to touch her as she went.

"Addison?"

"Yes, milady." Addison would not meet her eyes.

"Nothing. Thank you."

"You are welcome, milady."

Brontë watched Addison until she disappeared from sight. Without even realizing she had done so, Brontë moved into John's room and sank down into a chair. She felt drained, as if she were becoming ill, and yet strangely invigorated at the same time. "I am not even sure who won that battle."

ADDISON WALKED QUICKLY up the corridor and down the long hall toward the library. She'd expected this at some point; she just had no idea it would be so soon. Addison was not a stupid person; she was good with figures, and even better with her hands. But when she looked at words they seemed to blend together. Where everyone else seemed to be able to tell a "b" from a "d", Addison could not.

She still remembered how frustrated her father had been when he was teaching her how to write her name. Addison had excelled in math and art, but in reading she just could not comprehend the gibberish before her. Eventually the attempts at lessons had ceased, never to be mentioned again.

Addison opened the door to the library and looked around for a place to leave the trunk. Spotting an out-of-the-way corner, she sat the trunk down and headed toward the door. Passing a comfy chair, she spotted a book lying open on a leather chair. Picking it up, she ran her hands over the pictures.

"Did I leave this out?" she muttered.

Addison took the stairs two at a time up to the narrow walkway that surrounded the library and found the open space where it should have been. Carefully replacing the book, Addison stroked the spine, deep in thought. She had often wondered what the words there meant. Though she could not read, Addison was hungry for information. She came here as often as she could. It astounded her, the number of books in this quiet place. Several of them had portraits and other interesting pictures in them. Addison, herself an artist, found these books the most interesting. She would sometimes just stare at the text and try to see what others saw, but she could not. Her Papa had loved her, but even he had given up on her. It was the reason that he had taught her how to work with her hands, fearing that his tall and wide-shouldered daughter would be left in this world with no one and no way to take care of herself.

Addison knew that, as ill as her father had been, he had hung on because he was afraid for her well-being. Addison had miraculously led an uneventful life at Markby. The Lord's family had only spent half the year at the country estate in the past. Addison had grown up there, so none of the servants thought that the type of work that she did was unusual; it had simply always been so. When Lord John's father passed away, the large house in London was sold for reasons no one quite understood, leaving all of its nearly three-dozen servants without work. The country estate, Markby, was willed to his only son.

Addison remembered one of the last conversations she had had with her father before he passed away. Addigo Le Claire had no doubt in his mind the old Lord would have had him removed from the premises years before if not for his knowledge of blooded horses.

"Addison, please come here," Addigo called from his sickbed.

"Yes, Papa." Addison wiped her father's dark brow with a handkerchief. *"Are you feeling poorly, Papa?"*

"No, I feel much better today." Addison smiled; that was always his response to that particular question.

"I am worried for you, Addison. This young Lord is not as honorable as his father. The father, devil that he was, had honor; he would keep his promises. This one, I do not know. He has watched you for as long as I can remember with nothing but hate in his eyes. He will be trouble to everything he touches."

Addison held her father's hand and tried to understand what he was saying.

Other than handing him the reins to his horse, Addison had had little or no interaction with the young Lord. She, too, had seen his looks of hate and disgust, but she had assumed that it had been the fact that she was a girl being allowed to do a man's job. Addison had ignored it as she had ignored many comments about her size and how rough she was over the years. It was of no concern to her if this rich boy looked upon her with disgust. Addison could take care of herself, and she thought her Papa was worrying for naught.

"Papa, do not worry about..."

"You must listen to me, Addison. Do not underestimate him. That boy has resented you since birth because of who and what you are. And who or what he really is. Stay away from him. Promise me, if something should happen to me, you will go to your aunt in Paris. She has agreed to help you with your art. You must not stay here in this evil place. It will take you as it has taken the rest of us."

"Papa, Papa, I do not understand." Addison's father, exhausted by the effort of talking, fell into deep sleep.

Releasing her father's hand, Addison had quietly left the small cottage and started her chores.

Addison continued to stroke the spine of the book as she thought of her father. Over the last year, Addigo had grown more and more sick; she had begun to take on more of his duties. It had been so gradual that no one really thought much of it. When others would ask after Addigo, Addison would make up some excuse for his whereabouts. The old Lord, and, so far, the new one, rarely took notice of who did what as long as it was done. And Addison was meticulous about there being no cause for complaint. Even Wesley had to admit that she was an excellent worker. He had watched her enough to know; Addison had caught him sneaking around the cottage on more than one occasion. She had threatened to tell the Lord of his unwanted attentions if he did not steer clear of her home, and that had seemed to scare Wesley away, at least temporarily.

Addison brushed away the tears that streaked her sun-darkened cheeks; she unconsciously placed her hand over the letter that she had carried close to her heart for the last six months.

The new Lady of the house seemed to be different from the now-deceased Lord Senior and his spoiled offspring Lord John. She seemed to be very observant. Addison remembered watching from the forest as the wedding vows had been spoken. She wondered why this woman, girl really, would marry such a weak-spirited man as the new Lord. Something had drawn her to watch the wedding that day. She had been unable to turn away when the veil was lifted and she caught her first glimpse of Brontë, Lady Baptiste. She felt herself lean forward to get a better look, her breath coming in shallow gusts only to be halted completely when the Lady had looked directly at the area where Addison hid. Addison was sure she had been seen, but the Lady had looked away after a moment, allowing Addison to breathe once again.

Addison had spent all of her twenty-two years on Markby Estate. She had spoken to Lord Baptiste all of four times that she could remember. His cocky, almost feminine, strut was enough to make Addison frown. The way he dressed was also rather flamboyant. Both Lords, senior and junior, had an affinity for bright colors.

When Addison was fourteen she had taken to calling them the Peacocks of Markby and had received a hard smack on the behind from a very irate Addigo.

"Listen to me, Addison Mari Le Claire. You will not speak in such a fashion about the Lord and his son. At least not while we live on these grounds."

Addison frowned even now as she remembered the fear in her father's voice as he looked around, etched clearly as well across his dark handsome face.

"But, Papa, why do we stay? I am told that you are the best. Why do we stay here when you are barely paid enough for the work you do? They are taking advantage of you, Papa. You are worth so much more than this." Addison had gestured wildly at the two-room cottage that had at one time been used as a gamekeeper's hut.

"This is my home, Addison." Addigo sat down on the small cot that he slept on and pulled off his boots. *"Where would you have us go? There is so much more to it than you will ever realize. I know that you ache to paint, and I will write my sister in Paris when you get older so that you may go there to study. But as for me, I do not wish to leave here. Not until I find ..."*

*Addison was looking at her father with such utter joy that Addigo
had paused in what he was saying.*

"Paris, Papa? Me? Really?"

*In that moment, Addigo saw Addison for what she was, a child.
Even at fourteen she had been somber and a loner. Often mistaken for an
adult because of the way that she held herself, Addigo was aware that his
daughter carried the weight of the world on her shoulders. Not for the
first time, he wished that her mother had taken a part in her upbringing.
Addigo looked at his even-then nearly six-foot-tall daughter and wondered if he could have done anything differently. He looked into her dark
blue, intelligent eyes and felt pride. Addison, though stubborn, bad-tem-
pered, and headstrong, was a kind person with a good heart. A parent
could not ask for more than that from his only child.*

*He had picked her long lanky frame up off the floor and spun her
around as he had when she was a small child. They both had giggled gleefully at his antics, young Perry barking along with them. Addigo had
sent his daughter off to bed with the knowledge that one day her dreams of
studying art would perhaps be realized.*

Addison hurried down the narrow spiraling staircase as she
realized that she had lost track of time. The Lady was probably
wondering where she was. Her long strides carried her to the front
door in no time. She quickly grabbed one of the last two trunks,
carried it up the stairs, set it next to its mate and headed back down
to get the last one. Addison was on her way up the stairs with the
last trunk when she caught a flash of movement out of the corner of
her eye. Victoria, a blonde scullery maid with hands far too soft for
one with such a position, was standing at the top of the stairway.

"Good morning, Addison. My, that trunk must be heavy. You
must be very strong to carry it so easily." The ever-present grin
creased Victoria's lips and a less astute person would think the
woman quite comely.

Addison shifted the trunk from one strong shoulder to another
so that she could better see the simpering figure of the scullery
maid. Addison smirked for a moment, remembering the soft body
underneath the white and blue dress.

"I am sure you will be sore after you are done working today.
If you like, I would be happy to rub the muscles that ache tonight.
Then we could..."

Addison's eyes narrowed as the presumptuous woman went
into erotic detail about what she would be willing to do to help her
get over her aches and pains.

In a moment of weakness nearly a year ago, Addison had taken
the girl up on her thinly veiled offer of sex. The annoying little
strumpet had pestered her for weeks until Addison, sweaty and

dirty from stacking hay, had finally given in to her unwanted advances. Her intention had been to teach Victoria a lesson, and perhaps to gain some relief in the process.

Addison stared in disbelief at the promiscuous young woman.

"You know you want me, Addison. I have seen how you look at women when you think no one will notice."

"Perhaps I do, but what does my looking at women have to do with your offering yourself to me like a common trollop?"

While the insult would have offended most people, it did not seem to bother Victoria in the least. Addison watched as a look of amusement passed over Victoria's features. She had long since given up trying to pretend that she was something she was not. Promiscuous? Victoria had invented the word. She not only loved being loved; she used it to give her power over as many people as she could.

Addison had heard her say on more than one occasion that the only reason that she was still a scullery maid was because she chose to be; there was no pressure in the job. She loved telling anyone willing to listen that she could be head of the kitchen if it was her wish. Addison had often seen Mary, Beatrice or even Cook doing Victoria's job, their hands often chapped and red from the strenuous work. Victoria came and went as she pleased and was never reprimanded.

She used sex as her tool to get what she wanted, and from what Addison could see, she was doing quite well for herself. To Addison, the only difference between Victoria and a woman who sold her wares on the street was that Victoria was good at what she did because she liked it. Now she had set her sights on Addison.

"What is the matter, Addison? Are you afraid that you will not be able to pleasure me as well as the others?"

Addison felt her pulse quicken, then calm, as she forced herself to ignore the excitement in Victoria's voice. "I would rather be alone than bed you," Addison said as she continued her work.

The warm hand on her forearm was a shock to Addison, causing her to react without thinking. She dropped the pitchfork and grabbed Victoria's wrist. With a quick tug, Addison pulled her close and growled, "Did I give you permission to touch me, Victoria?"

"Come now, Addison, I know I am not wrong about you. When did you last bed a woman?" Victoria had tossed her head and continued in the same taunting tone, "You should be happy that I want to touch you. It is not likely that anyone else ever would."

As the pressure on her wrist increased, Victoria viciously continued her verbal attack, reveling in the fact that she had gotten a reaction from Addison. "You know, it really is a shame," she said, as she moved her hand down Addison's prominent cheekbones before Addison could jerk away in disgust. "You really are quite beautiful. All the men should be

*clambering for your hand, but they never will because you are more a man
than any man would ever be, is that not true, Addison? But I am sure you
do not care, do you, Addison? I am sure your dreams are not of strapping
young men, are they, Addison? You only covet women, is that not true?
Tell me, Addison, what would Addigo say if he knew what..."*

*Addison picked the maid up, threw her onto the bales of hay, and took
her viciously. Victoria had not only reveled in it, she had continued to
taunt Addison until they had both reached climax.*

Addison had regretted her loss of control ever since. The girl
had the most annoying habit of popping up wherever Addison was.
She had no business in the stables or the barn, but Addison would
often look up from shoveling hay or feeding the animals and find
her there, and nearly half-naked, at that. It was not that Addison
failed to find her attractive. She just knew what she wanted out of a
woman, and it was not to share her with everyone who showed a
passing interest. Addison truly did regret using the girl; however,
it was not as if she had been her first, nor was she anywhere near
her last.

"Victoria," Addison started to tell the girl to be done with her
incessant chasing, but another voice spoke first.

"Victoria, you have no business being on this side of the house.
Please return to the kitchen. I am sure that Cook can find something for you to do if you are bored," Brontë's mouth was set in a
stern line, her arms folded against some of the words she had just
heard.

"Yes, m'lady." Victoria escaped into the kitchen and Addison
wished that she could follow her.

Addison studied the new Lady of Markby with a guarded
expression; she wondered exactly how much of the conversation
she had overheard. Noting the red face of the Lady in question,
Addison was certain that she had been privy to all of the sordid
things that Victoria had said to her. She was used to such things but
she was sure that the Lady had never heard such bawdy talk.

"Milady, I ..."

"Addison, if you would continue what you were doing, that
would be most appreciated."

Face hot with embarrassment, Addison quickly climbed the
stairs, kicked the door open, and all but threw the trunk onto the
bedroom floor. She stalked back into the hallway, barely resisting
the urge to slam the door behind her.

Chapter
Three

ADDISON HAD HOPED to escape from the house without another encounter with the Lady. However, Lady Baptiste had not left her position at the foot of the stairs. They were saved from a possible confrontation by a knock at the front door.

Mary appeared in the foyer and opened the door to Doctor Quimby, who immediately held Lady Baptiste's full attention. Addison was able to slip, unnoticed, through the door and run to the barn, where she could lick her wounds in peace.

Addison viciously kicked a wooden pail that was sitting in the middle of the floor. She would teach Victoria a lesson for sure. Addison rolled up the sleeves on her shirt and threw her vest haphazardly into a corner as she began to shovel hay. After nearly two hours, the hay, which generally should have taken two grown men a full day to pile, was neatly arranged in a corner. As was usual, the hard manual labor had lessened Addison's anger to the point that she was no longer seeing red at the thought of Victoria's name.

She stiffened as she felt a presence behind her, pushed down the anger that threatened to well up in her anew. "Listen, you pig-headed woman, I have told you once, and I am not going to tell you again, leave me al—"

Addison turned around to look into the amused calm emerald eyes of the Lady Baptiste.

"Oh, milady, forgive me. I thought you were... someone else." Addison found herself floundering for the right words.

"Do not worry. I should have announced my presence as soon as I came into the barn; I just didn't want to scare you. You looked as if you were deep in thought."

Addison, feeling self-conscious, began to roll her shirtsleeves down over her muscular forearms.

"May I help you with something, milady?"

Brontë looked around the barn and then back at the tall woman who stood in front of her, the mask of indifference firmly in place again.

Brontë sighed, "Addison, I came to apologize. I am afraid that I was so disturbed by what I overheard Victoria saying that I took it out on you. I am usually not so unfair, and I am sorry for jumping to conclusions. I will talk to Cook about Victoria's language, as well as her behavior towards you, if you like."

"My...milady, if you do not mind, in regard to Victoria's behavior towards me...I would much rather talk to her myself. That way there will be no bad blood between us. After all, we still have to work here together."

"Of course, Addison. However, should she continue with her pursuit, please let me know, and I will make sure she is no longer employed at Markby."

"Yes, milady. Thank you."

"You are welcome." Brontë smiled and left Addison to her chores.

Addison watched her go, blinking her eyes in shock. Not only had the Lady apologized, but she had also offered to talk to Victoria on her behalf. Addison would have loved to let the Lady talk to Victoria, but she was too afraid of what would have come out of Victoria's mouth if her back was up against the wall. *No, it will be better if I deal with Victoria.*

BRONTË ENTERED THE house and went straight to John's room to check on him, then up to the office. There, neatly stacked on the desk, were the food receipts she had requested.

Brontë went over the receipts with a fine-toothed comb. To her surprise, she found little out of the ordinary save the sheer amount of food purchased. Brontë thought it odd that Markby purchased three times more food than her parent's fully staffed estate required. Still, all of the food had been delivered to Markby, and none of the items ordered seemed out of the ordinary, so she signed the receipts for payment and took them downstairs to Cook.

Cook's face had a constant jolly red flush, as she had spent half her life standing over steaming food pots.

"Cook, I just signed the receipts for payment, but I have a question for you. It seems like an awful lot of food was purchased last month; did you have a special occasion to prepare for? I am not talking about the reception, as I have yet to see the receipts for that."

"No, m'lady, I didn't. The food rarely peaks. It is always about the same, give or take a few things as I run out. I am very careful about how I plan my meals, you see."

"I see. Well, here are the signed receipts." Brontë turned to go and paused.

"Cook, is there any way you can get the receipts for the past few months?"

Cook thought about it for a moment. "Well, m'lady, Sellers will be by tomorrow morning to stock the pantry. I can ask him to bring them by."

"Good, and Cook, I would like to keep this between us for now. Understood?"

Cook nodded, "Yes, m'lady."

Brontë left the kitchen and almost ran into Wesley, who had either been eavesdropping or was in the process of licking the door.

"Oh, m'lady, please forgive me. I was just going in to talk to Cook about something," he explained nervously.

Brontë looked at Wesley for a moment and then, without a word, turned and left him standing where he was.

There was something strange about Markby, though she could not quite say what. Brontë decided that she would watch the servants closely, especially Wesley. He was definitely up to something. Cook, Beatrice, and Mary seemed to be hard workers, but Victoria was entirely too comfortable with herself. Thomas was nice, but had only been at Markby for a few months, and was unlikely to know what was going on. Brontë entered John's room and sat down in a chair next to his bed, absently sighing as she noted that there appeared to be no change in his condition.

That left Addison and her father, Addigo. Someone had said that Addigo had been the caretaker at Markby for twenty-four years. That would mean that Addison had been at Markby all of her life. For some reason, Brontë was sure that she could trust Addison. Her blue eyes mirrored the honesty in her heart. The anger she had felt when the sheriff had invaded her space had been plain, as clear as her hurt when Brontë had ordered her to continue in her duties earlier.

"Victoria." Brontë frowned. The things that woman had offered to do to Addison had made Brontë blush. She had no idea people did that to each other; any people, let alone two women.

Victoria had seemed suitably surprised to find that her graphic overtures had been overheard, but not to the point of fear, as she should have been. Brontë would have had every right to dismiss her on the spot, yet Victoria had reacted like the child who had been caught with her hand in the cookie jar, not at all like a servant about to lose her job. And why had she been so rude to Addison earlier? It was not as if Addison had said a word during that deluge of filth Victoria had been spouting. Brontë shook her head, deciding she was overacting because of the stress of John's accident.

DUE TO CONCERN over inflammation around John's collar-
bone, Doctor Quimby made twice-daily visits to Markby for several
days following the accident. On the third day, satisfied that the
Lord of Markby was out of immediate danger, he made a suggestion to the young bride.

"Lady Baptiste, if I may make a suggestion?"

"Of course, Doctor, please do."

"Are you aware that Wesley was responsible for taking care of
the late Lord Senior?

"No, I had no idea."

"Yes, he did an admirable job."

"I will talk to Wesley about taking over John's daily care."

"Thank you, milady, I was going to suggest that you might
want to think about getting one of the girls from the village, but
Wesley would be a better choice."

"What did the late Lord Baptiste die of, if I may I ask, Doctor
Quimby?"

The doctor hesitated before he apparently decided it would do
no harm to tell her the truth. "He had a liver ailment, milady."

"What caused it, Doctor?"

"It comes from indulging in too many spirits. He indulged up
until his dying day."

The doctor stayed for another few moments before bidding the
Lady Baptiste farewell.

Brontë caught Thomas as he walked by carrying a large tray
full of silverware. "Thomas, would you mind telling Wesley that I
would like to see him please?"

"Yes, m'lady."

Within minutes, Wesley was standing at the room's entryway.
"Milady, Thomas informed me that you wished to see me?"

"Yes, Wesley. I would like you to take on some added responsibility."

Wesley seemed to stand a bit taller at this and his eyes took on
a knowing assuredness that Brontë thought didn't quite fit his
usual humble body language.

"Of course, milady. If you like, I would be more than happy to
take over the day-to-day running of the house as well as supervising the keep and the goings on outside."

Brontë stared at the man who, in his eagerness to take on more
responsibility, had totally let his mask of servitude fall by the way-
side and now stood in his true form—an eager, conniving little man
who wished for nothing less than complete power.

"Wesley, once again you have overstepped your boundaries. I
do not need you to take over my duties at Markby; I am more than
capable of running this household. And I am sure that Addison and

her father are thoroughly capable of supervising themselves, as they have done so without any help to this point. I need you to take over supervision of Lord John." Brontë paused in order to calm herself. "I was told by the doctor that you have some experience in this area, and that you did an admirable job nursing the Lord Senior, so I would like for you to do the same with my husband." Wesley looked from John to Brontë and back again.

"But surely a girl from the village would be better suited for such work, milady." Wesley was nearly sputtering in his attempt not to become angry. "And what of my duties about the house?"

"Pass them on to Thomas. I am sure that he will be able to take on more responsibility." Brontë was beginning to suspect that Thomas was already doing the majority of Wesley's job, allowing Wesley time to meddle in others affairs to his heart's content.

"Thomas is but a boy; surely you do not wish me to become a wet nurse? I have been head man at this estate for nearly fifteen years, and I do not think that Thomas has the ability to do *my* job successfully."

Brontë was growing tired of the verbal sparring and decided to put an end to it before he started to believe that he was free to speak in such a manner to her.

"Wesley, perhaps I have not made myself clear. What I need right now is a nurse for Lord John. What I do not need is someone who supervises people who do not need supervision. So, therefore, I will let you make the decision in this matter. Either you are his nurse or you are without employment."

Aghast, Wesley's hand fluttered to his scrawny neck in shock, his mouth opening and closing as he struggled to either speak or breathe, his face paling past the point of normalcy. He finally regained control of his speech and answered, as he should have in the first place.

"Y-yes, of course, milady. Please forgive me; I had no idea how dire your need for my services in this matter really were. I had only thoughts of Markby when I made the suggestion."

Brontë decided to let him escape with his pride. "Of course you did, Wesley, but as I said before, I am more than capable of running Markby. I do, however, need your knowledge of the infirm at the moment."

"Yes, milady."

"I would like to go up to my room to take a nap. Please sit with Lord Baptiste until I return"

"Yes, milady, I will just go tell the others. It will be but a moment."

"There is no need for that. I will notify Cook, and if need be, she can inform the others of your whereabouts."

Brontë entered the kitchen to find Cook standing at the stove and a slender young woman sitting at a table eating what looked to be soup. Upon Brontë's sudden appearance, the young woman jumped to her feet, nearly spilling her soup in the process.

"M'lady, I am sorry. I didn't get a chance to have breakfast this morning, so I begged some of last night's soup off of Cook."

The girl looked like she was going to keel over from fright.

It took Brontë a moment to place her. "Your name is Mary?"

The girl nodded, still too frightened to look Brontë in the eye.

"Well, Mary, it seems to me that if you went to all the trouble to beg for the soup from Cook here, you should at least eat it before it gets cold."

"Yes, m'lady."

Mary glanced shyly at Brontë from under her eyelashes and all but collapsed into her chair, starting to shovel the soup into her mouth so fast that Brontë was sure she would choke. In no time, she had finished the soup, and after a rather graceless curtsey to Lady Baptiste and a heartfelt thanks to Cook, she was out the door.

Brontë looked at Cook wide-eyed and asked seriously, "Well, do you supposed she swallowed or just inhaled it all?"

Cook's jovial eyes crinkled at the sides as she opened her mouth and howled with merriment. Brontë dropped into the chair at the small table, much as Mary had, and joined her in her laughter. Cook walked over to the table, fanning her heated face with the bottom of her apron. She dropped into the other chair looking around her immaculate kitchen as they both calmed down. She made the mistake of sneaking a peek at her Lady, however, and seconds later they had both dissolved into laughter once again. By the time their laughter had run its course, they were completely at ease with one another, and Brontë seized the chance to ask questions, wanting to learn more of her new home and its inhabitants.

"So, Mary the upstairs maid is the daughter of Beatrice the downstairs maid?"

"Aye, that she is, m'lady. And despite her lack of graces, and forgive me, m'lady, any good sense, never a sweeter girl will you meet. The same with Beatrice, her mother; both of them work very hard."

Brontë nodded. She had spent nearly one-half an hour picking Cook's brain about Markby and its inhabitants. She was glad that Addison and Cook were not the only servants that seemed to earn their keep at Markby. "Cook, do you know why there are so few servants at Markby? From what you're saying, Mary will be my lady's maid now that Mother and her servants have gone, as well as acting as the upstairs maid. Not that you do not all do a wonderful job, it just seems like a lot of work for so few people."

Cook seemed to weigh her answer carefully. "That I do not know, m'lady. But years ago, when the young Lord's mother was here, there were at least ten others hired on from town that I can remember. Now, that may have been too many, but even then it was only for six months."

"So you, Wesley, and Addison and her father are the only servants that live here full time? What of Thomas?"

"Thomas lives in town when the house is closed, as do Victoria, Beatrice and Mary. He is a new one, but he seems to be doing right well. Of course it is hard to say because I only have information about him from Wesley, and in Wesley's book, no one can do a good job unless they have been here for ten years or so. Thomas was hired to be the carriage driver and to help out with the horses, as it was quite a bit of work for Addison to do alone, but Wesley has had him polishing the silver and handling many of the duties which rightly should have been his. The only job that Wesley has not pushed off onto that poor boy is locking up this house every night, and I think that is because he is afraid that someone will come in after *him*. Thomas has only driven the carriage once that I can remember, and I do not think he has ever worked with Addison at all."

"That must make her job very hard."

Cook nodded. "Not that she would ever complain, mind you." Brontë did not miss the pride on Cook's face when she spoke of Addison Le Claire "I think she has been doing the majority of the work around the estate because Addigo has been sick. She will not admit to it, though. That girl has been a hard worker since the day she learned to walk, and so beautiful, too. It is a shame that Addigo has kept her here. It is so lonely and out of the way she will never meet a husband here."

Brontë thought about the one-sided conversation that she had overheard between Victoria and Addison. Addison had not been mortified, as she herself would have been; instead she had looked impatient, as if she had heard it all before and it did not surprise her in the least. Brontë nodded and continued in her questioning.

"And what of Victoria?"

Cook's open face looked as though she had just eaten something bitter. "That one is good for nothing. Even Wesley works more than she does. She comes and goes as she pleases and makes no attempt to work; yet she is always first in line to collect her wages. Her mother Calliope started working here a few months after I did, but she quit working years ago. She was never much for hard work. I do not understand why she is allowed to do whatever she wants around here, but she has for as long as I can remember. I swear it is as if she had something over Lord Senior and that was the reason why she was given free rein." Cook quickly looked up to see what Brontë's reaction would be to her comment.

"But that does not make sense. The Lord Senior has been dead for months now. Yet she is still here and allowed to do what she wants?"

"Yes, m'lady, and I would not underestimate that one. She is hiding something, and she is just the type to drag this house through the mud to get what she wants."

The mysteries of Markby seemed to get even deeper with every new piece of information. Brontë filled Cook in on Wesley's new assignments, smiling as Cook glowed at the fact that Wesley would not be underfoot as much as usual. She also told Cook that she had heard Victoria say something unbecoming to her position and she should be cautioned to curb such bawdy language when at work. Cook promised to speak to both Thomas and Victoria about Lady Baptiste's expectations of them.

"Well, Cook, I should leave you to your work. I will need to go check on John before I can take my nap." Brontë found herself having a hard time keeping her eyes open.

Brontë was able to watch Wesley for a few moments before he noticed that she was there. He was writing something fervently in a small leather-bound book.

"How is he, Wesley?"

Wesley sprung up from his chair, dropping the book that had earned his full attention moments before in the seat behind him.

"Milady, the Lord is still sleeping peacefully. I will need to ask Thomas to help me turn him later so that we may change his sheets, to keep him from getting bed sores."

"Of course, Wesley, I am sure Thomas will be more than happy to help with that. I will return in a few hours."

"Yes, milady."

Brontë climbed the stairs to her room stifling two yawns behind the back of her hand. Looking down at the trunks marked clothing, hats, and books brought her mind back to Addison. She had deduced that Addison was unable to read, or she would have known that Brontë's shoes had no business in the library. Brontë had decided to let her take the trunk into the library rather than embarrass her by mentioning the error. She would need to remember to have Thomas switch them later.

The soft tap to her door interrupted her thoughts. "Come in."

"M'lady," Mary curtsied and looked down shyly at the floor.

"Mary." Brontë turned her back and stifled another yawn. Moments later she stepped out of her clothes and raised her hands above her head. As her sleeping gown was tugged down over her head she blinked a few times and yawned again.

"Will there be anything else, m'lady?"

"No, Mary, that should be all." Brontë's body craved sleep and she moved toward her bed without much thought. The small creak of the door as it was opened reminded her that Mary was still in the room. "Oh, and Mary?"

"Yes, m'lady?"

"Thank you."

"You are very welcome, m'lady."

Brontë lay across her bed and wondered at what type of life Addison had led without the joy of reading. *How do you escape, Addison?* She closed her eyes and fell into an exhausted sleep.

DEEP IN THE woods behind the main house, Addison Le Claire sat in a small converted tool shed, painting. She was in her own world of castles and knights and flying creatures of myth and legend. In the far corner of her colorful painting stood a blonde princess waiting to be rescued from her prison. Below, a fierce knight with a royal crest on his chest did battle against a fire-breathing dragon.

"Well, what do you think, Perry? Will she like this?"

The old hound looked up at the portrait and gave a soft but enthusiastic woof, then thumped her head back down on the wooden floor. Addison smiled. "Ahh, Perry, thank you for the effort, my friend. I know how tired you are today."

Addison draped cheesecloth over the painting and left the small building, calling to Perry as she went. Perry limped carefully from the shed, Addison waiting for her to get through the door before she closed it. Perry lifted her head regally and woofed again at Addison, to which Addison replied, "You are welcome."

Addison left Perry to make it back home at her own pace and headed over to the dog kennels. One of the younger dogs was set to have her first litter and she wanted to make sure that there were no complications. Addison remembered the day the Lord Senior had ordered the dogs moved into the woods. He complained that they made too much noise at night and he wanted them moved immediately. Addison's father had to work throughout the night building the kennels that housed them. Addison had secretly been pleased that she didn't have to go too close to that big monstrosity of a house to play with the puppies. Although, later, she had conceded that the Lord was right. The dogs did make entirely too much noise during the night.

Addison found Sophie resting comfortably on a bed of rags that Addison had set out for her. She gently touched Sophie's protruding stomach and her nose to check for any problems. "Good girl, Sophie. You are doing so well. Markby will have new babies come tomorrow."

Addison left the kennel, but instead of going into her house for the nap that she so badly needed, she continued into the woods behind her home. After taking a few turns and ducking underneath a low-hanging branch, Addison entered the glade that she and her father had found some years before. Her father said that many deer had probably given birth in the little secluded grove. Addison picked up a fallen branch and began to sweep away the leaves surrounding a mound of earth.

"Hello, Papa, I missed you today. But then, I miss you every day. Did I ever tell you that you were my best friend? I am sorry I have not been to see you in a few days, but a lot has happened. As you know, the Lord Senior passed away a few months before you left me. Then the Lord Junior married. Would you believe, the day after he was married, someone took after him with a gun? I am not sure if they will be caught. That sheriff does not know his arse from a hole in the wall. I am telling the truth, Papa. I feel sorry for the Lady, though." Addison stopped cleaning and sat back on her heels.

"You know, Papa, I didn't think I would like her, but she apologized to me today. She didn't have to, but she did." Addison shook her head and fingered the breast pocket of her shirt through her thick pullover.

"I hope you are not angry with me, Papa, because I did not send your letter to your sister. I will, I give my word. I just...there is so much that I do not understand. Who is my mother, Papa? Is she dead? Where is her grave? I buried you here because you asked me to, but where is *she* buried, and why would you not wish to lie beside her? Why didn't we ever visit her?" Addison finished cleaning the grave and fingered the handmade headstone. *Addigo Le Claire* was spelled out in painstaking but jagged letters.

"I know the headstone is not very nice. Perhaps one day I can have someone help me to make another that says more. I love you, Papa. I am glad you do not hurt anymore, but I miss you." Addison stood up and trudged back through the moist woods to her home.

Addison stomped her boots before entering the small house, clearing as much of the mud from them as possible. She was amused to find Perry already lying at the warm hearth, fast asleep. Addison hoped Perry did not suffer from too much pain, her joints tended to bother her on cold evenings. Addison pulled her wool sweater over her head and dropped the bracers that held up the soft, baggy trousers that she normally wore. Unbuttoning her shirt, Addison looked down at her wrapped chest, deep in thought. Victoria's body had been so different from her own.

Shrugging, she poured water into the basin and washed the paint and dirt from the day's work from her body before putting on a sleep shirt and heading out to another small shed that sat on the property. After doing her business, Addison walked back into the house and lay on the cot that for years had been her father's bed. She smiled as she felt Perry move closer to her. "Perry, I know you like to sleep near the fire. I will be fine." Perry whined a little and settled down half under the cot and half out. "Thank you for not leaving me, my friend." Addison wondered dreamily about the new Lady of Markby. "Brontë. What an odd little name. I wonder if she has friends, Perry?" Addison, who was more asleep than awake, smiled when Perry tried to grumpily answer. "I will watch out for her. She needs..." She never finished her comment. Addison and Perry slept. One of them dreamed fitfully while the other moved protectively closer.

Chapter
Four

BRONTË SIPPED HER tea groggily. John's horrible accident had left her completely drained. She had slept through the morning and, based on the low gray light seeping through the billowing curtains, it was already dinnertime. From the moment she had awakened her eyes had been drawn to a portrait of a little fair-haired, fair-skinned girl that hung above the fireplace. The smile on her face looked sad to Brontë. Mary had bustled into the room sometime later and Brontë stood to allow the servant to help her to dress.

"Mary, who is that girl?"

"Girl, m'lady?" Mary finished the last button on Brontë's dress and Brontë placed her hand over her now confined stomach and grimaced. "There, on the wall. The little girl with the blond curls and the blue eyes, she looks very familiar."

Brontë stepped forward and tried to make out the name on the portrait. "Lady...Elizabeth...I cannot read it, it is too tarnished."

"Oh, yes m'lady, now I remember. That is the Lady Elizabeth Markby, Lord Baptiste's mother. He found the portrait in a room of old furniture and clothes. He asked me to clean it and put it in your room."

"Really? Why would anyone put such a beautiful portrait in a room with old furniture in the first place?"

"I do not know, m'lady, that is why he asked me to hang it in this room. Perhaps it was the Lord Senior's doing. Perhaps he could no longer look at her portrait after she...." Mary blushed, realizing she had said too much. "Will there be anything else, m'lady?"

Brontë became aware that Mary was looking at her quizzically. "What? No. No that will be all, Mary, thank you."

Brontë continued to stare at the portrait long after Mary had gone. She felt sorry for John. Though her own mother was a bit much at times, she could not fathom life without her.

"John." Brontë abruptly remembered. Her stomach churned as she remembered the pallor on her husband's face the last time she had seen him. John Patrick Baptiste was her husband and yet he was a stranger, barely an acquaintance. Brontë was in a quandary about how she should feel. Surely she should be more distraught? Certainly she wanted no harm to come to John, or anyone else for that matter. It was just that feeling of foreboding that had haunted her since the day John had asked for her hand in marriage. Her mother had said that it was just pre-wedding nerves and that she would get over it by the wedding night.

She didn't know what was worse, the idea of sleeping with John or the fact that her mother seemed to be thinking about things better left unsaid. Thoroughly disgusted, Brontë had let the conversation drop and had waved a needlework magazine in front of her mother's face.

"Mother, did you get a new magazine today?" The question was all that was needed to launch her mother unrestrained into the merits of embroidery. Brontë pretended to listen as she got her queasy stomach under control. A full half-hour had passed before she was able to retreat to her bedroom. It was a lesson she would never forget. She had avoided any further conversations about sex with her mother. And much to her relief, she had been successful except for the occasional comment here and there.

Brontë was not looking forward to eating alone. The servants, she had been informed, ate much later in the evening, and even then, in their own quarters. Leaving the confines of her opulent but gloomy room, she made her way down the stairs and after a few quick seconds talking to Wesley regarding John's condition, she made her way to the dining room.

The large oak table could have easily sat more than twenty people. Brontë sat at the end of the table near the candelabra.

Seconds later, a beaming Beatrice made her way into the room with a large bowl of a steaming, fragrant soup.

"Good evening, m'lady, you look well rested."

"Good evening, Beatrice." Brontë smiled at the good-natured woman, and then blushed as her stomach made itself known. Brontë realized that she had not eaten at all yesterday. With the excitement of John's accident, she had not given much thought to food. Now her stomach made its displeasure obvious.

Picking up her spoon, she cautiously tasted the soup. Deciding that it was delicious, she gratefully tucked into it, albeit a bit more gracefully than Mary had. Brontë always enjoyed food. Although she had a huge appetite, she would always savor each and every bite slowly.

Beatrice, as Cook had said, was excellent at her job. She kept the courses coming as Brontë eagerly ate everything that was put in front of her. Beatrice had just put a small bowl of custard in front of

Brontë and was turning to leave when Brontë stopped her.

"Beatrice, please sit and talk for a moment."

Beatrice seemed surprised at the request, but she nodded and sat down in the chair across from Brontë. A soft sigh was the only indication that she welcomed the break.

"How long have you been at Markby, Beatrice?" Brontë asked.

"Since Mary's father passed away, so that would be nearly fifteen years, m'lady."

Brontë nodded and continued. "During that time, have you ever known anyone that hated Lord Baptiste enough to want to harm him?"

"Well, no, m'lady, not that I know of. I pretty much keep to myself."

"I understand." Brontë smiled. "But you will tell me if you should hear anything?"

Beatrice was saved from answering by a clamoring at the front door.

"Now who could that be at this hour?" she said to no one in particular. She excused herself from her Ladyship and bustled off to open the door.

A loud commotion in the front entryway caused Brontë to pause with the spoonful of custard only halfway to her lips. She groaned as she recognized the squalling coming from down the hall, one high and female the other equally high and without a doubt of the canine variety.

"Where is my daughter?" a loud, overly dramatic voice demanded.

Beatrice's much quieter voice answered and within minutes, a robust woman with blond hair piled high atop her head and a dog tucked neatly under her arm came rushing into the dining room, Beatrice trailing nervously behind her. Brontë was halfway from her seat when she was engulfed in a tight hug from her mother. The candles in the room dimmed, as if they too were being deprived of air.

"Oh, my dearest, sweet, little girl. And on the day after her wedding, no less. I came as soon as I heard." Brontë took a deep breath after she was released. "Why was I not sent for immediately?"

"Mother, with everything that has happened..." Brontë trailed off as her mother had already turned from her and was pouring a glass of water and settling herself across from Brontë.

"Yes, of course, you were probably too busy taking care of John to contact me."

Brontë flushed. She had not been too busy, she had not wished to deal with her mother, and although she had every intention of letting her know what had happened to John, she had not looked forward to sending word.

"Not to worry, dearest. Mother is here now and I am quite sure that I will be able to help you with the household duties."

Brontë sighed. Why did everyone want to take over her duties? "Mother, Wesley is taking care of John and I am seeing to Markby. Everything will be fine until John is able to see to things again."

"Wesley? *A man?* How could he possibly give proper care to Lord Baptiste?"

"Mother, Wesley took care of the Lord Senior. He has experience with the infirm. At this point there is really nothing I can do for John anyway."

"Brontë Bonnaella Baptiste, surely you do not intend to have one of the servants look after your husband? Why, that is utterly unacceptable!"

Brontë winced as the hated middle name was screeched, causing her mother's pet toy poodle to start his infernal whining.

"Mother, did you have to bring him?" Brontë glared at the creature, cozily tucked into a hand warmer, his beady little eyes peering back at Brontë with just as much malevolence.

"Of course, dear, you know where I go my darling Crumpet goes." Crumpet was actually Crumpet III. Although he was not related to any of his predecessors, he had their same attitude and hatred for anything that would come between Mother and the little dog.

"Well, please make sure that he does not get into anything."

"Oh, Brontë dearest, surely you are not still jealous of my little sweetie?" Brontë and her brothers had long since given up trying to blame anything on the Crumpets, their mother simply would not hear of it. Brontë and Crumpet III got along the least. "Mother, you know as well as I do that dog hates me. He...he waits until I am reading or not paying attention and then he barks as loud as he can...once he nearly caused me to fall down the stairs, I was so startled!"

"Oh, dearest, he was just playing with you, were you not, my sweet little Crumpet?" Brontë watched in disgust as her mother made kissing noises at the dog. Brontë could not resist making a face at Crumpet while her mother was not looking.

Crumpet showed his small fangs to Brontë once and then began his patented whining, immediately answered by Mother, who pulled Crumpet from the hand warmer and, to Brontë's great disgust, allowed the dog to lick her directly on the mouth.

Crumpet III had arrived when Brontë was thirteen years old, which coincided with the last time Brontë had kissed her mother. Brontë shuddered once at the thought of being licked on the mouth by the little infidel.

"Mother," Brontë tried to get her mother's attention away from the dog, as she had just eaten and her stomach had not quite settled. "As I was saying, I can handle the duties here at Markby until John recovers, there is no need for you to stay."

"Of course you can, dear, you are a strong one. I am sure that you would be able to handle it all. But it is a mother's duty to help her only daughter in times like these." She cleared her throat. "Has the doctor been here at all?" She looked around as if expecting him to pop out of the shadows. Brontë rolled her eyes at her mother's display.

"Yes, Mother, he said he would be by often until John regains consciousness. He's the one that recommended that Wesley look after John."

"Oh, well, then, if Doctor Quimby recommended it, then it must be what is best for John." She straightened in her chair and patted her coif.

"Oh, dear, I brought the rest of your books as well. They are in the carriage. That horrible woman in the trousers is helping to unload them. Why John has someone like that working for him is beyond me."

"Mother, her name is Addison and she grew up here at Markby. Besides that, she is a very good worker, so please do not call her a horrible woman. You and Father always taught us to be kind to our servants. I am truly surprised at you, Mother."

"Well dear, I am quite sure that none of our servants ever looked like that."

Brontë decided not to fight a battle she could not possibly win. Her mother's family had always been one step shy of the ruling class. She had married Mr. Havisham for money and didn't see any reason why Brontë should not do the same. When Lord John Baptiste came along with his wealth and title, it had been Mrs. Havisham, not Brontë, who had swooned when he had asked for her daughter's hand.

Brontë heard noise coming from the direction of the front entryway. "Mother, if you will excuse me, I need to tell them where to take the books." Brontë got to her feet before her mother could protest and walked quickly down the hall toward the front door.

Addison had just put down a heavy crate and was grumbling under her breath. "What does she have in here anyway?"

"Books," Brontë said.

"Oh." Addison looked down at the trunks, embarrassed at being overheard. "Shall I put them in the library, then, milady?"

"That will be fine, Addison, thank you."

Brontë smiled at Addison and received a wary smile in return.

The tall servant picked up the trunk and carefully walked past Brontë's mother, politely greeting her as she went by. Brontë's mother harrumphed her answer while both she and Crumpet III, who was in his normal position tucked under her arm, glared after Addison's lanky frame.

"Imagine her wearing those trousers as if she were a man."

"Mother, please do not speak of her in that way." Brontë rubbed tiredly at her aching temples.

"Oh dear, look at you, poor thing, you must be so tired. Why do not you show me where John is so Crumpet and I can sit with him a spell, and I will let you go and take a nap?"

Brontë nodded and decided not to tell her mother that she had awakened from her nap minutes before. She showed her into the room that was now John's.

"Why, you poor dear." Mrs. Havisham sniffled and blinked rapidly. "I had no idea that you were so badly off." She rubbed his pale forehead as if she could will him back to consciousness. "Brontë, are there no better accommodations for him than this? What if he should wake and find himself in the servant's quarters?"

"Mother, I doubt he will care where he is lying when he wakes up. Besides, we were trying to get him to the nearest bed possible, and this happened to be it."

"Well, dear, it just seems to me in a house of this size there has to be more comfortable rooms for Lord Baptiste to recover in than this." She gestured wildly with one hand while the other tucked Crumpet III more firmly under her arm, as if she didn't want him to catch germs.

Brontë looked around; noting that it was indeed small, though impeccably clean, as were most rooms at Markby aside from the library. Exasperated, she turned to her mother and was about to confront her about her snootiness when Wesley walked in carrying a shaving cup.

"Oh, forgive me, milady, I had no idea milord had visitors. Shall I come back then?"

"No, no, Wesley, please carry on. This is my mother, Mrs. Havisham."

"Mrs. Havisham, it is a pleasure to meet a lady of such high regard," Wesley bowed deeply. Brontë's mother dimpled and told Wesley what a fine job he seemed to be doing with Lord Baptiste, and that she had nothing but confidence in his abilities. After the mutual admiration ended, she exited the room, leaving a bemused Brontë to follow behind her. Brontë shook her head at her mother's hypocrisy as she followed her to the sitting room.

"So, Mother, how long will I have the pleasure of your company?"

"Dearest, I shall stay as long as you and John need me. Besides, dear, I think Doctor Quimby will appreciate the fact that he will not have to come all the way to our home for my treatments." She waved her hand in front of her face as if suddenly overcome by heat.

"What treatments? You are not ill, are you?" Brontë noted with concern that her mother's normally pale skin was flushed to a bright red hue.

"Well dear, Doctor Quimby has diagnosed me with 'hysteria of the womb' for which I receive treatments twice weekly."

"Is it serious, Mother?" Brontë was feeling quite guilty for the thoughts she had been having.

"No, dearest, Laura Burskill has the same thing, and so does my sister."

"So this only happens to older women, Mother?"

"Well, yes, dearest, I suppose so. Let's not talk about this right now, I am starting to feel quite tired."

"Oh, of course, Mother, I will go find Beatrice or Mary and have them show you to your room."

"Thank you, dear." Brontë frowned as her mother's face flushed once again and she fanned herself animatedly.

After Brontë's mother was comfortably settled in her quarters, Brontë decided to head down to the kitchen to see Cook. Just before entering the kitchen, Brontë overheard Cook's voice. "But it has to be her, Addison, look at those eyes."

"Cook, I am telling you, I started this long before the Lady even came to Markby. It is just a coincidence."

"Cook is right, Addison. That looks exactly like Her Ladyship."

"Good evening." Brontë pushed the door open and made her presence known.

Addison's smile disappeared instantly upon seeing Brontë. "Good evening, milady." Then she looked at the others nervously and said, "I should be going. I hope she likes it, Beatrice."

With one final look at Brontë, Addison escaped out the back door of the kitchen leaving the rest of them in thick silence. Brontë's curiosity got the better of her.

"What have you there, Beatrice?"

Beatrice looked down at the painting, then up at Brontë as if to decide if she could be trusted. "It is a painting, Lady Baptiste. Addison did it for my niece's birthday."

Brontë smiled at her and stepped closer. "May I see it?"

Beatrice studied Brontë's face before giving the large portrait over to the Lady.

Brontë carefully held the painting in her hand and looked at it with a critical eye. The painting was obviously for a child, yet she could tell that Addison was a very talented artist. Although the colors had been exaggerated, the beautiful lines and shadows blended to create a wonderful depiction of a dark knight battling a fierce dragon in front of a castle while a princess looked on from above.

It was the princess that caused Brontë to pause. The green eyes, the blond hair, even the facial features. Brontë's mouth dropped as she stared at the painting.

"It does resemble me, does it not?"

"That is what I say too, m'lady," Mary piped up eagerly. "But Addison says she painted the princess before you arrived."

"I do not think it looks like m'lady at all," Victoria said sounding like a petulant child.

"Oh, Victoria, it is so m'lady. Look at it." Cook took the painting and held it up and they all looked at the small figure in the window.

"She is very talented, is she not, m'lady?" Cook asked with affection in her voice.

"Yes, she is." Brontë agreed.

"This has to have taken a while to paint, it is completely dry. I only just came to Markby. I am quite certain that if I had seen Addison before, I would remember her."

"No doubt she would have remembered you, too," Victoria said in a molasses-sweet voice.

Brontë glared at Victoria, and then turned back to the image in question, thinking, *This has to be a coincidence.* Addison could not possibly have painted such an intricate painting in one day.

"No, Addison could not paint this in one day," she said aloud. "It is beautiful, Beatrice. I had no idea that Addison was a painter, or that she was this talented." Brontë handed the painting back to the beaming maid with a smile.

"Yes, m'lady, she did this one for my niece, but she has some wonderful paintings in her home that are just magnificent. Addigo said when she is ready, she is to go to Paris to study."

"Addison is to leave Markby to study in Paris?" Brontë was disappointed for some reason. The dark young woman seemed to be as much a part of Markby as the very foundation itself.

"Yes, m'lady, it is all she talks about. You should ask her if she would let you see the others, they are just wonderful," Mary piped up.

"I am sure the last thing m'lady wants to do is go tramping through the woods to see Addison," Victoria said.

Mary flushed and took a step back, her eyes submissively on the floor.

Brontë glared at Victoria. If there was one thing she hated, it was a bully, and poor Mary really was a sweet girl. "Why not, Victoria? You do not seem to mind tramping through the woods after Addison, why should I?"

Victoria's face turned a bright red, her thin lips tightening noticeably at Brontë's comment. She quickly excused herself and went off with the false announcement that she had work to do. Brontë knew she was being sharp with the girl, but she didn't like the way Mary, who had moments before seemed comfortable talking to her, wilted under Victoria's stronger will.

Thomas excused himself and hurried out the door, leaving the rest of them in awkward silence.

Noticing the discomfort in the warm kitchen, Brontë moved to put everyone at ease by telling Cook that she was quite famished and that she had come to beg for a snack. She asked Beatrice, Cook, and Mary to join her, which they all happily did. They spent a very pleasant few minutes munching on bread, cheese, and fruit while getting to know each other. By the time they had finished their snack, each person had a distinct impression of the other. All three servants decided that they liked the Lady Baptiste. They sensed that she could be strong enough to bring a welcome change to Markby. Brontë, on the other hand, was just happy that she seemed to have a good core group of people to help her run the household.

Brontë left the threesome in the kitchen to go check on John, who, according to Wesley, still had not stirred. Brontë sat for a moment with John. Feeling guilty about her lack of feelings toward this man, she awkwardly tried to hold his hand, but felt even worse when she still felt nothing other than a mild sorrow for his plight.

With some vague instructions to Wesley, Brontë left the still oblivious John and made her way up the long flight of stairs. She had felt more remorse for the fate of Crumpet I than she did for her own husband. Of course, she had been partially responsible for the snobbish little dog's untimely demise. How was she to know that Crumpet I would plop his fat self down behind the wheel of the carriage to get out of the sun? And how was she to know that, when the carriage started to roll slowly of its own accord, Crumpet I was far too fat and lazy to get up and get out of the way? She winced even now, a full fourteen years later, as she remembered the fate of Crumpet I. It was the beginning of the nightmare of the Crumpets. Crumpet II was a hideous little fellow who liked to jump into the boys' beds and urinate in them, whether the bed was occupied or not. Crumpet III, the current reigning prince, had always had an incurable dislike for Brontë and seemed to plot to get back at her for some imagined affront.

Brontë shook her head as she stood in front of two double doors. She had been so deep in thought about the Crumpets that she had walked by her own room and was now standing in front of the library. She decided that it might be a good idea to finish reading the book that she had started yesterday. Entering the library, she lit several candles and walked over to the chair that she had been reading in. She was surprised to note that the book was not where she had left it. After looking around the floor for the book, she decided to check the shelf.

It took Brontë only moments to find the missing book. *How strange. The place looks like it hasn't been used in years yet someone reshelves the book that I am reading.* Brontë remembered that Addison, as well as her mother's carriage driver, had been in the library that day to bring her books in, but could think of no reason that either of them would have for putting the book back on the shelf.

She shrugged and took the book back downstairs to go through her own trunks of books. Brontë was not quite sure what she was looking for, but she figured she would know it when she saw it. She had come to the bottom of the second trunk with no luck, and was contemplating giving up the search until another time, when she pounced on the book she was looking for, <u>The Artists Guide to Paris.</u> Brontë lifted the large hardbound book out of the trunk.

"Yes, this is perfect," she said to herself, as she thumbed through page upon page of photos and artists' impressions of the great city. The small captions told the names of each place and its history. Brontë had purchased the book two years ago and, after reading it cover to cover, had not picked it up since.

Brontë picked up the book and took it back to her room. She would give it to Addison tomorrow. Brontë smiled to herself, she was quite certain that Addison would enjoy the book immensely.

THE NEXT MORNING, Brontë met her mother in the hall, and with the prized book clutched firmly in both hands, she descended the stairs. She caught sight of Addison just as she attempted to make a quick getaway out the front door.

"Addison, may I have a word with you?"

Addison turned around warily and waited for the Lady to approach her.

"I found this. I thought you might..." Brontë shyly handed Addison the book. Addison gazed at the Lady for a moment, her face carefully blank. She opened the hardbound book and slowly turned the pages, studying each page with so much concentration that Brontë began to regret the gift immediately.

"This is wonderful," she said, her voice so low that Brontë had a hard time hearing it. Her eyes never left the page as she asked, "How did you know?"

Seeing none of the sarcasm of the day before, a very relieved Brontë said, "I saw your beautiful painting, and Mary said that you wanted to go to Paris to study. I remembered that I had this book. When my trunks arrived, I was able to go through them and find it. I thought you might like it."

"I love it." Addison did not look up from the book. "May I borrow it?" She looked up at Lady Baptiste quickly, "Just for a few days. I will take good care of it."

"Um, no." Noting the look of disappointment on Addison's face, Brontë rushed on to explain. "Addison, it is for you. You may have it."

Addison looked at her in wonder. Then the mask of non-emotion dropped into place once again. "Forgive me, milady, but I have money." Addison held out the book, her eyes still lingering on it.

"Oh, for heaven's sake..." Mrs. Havisham burst in just as Brontë was about to speak.

"Mother, please," Brontë interrupted the truculent woman before the tirade could begin. She had forgotten that her mother was still waiting for her at the bottom of the stairs. "Mother, would you mind going to breakfast without me? I will be there in but a moment."

Mother gave one last disapproving look at Addison, which Crumpet III seconded, and fairly stalked to the dining room with the yapping dog tucked under her arm.

Brontë turned back to Addison who, she noted, was looking at the pages of the book again, seemingly oblivious to the tension in the air or her mother's rudeness.

"Addison..." Brontë paused as Addison jumped. She had been concentrating so hard on memorizing the pictures in the book so that she might reproduce them later that she had forgotten that she was not alone. "Please forgive her behavior." Brontë gestured toward the hall down which her mother had disappeared.

"I understand; she does not like me. They never do." Addison's voice was completely devoid of animosity. She was simply stating a fact.

"Who never likes you, Addison?"

"Mothers. They hate me," Addison said, her voice nonchalant, as once again she became completely entranced with the images in the book.

"It is not that she hates you." Brontë fumbled for an explanation for her mother's rudeness, but had none.

Addison looked up from the book finally, and upon noticing Brontë's discomfort, began to shift from one foot to the other.

"What about your mother, Addison? She could not have hated you."

Addison's tall body went still; the mask of indifference slipped and Brontë was made privy to a well of pain so deep that she exhaled sharply.

"My mother, milady? She hated me most of all." Addison's mouth twisted into a smile, but Brontë could see the deep-seated pain in the set of her lips. Her heart went out to this strange woman.

Addison tried to give the book back to Brontë. Brontë, still struggling to comprehend and speechless from Addison's quiet statement, could only shake her head and refuse it. Addison held the large book close to her chest, her brown fingers pale, she held it so tightly. She looked solemnly into Brontë's eyes. The sarcasm and cynicism that she regularly showed a world that had never treated her very kindly was completely gone from her expressive eyes. "This is the finest gift anyone has ever given me. I will not forget." With that, she turned and left quickly. Addison's heart beat painfully in her chest as she attempted to escape the house that haunted her every nightmare.

Brontë watched from the open front door as Addison broke into a trot and then a sprint. In seconds, her tall form was hidden behind the trees, lost to Brontë's concerned gaze.

Chapter
Five

ADDISON HELD THE book tightly as she ran into the trees. Her heart pounding in her chest, she passed her home and ran deeper into the forest to her normal place of contemplation. She stumbled into the clearing where her father lay buried and sank to her knees in front of the grave.

"Papa...she gave me a book and there are pictures of Paris. You were right, it is very beautiful, and I will see it someday, but I need to know what happened to her first." Addison, as was her habit, cleared her father's grave until it was spotless. She then placed a bunch of wildflowers on his crudely crafted gravestone.

"Why does it hurt so much, Papa? I never knew her, but it still hurts just the same. I know that you would not like Brontë's mother. But even she would have never left her daughter. She loves her very much; I can tell." Addison sat for a moment with her head on her knees. Her heart felt like it would force its way out of her body through her throat.

"Forgive me, Papa. I am feeling sorry for myself. I did have you and you were always proud of me." Addison jumped up. "Oh, Papa, I should go. Sophie is going to have a litter soon, her first."

Picking up the large book, Addison hurried home. She had checked on Sophie before going to the main house with the cord of wood that Cook had asked for, but Sophie had still not progressed in her labor. She frowned; with such a large litter as Sophie's, one of the pups could have gotten turned around in the birth canal or, even worse, be stillborn and blocking the path for the others. Addison let nature take its course as far as uncomplicated births were concerned, but if Sophie looked like she was having problems, then Addison would intervene and induce labor, as she had had to do many times before with the horses.

Running into her small cottage, Addison carefully laid the prized book on the table, grabbed her work gloves and walked out to Sophie's kennel. Sophie's labor seemed to be progressing well, so Addison sat on the ground outside of her kennel to wait, just in case Sophie needed her.

An hour later, the first little mewl of a newborn puppy could barely be heard over the din of the other dogs in the kennel. Addison wanted very much to pick it up, but knew it would not be a good idea, so she contented herself with a proud grin as Sophie carefully cleaned the little pup and then settled back to wait for the next new arrival.

Addison was watching, still smiling, as Sophie licked the second puppy, when she heard the breaking of a twig behind her. Turning, her smile grew into a full grin as Perry slowly approached and sat down beside her. Addison scratched between her ears and Perry leaned her old head against Addison's side before settling down. They both watched proudly, as Perry's only daughter produced her first litter of puppies.

"She is doing a fine job, Perry." Perry looked up at Addison as she wrapped her arms around her long wool-encased legs and woofed once in agreement. Together the two would stand guard as the puppies came into the world.

BRONTË WATCHED IMPATIENTLY as her mother attempted to shove Crumpet III into a white pullover.

"Mother, why must he wear that? He has fur."

"Dearest, surely you wouldn't want my little baby to catch cold, now would you?"

"Why can't he stay here? We are only going for a short walk." Brontë forced herself to stop. She and her mother had quarreled throughout breakfast. Mrs. Havisham failed to see why it mattered how she spoke to Addison. The woman was, after all, only a servant.

Brontë frowned as she watched her mother struggle with the little dog. Brontë was used to her mother's behavior towards the servants, but never had she been so rude to anyone. It was as if there was something about the tall servant that brought out the worst in her.

"You look wonderful, my love. Are we all ready now?"

"Yes, Mother, I have been ready for quite some time," Brontë said.

"Not you, dear. I am talking to my handsome man Crumpet."

"Of course you are, Mother," Brontë left her mother to exchange saliva with her infernal pet and went to check with Wesley regarding John's well-being. She noted that Thomas and Wesley were changing John's bed linens. They had him turned on his side so that they could remove the soiled linens and put on clean ones. She looked at the angry purple color of John's back and shuddered.

Who could do such a thing? Brontë watched the man that was her husband as he was tended to and tried to decipher the turmoil that gripped her heart. It was as if she could not feel anything for him except for the sympathy that she would hold for any acquaintance in the same condition. Yet her heart had broken for Addison when she had witnessed the pain buried deep in the young servant's soul.

She wondered if she should try to talk to her mother about these feelings toward John on their walk. She had been on her way up to take a nap when her mother had called to her from the sitting room. In an obvious effort to quash the argument that had been so heated over breakfast, she had suggested that she and Brontë head out for a late afternoon walk on the grounds. Although Brontë was truly trying to avoid her mother, she could think of no polite way to refuse. Therefore, Brontë reluctantly went to her room where, with Mary's help, she changed into her dark walking dress and headed to her mother's room.

Mrs. Havisham huffily caught up with Brontë as she turned from John's room and the two women and the dog exited the manor house and set out on the rough path surrounding the estate. Brontë was trying to figure out the best way to broach the subject of her feelings, or lack thereof, but her mother never gave her the chance.

"My word, it is rather rustic here is it not, dearest?" Mrs. Havisham skirted a muddy puddle that sat squarely in the middle of the path. "You must miss Glen Grove awfully."

"I have not had time to think about town much, Mother. I have been here for only a few days, but much has happened. I have had very little time to feel sorry for myself."

"Nonetheless, I would hate to have to live here forever, dearest. I do not know what possessed Lord John to sell that lovely home in town. This is certainly fine for holiday, but who would want to live here year-round? It's so," Mrs. Havisham stated, wrinkling her nose as if something foul had wafted past, "so country."

"Come now, Mother, it is not as though Glen Grove is the middle of Leicester. There are barely three hundred people, and I am sure that if I miss society that much, I can have Thomas or Addison take me into town."

Brontë stopped and looked back when she noticed that her mother was no longer walking beside her. Concerned, she opened her mouth to ask her mother if she felt ill when she caught sight of Addison coming through the trees. She wanted to get her mother as far away from Addison as she could so as not to cause another embarrassing scene.

"I refuse to have any daughter of mine escorted into town by a- a girl in men's trousers." Mrs. Havisham was looking thoroughly scandalized.

"Mother, perhaps we should go back to the house now; it will be time for dinner soon. We can perhaps have another walk later; Wesley does not lock up the house until 9 o'clock." Brontë gripped her mother's elbow and started to steer her back toward the house, but Mrs. Havisham seemed to have other ideas. Jerking her arm away from Brontë, she began to walk contrarily in the opposite direction.

Addison, who had slowed her pace so as not to catch up with the Lady and her mother, was dismayed when Mrs. Havisham abruptly began to walk toward her.

Mrs. Havisham was carrying on an animated conversation with Crumpet III; she was not aware that she was headed in the direction of the very cause of her considerable ire.

"Mother, please stop." Brontë called out, exasperated by her mother's behavior.

Mrs. Havisham turned so quickly that Crumpet III let out a startled yelp. "Brontë Bonnaella Baptiste. Lady or not, I am still your mother and you will not speak to me as if I were one of your servants. I dare say you treat that...that *woman* with more respect than she deserves." This statement was spoken with much disgust and at the top of her voice. Brontë flushed, as she was sure that Addison would have had to hear the hurtful words, as well as her abhorred middle name.

Having said her piece, Mrs. Havisham turned back around haughtily to resume her walk, and stepped directly into a mud puddle.

Addison opened her mouth to tell her to watch her step, but was too late. She watched, mouth agape, as Mrs. Havisham's foot stuck securely, causing her to pitch forward.

"Mrs. Havisham!"

"Mother!"

"Yip!"

And then a loud smack as Mrs. Havisham and Crumpet III landed squarely in a mud puddle barely visible in the leaf-filtered light. Mrs. Havisham landed face down, her dress flipped inelegantly up to reveal two muddied petticoats and one startlingly white one. Crumpet III, still clutched in her out stretched hands, for once was silent. He looked around, confused, but surprisingly clean for the misadventure.

Addison, who had started to run as soon as she saw the Lady's mother begin to fall, skidded to a halt at the edge of the mud puddle. Brontë, who had also started to run to help her mother, arrived moments later, hampered by her walking dress.

Brontë and Addison stared at each other for a moment and then down at the hapless woman who had still not raised her head from its position in the mud.

Brontë opened her mouth once and then clamped it shut as her mother slowly raised her head revealing a face covered entirely with mud.

Addison was the one she saw first, which of course made her livid.

"You...help me up this instant," she demanded.

"Yes, Missus," Addison stepped one booted foot into the puddle and offered Mrs. Havisham a strong, callused hand. Brontë, who by this time had carefully picked her way around the puddle, now stood behind Addison and could see her mother's mud-covered face. She choked back a completely unladylike snort of laughter as her mother blinked owlishly at the hand Addison offered.

Crumpet III, still held in a death grip, had decided that he wanted his freedom. After a few strong twists, he triumphantly squirmed free of his captor. Unfortunately for him, this meant that he was dropped unceremoniously in the mud, leaving him, much like his owner, caked in the stuff.

Crumpet III, being a dog, proceeded to do what all dogs do when wet: He shook himself. Addison was able to jump out of the way just in time to remain free of the flying droplets of mud. Mrs. Havisham, however, was not so lucky, and more mud splattered her face and hair as she stared after her beloved Crumpet III, who was now high-stepping daintily out of the puddle.

Brontë again stifled a snort, but this time she could not contain the unladylike cackling that erupted from her mouth. Addison, still stoic as ever, tried to help Mrs. Havisham, who, hampered by the latest fashionable walking attire from London, was having a hard time getting to her feet. After two tries, Mrs. Havisham angrily rose to her full height and slapped angrily at Addison's hands. Addison, to her credit, still attempted gallantly to lead her out of the pool of mud.

Mrs. Havisham gave one angry look at the still-cackling Brontë and another chilling glance at the straight-faced Addison, and stomped off angrily toward the main house. Her expensive shoes sloshed loudly as she walked.

Unfortunately, Mrs. Havisham paid no attention to the mud on the bottom of her shoes and very nearly ended up on her face again, but through some miracle, or perhaps Addison's quick grab at the back of her dress, she didn't fall again. She snatched her dress away from Addison, her face dull red beneath its drying coat of earth, and stomped away still angry, though a bit more cautious. A bedraggled Crumpet III walked at her side whining to be picked up.

Addison and Brontë watched her stalk back to the manor

house. Addison looked at Lady Baptiste, who was still chuckling softly and watching after her mother.

"She is not going to be happy, milady," Addison said gravely as the Mrs. Havisham ran into the house and slammed the door behind her.

Brontë's grin widened as she looked at the straight-faced Addison before breaking into another fit of giggles.

"No, she will not. I will never hear the end of it, but it was worth it," she said.

Addison shifted from one foot to the other. "Milady, I was on my way to ask Cook to let you know that we had a new litter of puppies born today."

Brontë, still smiling at her mother's theatrics, turned to Addison, her smile getting even larger. "Puppies? Really?"

Addison nodded, her lips quirking at the corners, as the Lady seemed to glow with childlike anticipation.

"May I see them, Addison?" Brontë forgot herself for a moment.

Addison was stunned. She had not expected the Lady to want to see the dogs. The Lord Senior and his offspring never had anything to do with the hounds until they were ready for the hunt. Fear enveloped Addison as she wondered what she could do to curtail the Lady's enthusiasm. She was afraid that she would somehow stumble upon her secret. She was also a bit nervous of the Lady's reaction. Only a few of the village girls had ever visited, and that had merely been to exchange sexual favors. It was not that she was ashamed of her home. She and her father had put a lot of time into making it very cozy.

"Well, they do belong to you, milady." Fear caused sarcasm to creep into Addison's voice. She instantly regretted her words when the warmth of the Lady's smile receded.

"Whenever you have the time, just let me know, Addison. I really would like to see them." Brontë said goodbye and turned to escape the inexplicably awkward situation.

"What did I do to cause that?" Brontë said under her breath as she approached the manor house.

"Milady?" Addison called out. She had hated to see the disappointment in the Lady's green eyes.

Brontë paused to allow Addison to catch up to her.

"Milady, I need to check on the horses and attend to a few other chores. I can show you the pups afterwards, if you like?"

Addison was cursing herself for giving in; she should have just left well enough alone. But she had felt bad, and the Lady had looked almost stunned at her reluctance to show her the puppies. She studied the Lady's pensive face for a moment.

"I would really like to see them, Addison, if you have the time," Brontë said, her voice hesitant as she tried to determine Addison's mood.

"Yes, milady. Shall I fetch you after I am done with my work?"

"That will not be necessary, Addison, I am sure that I can find my way. Why do I not meet you there after I have dinner with Mother? Shall we say a few hours, then?"

"Yes, that will be fine. If you just follow the path and do not stray from it, you should have no problems finding the cottage. If you get lost, just follow the sound of the dogs; they usually make a lot of noise so it is easy to find your way there." Addison looked away from the Lady's bright eyes, feeling awkward in her rough work clothes next to the Lady in all of her finery.

"That should be fine then, Addison. I am looking forward to it." The Lady smiled again before leaving a frantically thinking Addison in her wake.

Addison hurried to the stables where she quickly fed and watered the horses, then headed over to the sheep to check on them as well. For once, her mind was not on her work. *What if the Lady wants to come into the house?*

Addison tried to think of a reason why she should not allow the Lady in and could think of none. Quickly tossing her well-worn saddle into a corner, she left the stable and trotted into the woods. Addison stepped into the warmth of her home and looked around the deathly quiet of the two-room cottage. Lying down on the cot with her arm draped over her eyes, she mulled the situation over in her head. Perhaps the Lady would simply come and look at the puppies and then be on her way. *After all, a Lady as fine as herself would not wish to stay out here for long, puppies or not.* Addison closed her eyes and tried to calm herself. Her quick mind devised a reasonable excuse if Lady Baptiste should ask after her father. Addison drifted off into a light slumber, thanks in part to the unusually quiet hounds and her confidence in her new plan of action.

BRONTË WAS NOT as lucky as Addison. Her home was far from peaceful; in fact it was utter chaos. Thomas was running out of the door as Brontë entered, practically knocking her over in his haste. He apologized, explaining that he was going to get the doctor. Brontë watched open-mouthed as the normally calm young man raced toward the stables as if Cerberus himself breathed hot at his heels. Mary and Beatrice were standing at the bottom of the stairs looking as if they had seen a ghost. Victoria was standing amongst all of the chaos looking like a well-fed cat. In the background, a high-pitched keening wail could be heard, to which

Brontë could only make out two words. "Doctor Quimby!"

"Mother!" Brontë stood at the bottom of the stairs, awestruck by the sheer amount of noise that her mother was making. Beatrice and Mary stood behind her as if she could protect them, while Cook came from the kitchen, nervously drying her hands on her apron. Wesley came out of John's sick room, promptly decided he wanted no part of this new turn of events, and went back in, closing the door behind him.

Brontë paled as her mother started screaming her name.

"Brontë, Brontë! I need you now." Victoria's malicious smile grew ten-fold as Lady Baptiste paled even further.

Brontë thought her mother should be on the finest stage in London. The way that she could pitch her voice to reach throughout the large house and yet still sound so pathetic and weak was simply amazing. If Brontë were not the object of her mother's interest at this moment, she would have been suitably impressed. As it was, she was incredibly reticent to answer her mother's summons. All, including Victoria, who was nearly glowing with glee at the unfolding drama, noticed this.

Brontë focused in on her glinting eyes, narrowing her own as she said, "You know, Victoria, it really is too bad you can only be happy when others are not. You could be quite pretty if your smile were not so self-serving." With that said, Brontë stomped up the stairs to see to her mother's needs, leaving a gaping Victoria behind her.

Brontë approached her mother's door cautiously. She listened for a moment, hoping that perhaps Mother was done with her tirade and had been so exhausted that she had fallen asleep. Brontë put her ear against the solid door and upon hearing nothing from the room, was prepared to make a stealthy escape when Crumpet III let out one sharp yelp.

"Brontë, are you there?" Mrs. Havisham called out in her most pathetic voice.

Brontë stood there fuming. *Just a few minutes alone with that dog, that is all I ask.* Steeling herself, she opened the door. Crumpet III immediately streaked through the open door and ran down the hall and out of sight.

Brontë entered the room and closed the door behind her she studied the woman in the bed. "Yes, Mother, may I help you with something?"

Mrs. Havisham lay on her bed with a cloth draped across her head, the back of her open hand placed dramatically on top of the cool compress to keep it affixed to her head, completing the image. Brontë recognized it as tantrum number ten. This was the worst type. It usually occurred when Mrs. Havisham felt some family member had wronged her. Although the exact issue was never brought up, she would rely heavily on said family member during her recovery process, often driving Brontë and her brothers to tears with her whining. It was an oddity that they expected, and accepted, from their mother.

"Brontë, dear, can you look in my bag and get my elixir, please?"

"Yes, Mother." Brontë frowned as she pulled the plain brown bottle from her mother's bag and shook the liquid content. "Mother, surely Doctor Quimby didn't prescribe this for you?"

"No, dear, I got it through another doctor. You know how Doctor Quimby can be. Now please give me my medicine, my womb is causing me trouble. Have those servants found Doctor Quimby as I asked?"

Brontë studied her mother with concern. She had no idea what 'hysteria of the womb' was; she had not had the time to look it up as of yet. "Mother, should I have Mary bring Doctor Richards, in case we can not find Doctor Quimby?"

Mrs. Havisham nearly sat straight up in bed. "No, no, dear, it must be Doctor Quimby. He is the only one that I allow to treat me."

Before Brontë could question her mother further, the doctor so named was at the door. Doctor Quimby was a handsome, though rather small-boned and delicate, man of forty. Having never been married, he was considered by many to be the most eligible bachelor in the area. To Brontë, he was always nothing but polite and efficient, however, she didn't see much by way of personality in the man.

"Lady Baptiste, it is a pleasure to see you again." He nodded politely and walked over to Mrs. Havisham, a look of utter exasperation in his gray eyes.

"What seems to be the problem *today*, Mrs. Havisham?" He asked as he checked her nodes, her pupils and her tongue. He took a few delicate sniffs and then looked up at Brontë. "Has she taken spirits?"

"Spirits? No, just some elixir."

Doctor Quimby looked down at Mrs. Havisham with something akin to disgust. "Mrs. Havisham, what did I tell you about taking untested medicines and home remedies? They could seriously harm you." The last was said as the doctor expertly reached under her pillow and pulled out the half-empty brown bottle of elixir, putting it into his pocket.

"I didn't know if you would come and I was so distraught, I needed something to help me calm down until you arrived."

Brontë watched as her mother whined and preened for the doctor at the same time. She did not understand her mother's behavior, but it was fascinating to watch.

"Mrs. Havisham, did we not speak of this the last time you had a reaction? You could treat yourself and not have to wait for me. Did I not give you the catalogue? Even your own magazines have them. Why do you not just order one?" He sighed as he looked down at the bedridden woman as if she were a small child.

"Well, I would be too afraid, Doctor. What if I do something wrong? I do not bother you too much, do I?" Brontë winced at her mother's whining voice.

"Forgive me, Mother, I shall take my leave as I am sure that you are in good hands with Doctor Quimby."

"Not yet, dear, but I soon will be."

Doctor Quimby had taken off his coat and was rolling up his shirtsleeves. Brontë shrugged, far too happy to escape to be concerned about the treatments.

After a lovely dinner, she told Beatrice to take something up to her mother after the doctor had left and went to go check on John's condition. As she left his room, she noted the time on the grandfather clock; it was just past six. She would need to hurry if she wanted to see the puppies and make it back in time before Wesley locked up for the evening. If she were to be locked out, she would have to walk all the way around to the servant's quarters in the dark to be let back in. She could, she supposed, ask Wesley not to lock the door, but she didn't want the nosy man to know her comings and goings.

Brontë was on her way to her mother's room to tell her she would be out for a while and to bid the doctor a good night, when a long low moan sounded from behind her mother's closed door. Brontë paused, her hand still raised to knock.

"*Ohhhhhhh*, Doctor Quimby, you are so good at this!"

"Please do not talk, Mrs. Havisham, there is a rhythm involved with this procedure," the doctor answered breathlessly.

"*Ohhhh*, yes you have found the right rhythm, Doctor Quimby...yes, right there...Oh yes!"

Brontë's eyes widened as she wondered what type of treatment would be giving her mother such pleasure. She really did need to look up 'hysteria of the womb'. Perhaps she could find out what the treatment was, as well.

"Mrs. Havisham, please let go of my hair so that we may finish your treatment!"

"Forgive me, Doctor Quimby. You have such wonderful hands that I was beside myself for a moment."

Unable to restrain herself, Brontë opened the door to find a furiously sweating Doctor Quimby and a compromised Mrs. Havisham, neither of whom noticed the pale figure standing in the doorway. Brontë quickly closed the door and suffered a moment in which she thought that her recently eaten dinner was going to come back up. After several moments of quiet, in which she had convinced herself that she must be mistaken, she raised her hand to knock and was stopped mid-gesture by another loud groan and her mother's voice.

"*Ohhhhh*, Doctor Quimby, You have found it...harder, harder... *Haaaarrrrrdddeeeerrrr.*"

Whatever else might have been said went unheard by Brontë, running horrified down the hall to empty the contents of her stomach into the opening of a very expensive vase.

Chapter
Six

ADDISON AWOKE WITH with a start. She jumped up, wondering how long she had been asleep. She had never had the need for a timepiece before, nor had her father. She had trained her body to awaken at four o'clock every morning just as she had trained it to fall instantly asleep when her head hit the pillow at midnight, when she usually finished her chores. Perry raised her head and watched with some interest as her usually calm housemate scurried around talking to herself.

"How could I fall asleep, Perry?" she asked, angry with herself.

Addison ran into the chilly bedroom, dropped to her knees, and searched frantically under the bed until her hand found the elusive items. She nearly crowed as she pulled out the large men's house shoes. Addison also retrieved a long button-down shirt from a box in a corner. She threw the shoes haphazardly in front of the fireplace, her heart aching for a moment as she remembered the number of times her father had done the very same thing as he prepared for bed. She placed the large shirt over the high-backed chair tucked under the crudely crafted table where she ate her meals. Then, grabbing a clean white shirt for herself, she turned to the basin to clean up. Addison cursed loudly as she realized that she had forgotten to fill the pitcher before falling asleep earlier. Normally she would do that at least an hour before she washed so that the water was at least room temperature. She would have to wash up with the freezing water directly from the well.

Addison briefly considered forgoing a wash, but after one surreptitious sniff of one of her underarms, she decided that she should most definitely scrub that offensive area, hard. She flushed at the thought of Lady Baptiste's reaction if she were to smell her right now. Grabbing an extra bucket, some soap, and the clean white shirt, Addison hurried outside.

Certainly, she would see Lady Baptiste long before she saw her. Addison stripped off her shirt and unwound the binding that kept her breasts from bouncing while she worked. Cursing herself

for forgetting a washcloth, Addison decided not to waste time
going back into the house and instead poured the water into the
extra bucket, which she sat on the edge of the well, and dunked her
old shirt into it to wash.

BRONTË STUMBLED OUT into the cool evening air. Taking a
couple of deep breaths, she started walking up the path that Addison had pointed out to her a few hours earlier. Her mind kept revisiting the horror she had witnessed in her mother's room. Surely
there had to be some explanation? Her mother was a married
woman! It was true that her father had let them all down in different ways on more than one occasion, but surely Mother would not
resort to infidelity, would she?

Brontë considered talking to her mother about the situation,
but that was quickly ruled out in favor of keeping her sanity. She
could almost hear Mother's whining voice as she pled her case.
Brontë's head pounded at the mere thought of the conversion. *No,
she decided, Mother is an adult and knows what is best for her own
well-being.*

But Doctor Quimby? Brontë shuddered. *Well, it is not as though
John is much better, and at least Doctor Quimby apparently knows what
he's doing.* Brontë snickered to herself, then felt guilty as she
thought of the unconscious John.

Brontë was so deep in thought that she didn't realize she had
wandered off the path. She had been walking for nearly twenty
minutes when it dawned on her that she should have reached Addison's home by now. Brontë felt an almost instantaneous urge to
panic, the remaining sunlight seeming to recede even as she
thought it, showing no deference to her plight. She was considering
calling out for help when she heard one lone bark.

"Addison said if I got lost, to follow the barking," she said
aloud.

Brontë stood completely still and waited for another bark to
lead her to Addison's home. She didn't have long to wait, and with
relief, she followed the sounds. Fifteen minutes later she spotted
three roofs in the distance. A small smile transformed her grim
face as she decided she would not tell Addison that she had been
lost; after all, it was a mistake anyone could make, and she was in
no mood to see that sarcastic smile directed at her.

Brontë continued to pick her way through the forest and was
just about to step out into the clearing that belonged to Addison
and her father when she halted abruptly. The smile of relief at
finding her way was still plastered on her face, as, stunned, she
watched a partially naked Addison dunk something into a bucket

and rub it vigorously with a bar of soap before proceeding to wash her face, neck, and bare chest. Brontë's mouth dropped open as she watched the woman, for that is most definitely what she was, wash her bronzed breasts and shoulders. Then, dunking the cloth in the clean water, she squeezed it out over her upper body to clear off the remaining soap.

Brontë closed her mouth and swallowed dryly as her eyes, of their own accord, went to Addison's breasts. She wondered how she could have ever mistaken this woman's body for that of a man. Addison had full breasts graced with brown dusky nipples that were, at this moment, hard from the gentle breeze and the cold well water. Brontë licked her lips as she gazed at the perfection of those nipples. Blood rushed to her center and pulsed there.

Strong brown hands worked the cloth over the flat planes of the tall woman's stomach and then back up to her breasts. Later, Brontë would wonder if Addison had known, subconsciously, that she was being watched, because her movements seemed to slow as she washed the sweat and grime from her body.

Addison scrubbed once more at her underarms before tossing the dirty water to the side and quickly cranking the pump up again to pour fresh water into her bucket. She unbuttoned her trousers, and before Brontë could even think to turn away from the scene, the trousers slid down strong legs to pool around booted feet and she stood naked to Brontë's hungry eyes.

Brontë knew she should feel badly for watching Addison, but she did not. Her eyes caressed the lean body revealed to her. "Oh, Addison, you are beautiful," she whispered to the unsuspecting woman. Something deep in her core told her that this was right, this was what she needed to see, and so she watched greedily from the forest as the diminishing sunlight helped to keep her safe from detection.

Addison wrung the excess water from the shirt and washed slowly between the folds of her sex, her mind already on the subject of Lady Baptiste and what she would say if asked the whereabouts of the elusive caretaker of Markby Estates. Thinking she had better hurry, Addison quickened her pace as her eyes kept watch on the path that she was expecting the Lady to be traveling. If she had looked to her left, she would have been in for a surprise.

Brontë whimpered as the strong brown hands worked the large cloth over the dark triangle of hair that hid Addison's womanhood, the muscles in her arms flexing rhythmically as she washed herself. Brontë didn't know whether to be relieved or dismayed that Addison was quickening her pace. Addison bent to pull up her baggy worn trousers. She left them open at her narrow waist, the bracers hanging at her sides.

Brontë felt her own sex clench and then become warm as she was treated to a tantalizing view of moist curls peeking from the open trousers. Addison obviously did not feel the need to wear any underwear whatsoever.

Brontë watched as Addison untied the brown leather band that bound her hair and then dunked her entire head into the bucket. As Addison stood, she threw back her head, sending droplets of water in all directions. After lathering her shoulder-length hair, she dunked her head again to rinse the soap from it.

Brontë felt her face flush. She didn't want to look away, but at the same time she felt that she should. Placing her hand on a nearby tree for support, she watched as Addison dumped the soiled water and cranked the bucket up again, pouring the clean water into the extra pail.

Addison's strong back muscles stood out in relief as she bent to rinse her hair. Brontë thought Addison's body was like a finely chiseled piece of artwork that she took painstaking measures to hide away.

Addison rinsed her hair a few more times before pushing her now-clean tresses back on her head and tossing the dirty shirt and soap into the bucket. She grabbed her clean shirt and, not wanting to get it wet until she could dry her hair, walked bare-chested and glistening into the cottage, shutting the door behind her.

Brontë blinked and took a deep breath. Her face warmed at the thought of being caught as she watched Addison bathe.

Closing her eyes, she could see every muscle and sinew of Addison's lean, bronzed body. Opening them again, her face still flushed, she leaned back against the tree, her stomach churning once again, but for different reasons. Unlike earlier, she did not feel as though she was going to lose her dinner. On the contrary, she was craving something. As these new feelings floated through her mind, she briefly considered returning to Markby without seeing the puppies and, most of all, Addison. However, she was afraid that she would not be able to find her way back without Addison's help. There was barely any light left now and it was starting to get cold. So, taking a deep breath, Brontë stepped from her hiding place and approached Addison's cottage door.

Addison, unaware that she had been observed, tucked her white shirt into her baggy trousers and pulled the bracers up over her broad shoulders. She had just tied her hair back neatly when she heard the tentative knock on the door.

She jumped up from the table to nervously open the door to Lady Baptiste. Addison was speechless as her heart pounded in her ears. She had noticed right off that the Lady was a beautiful woman; she always noticed beautiful women. However, right now, the Lady's skin was flushed and her green eyes had darkened. Her always perfectly coiffed hair looked slightly mussed and she had a light sheen of moisture over her upper lip. Addison's eyes lingered on the place above her lip for an inordinately long length of time before dropping to the Lady's small chest, which was rising and falling noticeably as if she were out of breath. *She looks like she has just been thoroughly kissed.* Addison's own lips parted as a vision of herself lying naked on the Lady's pale body in a thick forest instantly came to mind. Addison's mouth watered as she thought of the breasts that had to be hidden under all of those layers of cloth.

Like a rose. I want to pull the petals off, one by one, until I get to the center. Addison inhaled sharply at the thought and blinked twice, snapping herself and the Lady out of their stupor.

"Are you alright, milady?" Addison finally asked. "You look winded."

Brontë cleared her throat before answering. Before Addison had opened the door she had convinced herself that a clothed Addison was completely safe. Now it seemed she had been greatly mistaken. Not only was a clothed Addison just as dangerous as a nude one, but also, Brontë had not taken into consideration her overactive imagination, which helpfully provided visions of dark curls and dusky nipples. Brontë's pink-tipped tongue snuck between her lips, causing Addison's eyes to focus instantly there.

"Y-yes, why do you ask?" she finally managed to say.

"Because you look flushed."

"No, Addison, I am fine. Thank you. It just got a little cold, so I walked a bit faster than usual." Brontë was amazed at how quickly the lie came to mind.

"Are you still cold, milady?" Addison colored as Brontë's brow rose at her apparent concern. "I asked because I could give you my pullover to wear." Addison colored again as she realized how ridiculous it would be for Lady Baptiste to wear the pullover over her lovely green walking dress. Addison, once again, was feeling very common around the Lady Baptiste in all her finery.

"No, I should be fine, Addison, thank you."

"Would you like see the puppies now?" Addison gestured toward the kennels.

Brontë nodded and stepped back so that Addison could exit the cottage, closing the door securely behind her.

"Sophie had a nice sized litter, but I am afraid only six lived." Addison nervously began to chatter.

Brontë was glad for something to focus on. "Oh, no. Why did they die?"

Addison, who was used to animals dying in birth all the time, simply shrugged and said, "It was not meant to be. Six is still a very good litter, milady. Sometimes it is just nature's way of weeding out the weak. If the ones that cannot care for themselves perish, then that leaves more food for the strong animals. It is just the way things are. It happens that way in all of nature."

Brontë listened, riveted, as Addison spoke. They approached Sophie's single pen where she was currently feeding the six hungry puppies. Brontë opened her mouth to comment when she caught sight of the little bundles.

"Ooh, they are so small, Addison." Brontë grabbed at Addison's arm unwittingly as she gazed down at the amazing little creatures. She had never seen puppies before. All of the Crumpets had been boys and as far as she had known had never mated. Well, except Crumpet II, which, upon occasion, would take a liking to her oldest brother Albert's leg.

"How long before we can hold them?"

"I would say a week, milady, just to be sure. Sophie is a good mother, but we do not want to give her a reason to reject one of them. My father thinks that it is important that they be allowed to interact with just their mother for a week at first before introducing them to other things." Addison felt like kicking herself for bringing up her father.

But Lady Baptiste was far too busy staring at the tiny little puppies to notice or even think anything of it. "I really want to hold one," she said, putting her hand on Addison's arm, again unwittingly, but this time she left it there as they stood and watched the little puppies.

Addison was thinking she could stay here with the Lady forever when a fat droplet of water dropped from the sky. She frowned and tried to concentrate on the small warm hand that circled her forearm. It was odd, really. Aside from her father and maybe Cook she had never allowed anyone to touch her casually. But here she stood, actually relishing the warmth of the small hand on her upper arm. Addison peeked at the Lady out of the corner of her eye. Instantly, a rush of desire started from the tips of her breasts and worked its way down to her sex, then seemed to throb for a moment, making Addison feel self-conscious and afraid. She calmed greatly when she realized that Lady Baptiste would never know that she was having such feelings for her.

She had opened her mouth to comment when another fat droplet landed on the top of her head, and then two more. Addison looked up at the dark sky and decided that they had better leave now if they were going to make it back to the manor house before the skies opened up. She turned to the Lady to say as much when the skies opened up and started pelting down on both of them.

"Milady, we should get inside." Addison had to raise her voice to be heard over the rain.

Brontë allowed herself to be led back to the cottage, shocked by the sudden onslaught of rain. By the time they made it back to the cottage, both of them were thoroughly drenched. Brontë shivered as Addison instructed her to stand in front of the fire to keep warm while she went into the chilly bedroom to find some dry clothes.

Brontë watched as Addison fussed with the fire a bit to get it hot. She was bent over, her face turned toward the hearth, allowing Brontë to gaze at her without being observed. Brontë's eyes caressed her neck and shoulders, then the front of Addison's shirt. She paled and turned away. Addison's hardened nipples were clearly visible through the soaking wet white shirt. Every time she bent toward the fire, they pressed against the almost translucent fabric. Brontë shivered uncontrollably, her stomach churning, as she contemplated her unfamiliar feelings.

Addison quickly moved away, rushing to the back room, where she grabbed her two nightshirts, grateful that she had recently washed them both. She carried them into the only other room in the cottage, where the Lady was shivering violently in front of the fire. *She looks miserable,* Addison thought sadly.

"Milady, you need to get those wet clothes off." Addison spoke quietly, as Lady Baptiste seemed to be deep in thought.

Brontë looked up at Addison sharply. "N-no, Addison. I think I will be fine. Thank you. I am already starting to warm up." As if to belie her words, her body gave a particularly hard shudder.

"Milady, please, you will become ill if you stay in those damp clothes. Put this on. You cannot walk home with the weather as it is. I will run out to the shed and grab more wood for the fire so that you can have some privacy." Addison walked back into the chilly bedroom and returned with a cloth and the duvet from the bed.

"What about your father, Addison?"

Addison turned away casually. "He would not walk back in this, milady. He would shelter in the barn, most likely, so you have no need to worry." Addison felt a twinge of pain in her chest at having to lie about her father, but she didn't think she had any other choice.

"I will give you some privacy, milady." Addison was almost out the door when Brontë called to her, a note of exasperation in her voice.

"Addison, before you go, would you mind helping me with the buttons on the back of my dress? Mary usually helps me dress, but..." Brontë turned with her back to Addison, certain that Addison would comply with her request.

Addison, for her part, wanted nothing more than to tell the Lady to unbutton her own damned dress and run out into the relative safety of her tool shed. Surely there was some way that she could gracefully back out of this.

"Addison, please hurry." Brontë shivered again, hard, her voice dejected.

Addison was angry at herself for making the Lady stand there drenched because she could not control her own sexual cravings. Her fingers fumbled with the delicate buttons of the dress. She tried not to look at the pale skin being exposed to her at the back of the Lady's neck, but her own eyes betrayed her. Addison was never more grateful than when she reached the final button. Quickly turning away from the Lady, Addison almost ran to the door and jerked it open.

"I will give you some privacy, milady, while I go and fetch some wood for the fire." Without waiting for a reply, Addison shut the door behind her and walked slowly to the tool shed, allowing herself to be drenched by the frigid rains.

Lady Baptiste miserably stepped out of the layers of clothing. She briefly entertained the idea of keeping on her underwear, but decided against it, as they too, were uncomfortably damp. In three days' time, her whole world had been turned upside down. Everything that she had held as true and sacred was no more and she honestly did not know what to make of it. She had married a man she did not know, let alone love, to save her family from relative financial mediocrity. Then she had witnessed her mother engaged in some intimate act with a man not her father. And, worst of all, she had stood and watched as one of her own servants, a woman who dressed in men's clothing no less, had washed herself, and had drunk in the sight.

Brontë slipped the huge nightshirt over her head and sat down in a chair in front of the fire. She had enjoyed watching Addison, her skin flushed and her lips parted. She enjoyed looking at the woman's body that was so different from her own. But, how was that possible? She had felt nothing when she had seen what little she had of John's body. She had been thoroughly disgusted by whatever her mother—and, for all she knew, every other woman aged forty to sixty in the area—did with Doctor Quimby. Even now, Brontë's chin wobbled and her mouth twisted with disgust. It was, therefore, shocking to her that she did not feel that same disgust when thinking of what she had seen of Addison's body. *She is a perfect blend of femininity and strength,* Brontë thought. She frowned as she remembered the hurtful comments her mother had hurled at Addison.

"Well, Mother, you were wrong. Addison has nothing in common with my husband or father. Well, except father has bigger breasts." Brontë snickered and then felt remorseful for poking fun at her poor father, who at this moment did not know he was married to an adulterous wife.

She sat staring at the fire, shivering, then reached back and pulled the neatly folded duvet from the table where Addison had left it and wrapped it tightly around herself. The weight and seriousness of all that she had been through suddenly slammed down on the small shoulders of the Lady, and she forced herself to stifle a sob. Addison would be back soon and it would not do for her to see her crying. Brontë nearly jumped out of her skin as something cold pressed against her hand and a weight settled onto her lap. Brontë looked down into the sweetest brown eyes she had ever seen.

"Well, hello there. Who are you?"

Perry just blinked her eyes and continued to rest her head on the sad human's lap. She had watched her tall owner fret over the little one and had decided that she would watch over her, as well. Perry closed her eyes in bliss as the smaller fingers of this human found the spots that her owner's much bigger fingers could not. The dog's tail twitched for a moment before settling down again. Perry was so tired that it was becoming hard for her to keep her eyes open, but this was wonderful and she had no intentions of giving this up before she had to.

The door to the cottage swung open and Addison stomped in carrying a bunch of wood, which she placed into a metal bucket near the fireplace, careful to stay as far away from Lady Baptiste as she could.

"Addison, you are soaked!" Brontë cried out.

"Yes it is pretty bad out there. I see you met my friend Perry?"

Brontë smiled and opened her mouth to answer, but Perry lifted her head and woofed an answer for her.

Addison smiled at Perry, causing Brontë to notice for the first time that Addison seemed to lack the tension that always emanated from her body.

"Milady, forgive me, I didn't expect visitors. I am afraid that all I have is some bread and some leftover rabbit stew from yesterday."

"That sounds wonderful, Addison." Brontë had not realized how hungry she was until that very moment.

Addison walked over to the earthen cookware that sat on her stove and dished up two bowls, giving one to Lady Baptiste along with a spoon.

"Come, Perry, are you hungry?" she asked gently. "I have some left over rabbit stew if you like." She filled the dog's much larger bowl and set it down on the floor. Perry limped over to it and proceeded to wolf down the contents.

"I am just going to change in the other room and then I will join you two." Addison disappeared into the freezing bedroom to dry off and change into her sleep shirt.

Upon returning to the front room she watched as the Lady and Perry ate so fast that she thought about telling them both to slow down lest they both became ill, but decided it would probably do no good. Addison grabbed the only remaining chair and sat down to eat her food as well.

The women ate their meal in silence, each deep in their own thoughts. Brontë felt her eyes droop as the warmth of the room, the food in her stomach, and the sound of the rain all conspired to lull her to sleep.

Addison watched from across the table in amusement as Lady Baptiste's head fell forward a few times, her eyes blinking as she attempted to keep her head from falling into her empty bowl. Her heart warmed at the sight of the Lady trying to stay awake and failing miserably.

Addison stood quietly, and, after a few whispered words to Perry, she gently picked up the Lady Baptiste, and after some deliberation, placed her in the cot. She covered her with as many blankets as she could find and headed towards the bedroom.

"Addison, where are you going?" asked Brontë.

Addison turned to look at the droopy-eyed Lady. "Milady, the cot is too small; I will sleep in the other room."

"You took the blankets from there and put them on me. Please sleep here, Addison. There is enough room for both of us. You will be cold in there." The Lady's eyes closed again and Addison was left to make the decision to stay or go on her own.

Sighing, Addison eased onto the cot. She would stay on top of the blankets and just enjoy the warmth from the fireplace. It was a good plan, in theory. Addison even managed to fall asleep for a few hours. What she didn't count on was the fact that Lady Baptiste would start to shiver as the fire died.

Addison eased out of the bed, and, stepping over Perry, put the last three pieces of wood into the fireplace before returning to bed. Lady Baptiste's small body was shivering harder by the time Addison laid back down. With the four blankets between them, she wrapped her arms around the Lady's small frame and pulled her back against her much larger body to give Lady Baptiste the benefit of her natural body heat.

Addison held her for a few more moments, concern creasing her brow as the body bundled under the blankets continued to shiver violently from cold. Addison cursed under her breath and hopped off the cot. She lifted the blankets and climbed underneath them. The Lady's body instantly gravitated toward the source of heat, scooting back so that her backside was firmly pressed into

Addison's stomach.

Addison closed her eyes and forced herself to relax. The dark-haired woman lay completely still for ten minutes, trying hard to ignore the blood rushing to her center. She tried to straighten her legs to give the Lady more space, but Lady Baptiste just moved back further, this time aligning her hips with Addison's own. Addison placed her hand on the curve of her small hips and helped her snuggle even closer

"Mmm." Addison groaned and then promptly froze, arousal coursing through her body unchecked. She had a warm female body pressed intimately against her own and all she could do was hope against hope that she fell asleep soon. Addison closed her eyes and tried to ignore the persistent voice in the back of her head telling her that she could touch Lady Baptiste and no one would ever know.

Addison's body made the decision for her; her hips pressed into the warm curve of Lady Baptiste's backside for the first time.

Shock careened through Addison's system, causing her to jump reflexively as she realized how painfully aroused her body truly was. There was no turning back at this point, she needed relief or she would need to remove herself from this bed. The Lady's breathing pattern was still steady, while Addison's own was ragged. Addison stared at the fine hairs on the back of the Lady Baptiste's neck and, almost without realizing what she was doing, she eased her head forward and planted one soft kiss there. She waited for a reaction, holding her breath the whole time. The Lady continued to breathe deeply, her sleep undisturbed. Addison kissed the back of her neck once again, this time lingering and inhaling the sweet scent that was uniquely Lady Baptiste's.

Addison raised her hand to move the sleep shirt over the curve of the Lady Baptiste's milky white shoulder. Her fingers caressed the soft skin there as her ears listened for any change in breathing pattern that would mean that the Lady was awake. Getting bolder by the minute, her aroused mind continued to lead her down the path of no return as her right hand crept over the Lady Baptiste's side and found the sleep shirt's opening. When her seeking fingers finally crept under the fabric and down the Lady's warm flesh, her breathing had ceased to be anything near quiet. As her fingertips grazed hardened nipples, the smaller woman shivered again and then stilled. Addison felt some relief from the pressure between her legs.

It was not to last, however. Her body was becoming more demanding by the second. Addison thought briefly of relieving her own needs, but it did not seem appealing as her fingers continued to gently toy with the Lady's nipple. Finally, Addison scooted up in the bed a bit. She was then able to cup the Lady's breast fully.

She froze as the Lady groaned in her sleep. Addison closed her eyes and thought of what could happen to her if she were caught molesting the Lady in this fashion. She could not seem to stop herself. And it was with great relief that she noted the Lady's breathing return to the normal deep patterns of sleep.

Addison removed her hand from the Lady's sleep shirt, intending to go to sleep. But again, her body had a mind of its own, and the hand that only moments before had been fondling the Lady Baptiste's breast was now caressing the gentle curve of her hip and pulling her into the waiting curve of Addison's body. Addison, thankful that the Lady was a deep sleeper, began to move, tortuously slow, against the small body in front of her. Her fingers gently glided down the Lady's pale arm, leaving a trail of raised flesh in its wake, as her hips continued to move against the Lady. Addison wanted to crush Lady Baptiste to her, but she knew that would wake her for certain. So she continued with the slow maddening torment, her hand gently holding the Lady's hip as her own continued to move in a slow steady pace that was both giving her pleasure and driving her insane.

Addison could not get her erratic breathing under control and her heart was thudding painfully against her chest. A small groan escaped from her moist lips and her body jumped uncontrollably. Still, the Lady did not wake and Addison, who was fast approaching the release she needed, turned her face into her pillow. She forced herself not to tighten her grip on the Lady's hip as her next thrust sent a wave of pleasure crashing through her system. Addison let out a moan that was half a sob as she rotated her hips into the Lady again and was hit with a second wave that threatened to make her scream.

Face pressed firmly into the pillows, Addison lifted her hips from the bed and, with as little pressure on the Lady as possible, she held Lady Baptiste's hip steady and moved strongly against her one last time. The sob that erupted from her throat was sucked up by the pillow, as was the solitary tear that crept from one tightly closed eye. Addison's body continued to pulse for several minutes after her release, and she lay, stunned, staring at the back of the Lady's neck.

Addison did not sleep at all that night. The mantra of *What have I done?* kept her awake until dawn, repeating over and over again in her mind.

Chapter
Seven

A HOWLING DOG tore Brontë from the realm of a pleasurable dream. She frowned in her sleep and snuggled down on the warm mattress that seemed to be molded to her body specifically for maximum pleasure. A contented smile formed on her face as she snuggled down even further and the mattress shifted to allow her to get closer. A sigh escaped her lips and was mimicked by the mattress beneath her.

Brontë's eyes shot open; warm, sun-darkened skin greeted her. Slowly, she raised her head and found herself looking into the peacefully slumbering face of the caretaker's daughter. Almost fearfully, she looked down to confirm what she already knew. Apparently, during the night, she had rolled on top of Addison. She now lay with her legs on either side of the larger woman, the borrowed large sleep shirt hiked wantonly around her hips. Addison's right arm was around her waist and her left hand cupped Brontë's backside as if to help keep her in position.

Brontë's face flushed as she realized the absurdity of the situation. If she tried to extricate herself from the tangle of arms and legs, she was sure that Addison would wake up. Brontë's face went from hot red to pale white as she realized that her first meeting with the caretaker could be an awkward one, were he to come in and find her astride his daughter. With that in mind, Brontë began trying to remove herself from Addison's embrace without waking her.

It seemed Addison could be stubborn even in sleep. Every time Brontë would wiggle some part of her body free, Addison would gently cup her bottom and scoot her back up to her former position, a slight frown creasing her forehead until she had the Lady settled just so. Then she would relax back into her deep slumber, only to repeat the process seconds later. This happened three times before Brontë, flushed and out of breath, stopped to consider her alternatives.

Finally deciding that she would rather wake Addison than run the risk of having Addigo walk in and find them as they were positioned now, she leaned closer to Addison's ear and whispered her name urgently. "Addison?" The frown reappeared on the smooth skin of Addison's forehead.

"Mmm, sleep, my love," she whispered. "There is plenty of time for that."

Brontë flushed, a warm feeling settling in the pit of her stomach those words, "my love." She knew that Addison was talking in her sleep, but it was certainly more pleasurable than being called 'Milady' all the time.

"Addison, please wake up!" Brontë said as the hounds' barking became even more frenzied.

Addison gradually opened her eyes and stared into the most beautiful face she had ever seen. She smiled gently at the Lady above her. Her eyes focused on the Lady's lips for a moment as she unconsciously licked her own. Brontë, to her great chagrin, mimicked the action. They both stared at each other's now-moist lips. Brontë leaned forward. It was a slight movement, as much imagined as real, but it was enough to snap both of them back into reality.

They lay that way for several moments, frozen as if for all of eternity. Brontë was still straddling Addison's long length, her sleep shirt immodestly high on her thighs. She could feel the heat of Addison's hand on her bottom through the fabric. Two sets of eyes grew large simultaneously.

Brontë broke the spell first. "A-Addison?"

Still staring into Brontë's darkening green eyes, Addison replied without realizing it. "Yes, Brontë?"

Brontë inhaled sharply, swallowed, then shifted a little, which was a mistake, as she was pressed so intimately against Addison that it only increased the electricity between them. "I think someone is coming, Addison. It may be your father. We need to get up."

The Lady was whimpering now. Addison snapped fully into consciousness at the mention of her father. She inhaled deeply as she became aware of Lady Baptiste's position. She realized that she had probably pulled the Lady atop her during a dream of some sort. Addison knew what sort, but didn't want to travel down that road again; at least not until she was free to do something about the results of such heady thinking. Addison nodded in agreement and reluctantly removed her hand from the Lady's backside.

Brontë tried to ignore the chill that she felt when the warmth of Addison's hand left her body. She made herself move, even though her body protested that it was most comfortable where it was.

"I am sorry for waking you, Addison, but the dogs started barking and I was afraid that your father was returning," Brontë chattered while climbing off of the bed.

Addison was busy looking anywhere but at the Lady when a loud knocking on the door caused both to freeze. Brontë, who had gone over to pick up her now-dry clothing, clutched them to her chest and looked fearfully at a motionless Addison.

Addison never had visitors, so she too was shocked that someone would be knocking on her door so early in the morning. Putting her finger to her lips, she quickly hopped up off the cot and gestured for Lady Baptiste to follow her. She opened the door to the chilly bedroom and quickly stepped into her trousers. Brontë was glad that she had convinced Addison to sleep out front with her because this room was freezing. Her teeth started to chatter as she nervously looked around for somewhere that she could dress in private.

Addison shook her head, leaned close, and whispered in her ear. "My lady, let me see who is at my door, then I will help you dress. I am assuming you do not want anyone to know that you spent the night here, correct?"

Remembering the way she had draped herself over Addison during the night like some wanton hussy caused Brontë to blush again.

Addison perceived the blush as an indication of Brontë's shame at having spent the night with her. Shaking off her feelings of rejection, Addison nodded her head in understanding. "I will try to get rid of whoever it is quickly. You just be as quiet as possible."

Before Lady Baptiste could respond, Addison hurried from the room to the demanding pounding at the front door. She was just about to open it when she glanced down at the numerous blankets on the cot. Thinking of the shivering Lady, she quickly grabbed one and tossed it through the door, startling Lady Baptiste.

"Try to keep warm," Addison said as she closed the door.

The pounding at the front door had become even more demanding and Addison had a scowl on her face as she finally opened it. Whoever it was had better have a good reason for attempting to knock down her door at such an early hour.

Addison swung the door open with such a fierce scowl that a more intelligent person would have turned on their heels and beat a hasty retreat. The sheriff, however, was not known for his intelligence. He stood his ground arrogantly, taking in Addison's unkempt hair, wrinkled sleep shirt over mud brown trousers, and bare feet.

"Surely I didn't wake you, Miss Le Claire?"

Addison frowned at the way the annoying man put emphasis on 'Miss'. "Yes, you did wake me."

"Oh, well, I am sorry, Miss Le Claire. I am actually here to see both you and your father. Is he here?" He stepped into the house without waiting for an invitation. Once again, Addison retreated so as not to have to come in contact with his belly.

"No."

"Why, Addison, I was under the impression that you were an early riser," he said in a falsely placating tone.

"What do you want, sheriff?"

"Ah, well, I am here to take written statements from you and your father," he said. "Where is he? Surely he is not still in bed?" The sheriff began walking towards the closed bedroom door, his intent obviously to look within.

"My father has already gone to the stables, sheriff. You can no doubt speak to him there." Addison hoped that the sheriff would give up upon not finding Addigo in the stable and simply return to town.

The sheriff stopped mere steps from the bedroom door and turned what he was sure was his most charming smile on Addison. "Now, that is strange. I stopped there first before coming here. I thought you might both be there, but no one has even fed the animals yet."

Addison glared at the sheriff and grudgingly admitted that perhaps she should watch him a bit closer. The man could stumble onto her secret before she was ready, and that simply would not do.

Making a decided effort to appear calm, Addison dropped her folded arms and tried to give the sheriff a smile. "Again, is there something I can help you with, sheriff?"

The sheriff chuckled, thinking that his charms worked on the entire female population, even big ones like Addison Le Claire.

Cockily, the sheriff sat down at the small table that graced the center of the room and pulled some folded papers from his right breast pocket. "Well, the reason I am here is to get you and your father's statements as to your whereabouts on the afternoon Lord Baptiste was shot."

Brontë had eased open the door to the bedroom just a crack so that she could see who the visitor was. She was only able to see the sheriff's back and the angry scowl on Addison's face as she looked down at the man.

"Well, my father is not here," Addison said through clenched teeth. "So if you leave those, I am sure that one of us will get them back to you." She had already turned to show him to the door, but the sheriff's only movement was to stretch his feet out in front of him and study Addison from under his heavy lashes.

"Well, that should be fine for your father's, but since I am here, why do you not go ahead and give me yours?" He pulled out a pen and smoothed the creases in the stack of papers.

"Sheriff, I do not have time for this," Addison said. "I am

already late as it is." She would not admit her inability to write to this arrogant man.

"Forgive me, Miss Le Claire. I will not take much more of your time. I took the liberty of writing down your statement after you gave it to me. All you have to do is sign on this line and that should be all that I need from you." The sheriff's mouth twisted into a toothy smile.

Addison slowly approached the table and took the seat across from him. She picked up a sheet of paper and stared at it for a moment.

"Oh, do forgive me." The sheriff smiled. "That one is your father's, here is yours." He handed her a second stack and Addison nervously rubbed her sweaty palms on her trousers and picked them up. She studied them, but aside from her name she could not make out any of the other words on the papers.

"I think I am going to wait until I can talk to my father before signing this."

The sheriff snorted. "Whatever for? There is nothing written here that you did not tell me yourself." He looked Addison up and down once more before standing to leave. "Very well, if you insist. Actually, it is a good idea that you discuss things with your father. It is always better to get a man's opinion, and since you have no husband to take care of things for you..."

Addison bit back a retort. She was just relieved that the nosy man would be leaving soon. Her thoughts had turned to the Lady Baptiste when she became aware that the sheriff was still speaking to her and had managed to step closer to her without her even realizing it.

"My wife died giving birth to our fourth child. I am in need of a wife and you are too old not to have a husband. Shall I speak to your father about an arrangement the next time I see him?"

Brontë clamped her teeth down over her lip and her eyes shot daggers at the sheriff as he advanced on Addison. *How dare he all but accuse her of shooting Lord John, and, in the same breath, nearly ask her to be a wet nurse for his heathen children?*

Addison's chin dropped as she stared incredulously at the still-advancing sheriff. She was still frozen in shock when the sheriff raised his hand, presumably to stroke Addison's cheek. Addison's left hand shot up and caught the man's fingers in a tight grasp.

"Sheriff, are you asking me to marry you?"

Brontë could not see Addison; her voice, however, almost sounded like she was actually quite pleased with his offer. If not for the white-knuckled grip that Addison had on the sheriff's pudgy fingers, she would have assumed that she was eavesdropping on a romantic marriage proposal.

"Let go of me, you stupid cow," the sheriff gasped, his normally pink face paling to a sickly white, beads of perspiration breaking out on his forehead.

"Now, Sheriff, is that anyway to talk to someone you wish to take care of your offspring?" she asked again, just as sweetly. "Ooh, I am quite certain you will want me to squeeze out a few new ones as well."

Each of Addison's sweetly spoken words was punctuated with a squeeze to the now-bloodless fingers she held in her hand. The sheriff sank to his knees and Addison knelt so that she could keep her grip on his fingers.

"Oh, my, Sheriff, look at your fingers; they have gone white. I think that I cut the blood flow to them." Addison screwed her face up as if in thought. "I think you should go before I cut the blood flow to other body parts that you might need if you plan on increasing that lovely family of yours."

The sheriff, still trying to regain his composure, got clumsily to his feet, while Addison rose smoothly to hers. He turned to go.

"Sheriff? Do not come back out here without sending word first. A girl needs her privacy." The sweet tone of voice was still present, but Brontë shivered as Addison's fists clenched and she took one step towards the cowering sheriff.

Brontë swallowed. She had been right. Addison was not one to be played with.

The sheriff nodded and fumbled with the door for a few seconds before he managed to open it and scurry out.

Addison watched the man go with a scowl creasing her brow. She closed the door and approached the scattered documents on the table. Momentarily forgetting the presence of the Lady in the back room, Addison glared down at the words printed on the pages. They might as well have been a foreign language for her understanding of them.

Addison slammed the papers down on the table and placed her balled fist to her forehead. Her head had begun to pound, just as it always did when she tried to decipher words on paper. Her father's frustration with her inability to comprehend had now become her own. '*You must learn to read if you ever expect to be anything more then a servant.*'

'*If you can be a servant, why can't I?*' she had mumbled to his retreating back.

Addison was so lost in thought that she had forgotten the fact that the Lady was still hiding in the chilly back bedroom. She opened her mouth to call out that it was safe for her to come out when she heard a throat being cleared behind her.

"Addison, would you help me, please?" Brontë turned her back and without a word Addison began to button her dress. "I think I may be able to help you."

Addison frowned at the back of Lady Baptiste's head before finishing her task. "Help me?" She repeated. "Help me with what, my lady?"

"I know, Addison." Brontë turned around and met Addison's gaze. "You do not have to keep it a secret, at least not from me."

Addison wiped her face clean of emotion as she waited for the Lady to continue. She could already see her plans falling apart if the Lady had somehow found out that her father had passed away months before.

"Addison, I am sorry, but I know you cannot read."

Addison's short-lived moment of happiness that she had not been found out was quickly replaced by embarrassment and then, as usual with Addison, anger. "Who told you that I could not read?" she asked angrily.

"N-no one had to tell me, Addison. I have known since the day that you put my shoes in the library."

There was a moment of awkward silence in which Brontë began to think that perhaps she had overstepped her boundaries by interfering with Addison's private life. She opened her mouth to apologize, but Addison spoke first.

"I have tried, you know."

Brontë frowned. "Have tried what?"

"To learn to read," Addison answered heatedly. "My father said he would teach me what he knew, but we never seemed to have time. I tried on my own, but I do not think I see what everyone else sees."

"What do you see, Addison?"

"It is hard to explain. I just think that everyone sees something that I do not. None of it makes any sense to me. I try to look at the words, but nothing looks the same. I go to the library," she looked up quickly. "After my work is done," she added, as if assuring Lady Baptiste that she did not do it when she should be working.

Brontë smiled, encouraging her to continue.

"I try to read the words, but they do not make sense to me, so I end up just looking at the books with the beautiful drawings." She shrugged dejectedly.

"Addison, can we at least try? Please, what harm would it do? There is so much more to books than just looking at the pictures."

"Do you not think I know that?" Addison jumped to her feet. Her intention was to slam out of the cottage and run to speak to her father, but the look on the Lady's face stopped her.

"Please forgive me, my lady. I did not mean to yell at you," she said, as she sank back down in her chair. "It is just that when I was younger, some of the kids in town would say that I was dumb and stupid. I do not understand why I cannot read, but I do not *feel* ignorant. My father says that not everyone can do everything. I can paint pretty well, but he never could. All of his paintings look like a child made them." Addison smiled, remembering.

Brontë gasped. "It was you! You are the one that oiled the ladder and replaced my book?"

Addison flushed. "Yes, I suppose so. I try to keep it up in there; it seems such a shame that people who read do not take advantage of it." Addison shrugged. "I go there sometimes to think and get ideas for paintings. I used to bring books home that looked interesting and my father would read them to me. The one that you were reading was one of our favorites. I thought I had forgotten to put it back. I almost know all the stories in it by heart."

Last night Brontë had been too cold and unhappy to look about the cottage. But now she saw that nearly every wall was covered with Addison's art. She examined each one with amazement. Some of them had clearly been done when Addison was a young girl but even then Addison's talent was obvious; her art was as refined as any that Brontë had ever seen. She turned around and noted with some trepidation that Addison was watching her as she admired the paintings.

"Addison, will you at least consider trying? I should get back to the manor house before I am missed, but would you at least agree to let me try to teach you?"

"I will consider it, my lady," Addison said, and was rewarded with one of the most beautiful smiles she had ever seen.

"Oh, thank you, Addison. You won't regret it." With a final goodbye, Brontë was out the door and walking quickly up the path toward the manor house.

Addison watched her go until she was but a speck. She shook her head and smiled at Perry, who had somehow managed to sleep through all of the excitement and was just now crawling, ever so slowly, from under the rumpled cot.

"Perry, did I just tell her that I would think about it? What have I gotten myself into?" Perry's mouth stretched into a large slow yawn before she limped over to inspect her empty food dish.

Chapter
Eight

BRONTË HURRIED DOWN the path, her step fueled by her exhilaration. She could not believe that Addison had agreed to allow her to help. She slowed her pace as she reached the manor house, fearful of being questioned by her mother, or, worse yet, being seen by one of the servants in her rumpled clothing from the day before.

Luck was with her, however, as she entered the house unseen by anybody and was able to make her way up to her bedroom seconds before Mary entered with her tea.

"Oh, there you are, m'lady," Mary's face looked worried. "I tried to find you last night, but..."

Brontë felt a surge of panic; of course Mary would have come up to help her to bed. "Mary, please forgive me, I fell asleep in the library. It is not your fault at all."

"Thank you, m'lady," she said with some relief evident in her voice. "M'lady, if you would be so kind..."

"What is it, Mary?"

"Well, it is my mother, she would not be happy with me if she knew that I allowed you to sleep in your clothes. It is just that I was so very tired and I did not think to look in the library."

Mary looked as if she was going to cry and Brontë felt incredibly guilty. She grabbed Mary's work-hardened hands. "It shall be our solemn secret, Mary. No one need ever know."

"Oh thank you, m'lady."

Brontë was still feeling guilty about allowing Mary to take responsibility for something she had no control over when she walked downstairs an hour later. After exchanging a few words with Wesley about John's condition, she made her way to the library.

Once inside the library, Brontë tirelessly sought out as many books as she could that she felt would not only help Addison, but would be of interest to her. She found several children's books that she assumed had been in John's family for years. She also found numerous portrait books and a few books about touring Paris on a small budget. Satisfied that she had probably found enough books for now, she was in the process of carrying the armload to her room when it occurred to her that she had intended to look up her mother's illness in the medical dictionary.

Brontë opened the heavy volume and carefully turned the thin pages until she came to what she was looking for. Brontë read under her breath:

"*Hysteria of the Womb:* An ailment found commonly in women between the ages of forty and sixty. Most common behavior exhibited in patients suffering from this condition is overwhelming or unmanageable fear or emotional excess."

Brontë nodded. She was sure that her mother suffered from emotional excess. That passage described her mother almost exactly. Scanning through the text for a moment, Brontë finally found what she was looking for.

"Hysteria of the Womb can be treated successfully by the induction of *Hysterical Paroxysm.*"

"Hysterical Paroxysm? What does that mean?" She quickly scanned the book. She found the definition further down the page. "Here it is." Brontë ran her finger along the passage as she read.

"*Hysterical Paroxysm:* The manual manipulation of the female genitals," Brontë paused before finishing in disbelief, "for the purposes of inducing orgasm."

Brontë backed away from the book as if it were a living entity. Her hand covered her mouth and she looked around for somewhere to release the bile that had risen in her throat. Finally, Brontë was able to control her nervous stomach enough to allow her to leave the library. The books she had spent two hours gathering were left on the floor of the library, forgotten.

Brontë nearly made it to her bedroom door without incident but was stopped by a tentative voice hailing her. Warily she turned and gave Mary a sickly smile. "Yes, Mary?"

"Forgive me for disturbing you, m'lady, but this package just came. The rain blurred the address label but I thought I should just deliver it to you."

Brontë nodded, took the rather large package from Mary and escaped to her room where she lay down tiredly with her arm resting on her moist forehead. Her mother was depraved, and worse yet, based on the lusty way she had watched Addison bathe herself, she had obviously passed the trait on to Brontë as well.

Brontë flushed as her thoughts went to Addison Le Claire and what she had witnessed the night before. Sighing, Brontë sat up, nearly knocking the large brown package to the floor.

Curious, Brontë picked up the box and shook it a few times before deciding that she would have to open it to determine its rightful owner. Brontë ripped off the paper to reveal a black case roughly the size of a book. Carefully opening it, Brontë picked up the small metallic instrument and examined it thoroughly. It sat neatly in her hand and the top was painted an attractive periwinkle. Turning it over, Brontë saw a small key, which she turned, causing the object to vibrate. "It must be some type of tool that John ordered." She was returning the tool to its box when she noticed a small hand-written note tucked behind a rather elegant looking silk ribbon that said *Milton Church Vibrosage*. Brontë removed the thin notepaper and opened it.

Dear Mrs. Emily Havisham,
    At the request of your physician, Doctor Eli Quimby, we are proud to offer you this, one of our most popular massage units. We are positive that with daily use of our unit, you will look and feel so vibrant that your friends will notice the immediate change. Please note that due to the delicate nature of this equipment, we will no longer accept returns or exchanges on this product.

Yours truly,
Iona Fue

My God, what does one do with something like this? Brontë scanned the box and found a small booklet of instructions. She read for a moment before closing the booklet, red-faced, and placing it back in the box. After the ruckus her mother had put up the last time she had received her 'treatments,' Brontë was determined that she not test this new 'medical procedure' in her home. She could already hear her mother's voice screaming down the halls of Markby.

Embarrassed at the direction her thoughts had taken, she got to her feet and, in an effort to keep busy, headed back to the library. Not even glancing in the direction of the medical dictionary, she gathered the books that she had left earlier; her intention was to go through each of them to determine which she thought Addison would like most.

Once again, however, she was interrupted before she could retreat behind closed doors.

"Brontë, are you there, dearest?"

Brontë grimaced. It was as if her mother had four ears. She could hear people through closed doors.

"Mother, I will be there in a moment," Brontë said.

She set the books on her desk and slid the black box and the torn wrapping paper underneath her bed for consideration at a more opportune moment. Brontë closed the door behind her and quickly made her way to her mother's room. Opening the door, she noted that her mother did not look much different from the last time she had seen her. *So much for the effectiveness of Doctor Quimby's treatment,* Brontë thought wryly.

"May I help you with something, Mother?" Brontë looked around the room so as not to have to look at her mother for too long.

"Yes, would you mind pouring a glass of water for me, dear heart? I am simply parched." Mrs. Havisham pointed weakly to the water pitcher within arm's reach of her. Brontë sighed lightly, poured the water into a glass, and handed it to her mother.

"Will that be all, Mother?" Brontë inquired hopefully.

"No dear, just one moment."

Brontë was forced to wait as her mother took several deep breaths after each swallow of water. After having enough, she handed the glass to Brontë instead of setting it down on the bedside table just to her right.

Brontë knew from experience that her mother would not say what was on her mind until she felt that Brontë had stood around long enough. "Brontë, I have been meaning to talk to you about that *Addison* girl."

"What about Addison, Mother?" Brontë steeled herself for what was to come next.

"Forgive me, dear, but I do not think she is at all appropriate. I think that you should talk to her father and tell him that her behavior is inappropriate for a servant at Markby Estates."

Mrs. Havisham folded her fingers just above her duvet and peered at Brontë. "If he is incapable of making sure that his daughter receives the right training, then perhaps he should not work here either, in my opinion." Mrs. Havisham harrumphed. "Imagine if Mildred or one of the other ladies were to ever come by for tea and see that, that woman walking around in those *trousers.* Her skin is so *brown.*" She whispered the last few words as if they were expletives.

Brontë unsuccessfully tried to hide her shock. Addison could be gruff, to be sure, but for some reason she had gone out of her way to be polite and accommodating to Mrs. Havisham. In return, the woman was suggesting, no, insisting really, that Brontë remove her from her duties, and her father as well. Brontë felt the hairs on the back of her neck stand on end as she stared at the self-satisfied smirk on the older woman's face.

"What has Addison ever done to you, Mother?"

"Why, what do you mean, dear?"

"What has she done to you to make you treat her in such a

way?"

"Why would she need to do anything to me, dear? I am simply stating that I do not feel her appearance and behavior is appropriate for people of our stature."

"Appropriate behavior?" Brontë's voice had risen nearly two octaves. "Surely you do not believe that what you are doing is appropriate behavior?"

"What is that supposed to mean, Brontë Bonnaella Baptiste?"

Brontë winced again as the hated middle name was screeched at the top of her mother's lungs. Brontë had had about all she was willing to take. Addison deserved more respect than any of the pampered servants that her mother employed and yet her mother had, for some reason, taken an instant dislike to Addison and was attempting to get her fired from her job. For the life of her, Brontë could not figure out why.

"Mother, please. I do not wish to listen to you speak about Addison in this way."

Mrs. Havisham looked at Brontë as if she had struck her. "I am your mother, Brontë!"

"That is correct, and I always thought we were taught to treat people with respect, but now I know that I obviously missed the part of the lesson where you said it only applied as long as the people are just like us."

"How dare you take her side over mine!"

"Her side, Mother? She has no side. She has no idea that you are even speaking of her in this manner, how could she have a side?"

"I do not understand why you are so upset. I am simply saying her appearance and behavior are not suitable for this home."

"Mother, this is my home, not yours, and until John wakes up, I am the only one that can make the determination of what is suitable and what is not."

"But why does she have to dress that way and do such manly work? It is just unbecoming, I tell you."

Brontë was only just able to stifle the impulse to point out that Doctor Quimby's treatments were more unbecoming than anything that Addison might do. "Mother, Addison was born here, this is her home just as much as mine. I would never ask her to leave, and besides, she is the best worker we have here. From what I understand, the place would fall apart without her. If someone were to be uncomfortable with her appearance, then I am sorry, there is nothing I could do about that, as she is a necessity at the Estate. I am sure that there will be other places that they could visit besides Markby."

"Are you saying that I am not welcome here?" Brontë's mother looked as though she would burst into tears.

"Of course not, Mother. I love you. You will always be welcome in my home. But this is Addison's home, too, and it always will be, for as long as she wishes." Brontë sat on the edge of her mother's bed, feeling drained.

Brontë's mother sniffed and was silent for a moment. Then she said, almost slyly, "And what of your husband? Surely he will not like the fact that you are being so nice to her."

"Mother, I am no nicer to her than any of the others."

"I saw you give her that book, Brontë."

"Mother, you give your servants Christmas gifts every year." Brontë said, trying to remind herself to stay calm.

"Well, that is different." Mrs. Havisham sniffed.

"How so, Mother?"

"My servants are not so crass. It is hard to find good people. You have to give them a little extra to keep the good ones."

Brontë rolled her eyes. Not one of her mother's servants could hold a candle to Addison. They all did their jobs and were exceedingly polite, but not one of them would go out of their way to do as good a job as Addison.

"Well, dearest, I just hope you do not pay her much, because I think you would be better off with a boy in her place and that is all I am going to say about that."

Brontë tried to make small talk with her mother, but was increasingly aware of the undercurrent of tension between them. Brontë gave her mother another glass of water and retreated from the room.

Brontë was on her way to see John when she passed by his office. Something her mother had said made her take a few steps back and enter the room. The office looked as if it had not been changed since the Lord Senior's death. The obscenely large wooden desk and its cavernous leather chair did not seem to suit John's disposition. A brass and oak box resting on one corner of the desk begged Brontë to investigate its contents. With a husband lying unconscious from a gunshot wound in a nearby room, the irony of the exquisitely crafted dueling pistols, nestled in satin, was not lost on her. With a shake of her head, Brontë sank into the large leather chair and focused her attention on the reason she had come into the office in the first place.

Pulling the salary ledger from the desk drawer, she turned to the page containing Addigo Le Claire's name and inhaled deeply in disgust at the paltry sum of money he was being paid. As she began to turn the page, Brontë noted there was a marked difference in Addigo's most recent four signatures. The first few, although not the neatest she had ever seen, were certainly neater than the crookedly scrawled Addigo that had been placed on the line for the last four months. Unsure of the meaning of this discovery, she continued to scan through the ledger and was stunned to find that Addison's name was not listed at all.

Brontë shook her head and was about to close the book when she caught sight of Mary and Beatrice's salaries, which were twice the amount that Addigo was being paid. It did not make sense. Brontë was well aware of the inequality in pay amongst men and women. It was unheard of to have a man of Addigo's supposed skills making less than a new upstairs maid such as Mary.

Brontë checked Thomas's salary, thinking that he, being the newest servant, would make less than anyone, and was startled to note that his pay was higher than everyone's with the exception of, to Brontë's stunned amazement, Victoria. Shockingly, Victoria made more money than all of the other servants.

This one fact alone was enough to convince Brontë that Victoria not only had some hold over Lord Senior, but that the hold extended to John as well.

Brontë sat back in the leather chair with a frown, trying to figure out what the secret could be. Why was Victoria making so much more than the oldest male servant at the estate? Why would Addigo make so little, and, even more curious, stay on when he could no doubt make much more money elsewhere?

Brontë had noted that, according to the log, everyone would be expecting to receive his or her pay the first Tuesday of the month. "Which means today," Brontë said to herself.

She would ask Addigo about the discrepancy in pay when he came to pick up his wages. After writing down a few figures, Brontë went in search of Thomas so that he could drive her into town. Brontë went in to see the manager of the small bank that sat in the center of town. Luckily for her, the doctor had mentioned to him John's situation, so he approved her withdrawal from the Markby accounts and she was on her way back to the estate within fifteen minutes.

After eating a delicious meal, Brontë retreated to the office, where she went over the books just to make sure that she had not missed anything. She noticed that the rise in food cost seemed to coincide with Victoria's arrival at the estate. Brontë figured that was a coincidence, but she also noticed something else disturbing. After turning several pages in the large leather bound volume, she was able to ascertain that Addigo Le Claire was making the same exact salary as he had the day he had first started working at Markby Estates. She still could not find any wages listed for Addison. It truly made no sense. Either her wages were not being recorded or Addison was working for free.

Brontë was interrupted from her reverie by Victoria's appearance. "I have come to get my wages, m'lady."

Brontë's mouth twisted. *Of course you would be the first to come for your pay.* She wordlessly handed Victoria the large sum of money. She considered questioning the woman about her pay rate but decided against it. If Victoria were up to something, it was unlikely she would admit to it just because Brontë asked. Brontë decided to allow her to take her money and run, for now.

Mary was next. She shyly explained that she would be going to buy fabric for a new dress with her money.

Brontë smiled at her and after a few more pleasant words, Mary hurried out so that her mother could receive her wages next. Brontë made sure to tell Beatrice what a fine job Mary did, causing Beatrice to flush with pride. Wesley came next, followed closely by Cook and finally Thomas.

Brontë waited nearly an hour for Addigo to come and receive his pay. She filled the time by scratching out notes for herself regarding the discrepancies in the books. She was so into her own thoughts that she did not hear the first time Addison cleared her throat.

Brontë looked up and could not help but smile at the tall, strong, young woman that stood in the entryway. The battered hat that she had worn the first time Brontë saw her was now being turned anxiously in her hands.

"My father asked me to pick up the wages, my lady."

Brontë nodded. "Please come in, Addison."

Addison seemed to hesitate before entering and shutting the door behind her. Still turning the hat, she sat down in a chair across from Brontë and waited.

"Addison, I know how much Addigo makes, but I cannot seem to find record of your wages here. I am sure it is merely an oversight?"

Addison looked down at her hat. "There is no mistake, my lady. My father and I share the wages."

Brontë's jaw dropped. "B-But how is that possible? You work harder than anyone on this place."

Addison smiled uncertainly at Lady Baptiste and sat a little taller in her chair. "I try to work hard, my lady. I like my work," she said, and shrugged as if that should be explanation enough.

Figuring the stoic young woman would not tell her anything else, Brontë chose a different direction for her questioning. "Addison, I would like to see your father. Will you let him know that I would like to meet with him today, please?"

The blood drained from Addison's face as the moment she had feared was finally at hand. "My lady, he is not feeling well. May I help you with something?" she asked, hating herself once again for the never-ending lie, but telling herself that it would be worth it when she came face to face with her mother.

"I see. I was going to come by to see you tomorrow anyway. Perhaps I could talk to him then?"

Addison opened her mouth and closed it again. The decision to pick up her father's wages had been a difficult one. Deciding it would be more suspicious if someone did not pick up Addigo's pay, she had come, hoping that Lady Baptiste would not think it odd. After all, in the past, Lord John had barely looked up from his lunch long enough to hand out wages.

Brontë sat back in her chair and looked at the strained young woman in front of her, taking in the tired face." He is not sick, is he, Addison?" she guessed.

Expecting an immediate denial, she was not prepared for Addison's reaction. She froze, her eyes closed, and the most defeated look that Brontë had ever seen came across her face, leaving behind the features of a scared young woman.

"You can trust me," Brontë said as she leaned forward and put her hand over Addison's. "You can trust me, Addison," she repeated.

Addison closed her eyes and sighed. She opened them and looked directly into the Lady's compassionate green eyes.

"My father...he died, my lady." Addison's voice broke as she told someone for the first time that the only person who loved her unconditionally was no longer alive. It made it all the more final for Addison.

"Oh, Addison." Brontë gripped Addison's hand under her own and Addison curled over her fingers, but refused to look up at her as she continued to speak.

"I have been the sole caretaker here at Markby for over six months, ever since he got too sick to work. I took his wages but I made sure that the work was done just as he would have done it." She looked at Lady Baptiste and then down at their entwined hands. *My hand is so much bigger and rougher than hers.* The thought made her sad.

"Of course. You do a wonderful job. You had every right to be paid for your work. Quite frankly, I do not understand why your father, or you, for that matter, would stay on for such a paltry sum."

Addison did look up then. "Well, I have my suspicions about my father, but as for me, well, I am a woman, my lady. I thought it would only be so much time before the Lord noticed that I was always around and my father never was. So I decided to make as much money as I could before I was asked to leave."

"It is not very much money, Addison."

"No, but then, I do not need much. I hunt and fish for most of what I need. I also have a small garden in back of my cottage. I save most of the money for when I..."

"For when you—?" Brontë urged her to continue.

"For when I leave. My aunt in Paris is expecting me soon. I am to study art."

Brontë ignored the sinking feeling in her chest and decided to plow on as long as she had Addison talking. "Addison, there is one other thing I do not understand. Why did your father stay for so long? He could have found better pay anywhere."

"It is a long story, and I am not certain of the facts myself, my lady. "

"I understand, Addison. I do not wish to upset you. The whole situation looked odd. I wanted to be sure that I did not overlook something."

Nodding, Addison stood, hat in hand. "Thank you, my lady," she said and walked toward the door.

"Addison, you are forgetting something." Addison turned to the Lady with a worried frown.

"Your wages."

"My lady?"

"You are forgetting your pay, Addison. Is that not what you are here for?"

"Yes, but...thank you, my lady." Addison gave her a crooked smile and picked up the envelope that Lady Baptiste pushed towards her. Addison frowned and looked into the envelope.

"My lady, this is too much," she stated quickly.

"No, it is not, Addison. I am sure that discrepancy was an oversight on my husband, and Lord Senior's, part. I raised your wage and gave you back pay for the last few months."

"My lady, I cannot take this." Addison made to hand the envelope back.

"Did you not work for it? Did you not earn it?"

"Yes, my lady, I work very hard," Addison knew she worked hard and deserved far more than she normally earned.

"Well then, I think you should stop arguing with me and take your money."

"Yes, my lady." Addison gave her a small smile and was just about to leave when Lady Baptiste called her back. Turning warily, Addison waited for what came next.

"I would like to start tomorrow, if that suits you, Addison?

"Start, my lady?" Addison said, her voice flat.

"Surely you have not forgotten already? The reading and writing lessons?"

Addison's face cleared. "Oh. Yes, tomorrow should be fine."

"What time shall I come by?"

"Well, how about half past six? I should be done with my chores then."

"Half past six it is, Addison. Oh, and Addison, I just want to thank you for trusting me. I want you to know that I will never betray your confidence."

Addison gave her a genuine smile that nearly stole Brontë's breath away. "I know, my lady. I will see you tomorrow."

"Goodbye, Addison."

"Goodbye, my lady."

Brontë waited until the other woman left before taking a deep breath and shaking her head. It was amazing that Addison had run the estate so well, for so long, that no one even suspected that Addigo had passed away.

Brontë drummed her fingers on the smooth surface of the desk. Markby Estate seemed to have many mysteries. Brontë was sure that Addison was the key to some of them, but she was not sure just how. Brontë got up from her chair and stretched. After taking one final admiring look at the dueling pistols, she left the office, shutting the door behind her. She spent most of the day relieving Wesley by sitting and reading to John, but Addison Le Claire was never far from her thoughts.

Chapter
Nine

THE NEXT DAY went by quickly for Addison. She was whistling for all she was worth, a habit her father had oft attempted to discourage, but one he secretly appreciated, as Addison was an excellent whistler. The highs and lows that she would hit while she worked would often make Addigo pause and smile. She only whistled when she was exceedingly happy.

Addison brushed her horse Magnus until his coat shone from her efforts. After one last gentle rub to his nose, she closed the barn door and trotted home. Addison firmly believed there was no reason to walk when she could run. She reached her cottage in no time and quickly stripped down and washed so as not to offend the Lady.

After putting on a clean shirt and smoothing her hair, Addison walked about, cleaning the place as best she could, unable to relax. She had been that way since the night before, unable to sleep in her excitement over the Lady's acceptance and the fact that they would be spending time together.

Addison paused momentarily as she removed a rag from her sink. "Why am I so excited about this afternoon?" she wondered aloud. "She is coming here to teach me, not play hide the potato."

Addison sat down heavily, looking around the small snug cottage. *Why would she bother? It is not as if I need to read to be caretaker, do I?* Remembering how Lady Baptiste had smiled at her made Addison sit up taller. *Regardless of why she wants to teach me, I will try as best I can to learn.*

A knock at Addison's door caused her to jump to her feet, inadvertently knocking over a chair, which she quickly righted as she smoothed her hair back and adjusted the leather tie that kept it out of her face.

Opening the door, her nervousness was forgotten as she had to lunge to keep the stack of books that Lady Baptiste carried from toppling over. She caught two and then removed another two from the top of the stack to reveal a grinning Brontë. Addison could not help but grin back, albeit uncertainly, at the charming young woman.

Brontë breathed thanks and blew a strand of hair from her face. Her sparkling green eyes took in the flush of Addison's ruddy complexion.

"I did not think I would make it."

"That is a lot of books, my lady. Surely they are not all for me?" Addison said, her eyes growing large.

Brontë's grin widened as Addison stepped aside to let her into the cozy little home. She breathed a sigh of relief as she set the heavy books down. "Forgive me for being so late. I forgot that Wesley asked for the day off. I had to wait until Thomas was done with his chores so that someone could sit with Lord John."

Addison swallowed guiltily as the Lady passed her, smelling of powder and roses.

"I have not asked about Lord John's health. With everything that has been going on..." Addison shrugged apologetically.

"There is no change, really, Addison," Brontë said calmly. "Has the sheriff been by to bother you again?"

Addison smirked. "No, my lady. I think we have come to an understanding."

"I think you have, too."

Addison shifted nervously under the penetrating green gaze. "Will the table be all right to start, my lady? I do not have any place else for us to sit except the table around back, but it is dusty out there and I would hate for you to get your pretty dress dirty."

"This will do fine, Addison." Brontë blushed at the veiled compliment as she sat down at one of the surprisingly comfortable hand-hewn chairs.

"I went to the library and picked out a few books I thought you might be interested in reading. I thought I would bring them over all at once."

Noting the wary looks Addison was giving the books, Brontë cleared her throat and attempted to put Addison at ease. "Addison, if you are not up to this today, we can try again tomorrow."

Addison shifted once more and then, in a rush, she sat down on the bench across from Lady Baptiste. As she straddled the bench she unconsciously gripped its sides, her eyes now riveted to the book on horses that Brontë had grabbed as a last minute addition to the stack.

"No, I want to. It is just that they are so large," Addison said in a voice so quiet that if Brontë had not been paying such close attention, she might have missed the comment altogether.

Brontë watched as one long brown finger traced the edge of the book. Instinctively, Brontë's hand covered Addison's in a gesture meant to be soothing. The contact sent the familiar feeling of completeness flowing through Brontë as it had when she had watched Addison bathe from the woods. Brontë quickly removed her hand and began rifling through the satchel that she had carried with her in search of writing implements.

"We should get started before it becomes too late and you are stuck with me again." Brontë laughed to hide her embarrassment. Addison joined in, although she could think of worse things to wake up to than those shapely legs straddling her waist.

Do not think about that right now, Addison told herself, watching as Brontë shuffled through her items and finally came up with a children's primer.

Addison looked away as she recognized the book that she had tried to read on her own several times without success. "I cannot."

"You cannot?"

"No!" Seeing the light dim in Lady Baptiste's eyes slightly, Addison instantly regretted her brusque response. The Lady was only trying to help, and here she was treating her as if she were the enemy. A voice in the back of Addison's head promptly replied, *She is the enemy.* Addison looked into the hurt green eyes of the Lady in question and decided, *No, she is not the enemy, she is trying to help me and she does not even know me.*

"P-Please, I didn't mean to sound so angry. I do not want you to be disappointed." Addison was unable to continue to look into Lady Baptiste's eyes.

"But, why would I ever be disappointed in you?" Brontë asked.

"Because I cannot read that one," Addison said even though her throat felt constricted. "I have tried before and I could not read it."

"Addison." Brontë paused not wanting Addison to hear the lump that had formed in her throat. "Addison. I brought the books so that we could maybe gauge where we should start. I do not expect you to already know. I am already making a mess of this." Brontë wrung her hands underneath the table and thought hard about what she wanted to say to the proud young woman.

Addison cursed herself again. Clenching her fist, she decided to at least give it a try. "I can write my name and my father's name, but that is all."

Addison continued to look down at the table for a moment and then she forced herself to look up and was immediately blinded by the most brilliant smile that she had ever seen. Once again, she was forced to respond with a weak smile of her own.

"Addison, that is wonderful, we can start there," Brontë said, as she quickly scribbled a few words on paper, purposely making them large, and turning it to Addison. "This is your name, and this is your father's." Addison nodded vigorously. At least she could recognize those two words.

"Did you know that you could make several words out of the letters you already know how to write?" Brontë carefully spelled out the word 'dog' on the paper in large letters, noting that Addison's intelligent eyes followed her every move. "Do you recognize this first letter, Addison?"

Addison stared at it for a minute and answered, "It is a *D*, my lady, like in my father's name, and mine."

"Yes, that is correct. And this letter, it is in both your names, too."

"It is an *O*, my lady," Addison answered, quite pleased with herself at having answered all of the questions correctly so far.

"Yes, that is correct. Now this one?" Brontë pointed to the *G* and Addison immediately answered that it was a *G*.

"Addison, do you think you can write that word out for me?"

Addison took the pen, dropping it once before painstakingly writing the three letters on the paper. When she was finished, she handed the paper to Brontë, who studied it as Addison shifted uneasily in her seat.

"Excellent," she pronounced, causing Addison to smile against her will. She seemed to do that a lot lately. "Now, can you tell me what it says?"

Addison's smile started to slip as she looked down at her own crooked and unevenly spaced letters.

Brontë jumped up from her chair and joined Addison on the bench. Addison, who sat straddling the bench, moved back to give her more room. With only the smallest help from Lady Baptiste, she was soon able to sound out the word, pronouncing it, "Dog!" and grinning proudly.

"I have an idea, Addison. You could put a drawing under it to help you associate the word with its meaning. We could even hang it up so that you could look at it whenever you wish."

"Hmm," Addison took the paper and mumbled, "It may take a moment."

Remembering how shy Addison was when it came to her art, Brontë acted as nonchalant as possible. "I shall look at these books while you sketch."

"Thank you." Addison said as she once again picked up her pencil. Relieved that she could now do something that she did well, she threw herself into making a sketch of Perry, periodically looking up to see if Lady Baptiste was peeking at her work before going back to her drawing.

Brontë watched Addison's movements out of the corner of her eye. As she drew, she expertly shaded with her finger and every so often she would pause to observe Perry. Although Brontë could not see the sketch, she was positive that Addison was doing a wonderful job.

Brontë tried to concentrate on her book, but was having a hard time as she thought of the complicated young woman sitting next to her. Addison unconsciously tapped her foot as her hand quickly moved over the paper at different angles and lines turned into a small image of the companion that she so loved. Perry, for her part, was a perfect model as she now lay near the hearth with her feet in the air, lightly snoring.

Addison finished and was about to show it to the Lady when she paused, her nostrils flaring as the powdery floral scent that was Lady Baptiste floated past. Addison, still in her sideways position on the bench, was able to steal a few quick unobserved gazes at the smaller woman's somewhat pale skin and delicate features.

Lady Baptiste wore her hair down in the back tonight, making her look younger but more approachable. Addison watched her lips move slightly as she read, and moved forward trying to hear what she was saying. If she moved any further she would call attention to herself, so instead she contented herself with just watching the Lady's moist lips move as she read from her book. Brontë was so deeply engrossed in her book that she was unaware of Addison's deepening perusal. Finally, shaking her head, Addison picked up the paper and studied it before placing it in front of the Lady.

Brontë looked down at Addison's sketch. It was just as detailed and beautiful as she had thought it would be. She smiled and turned to Addison uttering, "It is beautiful..." Her words trailed off as she realized how close Addison now sat to her. "So beautiful," Brontë whispered, her eyes riveted on Addison's. Her lips parted and her traitorous tongue flicked out teasingly before disappearing again. Addison moved a little closer until she was nearly touching Lady Baptiste, but not quite.

Brontë nervously turned back to her book, her head bowed as the heat from the woman next to her served to keep her aware of the tension that was now between them.

"No, you are the one who is beautiful," Addison whispered, causing Brontë to close her eyes as the warmth of Addison's breath caressed her ear, the soft curls stirring above her earlobe and sending a chill down her back and straight to her nipples. Brontë lifted the book higher, hoping to hide the evidence of her arousal.

"Lady Baptiste, please look at me."

"No."

"Why?" Addison asked even though she knew the answer.

"Because I should not. I cannot." Brontë said softly.

"What harm will it do, my lady?" Addison raised her hand to Lady Baptiste's back as she moved even closer. She sat so close to her that the Lady's dress lay over Addison's outstretched legs. "What harm will it do?" Addison repeated, her voice husky in Brontë's ear. "Are you afraid?" she asked, unable to hide her own fear of the answer.

Brontë shivered. Addison gently caressed her back, unconsciously trying to soothe the Lady as she moved closer. "Please look at me, my lady."

Brontë's vision blurred as she made an attempt to blink back her tears of frustration.

"What do you think will happen if you look at me?" Addison asked as she allowed her fingertips to graze the Lady's soft hair.

Brontë closed her eyes as she inhaled Addison's spicy scent. "I do not know," she said under her breath.

"But I do know, my lady. I know."

Addison leaned forward and placed a gentle kiss on the corner of her eye, tasting the salty tears that threatened to fall. She held her breath waiting for some reaction, any reaction, but the Lady just sat there. Only her profile was visible. Addison placed her warm hand on Lady Baptiste's back once again and gently pulled her closer.

Brontë trembled as she felt the heat of Addison's hand through the layers of clothing.

"You do not have to be afraid," Addison whispered as her own heart pounded staccato in her ears. She kissed the pale temple in front of her, then closed her legs and placed her arms loosely around the smaller woman until she was holding her cradled close into her body. She kissed her gently on the temple again, and then her cheek, before kissing the corner of her quivering mouth. Brontë trembled, and Addison pulled her closer, closing her legs more tightly around her.

"My lady?"

Brontë refused to look up as her stomach lurched and settled. How could she feel this way for Addison and feel nothing for her husband? Addison placed her hand over the Lady's and caressed the top of it as her unbound breasts pressed firmly against Lady Baptiste's arm.

"I want to kiss you," Addison said gravely.

Brontë shook her head, but could not move away from Addison even had she wanted to.

"May I kiss you?" Addison's heart was still hammering in her chest. "Please. It feels like I have wanted to kiss you for such a long time." Addison continued to caress the Lady's back as she spoke.

Deciding to take a chance that she was not alone in feeling as she did, Addison turned Lady Baptiste's chin toward her and, focusing on her lips, leaned in close.

Brontë froze with the first caress of Addison's warm lips to hers. Both pairs of eyes closed and Addison's hand went up to touch the soft tantalizing skin of the Lady's neck and jaw line.

A whimper left Lady Baptiste's throat and seemed to travel straight to Addison's sex, where it hovered, nagging her with the power of her own need. Addison groaned a little and pulled the Lady even closer, crushing warm lips into her own. Feeling small breasts press into her chest, Addison felt as though she might lose all control. She needed to be closer, but there was too much material between them.

Addison's hand went up of its own accord to touch the Lady's breast. Brontë stiffened as her nipples responded to being caressed for the first time. Addison slowly ran her thumb back and forth over the hard point that was becoming more and more pronounced by the second.

Brontë became aware of Addison's harsh breathing, and her own. "We have to stop," she moaned, as she was unable to free herself from Addison's needy mouth.

"No, we do not. We do not have to stop," Addison said against soft lips.

"Yes we do," Brontë moaned and put her hands up to push Addison away, causing both of them to freeze as one of her hands inadvertently cupped Addison's breast. Brontë looked into Addison's blue eyes and turned away from the depths of desire that she saw there.

"Addison, we cannot do this. I am a married woman, Lady of Markby. I just cannot!"

"I know who you are, Lady Baptiste. Every time I say your name I am reminded of who you are," Addison said, her eyes still riveted to the Lady's lips.

Brontë squirmed under the heat of that hungry gaze. "Addison, please stop looking at me like that," she pleaded desperately as she forced herself to bow her head rather than jump on this enigmatic woman before her.

Addison's body stiffened and she sat up straight. Taking in the shaky appearance of the Lady before her, Addison's hands dropped to her own legs, which she gripped painfully. Scooting back along the bench and away from the object of her desire was one of the hardest things Addison had ever done. Brontë, for her part, shivered. She was not sure if it was from the loss of heat from Addison's body or the loss of her touch. One of the dogs howled, drawing Addison's eyes toward the window.

"It is nearing eight o'clock, my lady. Perhaps we should get you back to the manor house." Her regret was clear in her words.

Brontë stood and, without looking at Addison, picked up her

satchel and approached the door to the cottage.

"My lady, will you allow me to walk you back this time? I will stop within the trees so that no one will see me."

Brontë looked up this time and found that Addison was looking anywhere but at her. "I would like that very much, Addison."

Addison smiled and opened the door for Lady Baptiste and they both walked out into the much-needed cool air. They walked for a few minutes and then both decided to speak at the same time.

"Addison, I am—"

"My lady—"

Brontë laughed nervously while Addison just smiled down at her in the dim light of the evening.

"Go ahead, Addison."

Addison nodded and thought for a moment about what she wanted to say. She opened her mouth and spoke from her heart. "I did not mean to make you feel uncomfortable or afraid back there. I have wanted to do that from the moment I first saw you, I think." *Stupid*, Addison chided herself mentally, as she was greeted with silence.

"You did not scare me, Addison. It-I have never been kissed like that before," Brontë said.

"Never?"

"No, never."

"You deserve to be kissed that way all the time."

Brontë glanced quickly over at Addison, but all she could see was Addison's strong profile as she walked, her hands in her pockets, shoulders tensed. She glanced away, blushing as she thought about how those hands had felt on her neck and how strong the arms had felt around her.

Brontë kept walking for a moment longer before she realized that Addison was no longer beside her. Turning back she saw Addison watching her with an unreadable expression on her face.

"This is as far as I should go, my lady."

Brontë looked around, noting the edge of the tree line and the path that would lead her right to the door of the manor house.

"I will wait here until you are inside, Lady Baptiste." Addison said and then felt odd at allowing the Lady to see how much she cared about her well-being. For some reason, it was important for her to keep the Lady safe. So, hands in pockets, she waited for a response.

"When we are alone, please call me Brontë." Brontë shyly stepped forward and placed the sweetest kiss Addison had ever felt on her cheek.

Addison stood there stunned long after Brontë's gentle caress had ended.

"May we study tomorrow?" Brontë asked the still-silent Addison.

Addison nodded vigorously and then looked away, embarrassed.

"I will see you tomorrow, then?"

Addison nodded again and was able to muster a small smile for Brontë. She stood rooted to her spot watching as Brontë hurried down the path and disappeared behind the doors of the manor house.

A wide grin suddenly erupted across Addison's face as she turned on her heels. Where she normally would have trotted back home, she decided instead to enjoy the beautiful and unusually clear night by walking slowly. The birds were silent as a long thin whistle rent the air, peaked and dove melodiously before filtering off into the night.

BRONTË SAT IN front of her mirror brushing her hair, her mind wandering over the events of that day. Always returning to the kiss. She wondered if she had somehow done something to make Addison think that she wanted to be kissed. She flushed as she remembered the warmth of Addison's mouth as it had covered hers. The tenderness had been new to her. Addison had held her as if she were a precious gift. Brontë stopped brushing for a moment and then continued her strokes, having lost count a long time ago.

She had entered the house as if in a dream and had listened in apparent attentiveness as Thomas told her that, as she had expected, there were no changes in John's condition. She had been unable to escape to her room for half an hour, as every servant in the house seemed to need to speak to her about something or other. With Mary's help she had gone through her nighttime ritual automatically, her thoughts continuously playing the last few hours over in her head. Brontë felt that she should be mortified, or at the very least scared. Instead, all she felt was anticipation.

Brontë slowed her brushing. *This is how I should have felt when I married John, not that all-consuming dread.* Brontë set the brush down and climbed into her bed. Upon closing her eyes, her last thoughts were of Addison and how good it had felt to wake up with her. Her heart rebelled as her mind replied that she would probably never experience such warmth again.

Chapter
Ten

THE DAY SEEMED to stretch endlessly for Addison. She was nearly twenty minutes late for her lesson when she came trotting up the path toward her home. Her heart leapt to her throat as she saw Brontë waiting for her at her front door, another book in hand. Addison curbed the wide smile that threatened to break out on her face.

Brontë felt her resolve slip the instant she saw Addison, but she was certain that what she was about to say was best for both of them. Situations like yesterday's could never be allowed to happen again.

"My lady, forgive me for being so late. If you will give me a minute, I will wash up and we can get started."

Addison smiled widely this time, unable to hide her joy at seeing the blonde woman once again. She had fretted all day wondering whether the Lady would show up once the gravity of their situation set in. Yet here she stood, and Addison felt like whistling again.

Addison reached around Brontë to open the door for her, bringing her so close that her hand brushed across the crisp fabric of the Lady Baptiste's dress. The Lady jumped, causing Addison to straighten and step warily away from her.

"I am...I was only...the door was open. I do not lock it. You may come right in anytime you like." She swallowed down the gloom that threatened to overwhelm her as she realized there would be no repeat of yesterday's pleasantries, and motioned for Brontë to precede her into the cottage.

Both Addison and Brontë were businesslike in their questions and responses to each other. Both women silently hoped the other would voice some displeasure over the uncomfortable atmosphere, but neither had the courage to do so. The mood seemed to thicken as Brontë watched Addison struggle to write the letters as she had instructed. She tried desperately to think of something to say; if anyone were going to ease the tension, it would have to be her.

"A-Addison, have you always known how to ride?" she asked.

"Mm hmm, for as long as I can remember," she said without looking up.

Well, so much for that idea. Brontë settled in for what she thought would be a long strained hour.

Addison frowned down at the paper that she was writing on, her mind not on the lesson in the least. She had come up with a plan to spend more time with Brontë that very morning. It had been a good plan, and Brontë had even given her the opening to bring it up, but she had not mentioned it for fear of rejection.

"I can teach you if you want to learn." Addison froze as a voice sounding a lot like her own blurted out what she had been thinking about all day.

Brontë's mouth dropped. She had always wanted to ride, but her mother abhorred horses and had instilled a fear of them in all her children, especially Brontë, the only girl.

"I-I would love to, Addison..."

Addison looked up, a wide grin on her face.

"But..."

Brontë winced as the grin dropped from her companion's face to be replaced by a wary look.

"I understand, my lady," she said, trying to hide her disappointment.

"No. No, Addison, you do not."

"Of course I do. You are regretting yesterday, I understand that and I was not expecting to—"

"I am afraid of horses," Brontë blurted as Addison accurately described her thoughts before entering the cottage.

"Afraid?" Addison frowned totally befuddled. "But why? Have you been hurt by one or fallen off?"

"No."

"Well, do you know why you are afraid of them, Brontë?"

"My mother. She never liked them. She said they were dirty, smelly, mean creatures. She would not allow my brothers or me near them. Even the miniature ponies at the circuses that come through town." Brontë sniffed as she remembered how all the other children had been allowed to ride, some having photographs taken while she and her brothers had been forced to watch from a '*safe distance.*'

"I do not think they are dirty at all if their owners take care of them. You happen to be the owner of some wonderful horseflesh, my lady." Addison warmed as she proceeded to tell Brontë about every one of the six purebreds that were now in the stable.

"There is also a young mare that I have been working on for a few months now, and she is just about ready to be ridden."

"Really?" Brontë was fast joining in Addison's enthusiasm.

"Yes, really. Her name is Cinnamon, and I am sure she would be perfect for you in a few months!"

"But-But, Addison I cannot ride."

"I shall teach you; it is easy." Addison turned fully to Brontë and, in her enthusiasm, forgot her disappointment at finding Brontë so standoffish. "Please, Brontë, I will not let you get hurt."

Brontë swallowed, deciding she loved the way Addison said her name. Disregarding twenty years of inbred fear, Brontë nodded her assent. Addison made it all worthwhile by giving a brilliant smile and turning quickly back to her lesson, leaving a blinking Brontë to stare at her. *My God, is my mother daft? Addison Le Claire is nothing short of beautiful.*

The lesson went more smoothly after that. Before the Lady left for the evening, they made plans to visit the stables the following day. Brontë fairly floated through the front doors of Markby, up the stairs and to her room.

She was sitting in front of her dressing room table when it hit her. Her brush suspended in midair as she remembered her first encounter with Addison. *She does not ride sidesaddle!* The thought of someday riding in the same manner made her smile, until she remembered how large Addison's horse was.

"Oh, my, what have I gotten myself into?" Brontë wondered aloud. Her mind was so focused on her fear of horses that she forgot completely that she had not had her talk with Addison regarding the kisses that they had shared.

BRONTË WALKED INTO the kitchen intending to solicit a post-breakfast/pre-lunch snack from Cook, as was her habit, and was disappointed to find the kitchen unusually empty. Not once had she gone looking for Cook and not found her hovering over a steaming pot. Curious, Brontë noticed the back door leading to the stables standing wide open. Peering out the door, she was surprised to see every last one of the Markby servants gathered around the stable yard.

Brontë strained to see what they were looking at but Thomas was sitting on top of the fence, blocking her view. Curiosity won out and Brontë approached them from behind, the wind carrying their strange conversation to her.

"This is so exciting," Mary said.

"Shh, you must not speak too loudly. You could frighten her," Beatrice whispered.

"I do wish she would hurry." Wesley was trying his best to sound bored, though he did pitch his voice to a low whisper.

"I dare say that one of these days she shall fall to her death."

"Victoria, Addison is always careful, she will not be hurt." Brontë noted a current of fear in Cook's voice.

Brontë approached the fence and squeezed in between Thomas and Mary. Mary opened her mouth to greet Brontë, but Beatrice shushed her again and pointed to the ring.

There in the center of the stable yard stood Addison with a horse that she seemed to be leading around in circles by a bridle. The horse was fully saddled; however, it had some type of blindfold over its eyes and a bag of what looked like grain draped over the saddle.

Addison had been waiting for months for this moment. Her favorite part of breaking a horse was when she was finally able to mount them for the first time. She had hand-fed Cinnamon apples and carrots for months before even progressing to the equipment. She had spent days rubbing the halter over the horse's body to get her used to the smell and feel of it. Addigo often said that Addison had the patience of a saint when it came to horseflesh. She loved them and often let them dictate when they were ready to progress to the next level.

Still whispering to Cinnamon, Addison removed the heavy sack of grain from the saddle. Cinnamon shied away, but calmed at the sound of the tall, dark-haired woman's voice. "Do you trust me, Cinny? I will not hurt you."

Addison reached in the top of her boots, keeping her eyes firmly on the brown mare. She pulled out her well-worn gloves and placed them on her hands.

"Here she goes!" Beatrice whispered while Cook just nodded, riveted.

Brontë was starting to get as excited as the others though she had no idea what to expect next.

Suddenly, Addison was astride the small brown mare and had ripped the blindfold from its eyes. Brontë's mouth dropped as Addison whooped with joy and the mare jumped into the air, her eyes rolling wildly, and proceeded to do her very best to dislodge the tall woman from her back.

Thomas screamed and clapped his hands. "I think this one will get the best of you, Addison!" The sound of his voice seemed to madden the horse further and Cook whacked him on the back of the head. "Hush," she said, her eyes glinting. "You will only make her buck harder, you fool. What are you trying to do, get her killed?"

Brontë clutched the fence so hard that splinters of wood pierced her palms. The horse twisted in mid-air and kicked out, causing Addison to lose the hat that had miraculously managed to remain perched on her head until then.

Brontë stopped breathing altogether when the brown mare seemed to put all of her energy into one final kick and Addison lost her grasp on Cinnamon's reins, hanging on by the sheer strength of her thighs. Brontë leaned into the fence in order to keep herself from falling over in fear; she expected Addison to come flying off the horse at any moment. But minutes later, Addison still sat atop Cinnamon, who was allowing her to lead her in circles around the stable yard, still snorting but otherwise under control.

Addison was grinning rakishly when she passed the fence that was crowded with her spectators. Her smile broke when she looked into one set of angry and frightened green eyes.

"Oh, no." Addison jumped down from the horse. "Thomas, take Cinnamon!"

Thomas was at Addison and Cinnamon's side almost instantly. Brontë was already stomping off toward the front of the house, only just managing to avoid stepping into a large pile of steaming horse manure, which only served to enrage her further.

Addison hurriedly handed the reins to Thomas, and after scooping her hat up off the ground, she leaped clear over the fence between Cook and Beatrice and took off while smashing the hat down on her head.

"How does she do those things?" Mary wondered aloud as they watched Addison leap over the fence and go streaking across the yard after the inexplicably angry Lady Baptiste.

"I think it is the trousers," Victoria answered just as bemusedly. Cook snorted.

"Well, I think I could do some of those things if I dressed like that," Victoria insisted.

Beatrice and Mary snickered as Cook just shook her head.

Addison caught up with Brontë and tried to cut her off before she entered the house. Brontë turned and began walking toward the side of the house.

"My lady, please, why are you so angry?" Addison was out of breath as she trotted alongside Brontë.

"You were going to try to put me on that wild horse!"

"But, Cinny is not..." Addison flushed at the way she was pleading with Brontë. She noted with some relief that although they were still in view of the other servants, they would not be able to hear her.

"You said she was perfect for me! It was all you could do to stay on her and you ride bigger horses than that all the time!"

"But, I had it under control—"

"Of course you did," Brontë yelled. "That is why you almost got thrown off!"

"My lady, please..." Addison was huffing badly now. Between

the wild ride on Cinnamon and running after Brontë, Addison was not sure if she could continue this pace.

She reached out to grab Brontë's hand to get her to slow her pace, but it jerked away before she could get more than her fingertips on her. Hurt but determined, Addison tried again, this time succeeding in grabbing Brontë's hand. "My lady. Lady Baptiste, please let me—"

Brontë abruptly stopped, Addison skidding to a halt a few steps ahead of her. Addison had to place her hands on her knees as she tried to catch her breath. "For such a small person, you sure do walk fast." She smiled at the still-angry Brontë and cleared her throat nervously when the smile was not returned.

Straightening, Addison tried to make eye contact with the Lady, but was unsuccessful as Brontë stood with her arms folded and her eyes focused on some far-off object.

"That is how all horses are broken. They all react like that. Cinny was actually better than most. She has a sweet temper; it is just that she has never been ridden and was scared." Addison was sure to keep her tone gentle; she did not want to further aggravate the situation.

"Why would you ask me to ride a horse that has never been ridden if they all react like that?" Brontë asked, still angrier than she had been in a long time and unsure of what exactly she was angry at.

Addison ripped her hat off her head and twisted it in her hands, leaving her already wild mane of hair standing out in every direction.

"But I had no intentions of letting you ride Cinnamon until both of you were comfortable. I was going to teach you to ride on one of the other horses. I just thought Cinnamon was so sweet that you might like her as much as I do. Once she is fully trained, of course."

Brontë still looked angry, but Addison did not know what else to say, so she just stood there twisting her hat until it was nothing more then a wrinkled mass in her brown hands.

"You could have been killed!" Brontë said, her voice breaking with emotion on the last word.

Addison wordlessly enveloped Lady Baptiste in her arms as Brontë sobbed into her neck. "Why would you do something like that?"

Addison shook her head from side to side, not having a clue as to why the small blonde in her arms was so upset.

"It is my job, Brontë." She shrugged and held the smaller woman more tightly to her body.

"Well, I think that should be Wesley's job now," she said, her voice muffled by Addison's shirt.

"I enjoy it, though. I would do it for free if I had to," Addison told her quietly as she rubbed the Lady's back.

"Forgive me," Brontë said, her voice still thick with unshed tears. "I was afraid for you." Addison flushed and handed Brontë a neatly folded white handkerchief. Brontë wiped her eyes and blew her nose into it.

She started to give the handkerchief back to Addison, but then thought better of it as she had deposited more than just tears into its pristine white folds. "I will wash it for you and return it later," she said, refusing to look up for fear Addison would be laughing at her.

"You may keep it if you wish. I have several."

Heat permeated Brontë's cheeks as she thought of the spectacle she had made of herself in front of Addison and all of the other servants. "I am afraid that I have acted badly. It seemed as though that thing was trying to kill you."

Addison smiled down at the embarrassed Lady, warmed that she seemed to care so much about her safety. "All horses have to be broken at some point. They almost all act like that. They are not trying to kill us, they just are not used to being ridden. How would you feel if someone tried to ride you?" Addison asked, and then could have kicked herself as she and Brontë both blushed as they remembered Brontë doing very nearly just that to her.

"I do not suppose I would like it?" Brontë asked.

"N-no, I do not suppose you would." They shared a long moment in which both of their imaginations painted portraits that caused each to color. Addison broke the spell first. "Would you be willing to try a different horse? Perhaps just visit with her? Then, if you still do not want to learn how to ride, I will understand."

"Addison, I have to be honest with you. I do not think there is anything you can do or say that would ever make me like getting up on one of those beasts."

"Would you be willing to meet me in the stables before our lesson today? I can show you the horse I would have taught you on. You do not even have to touch her if you do not want to. Please trust me?"

The blonde woman recognized the words as being similar to ones that she herself had used when speaking to Addison. "I do trust you, Addison, but I cannot promise that I will want to ever ride those beasts." She wrinkled her nose and shuddered.

"That is fine; I will not insist. But I think you will find that, after a while, you'll like them as much as I do."

Brontë nodded, although she secretly knew that she would never like them as much as Addison obviously did. For one thing, they did not smell very good.

"Brontë, may I escort you back to the house?"

Brontë looked up, noting for the first time their surroundings. The path that they were on was not only in full view of the house, but also in full view of the other servants who at that moment were trying to look busy when they had only moments before been nosily watching Brontë and Addison interact with each other.

"Yes, Addison, I would like that very much."

Addison gallantly offered Brontë her arm, and then thought better of it as Brontë looked up at her, surprised. She was just about to make a sarcastic remark when Brontë took the offered arm and motioned for her to lead the way.

Addison headed in the direction of the main house, telling herself that the reason for her small steps was so that Brontë could keep up, and not because she wanted to make the moment last forever.

"Would you look at that? Looks like our Addison has found herself a friend," Victoria said.

"Well, I for one think it is wonderful. A girl her age needs some friends. Must get very lonely living out there with just her father," Beatrice answered, eyes riveted to the strolling couple.

"Hmm, I wonder when they became so close," Victoria grumbled as she watched the two women walk arm and arm toward the manor house.

Chapter
Eleven

BRONTË SAT IN John's room pretending to read a book. In truth, she was thinking of a tall, dark-haired woman with a smile that could light up the darkest of hearts. Addison's attitude toward her had changed so much. A week ago, if you had told Brontë that Addison would try to explain herself, and run after Brontë to do so, Brontë would have been the first person doubled over with laughter.

Addison seemed to be going out of her way to prove to Brontë that she was willing to take whatever Brontë was willing to give in the friendship. Brontë looked down at her unconscious husband; his pale features still made Brontë uncomfortable. She struggled with her feelings, or lack thereof, where John was concerned. She wanted to be the devoted, concerned wife, but how could she? She had barely known John before she'd married him.

Most of what Brontë felt was fear, fear of the unknown. More out of habit than any real sentiment, Brontë lay the book face-down on her lap and reached down to push her husband's dark hair back from his forehead. Why could he not make her feel the way Addison had? Why had the tips of her fingers gone numb when her lips and Addison's had met that one time, and yet John's kisses left her feeling sullied and unloved? Brontë was so deep in thought that she almost missed the small movement of John's eyelids.

"John, can you hear me?" Brontë choked out. Jumping to her feet she opened the door and yelled, "Thomas, Mary, Beatrice, come quickly!"

Brontë did not stay in the door long enough to see who was the first to come thundering into the room; she turned back to John, who was once again lying as still as a statue.

"John, can you hear me?" Brontë asked again.

"What has happened, milady? Has the Lord awakened?" Wesley asked as they all crowded around John's bed and peered hopefully at him for any signs of movement.

"Yes, his eyes flickered for a moment."

"Oh, that." Wesley waved his hand and crossed his arms over

his chest. "That means nothing. He has been doing that for days now, but he has yet to open his eyes."

"He has been...and you did not tell me?" Brontë was livid.

"Milady?" Wesley turned ashen as the Lady's face turned a scarlet red. "I thought..."

"Wesley, you have no right to think for me. You do not make the decision whether I should know something or not. I am giving you this last chance in deference to your many years of service to this estate, but this is it."

"Yes, milady." Wesley looked properly chastised and Brontë had no choice but to let the subject go for the moment.

"Wesley, please let Cook know that John has had a good turn and that I will not be having dinner." Brontë wanted Wesley out of her sight before she said something that they might both regret later.

"Yes, milady." Wesley, grateful for the reprieve, scurried to do Brontë's bidding.

"Mary?"

"Yes, m'lady?" Mary stumbled forward, afraid that she was next to be on the receiving end of the Lady's temper.

"Go and find Addison; have her come here immediately."

"Yes, m'lady."

Brontë watched Mary scramble out of the room and then turned to Beatrice. "This is a good sign. Beatrice, would you please go get some fresh water? I want to wash his face and hands."

Beatrice left Brontë alone with the stranger that was her husband. Brontë stared down at his handsome features. "John, can you hear me? Please wake up."

Brontë waited, but there was still no response. She was leaning over John, her hand on his forehead, when Addison came into the room.

"Brontë?"

"Oh, Addison." Brontë threw herself at the tall servant. Addison wrapped her arms around Brontë and, moving her into the room, shut the door behind her.

"What has happened? Mary said there was an emergency. Have you been hurt?"

Addison eased Brontë away from her and grazed her fingers down Brontë's moist cheeks.

"I think I saw John open his eyes."

Addison could not help it; she stiffened, her eyes going over to the still figure of the Lord of Markby. She was starting to wonder if the stress had caused Brontë to imagine the whole thing when she caught a movement out of the corner of her eye.

"Brontë?"

"Yes?"

Addison moved her away from her body and turned her so that she was looking at the bleary blue-eyed stare of the Lord of Markby. Everything stopped; not a sound was uttered until John's eyes closed again, releasing Addison and Brontë from their prison.

Addison reacted first by opening the door and yelling for Thomas. "Thomas, fetch Doctor Quimby! Tell him Lord Baptiste has opened his eyes."

Beatrice was approaching with a heavy bucket of water, which Addison quickly took from her and deposited in the chair next to the silently weeping Brontë.

Addison put her hand on Brontë's shoulder and gave it a squeeze before stepping back just as Mrs. Havisham came rushing into the room, followed closely by a yapping Crumpet III.

"Brontë, Beatrice just told me that our dear Lord John has awakened. Please tell me that it is true. We have been so overcome with grief!"

"Mother." Brontë closed her eyes and took a deep calming breath. "Mother, please."

"Oh, I am sorry, dear. What is it?"

"John is not awake. He only opened his eyes for a moment. He looked at Addison and me and then he closed them again."

"*Addison?* What on earth was she doing in here?" Brontë's eardrums started to itch from the shrillness in her mother's voice.

"Mother, please, this is not the time or place. I asked her to be here."

"Well, I certainly do not understand why!" Mrs. Havisham's sharp voice followed Addison as she slipped unnoticed from the manor house and retreated to the relative safety of the stables.

Addison waited in the stables, telling herself that she was not waiting for Brontë, that she was just staying around in case she was needed. It was nearly seven in the evening and dark outside when she ran out of busy work. She had watched Doctor Quimby come and go twice, but had seen no sign of Brontë.

She stood looking up at the monstrosity of a house for a moment before heading to her own home, where she would toss and turn for hours before finally getting up and starting a new portrait of a blond-haired, green-eyed woman.

BRONTË WATCHED SILENTLY as Doctor Quimby looked into John's eyes and checked his sutures and bandages. He carefully put away every one of the tools that he had used in his examination before turning to speak with Brontë and Mrs. Havisham.

"Well, it looks like he is coming out of it."

"Oh, thank goodness," Mrs. Havisham breathed. Brontë just sat quietly waiting for Doctor Quimby to finish.

"He is not out of danger yet, but I will admit that he looks a lot better than he did when I saw him last. His skin seems to be regaining some of its color and if what Wesley says is true, he has probably been coming in and out of consciousness for a few days now."

Brontë's lips tightened at the mention of Wesley's name. "Doctor, is there anything I can do to help him come out of this?"

"No, Lord Baptiste will have to do the work himself. He seems to be healing nicely. The rest is going to depend on how badly he wants to recover. I will caution you, though. He may sleep for a while, so do not expect him to awaken for another day or so. He will probably fade in and out before he completely regains consciousness."

After some final instructions for care, Doctor Quimby left, leaving Brontë and her mother alone in the room with John.

"Well, dear, why do you not join Crumpet and me for a little dinner? You heard Doctor Quimby, Lord John will not come out of it tonight, so we may as well keep our strength up."

"Mother, I think I will sit here for a while. I am not very hungry."

"Very well, Brontë. I am going to go fetch Crumpet. If you need us, we will be in the dining room."

Brontë turned back to John after her mother left. She sat unmoving for an hour before she finally rose to her feet and trudged up the stairs to her room. She had nearly reached the top when she remembered Addison and the fact that she had not seen her after her mother had pushed her way into the room.

Brontë had just moved past John's dark office when a sound inside made her stop. Pushing open the partially closed door, she was about to step inside when she was grabbed and shoved violently back, her head crashing with a thud into the wall. Brontë slid to the floor, dimly hearing the intruder's retreating footsteps echoing down the hall.

"Stop!" Brontë screamed out as she struggled to her feet, nearly slipping on a piece of paper on the floor. The front door slammed, and Brontë's body relaxed slightly. Her relief only lasted moments. The intruder was gone; he had boldly left through the front door as if certain no one would be there to stop him. That suggested a familiarity with the house that caused her chest to tighten.

Brontë was bending down to retrieve the paper when she heard the running footsteps of the servants responding to her scream. Brontë's hands trembled; she closed her eyes as the dim hallway began to blur. She tucked the small scrap of paper into her sleeve as a panting Cook came running up to her, followed closely by Beatrice and Mary.

"Lady Baptiste! Lady Baptiste! Are you hurt? We heard a scream." Cook's worried voice snapped Brontë out of her shock.

"Are you alright, m'lady?" Mary asked.

"Should we fetch Mrs. Havisham, m'lady?" Beatrice asked.

"No!" Brontë croaked. "No, I am fine, Mary."

Thomas ran up then. "Whoever it was ran into the woods. I could not catch them. Did you see anything, m'lady?"

"No, it was too dim in the hall and I was not expecting someone to come running out. I had just enough time to scream."

Wesley and Victoria came hurrying up at that moment, looking for the entire world like they had been caught with their hands in the cookie jar.

"Where have you two been?" Cook's eyes bored into Wesley until he looked away, ashamed.

"Wesley was helping me find something in the pantry," Victoria answered for both of them, running her hand over the messy bun at the back of her head.

Brontë missed entirely the looks of disgust that Cook, Mary, and Beatrice exchanged, for they all knew what Wesley often found in the pantry.

"Harrumph. Well, since no one else has thought of it, I think we should send Thomas for the sheriff before the thief gets away," Wesley said in a superior voice.

"Thief? Has something been stolen?" Beatrice asked, looking around the hall as if she could do a mental inventory of its contents.

"Well, he came out of the office, but I, for one, would not know if anything was missing just by looking," Brontë said.

Wesley imperiously turned to Thomas. "Well, boy, what are you waiting for, a map? Did you not hear me? Go and fetch the sheriff!"

Brontë, still angry with Wesley over his failure to tell her about John's improving condition, decided to extract a little revenge and interrupted. "No, Wesley, I have a better idea; you fetch the sheriff and Thomas will find Addison."

Wesley, aware that he was on thin ice with Lady Baptiste, simply nodded and excused himself. Thomas was right on his heels, a satisfied smirk not well hidden on his lips as he went.

"M'lady, should we try to at least look at the Lord's office to see if anything has been stolen?" Mary asked.

"I do not think so, Mary. I think we should leave the place as it is so that the sheriff can be the first one to enter. We do not want to inadvertently destroy clues."

Mary looked around the hall as if the intruder would jump out of the shadows at any moment. Brontë suggested that they wait in the sitting room for the sheriff and they all trooped downstairs.

Brontë checked in on her mother, who was happily embroidering a pillow while holding an animated conversation with Crumpet III about "Who is mummy's little man?" Brontë sighed, for once glad of her mother's total absorption in the little creature.

Brontë walked into the sitting room and sat down next to Cook, who patted her hand kindly as they waited for the sheriff to arrive.

Brontë stood as she heard the front door open and the sound of heavy footsteps muffled by the carpet on the stairs. "Where are they, Thomas?" Addison's frantic voice called out.

Brontë called out. "We are down here, Addison. In the sitting room."

Addison's boots could be heard taking the stairs three at a time before she barreled into the sitting room. She was almost upon Brontë before she stopped herself, forcing her hands into her pockets to keep from taking the Lady into her arms.

"Bron—my lady, are you hurt?" Her voice was low, as her eyes asked and told more than she could say in front of the others.

Brontë flushed and looked down. "I am fine, Addison. I just had the breath knocked out of me."

"Did you see who it was? Can you give a description?" she asked, her voice still soft and caressing.

"I chased whoever it was into the woods, Addison, but I did not see him," Thomas offered, but Addison barely acknowledged his heroism; her attention was completely focused on Brontë.

"Are you sure you are all right? Perhaps you should sit down; you just received a fright."

Brontë was feeling a bit dizzy, but not from the fright of finding the intruder. Addison's penetrating stare was causing her heart to beat irregularly and her skin to feel flushed. Nodding, she sat back down on the couch next to Cook.

Addison pulled up a chair and sat it next to Brontë, blushing as Cook gave her a wide-eyed grin, but she only shrugged. She could not try to explain her feelings for Brontë to the woman who had been the only mother figure she had known for her entire life. She shifted in her seat, feeling uncomfortable. Brontë looked around to make sure no one was looking before she briefly covered Addison's hand with her own. She barely had time to remove it before the sheriff and Wesley came barreling into the room.

"Did anyone touch anything?" the sheriff asked, breathing heavily.

"No, we did not, Sheriff," Brontë answered.

"No one leaves this house until I get back, is that understood?"

"Sheriff, why would we leave? We have been waiting here for

you this whole time." Brontë's voice had risen and her mouth tightened in exasperation.

"I am merely stating the obvious, m'lady. You never know what some people understand about the law and what others do not."

Brontë shook her head; the man was truly annoying her.

The sheriff went upstairs while the others sat in the sitting room waiting for him to return. The sheriff reappeared in moments. He shifted his belt and looked about the room before addressing the Lady Baptiste.

"Lady Baptiste, did you happen to see the intruder?" His voice was carefully modulated to convey just the right amount of boredom and intelligence, or so he had told himself when he practiced nightly.

"No, I did not see him," Brontë answered apologetically. "Whoever he was, he slammed into me and was running down the hall before I knew what was happening."

"Thomas, what about you? Did you see anything?" the sheriff asked.

"No. I did go after the intruder, but I did not see much. It was already dark out and he was moving fairly rapidly. I do believe he was tall. Much taller than me."

"He was tall, you say? Very interesting. You both seem to feel that it was a man. Why is that?" The sheriff looked at Brontë and Thomas with a superior look on his face. "Did you see enough of the intruder to ascertain it was a man?"

"Well, no, I suppose I just assumed." Brontë answered first.

"And what about you, Thomas? Did you see enough of the intruder to be certain that it was indeed a man?"

"No, it was dark, as I said," Thomas rushed to reply.

"I see. Well, I suppose that it was good fortune that I found evidence." The sheriff looked at each and every one of them, his gaze lingering on Addison.

He reached into his pocket and pulled out a handkerchief. Opening it, he extracted a small bit of brown cloth and held it up so that everyone in the room could see it.

"What do you have there, sheriff?" Brontë had to squint in order to see the minuscule object.

"Whoever was in your husband's office was looking for something, m'lady. He or she had every drawer in the desk open. When they heard you approach, they no doubt panicked, snagging their trousers on the desk drawer in the process of escaping and inadvertently leaving this clue behind."

The sheriff gave his audience a moment to catch up to his intellect. His self-satisfied smirk widened further as he announced,

"The intruder seems to be wearing brown work trousers, much like the type you are wearing now, Addison."

Addison jumped to her feet, taking a step towards the sheriff, her fists balled, her jaw tightly clenched.

"Addison, no!" Brontë's voice left no room for anything other than complete obedience.

Addison froze, her furious eyes conveying to the smirking sheriff how close he had come to physical harm.

"M'lady, I am afraid I will have to ask your *servant* to remove her trousers. I need them for evidence," he said, an insincere apologetic smile breaking across his face.

Mary gasped, scandalized, and Victoria giggled for a moment before Brontë silenced her with a scathing look.

Brontë rose from her chair and walked towards the imperiously smiling sheriff; his smile slipped a little as she approached.

Addison felt her stomach tighten painfully as angry, frustrated tears prickled at the back of her eyes. She wanted to do the sheriff harm for what he had said in front of Brontë. If anything, this was revenge for her refusal of his marriage proposal, but if Brontë believed him...Addison felt the anger rise again. She was almost to the breaking point when she felt Brontë come to a standstill beside her.

Addison was afraid to look at Brontë for fear she might see distrust in her eyes. She continued to stare her anger at the uncaring sheriff, her fists clenched and her back ramrod straight.

"How dare you." Brontë's voice was so guttural that everyone in the room jumped, including Addison.

"M'lady..." The sheriff looked like a child whose hand had just been slapped.

"How dare you come into this house and accuse one of my servants of something with no more proof than a scrap of cloth?"

Addison's face relaxed visibly; she had to fight down the urge to laugh at the disbelieving look that crossed the sheriff's face.

"Sheriff, look at Thomas's trousers." Brontë pointed fiercely at Thomas; everyone in the room turned to look at his trousers, causing him to blanch and then glare angrily at the Lady, his mouth opening to speak as he took a step forward. Brontë held up her hand and silenced Thomas as she continued, "They are of the exact same color and cloth as Addison wears, are they not?"

"Well, yes, m'lady." Everyone in the room could see that the sheriff had not considered this at all.

"Did you ask him to remove his trousers? His are in far worse condition than Addison's. In fact, do you see any tears or rips in Addison's trousers at all?"

Addison folded her arms in front of her chest, confident that she had none in hers...for once.

"No, m'lady, but—"

"But?"

"Perhaps she changed them. She certainly had time."

Brontë smacked her lips disgustedly. "Why would you ask Addison for her trousers and not Thomas?"

"Well, I do not think..."

"That is correct. You did not think, did you? Nor did you think of the fact that half the village wears the same kind of trousers when working."

The sheriff flushed as he realized that he had made a tactical error in thinking the Lady would just calmly agree to whatever he suggested.

Addison was grinning widely now. She stole a quick peek at the fuming Brontë and had to turn away before she swept the smaller woman up into an embrace and kissed her. No one had ever taken up for her the way the Lady was now. Addison was quite frankly enjoying it.

"Sheriff, allow me to see you to the door; I am sure you will want to look around outside before you leave." Brontë grabbed the sheriff's elbow and guided him out of the sitting room.

"Well, I thought I would wait until morning before I look about. It is very dark out there."

"Oh, but surely, Sheriff, you realize the clues might be gone by morning. You are better off looking around tonight."

"Yes, of course," the sheriff agreed huffily, and Brontë led him out of the room and to the front door.

Brontë pointed into the dark night. "I think Thomas said he ran around to the side of the house."

"Yes, m'lady," the sheriff said resignedly and walked out onto the porch. "M'lady, I think I should warn you—Addison Le Claire is not to be trusted." The sheriff dropped his voice as if to sharing a tasty bit of gossip. "I think you should be very careful about allowing her to remain in your household while the Lord is so ill."

"Now, Sheriff, perhaps you can clear something up for me?" Brontë assumed his conspiratorial tone and leaned forward, almost laughing when the dimwitted man leaned forward as well. "When, exactly, did you start thinking Addison was not to be trusted? Was it before she refused your hand in marriage, or after?"

The sheriff stared at her incredulously before sputtering something about searching for clues and stomping off. Suddenly there was a loud thump and moments later the air was rent with the sound of cursing. Addison and the rest of the servants came running down the hall. Addison came to a halt just behind Brontë, who was still standing in the open door looking into the pitch-black night. She turned to Addison with an angelic look on her face.

"Oh, Addison, I meant to ask you to clean up that large pile of horse manure, but it slipped my mind entirely."

"Horse shit! I have fallen in horse shit!" The sheriff screamed at the top of his lungs.

Brontë shuddered. "My word, that man is crass, is he not? Do not let him back in the house until he washes."

With that, she closed the door and, with another smile for her guffawing servants, she left to go check on her mother and John.

Surprisingly, Mrs. Havisham had slept through the whole thing, her head tilted to the side, mouth slightly agape and emitting a soft steady buzz. Crumpet III lay on the floor next to her, small growls rumbling in his throat as he dreamed. Brontë shook her head. How anything could sleep through all of that noise was beyond her. The thought of sleeping sent her eyes to John's prone form. *A caring wife would wipe his brow and straighten his bedding,* her mother's voice taunted. Overwhelming weariness made it impossible for her to do anything besides trudge up the stairs toward her bed. "Tomorrow. Tomorrow will be better."

Chapter
Twelve

"ADDISON, MAY I speak with you for a moment?" Brontë caught Addison as she was reaching for the door handle.

"Of course." Addison tried valiantly to keep the uneasiness from her voice; she followed Brontë up the stairs and down the hall.

"I hope you do not mind, but I am not comfortable going into the office right now." They entered the library and Addison sat at the edge of the couch, her back straight, and waited for Brontë to speak first.

"I found this note after the intruder ran away. I would like to read it to you and get your opinion. It looks as if it's been burned and torn in two, but this is what I can make out." Brontë opened the small scrap of paper and read it for the first time aloud.

My Dear Lady,

> I am writing you because of my concern...
> It has come to my attention that you...
> an unhealthy relationship with...
> should cease or...

Signed,
A friend.

Addison jumped up from her seat and leaned over Brontë's shoulder to stare down at the note she could not read, a scowl creasing her brow.

"That sounds like a threat," she growled.

"It sounds that way to me, as well. It also looks as if someone was trying to destroy it when I interrupted."

"But that does not make sense, Brontë. Why go to the trouble of writing it, bringing it here, and then try to destroy it?" Addison asked, as she paced back and forth in front of the seated Brontë.

Finally, she sat down heavily next to Brontë. "I know you

probably do not know whether you should continue to see...teach me, but I would like to continue our lessons. I know the note looks bad, but no one could possibly know..." Addison gestured feebly with her hands and Brontë nodded in understanding. Addison went on, "I would never say anything to anyone, and I know you have not; perhaps it is just someone guessing at the extent of our relationship."

Brontë turned away from Addison, a feeling of foreboding curling around her heart as it occurred to her for the first time that she could be putting Addison in danger. After all, John had been shot; perhaps whoever it was would now go after Brontë. She was startled out of her thoughts by warm hands over her own.

"My lady. Brontë. Please. I," Addison struggled with what she wanted to say, "know that you are uncomfortable with what happened in the cottage, and I will not force the issue. But I would like to ask that you still teach me to read." Addison flushed bright red with embarrassment, already regretting her decision to allow Brontë to see how much she cared.

"Addison, I do not care about myself, but what if it is someone who is out to hurt John and me? You could be hurt if you are around me. I cannot let that happen." Brontë grabbed Addison's hands as she attempted to pull away. "I care about you, Addison."

Addison froze, still refusing to look at Brontë. "Then do not pull away from me," she growled.

"I-I will not pull away." Brontë gripped the fabric of her dress in her hands in frustration. "I am afraid."

"I know," Addison croaked and cleared her throat. "But we do not know what the letter said, it could have been anything. I will not let anyone harm you if I can help it, Brontë. I will stake my life on that."

"No, Addison! Do you not understand? That is exactly what I am afraid of. I do not know what is going on. Someone has shot my husband, and now I find this note. I do not want you hurt because of some need for revenge against John, or myself for that matter."

"I understand that someone could be guessing about our relationship and by some chance, they are getting pretty close to the truth. I understand that you are scared right now. And I understand that you said you care about me. But forgive me, Brontë, I will not just walk away from what I feel."

"Then what do we do?" Brontë's heart fluttered with happiness. Even in this tense moment, she thrilled to hear Addison's quiet words. She stowed the little speech away in the back of her mind, as Addison sat back on the couch and appeared to be in deep thought.

"I think we go on as usual, as if we never found the note,"

Addison answered with more calm than she actually felt.

"Why bother acting as if we never found it?"

"Well, look at it. We do not know what the other part of it says. All we know is that it has been burned; it could mean just about anything." Addison shrugged, knowing she was grasping at straws but continuing anyway. "The point is, if this is a serious threat, whoever sent it will make themselves known to us soon enough."

"That is true, and I suppose if we stop having our lessons and the person does not reappear, we would always wonder who it was."

"Exactly," Addison said.

"But what if this is the same person responsible for shooting John? I find it hard to believe that two such awful things would happen in such a short span of time and not be related."

"Perhaps they are and perhaps they are not, Brontë, but what good is it to try to guess at this point? As I said before, either it is a prank, a misunderstanding, or a true threat. In any case we have no other alternative but to wait."

Brontë agreed, not entirely impressed with Addison's reasoning, but unable to come up with anything better.

Addison got reluctantly to her feet. "It is getting late; I should go. Tomorrow I shall search the grounds for footprints. It will tell me what direction our intruder came from. In the meantime, perhaps you should keep the doors locked at all times and only you should have the key."

"That is a wonderful idea!" Brontë brightened.

Addison snickered evilly. "You shall no doubt have to pry the key out of Wesley's hand. He is going to have a fit when you take away even more power from him."

"He would not dare," Brontë growled. "All I need is one reason and I do not care if he is the last servant on earth, he is out of a position."

"My, he seems to bring out the best in you. Such venom for one so small."

"Does he not bring out the best in most people?" Brontë asked sarcastically as she and Addison approached the door.

Addison shrugged as she allowed Brontë to exit the library ahead of her. "Yes, I suppose he does. He never really bothers me much, though, with his sniveling and conniving. I know I cannot trust him and so I stay away from him." She laughed derisively as they reached the front door. "Same thing with Victoria. I try to stay away from both of them unless I absolutely have to deal with them, and even then I am quick about it." Addison shifted nervously on her feet, feeling odd about having to say goodbye to Brontë.

"Will I see you tomorrow?" Brontë blurted out and looked

away, embarrassed.

"Yes, I would like that very much."

"Tomorrow it is."

Addison smiled and went to step out into the cool night air.

"Addison, you will be careful?"

"I will, Brontë. I always am." Addison quietly closed the door behind her and waited for Brontë to lock up.

As she walked away, Addison wondered if that was how it would always be between them. Something forever keeping them separated. She didn't know when or how her feelings for the Lady had reached this point, but she didn't like to think of her in any type of danger. Addison stopped in the darkness, her brow furrowed before she continued on her way.

She said she cared for me! A large grin spread across her features before she remembered that Perry and the rest of the dogs would be wondering what happened to their dinner. She broke into a run.

BRONTË WAVED TO Addison as she walked up the path. It was now Addison's habit to watch each time Brontë came for a lesson. Brontë was therefore surprised when Addison ran into the cottage and shut the door behind her; she usually watched until Brontë reached her just in case someone tried to harm her. She and Addison had been making excellent progress since the scare at the house. A torrential rain had proven to be the intruder's cohort. Any evidence left behind that night was washed away by the following morning. A giggle escaped Brontë's lips and evolved into a snort as she remembered their first lesson after the incident.

"The only thing I found was the sheriff's pocket watch deposited in the manure. He rolled around so much it was encased in the stuff," Addison had said as she diligently created her letters.

"Oh, that *is* awful." A smile stretched across Brontë's lips. "He checked it constantly. I am sure he was just ill when he realized he lost it."

"Oh, no, Brontë. I returned it to him." Addison had bent closer to her paper her tongue stuck out the side of her mouth as she worked on the drawing to go with the new word she had just learned to write.

"You returned it? I-is that not rather repulsive, Addison?"

"Yes, Brontë, quite."

Brontë had continued to stare at the top of Addison's dark head but Addison had not looked up, her hand moving rapidly over the paper. "How, may I ask, did you accomplish this?"

"You asked me to clean up the manure, did you not?"

"Well, yes, Addison, I did." Brontë wrinkled her nose. She certainly had not meant for Addison to root around in it.

Addison picked up her piece of paper and appraised it before a nod of her head told Brontë that she was pleased. "I shoveled his pocket watch into a sack, along with the manure, and left it on the porch of his office." Addison held up her lesson proudly. A donkey with an arrow pointing to its hindquarters had been expertly drawn and beneath it with painstaking care Addison had written the word 'sheriff.'

Brontë covered her mouth, unable to suppress her unladylike gulps of laughter. She and Addison had accomplished nothing else for the rest of that day. That had been well over a week ago, and with no news from the sheriff, and no attempts at more contact from the intruder, Brontë had slowly begun to relax. The only problem now was the fact that her mother was refusing to go home, stating that it was her duty to stay and support Brontë as long as John was still flitting in and out of consciousness. Her mother's sudden sense of responsibility was making it hard for Brontë to slip away.

She and Addison had taken to meeting twice daily, once to feed Cinnamon and her mother Sage in the afternoon, and again in the evenings for the reading and writing lessons.

This afternoon Mrs. Havisham had insisted that she and Crumpet III keep Brontë company and therefore Brontë had not been able to slip into the stables to see Addison. She had missed their quiet conversations about nothing while feeding the two horses. She had even begun to like Cinnamon, or Cinny as Addison called her, although she still preferred her mother, the much calmer Sage. Brontë reached Addison's door and raised her hand to knock. Although Addison had often told her to come right in, Brontë still insisted on knocking as a courtesy. Before she could bring her hand down, however, an unusually excited Addison wrenched the door open.

"I have something for you," Addison blurted, and then blushed at the surprised look on Brontë's face.

"A surprise? And it is not even my birthday." Brontë smiled. "May I come in first, or am I to have my surprise here in your entryway?"

"Oh. Yes, of course. Do come in."

"Thank you." Brontë laughed for the first time that day. She walked into the warm cottage, removed her cape and laid it over the back of the chair that she had taken to sitting in as she and Addison worked on her lessons.

"So, what do you have for me?"

"I hope you will not think I am pushing you, but I thought of them the other day and, well, they are just so perfect I wanted to give them to you."

"Fine.   What are they?" Brontë was starting to feel as excited as Addison.

"Wait right here."

Addison looked her up and down just long enough to bring a pink hue to Brontë's cheeks, and then disappeared behind the bedroom door. She was back in seconds with a neatly tied package in her hand. She handed the package to Brontë solemnly. Brontë took it and sat down in her chair to open it. She looked up at Addison as she noted the neatly folded white shirts and the brown trousers in the package.

"Oh, Addison!" Brontë held up the clothes, noting the neatly embroidered rose on the collar and shirtsleeve.

"Where did you get these?" she breathed as she fingered the rose and ran her hand over the trousers.

"They have been in a trunk in the back for as long as I can remember. I thought of them the other day while we were feeding the horses. I thought they might fit so I took them out and washed them, then I thought you might like something pretty, so I..."

Brontë gaped at Addison. "You did this embroidery?"

"Well, yes." Addison wished she had told Brontë that they had already been like that when she found them. "You do not like it?"

Brontë continued to stare rudely at Addison. "Like it? I think it is exquisite; it is far better than my mother's."

"Well, it is not my best work. I rushed because I wanted to give it to you today."

"Not your best?" Brontë looked down at the exquisite needlework. The stitching was so small that she could hardly see it. "Who taught you how to do this?"

"Beatrice did, a long time ago." Addison grabbed a pail off the sink, her face still pink. "I do not really get a chance to use it much. You can see if they fit if you like. I should go and feed the dogs."

"Will you help me before you go?"

"Of course." Addison quickly unbuttoned Brontë's dress.

"You are good at undressing me," Brontë said as she stared down at the new clothes. The slamming of the door was the only reply she received.

Brontë fingered the delicate rose, grinning as she thought of her mother's reaction if she knew that Addison had created it. Mrs. Havisham had long since given up on teaching Brontë needlework, as she had no eye for it whatsoever. Her grin faded as she looked at the trousers.

"I cannot wear..." Mortification caused tears to fill her eyes. She had never worn trousers, never even considered wearing them. Indeed, the simple idea of it left her feeling naked and exposed. But Addison had gone through so much trouble, and she did look quite comfortable in them herself. "It is not as if anyone will see me."

Brontë came to a decision. She would wear the clothes for Addison. To do anything else would be to insult someone that she had grown to care about a great deal.

Brontë carefully stripped down to her undergarments and slipped on the white shirt and trousers, tucking them into the waistband as she had seen Addison do and peering down at herself. She looked down at her legs in the formfitting trousers and was surprised that she did not feel half as embarrassed as she thought she would. "Somehow they seem to look better on Addison than they do on me," she murmured as she heard Addison enter the front door with a slam.

Brontë poked her head out the bedroom door and spotted Addison sitting at the table, her head bent as she mouthed each letter she wrote. Brontë cleared her throat and stepped out of the bedroom. "Well, what do you think?"

Addison looked up, and after a cursory look at Brontë, went back to her lesson. "I am sure they will do for now."

"I will just go change and we can start on those new words." Brontë said, happy that Addison did not make her feel self-conscious in the revealing trousers.

"That should be fine, Br..." Addison trailed off as she was treated to her first real look at Brontë's derrière as she walked into the bedroom, shutting the door behind her.

Clamping her knees together, Addison hunkered lower on the bench and stared blindly at the words she had been painstakingly writing not moments before.

"Addison, you are so ignorant," she growled under her breath. A noise sounding suspiciously like a gurgling chuckle emanated from under the cot.

"It is not funny, Perry; her arse looks like a, like a damn apple in those trousers." Another snuffle emanated from under the cot. "How the hell am I suppose to study my lessons when all I can think about is studying her arse?" Addison growled to herself before she grumpily continued with her lessons.

ADDISON'S READING HAD improved so dramatically that Brontë had agreed to take the next day off. After much cajoling and begging from Addison, she had even agreed to go out riding after Addison finished work. Both women had been looking forward to spending time together all day. It had been surprisingly easy for Brontë to slip out of the house in her new riding clothes. She found Mary to be an agreeable confidant as well as a competent lookout. Addison was waiting with Sage already saddled when Brontë arrived. Addison made it a point not to look at the Lady's backside as she tried to hand over the reins to Sage.

"No, Addison. She's too big."

"Come on, Brontë. This is Sage, remember? She would not hurt you."

"I know, but she's so high."

"Please, Brontë. I even put on this smaller saddle for you. Anyway, Sage likes it much better than the larger one."

"No." Brontë shook her head and scowled down at the ground.

"What if I get up there with you? We could ride together."

Brontë pursed her lips before grudgingly nodding. "You have to promise that we walk slowly and we only go to the stream and back."

"You have my word as, as a caretaker's daughter." Addison bowed deeply.

Brontë gave Addison another distrustful look before allowing herself to be led closer to Sage. "Are you sure she will not rear up?"

"Positive," Addison said. "This is what I want you to do. Put your foot in this..."

"No."

"What do you mean, *no?* You do not want to ride? You've changed your mind already?" Addison asked, exasperated.

"No, I mean I refuse to get up there before you do." Brontë crossed her arms stubbornly, prepared to walk away if need be.

"I shall get up first, but I want you to sit in front of me so that you can see everything."

"Fine." Addison easily pulled herself into the saddle and then helped a shaky Brontë up in front of her. Sage was being the perfect lady and held almost completely still as Brontë got settled into the saddle.

"F-forgive me, Brontë, this saddle is not really meant to seat two comfortably." Addison tried to move back to allow Brontë more room, but they still ended up pressed intimately against each other.

"It does not bother me, Addison." Brontë was far too nervous to worry about how close Addison sat.

"First, I would like you to take the reins. As I told you before, you should give her a little squeeze with your legs and lead with the reins."

"Fine."

"I am ready when you are." Addison loosely held Brontë's hips, more to support Brontë than from any real fear of falling off. Brontë weakly squeezed at Sage's sides. Sage took a few steps before stopping, unsure of the weak commands and not wanting to do the wrong thing.

"Hmm, that was good, Brontë, but you have to do it with a little more authority. Sage is a horse that beginners and children love to ride because she ignores anything but the most obvious commands. Try again."

"A little more authority, she says." Brontë nervously gave another squeeze to Sage's side and a barely audible click of her tongue. Sage took three steps this time before stopping. Addison shook her head; this was going to be harder than she thought.

"Here, let me show you." And before Brontë knew what was happening, Addison had moved even closer in the saddle. Placing her legs over Brontë's, she pressed firmly in on Sage's sides and gave an authoritative click of her tongue. To Brontë's dismay, they began to move forward.

They had gone a few yards before Addison pulled up on the reins and tapped Brontë on the shoulder. "You do not have your eyes closed, do you?"

"No, of course not!" Brontë lied.

"Good, because the only way you are going to get over your fear is by facing it."

"Why did we stop?" Brontë asked, trying to change the subject before she blushed guiltily.

"Well, it is the way you are moving."

"What do you mean, the way I am moving? I am not moving at all."

"Well, that is what I mean. You need to move with the horse, not against her. If you move with her gait, it is easier on both of you when you learn to canter and gallop."

"Gallop? Addison, I think walking is fine. I am already feeling a bit dizzy as it is."

"Would you prefer that we walk for a while?" Addison asked, concerned.

"Addison, forgive me, I am afraid I am being worse than a child about this."

"No, my lady, you are doing fine," Addison answered earnestly, causing Brontë to feel even worse.

"So, how do I need to move?"

"You just need to try to move with the motion of the horse. Not so stiffly. Here, I will show you." Addison once again covered Brontë's legs with her own and urged Sage forward. She handed the reins to Brontë and placed her hands over Brontë's hips.

"See how Sage is moving? You should try to move your body with her a little, like this." Addison scooted forward and urged Brontë's body into a rhythm similar to her own, though slightly exaggerated to make a point.

"Yes, you have it!" Addison breathed, delighted that Brontë

was catching on. "Shall we have Sage go a bit faster?" After receiving an uncertain nod from Brontë, she squeezed her legs around Sage again and gave her a click. Addison coaxed Brontë's hips into the motion that she wanted until they were moving in perfect unison.

Oh my God, this is heaven, Brontë thought, as she felt the wind whip through her hair and the trees start to speed by, albeit slower than in a carriage ride.

Oh my God, this is hell, Addison thought, as Brontë's backside moved rhythmically against her hips. Addison was fast coming to the conclusion that Brontë's backside was a region that she needed to stay as far away from as possible, as it seemed to have some type of special power over her.

Addison wanted very badly to make Sage go faster, but she didn't want to risk scaring Brontë, so she simply tried as best she could to scoot away from her.

"This feels wonderful," Brontë crowed, causing Addison to groan from behind her.

Addison closed her eyes; her head falling slightly back as she tried to think of anything other than the woman in front of her and her body's growing need.

A shift of the small body in front of her gave Addison enough time to sit up straight and wipe the pained grimace from her face before Brontë turned in her seat to give her a radiant smile.

"Do you have an idea where you want to stop, Addison?" Brontë asked, exhilarated by the fact that she was riding a horse.

Addison cleared her throat and pointed. "There under that big shade tree? I got some sandwiches from Cook so we can have lunch over there."

"Oh, that should be fine," Brontë said excitedly as she turned around in the saddle. She didn't see Addison slump forward with a tormented look on her face.

Brontë waited patiently as Addison got down off the horse as if she were eighty years old. Having seen Addison hop off Cinny, Brontë was instantly suspicious.

"Addison, what is wrong? You are not hurt, are you?"

"I am fine; why do you ask?"

"You are walking strangely, and you look so stiff."

Addison helped Brontë down before answering. "Oh, no. I think I may have strained something while working," Addison explained, not looking at the Lady as she told the little white lie. "Are you hungry, Brontë?"

Brontë replied enthusiastically and Addison thanked whoever was listening for Brontë's avid appreciation of food. As she happily went to spread out the blanket that Addison had given her, Addison prayed furtively for some way to keep from having to ride behind Brontë all the way back home. A few minutes later Addison gave Brontë her sandwich. She watched Brontë eat the food slowly, eyes closed, savoring every bite. Addison closed her eyes briefly as well and tried to nonchalantly cross her legs. Still gazing through her lashes at the oblivious woman in front of her, Addison sighed heavily. It was going to be a long day.

Chapter
Thirteen

BRONTË TUCKED HER riding clothes neatly into a small trunk that she kept under her bed. The ride yesterday had been wonderful; she had enjoyed spending time with Addison. Brontë grinned to herself as she proudly remembered her first ride alone. After lunch and a few minutes lounging lazily under the shade tree, they had decided to go back. Addison, poor thing, had come down with a fit of cramping in her legs so intense that she had been forced to jump hurriedly off of Sage's back. Brontë had originally thought it had been a ploy to get her to ride Sage alone, but one look at Addison's uncomfortable expression had put that suspicion to rest.

Brontë was still worrying about Addison when a loud pounding on her door caused her to jerk upright. "Come in," she called out. Mary opened the door quickly; her face had gone white.

"M'lady, come quickly; something has happened!"

Immediately Brontë's thoughts went to the letter and the thinly veiled threat it contained. Picking up her skirts, she ran down the hall as fast as she could behind Mary. She had traversed the stairs and was almost out the front door before she realized that Mary had stopped at the entry to John's room.

Brontë could hear her mother's wailing. Wesley was currently placing a cool cloth over John's head while Victoria, Thomas, Cook and Beatrice all hovered around the bed indecisively.

"What has happened? Has something happened to John?" Brontë was pushing her way towards John's bed when she was engulfed in her mother's arms.

"Oh, Brontë, is it not wonderful?"

"Mother, please, what are you talking about? What has happened?"

"It is Lord John, dearest; he is awake." Her mother moved out of the way and Brontë was able to stare into the blue eyes of the stranger whose last name was her own.

"John?"

Brontë walked slowly over to him and knelt at the side of the bed, the room behind her utterly quiet. Not knowing what to say or do she simply held his hand in hers and waited.

"Water." John's voice was raspy beyond recognition from weeks of disuse.

"Would one of you please get Lord John a glass of water?" Brontë said, not taking her eyes off John.

"Oh, John, we were so worried about you. Poor Brontë was nearly beside herself with grief." Mrs. Havisham wrung her hands happily over John's bedside.

"Mother, I am sure John is too tired to discuss this with you now. I am sure he would prefer to quench his thirst and go back to sleep." After accepting the glass from Mary, she helped the silent John take in as much of the water as he could and then eased him back down in his bed.

"What...happened?" Brontë had to lean closer to hear what he was saying. She considered telling John what she knew, which was not much, but decided against it, as she was sure that he would be asleep in moments anyway.

Brontë turned towards the others in the room. "Thank you all for your concern, but Lord John needs his rest. I shall call for you if you are needed. Until then, if you all would continue your duties as usual it would be most helpful."

As they all started to move away from the door, something occurred to Brontë. "Has anyone called for Doctor Quimby?"

"I was about to go when I saw Addison riding out. She said she was going into town already and that she would let him know first thing."

"Thank you, Thomas."

Brontë turned back to John, and with some relief noted that he had already fallen back to sleep. The room was now empty but for her mother and a surprisingly quiet Crumpet III.

Brontë idly washed John's brow and hands as she wondered briefly why Addison would be going into town. Based on a few remarks Addison had made, she had assumed that she rarely, if ever, went into town anymore.

A light snoring broke her from her reverie. Looking down at John, she noted that, although his skin still held a slight pallor, he looked much better than he had in the past few weeks. Brontë smiled resignedly as she noted that it was her mother that was snoring, not John. Apparently her dramatic performance had worn her out completely. Brontë finished cleaning John up and stood slowly. She suddenly regretted not taking Addison up on her suggestion yesterday that she walk back as well instead of riding Sage. Her rear end felt extremely tender from its hour or so in the saddle.

Bending her back and stretching her arms above her head, she went over to her mother and was prepared to tap her on the shoulder when she received a growl from the dog curled in her lap.

Hissing at Crumpet III, Brontë called her mother three times before giving up. She placed a small blanket over her mother's legs, and left the room. After checking the door to make sure that it was locked, she went upstairs to the quiet sanctuary of the library to contemplate the events of the last few hours. As much as she tried, Brontë was ashamed to find that her thoughts rarely stayed on her husband and quite often strayed to the caretaker's daughter.

"WHAT DO YOU mean, there are no records?" Addison leaned across the desk, her jaw clamped so tightly that she found it hard to enunciate.

"Forgive me, Miss. We didn't start keeping records until about fifteen years ago. There really was no need, you see. There were so few people and we all knew each other. But when the town started growing and we started receiving people from every which place the town folk thought it necessary to keep track of everyone," the old clerk explained in his quaking voice.

Addison scowled. "So am I to understand that you would not have any records of my birth?"

"No, I am afraid we would not unless you were under the age of fifteen, and I must say that you are a bit big to be fifteen." He started to chuckle, but decided against it as he was treated to a stomach-churning scowl.

Addison glared at the little man. Muttering a sarcastic, "Thank you for your help," she turned to stalk out of the office, her back ramrod straight.

"Wait! Did you try old Doctor Thatcher?"

Addison thought for a moment. "You mean Doctor Quimby? I do not think he delivered me."

"No, I am referring to Doctor Thatcher. He was the doctor here back then. This area was so small that we shared a doctor with Glen Meadow. Doctor Quimby didn't come until much later."

"I shall try Doctor Thatcher, then. Thank you." Addison said feeling a bit better as she walked down the street toward Magnus.

She had just reached him when she spotted two young women strolling arm and arm down the sidewalk, both of them carrying fans though it was far from hot. Addison considered being rude by stepping off the sidewalk and acting as if she did not see either of them.

One of them, Agnes, had always hated her for no good reason. The other, Diana, had been a frequent visitor to the cottage on days when Addison knew Addigo would be working late with one of the horses. Addison smiled slightly to herself as she remembered the days of her youth, and from the slight flush to the now-married Diana's face, she was sure that the other woman remembered those days just as well.

Addison nodded as the two women walked past, but only received a lingering look from Diana and a blatant lifting of the nose from Agnes. Addison recognized the look from Diana for what it was, an offer to get reacquainted. Addison glanced at the two women as they continued down the street before turning Magnus toward home. Not too long ago Addison would have taken Diana up on her silent offer of comfort. But for some reason, even though she was driven to relieve herself almost nightly because of thoughts of Brontë, she could not bring herself to take either Diana or Victoria up on their offers.

Surprisingly for such a small town, Addison had never lacked for a willing partner to experience pleasure with. Although never interested in boys, she knew at a young age that she enjoyed the female body. She had learned at thirteen that many of them did not mind a few shy kisses and even some handholding and at sixteen she learned that it could lead to much more with some of them. By the time she was eighteen, Addison was enjoying visits from a couple of steady *friends* from the village. Addison chuckled as she remembered one of the few times she had visited one of them in the village and had nearly been caught. She had been forced to jump out the window while pulling up her trousers, the girl's father hot on her heels. Luckily for her, having only seen her from the back and in the dark, he had assumed that she was a man. Unfortunately for the daughter, however, he had feared that she might become pregnant and had married her off to the first lout that had asked for her hand.

Sighing, Addison dismounted Magnus and began to remove his saddle, her mind still going over the day's events. She wondered at what point she would be able to get away from the estate long enough to ride over to Glen Meadow and talk to this Doctor Thatcher about her mother. Addison was not even sure what she would ask; she just hoped that he had some clues to her mother's whereabouts and what had made her leave Addison so soon after her birth.

Thoughts of Doctor Thatcher caused Addison's thoughts to progress to Doctor Quimby. Addison had been avoiding the subject all day, but her mind would not let her forget Thomas's exact words as he had run into the stables. "The Lord has awakened!" In a confused fog of emotions, Addison had told him that she was on her way into town and would find Doctor Quimby and send him back as soon as possible.

And so she had. She had found him at Lord Smythe's house,

giving his wife some questionable treatment. Addison smiled as she wondered what the treatment entailed; it had sounded similar to one she herself had given some of the village girls on many occasions in the past.

Addison closed the stable doors and walked toward home, unable to keep herself from glancing toward the manor house as she went. "The Lord has awakened!" The phrase kept filtering through her mind as she wondered how Brontë was feeling at this very moment.

Brontë rarely said anything about the Lord during their lessons, and when she did it was as if she were talking about a stranger. Addison shook her head as she opened her front door and immediately went to fill Perry's water bowl. "Well, Perry, I do not think we will be seeing much of the Lady around here for a while."

With a sinking heart, Addison left Perry to her meal and went to feed the other dogs. After spending time with the puppies, she went back into the cottage. Sitting down at the table, Addison pulled out her books and several pieces of paper and, with a resigned sigh, began going through her lessons on her own. Every so often she would pause as thoughts of warm words of praise and green eyes filtered through her consciousness.

WESLEY HURRIED ALONG the hall clutching Lord John's clean linens to his chest. His mind was still on Lady Baptiste and her apparent stiffness toward him. He frowned, *How was I to know that she was interested in every move and sigh Lord Baptiste made? The way she and Addison looked at each other, he had thought she could not have cared less whether the Lord awakened or not.* Wesley sighed; he had considered looking for a new situation, but he would hate to have to start over somewhere else.

"Oh, no, oh, oh..."

Wesley paused mid-stride, his eyes growing larger as Mrs. Havisham's agitated voice reached him through her thick bedroom door. *"Ohhhhhhhhhh."*

Wesley immediately dropped the linens, his heart pounding in terror, as he turned first left then right. He wanted to get Thomas, or at the very least Cook with her rolling pin. Someone was obviously hurting the poor woman. He needed to find help fast. He turned and ran down the hall to the stairs. He halted as he realized that by the time he had found someone to help, poor Mrs. Havisham could be hurt, or, worse yet, killed. *However,* Wesley thought, his head tilting to the side, *if I were to save the Lady's mother, it would make me a hero and no doubt ensure my situation for life.* With that thought in mind Wesley shakily retraced his steps. He wiped one thin hand across his sweaty brow and looked around for a weapon. Spotting a vase in the corner, Wesley picked it up and cautiously approached the door.

"Ohhhhhhh myyyy gooooddnnneeessss!" The volume of the scream galvanized Wesley into action. He turned the doorknob with one hand while clutching the vase with the other and rushed into the room. "I am coming, Mrs. Havisham!" He held the vase aloft, ready to smash it over the head of Mrs. Havisham's attacker.

Wesley skidded to a halt, his mind freezing. A foul-smelling substance began dripping from the vase, landing squarely on his head and shoulders; he stood stiffly, his gaze locked on the unfortunate Mrs. Havisham.

Neither moved as Beatrice and Mary came running in behind Wesley. All three servants stood gaping at the unlucky woman, who was so shocked to find herself with an audience that she forgot that she had both of her legs sticking straight up in the air. Wearing nothing but a corset, stockings and, for some odd reason, her shoes, her hand was still frozen in its place between her legs.

"Oh, my!" Mrs. Havisham wheezed in a high-pitched voice.

"Oh, my!" Beatrice and Mary gasped in equally high-pitched voices.

"Oh, my!" Wesley echoed in the highest voice of them all.

Beatrice came to her senses first. She made a small curtsey while keeping her eyes focused on the floor.

"Forgive me, Missus, we thought we heard screaming and with all the goings on here of late..." Beatrice trailed off and decided that a hasty exit would be in order. Pulling the dumbfounded Mary with her, she began to back out of the room. She reached out a hand to Wesley and was about to grab his arm when she noticed he was covered in something foul. She hissed his name urgently instead.

"Wesley! Wesley, it is time we took our leave. Now!"

Still in shock, Wesley mimicked Beatrice by performing a curtsey of his own as he mumbled, "Forgive me for the inter—" He broke off as the realization of exactly what he had interrupted flashed through his mind. He hurriedly closed the door behind him and all three scampered away from Mrs. Havisham's den of disrepute.

Mrs. Havisham lay in her bed, her legs motionless and immodestly ajar, her eyes still wide with shock and mortification. She looked over at Crumpet III who had been watching the strange goings-on from his place on the window seat.

"W-well, Crumpet...perhaps it is time we went home."

"MOTHER, THIS IS so sudden. Are you sure you do not wish

to stay a few more days?" Brontë was genuinely confused by her mother's sudden, though not unwelcome, departure.

"Uh, no, dear. I think it would be better if I went on home. I am sure your father is lost without me."

"Mother, I thought you wanted to stay until John was recovered?"

"Yes, well. Dear, I am quite certain that you can handle helping the Lord without me. I am just a little worried about your father."

Mrs. Havisham gave a wary look over Brontë's head at the servants who had, as was the custom, all lined up on the porch to bid farewell to the departing guest.

"Well, Mother, in that case, I suppose you should go home to see about Father. Perhaps you can come back soon?" Brontë asked politely, her mind already celebrating her mother's early departure.

"Er, perhaps, dear, but I am sure that it will be a while before I get the house in order. I doubt I will be up to visiting anytime soon." And with one final wary look at the servants, she clambered into the carriage and closed the door firmly behind her. Brontë reached up and squeezed her mother's hand and was rewarded with a nervous smile before the carriage took off with an uncharacteristically quiet Mrs. Havisham and a yipping Crumpet III.

"Oh, do shut up!" The startled yip of Crumpet III was the last the servants of Markby Estate would hear from Mrs. Havisham and Crumpet III for a very long time.

Brontë watched her mother leave. She finally shrugged her shoulders and turned to the servants, all of whom (with the exception of Thomas, who was driving Mrs. Havisham home) stood solemnly watching the carriage disappear down the road toward town. "Oh, well, it will be nice and quiet around here again," she commented, continuing into the house. She paused as she heard the uproarious laughter from the servants behind her. She thought about going back to find out what the joke was but decided against it as she had not been in the mood to laugh for quite a while.

THOUGH ADDISON HAD predicted that she would not see Brontë much, deep down she had hoped that Brontë would try to visit. Unfortunately for her, Lord Baptiste seemed to be progressing in leaps and bounds. To no one's great surprise, the Lord was unable to feel even the heaviest of pressure put to his legs. He would no doubt be confined to a bath chair for the rest of his life. However, other than that, his recovery, according to Doctor Quimby, was nothing short of miraculous. Addison had taken to eating lunch with Cook occasionally under the guise of being social. It was far from her usual custom. Although not necessarily a quiet person, Addison was definitely not one for small talk or gossip. The last few weeks, she had made time to do just that, to Cook's great amusement. Though there had been no threats against Brontë or herself in the last few months, she still worried about Brontë's safety.

She would come in, sit down, sip tea with Cook, and ask all her normal day-to-day questions before, as discreetly as she could under the circumstances, asking about Brontë.

Cook tried to be as honest as she could be without upsetting Addison. The Lord, it seemed, gained more and more strength as each day went by, but Brontë got more and more tired, to the point that Cook was tempted to suggest that she take a break and let Wesley go back to seeing to John's care.

The happy-go-lucky woman of weeks earlier was gone, replaced by a tired young woman who tried to look happy but failed miserably.

"Addison, when did you last see Lady Baptiste?"

Addison stopped munching the biscuit she was eating and looked down into her tea. "I saw her once last week as she was walking up the stairs, and I saw her a few weeks before that. It has been a while."

"I am curious...did she looked tired to you?" Cook's well-trained eye caught the stiffening of Addison's body.

"What are you asking, Cook? You do not think she is sick?" Addison asked, instantly concerned.

"No-o, it is not that." Cook paused just long enough to make Addison even more agitated. "Lord John is very demanding. Every time I turn around he is banging on the floor with that cane or calling for her, and she is running to bring him this or fetch him that. Even that mother of hers finally decided to go home, saying that the Lady barely had time to do anything but cater to the Lord's needs." Cook saw no reason to tell Addison that the woman had left in order to save face. *Better to let her think Lady Baptiste is being run ragged, then perhaps she will say something to her about it.*

Addison did not know why, but she felt angry.

"I remember she was quite fond of going for her walks during the evenings," Cook hinted. She knew much of that time had been spent with Addison. "You also mentioned she was helping you with your reading, is that not right?"

"Yes, she was, but I have not seen her in some time. I thought she was too busy."

"Hmm, yes, I suppose she is, but one so young should never be that busy. Especially as she has no children to tend to." Cook was enjoying herself immensely. It didn't take a lot to figure out that these two missed each other's company. She had often caught Brontë staring out at the stables, probably in the hopes of catching site of Addison. Cook was never one to put her nose where it was not wanted, but Addison was like a daughter to her and Lady Baptiste was fast becoming someone that she cared about as well.

"No, I suppose not," Addison agreed, not exactly sure what she could do about it, but she was determined to try to see Brontë. She had just started thinking of things she could do to bring her in contact with the Lady when Brontë rushed into the kitchen carrying used dishes and a cloth draped over her arm.

"Cook, have you seen Thomas and Wesley?"

Addison had rarely seen Brontë with a hair out of place, but right now she looked tired and disheveled. Her flushed face darkened even further when she noticed Addison sprawled in a chair, sipping tea.

"M'lady, Thomas went into town to get the Lord's new chair, remember? And Wesley has the day off." Cook looked from Brontë to Addison and back again.

"Oh, I had forgotten," Brontë said, disappointed, before focusing on Addison.

"Good afternoon, Addison."

"My lady," Addison answered apprehensively, as they both had trouble meeting each other's eyes. Addison's heart sank. She and Brontë had seemed to be growing closer before, but now that Lord Baptiste was awake, there was an almost tangible tension between them.

Cook discreetly went into the pantry to give the two nervous women time to talk.

"Addison, I regret that I have been unable to come by for the lessons. John just takes up so much of my time."

"I understand, my lady."

"I would like to continue them soon, though."

Addison nodded, afraid to speak.

Brontë desperately looked for some minuscule degree of the comfort that they had managed to gain in each other's presence.

"I even miss riding," she blurted out.

"Really?"

"Yes, I really do," Brontë lied, and would have gladly done so again to see the brilliant smile that appeared on Addison's face.

"Perhaps when things get better we could go riding again? When you have more time, of course." Addison could have kicked her own rear end for making the suggestion. It was not as if the Lady didn't have enough to do.

"I would love to."

"As would I."

They smiled at each other for another awkward moment and then Brontë turned reluctantly to leave.

Addison's smile began to fade as she watched her leave, when Brontë suddenly turned around.

"Shall we say tomorrow, then?"

"Tomorrow, my lady?" Addison asked, confused.

"Yes, perhaps we could go riding tomorrow if you have the time."

"I would like that, my lady."

"Addison, I liked it better when you called me Brontë."

"I would like that, Brontë." Addison smiled again and was about to say more when a loud banging sounded from the second floor of the house.

"I should go." Brontë said hurriedly and rushed out of the door before Addison could say another word.

Addison made her way back to the stables, jauntily whistling a tune. After she completed her chores, she would clean and oil Brontë's saddle. Cinny was progressing nicely, so she thought she would let Brontë ride Sage while she rode Cinnamon. She was still whistling, mucking out the stalls, when Thomas came in.

"Addison?"

"Yes, Thomas, I will be right there," Addison called, as she walked out of the stall, rolling her shirtsleeves down. She was still in a great mood after speaking with Brontë so she had a wide smile on her face, which he tiredly returned.

"Lady Baptiste asked if you would help us in the manor house."

Addison's heart leapt at the possibility of seeing Brontë again.

"Of course. I would be happy to." Addison was already walking toward the house as she spoke with Thomas following closely behind her.

"Lord Baptiste has decided that his room is too small and wants to move back into his own room. But Wesley is not here to help get him up the stairs. I tried to lift him in his chair, but it was just too heavy. All he could do is complain about how much I was jostling him." Thomas sucked his teeth in disgust as he rubbed his back.

Addison had ceased to listen to Thomas's complaining after he mentioned that the Lord wanted to move back into his own room.

Addison felt sick. Once long ago she had entertained herself by sneaking through out the estate, entering its every room, and studying each curiosity with adoration. One such curiosity had been the private doors between some of the larger rooms. She remembered wondering why it was necessary to have doors inside the rooms when all one had to do was enter the hall to go to the

next room. The need for privacy had never occurred to her eight-
year-old mind.

The idea of John somehow using that door, of Brontë sleeping
with him, caused Addison's heart to ache. A churlish male voice
and a softer calming one interrupted her thoughts.

"Well, where is she, then? I do not want to sit here all day."
Lord John Patrick Baptiste growled.

"Here she is," Brontë breathed, relieved, as Addison and Thomas appeared in the entryway.

Addison's heart sank even further. She had not seen Lord Baptiste since he had first awakened, but she had not expected him to
look so healthy. The only real indication that there was anything
wrong was that the tall body was stuffed into the wooden bath
chair.

She is his wife, she told herself, but she could not help but wish
that the Lord would stay in the room downstairs where he would
not be able to put his hands on Brontë.

"Well, are you going to stare all day, girl, or help get me up
those damned stairs?"

Brontë flinched at John calling Addison a girl. It was one thing
for him to do it to her and another entirely to call Addison a name.
"John, please, Thomas and Addison will do the best they can. You
need to be patient."

"Patient? I do not need to be patient! Who told them to put me
in here in the first place, Brontë? This is the servants' quarters, for
God's sake."

It was an old argument, one they had been having since day
three of his recovery. Her mother had been right. John saw no reason he should be uncomfortable in the servant's quarters when he
could be resting in his own room. It made no difference to him that
it was more convenient for the person bringing him food if he
stayed downstairs. He didn't care that it would have been next to
impossible to have carried him upstairs without hurting him more.
No, Lord Baptiste only knew that he was inconvenienced, and
when he was inconvenienced, he took it out on the closest person to
him, that person being Brontë.

Addison's lips tightened. It was not the first time someone had
spoken to her in such a manner and it would not be the last, but his
tone of voice with Brontë made her angry.

Brontë sighed and walked behind John's new chair. She
started to push him out of the door as the other two turned to follow.

John slammed his cane into the floor. "Let Thomas do it." Wesley had originally given John the cane so that he could reach some
things on his own. He never tried, of course; the cane was only used

for pointing and banging on the floorboards when he felt he had been left unattended for too long. Thomas stepped forward and pushed John into position. John placed the cane across his lap. "Try not to bang me around as much this time."

He sat that way for the entire twenty minutes that it took to get him and the chair to the top of the staircase.

"John, if you will wait here, I will make sure the bed is turned down and everything is out of your way."

"Where else would I go, Brontë?" If Brontë had not known the man better she would believe him to be truly amused by her slip. But she had learned to know him as she had tended him, and his emotions did not run to humor of late. Brontë's eyes lingered on Addison's for a moment before she turned to climb the stairs.

"I will run down and get the rest of your things, m'lord." Thomas huffed, still out of breath from the laborious lifting of John's considerable bulk, plus the heavy wood chair.

Addison found herself alone with a man she had avoided most of her childhood.

"So, Addison, we are finally alone."

Addison didn't say anything. She felt a slight sense of unease but pushed it away. The man was confined to the bath chair; he could not even move without someone else's help. Addison began to feel silly; what did she have to fear of this man? In the worst of situations she was quite capable of taking care of herself. So, with that in mind, when Lord Baptiste gestured for her to come closer she did so, thinking that he might require assistance.

She noticed the predatory smile marring his otherwise handsome features too late. Addison's breath left her chest and tears instantly filled her eyes as the cane was slammed down onto her foot.

"Stay away from my wife," he growled, sparks turning his blue eyes ice gray.

Anger and pain flowed through Addison. She took a step toward Lord Baptiste who was looking at the cane, a frown creasing his forehead. He smacked his lips completely ignoring Addison. "This cane belonged to my father. Now look at it, it's split nearly in two." Addison blinked back tears and walked away from him, telling herself if she did not she might do something she would come to regret.

"Now I shall have to find something else to help me *reach things*, won't I, Addison?" he called to her as she limped down the stairs, a hint of a laugh in his voice as if they had just shared some private joke.

Chapter
Fourteen

THE FOLLOWING DAY dawned clear and crisp, just as Addison had hoped. She had already saddled both Sage and Cinnamon and was ready to go when Brontë arrived, apologizing profusely for being late.

"John did not seem to want to lie down for his nap today."

"I understand. I am just glad you are here." Addison ducked back behind Cinnamon, under the pretense of checking something on her saddle, so that Brontë would not see her silly grin.

"Are you ready?"

"Yes, I suppose so," Brontë said nervously.

"Do not worry, Brontë; you never forget how to ride. Here, let me help you up."

Brontë acquiesced, and in minutes she and Addison were leisurely riding the horses down a path unfamiliar to her. Addison told her that she and her father would take this route often when they would go for rides together.

Addison pointed out several strangely shaped trees as well as some areas where she and her father had come across wild animals.

They were enjoying the day, the warm breeze, and one another's easy company. Brontë's smile spread across her face, only to fall away as she spied the large boulder completely obscuring the path.

Brontë hissed disappointedly. "Oh, well, I suppose that is the end of that. Shall we head back then?"

"Yes, I suppose so. It is too bad. There is a very nice pond just around that bend. My father and I used to fish there. I could come back and move the boulder, and in a few days we could come back?"

Brontë's mouth gaped open. "Addison, you cannot move that boulder. It is too large."

Addison grinned. "You do not think I can move it?"

"I know you cannot," she said, making sure to put her nose in the air and looking every bit the aristocrat.

"I can, too."

"Prove it," Brontë said with a grin

"And what do I win if I do it, *my lady*?" Addison was unable to keep herself from returning the imp-like grin that Brontë now wore.

"Well, I have not given much thought to it. I am quite certain that you shall not win and I will in all likelihood be the victor. Therefore, if you insist on this fruitless wager, I suppose I shall be obligated to do nothing less than your chores for the day. If you win."

Addison promptly threw her head back and howled. Through her mirth, she asked, "Do you really believe that you are capable of doing my chores, Brontë?"

"Of course I am *capable*." Brontë said while trying to look indignant. "I am stronger than I look. I thought the idea of me doing chores might appeal to you, but I have no intention of losing, so really, this is a frivolous conversation."

"Brontë, forgive me, but I cannot imagine you mucking out the stables or tending the sheep." Addison stood in her muddy riding boots with her hands on her hips, staring fondly at the Lady Baptiste.

Brontë narrowed her eyes and Addison raised one eyebrow, trying to look frightened. Brontë noticed again that Addison was favoring her right foot and wondered if she should ask about the injury. Perhaps she should ask Doctor Quimby to look at Addison's foot. She instantly shied away from that idea, fearful of what his cure might be for a foot injury. Suddenly she had an idea.

Her mouth stretched into a large grin. Her eyes sparkled mischievously as she smiled down at the dark-haired woman. "If you win, I will be your servant for the day. I will do anything you want, starting with washing and rubbing and, and kissing your feet."

Addison's mouth dropped, and in a perfect imitation of Wesley, she allowed her weight to settle on one foot, right hand fluttering at her chest.

"Oh, my!" she breathed in a high nasal voice.

They both howled with laughter.

"Fine." Brontë gasped as she wiped the tears from her eyes. "But if I win you have to wear a dress for the entire day, with corset and underpinnings and everything."

Addison's eyes grew wide and then narrowed as she started to protest the severity. Brontë was grinning, fully expecting Addison to back out.

"That shall be fine," Addison said, looking at the boulder.

Brontë's smile faltered. "Addison, are you sure? You cannot really move that boulder. It must weigh more than this horse."

"Mm-hmm, I am sure that it weighs at least that much. You

should have no trouble with our little wager then, my lady. Unless you are afraid that you may lose?"

Brontë looked down at the tall figure in front of her. Addison was undoubtedly stronger than any other woman she knew and no doubt many men as well. Still, the boulder was enormous; three men would not have been able to lift it.

"I do not believe that I should be the one in fear," Brontë said. She really had no desire to see Addison's strong body covered with a lot of cloth, but it was the only thing she could think of that would give Addison pause.

"Shall we shake on it, then?" Addison said and reached up to offer Brontë her hand. Brontë took the offered hand and gave it a firm shake.

Addison shook her head and said sternly, "You know, my lady, you really should not wager against me."

"I am not wagering against you, Addison, I am wagering for the stone. It has to weigh a ton."

Addison turned to look at the boulder in question and said contemplatively, "Hmm, it is probably no more than a quarter that, my lady."

Brontë rolled her eyes. "The point is, you cannot lift it."

"I am not going to lift it."

"What?" Brontë stared at Addison suspiciously. "We had a wager, Addison Le Claire, and if you are not going to lift it then I suggest that we return at once so that I may consult my mother's magazines for a suitable pattern."

"The wager was that I must move the boulder from the road. You did not say that I have to lift it to do so."

"How else are you going to move it?" Brontë asked cautiously, already having the distinct feeling that she had been tricked.

"Shall I show you? It should not take long. My foot hurts badly; those rubs and kisses shall be most appreciated." With that, Addison walked away, leaving Brontë to sputter out a reply that was heard only by herself.

Addison stood with her legs apart and studied the boulder much longer than she actually needed to. She wanted to make this good, so she was going a bit overboard with the dramatics. Besides, she was enjoying the Lady's playfulness. She would, of course, let her back out of the wager, but not before she teased her mercilessly. And not before she at least got her feet washed and got a few rubs.

Addison chuckled to herself as she thought of how put out the Lady would be when she realized that she had been tricked.

Brontë watched, her eyes narrowed, as Addison went to the side of the road, looked around for a moment and picked up a fairly large boulder. Brontë grinned as she noticed that Addison was already breathing heavily and the rock that she had in her hands was not even half the size of the boulder she had to move to win the wager. Brontë settled back in her saddle smugly. Addison looked up at her once during her preparations and gave her a smug grin of her own. Brontë's grin slowly slipped away as she realized that Addison was not in the least worried, which meant she had something up her sleeve and that she, Lady Baptiste, would be kissing feet very soon indeed.

Brontë wrinkled her nose, having completely forgotten that she was the one who had proposed the wager. Addison crowed from the side of the path as she found what she had been seeking. She picked up a small uprooted sapling and, with her uninjured foot, cleared the branches from it. Stepping back onto the path, she gave Brontë another grin and turned to wedge the end of the tree under the large rock while using the smaller rock as a fulcrum.

Brontë, who was still trying to catch her breath after being on the receiving end of Addison's dazzling smile, almost missed the whole thing. She had just looked down when the boulder started to move. Addison gritted her teeth and put all of her body weight onto the sapling trunk, crowing again when the boulder started to roll slowly off the path. Addison limped behind it and gave it another strong push, then watched as it rolled off the path.

She then stood with her hands on her hips, grinning up at Brontë. "Well, it is moved. So shall we head back so that you can get on with paying up on our little wager?"

"Sur-surely you do not expect me to actually kiss your feet, do you?" she asked with a horrified look on her face.

"Why, yes, I do expect you to kiss my feet. After all, you are the one who made the wager, not I."

"B-but, Addison?"

"Yes, Brontë?" Addison was sure that Brontë was about to back out as gracefully as possible.

Addison continued to smile at her, her arms folded as she waited to see how Brontë handled the situation.

Brontë's eyes narrowed as she noticed Addison's smug expression. Sitting straighter in her saddle, she looked down at Addison confidently. "Shall we get the horses back to the stable?"

The ride back was a quiet one, Brontë trying to think of a way out of the wager and Addison trying to think of what Brontë would do to get out of it.

Addison finished brushing her horse down first and offered to help Brontë, who had refused her help and seemed to be taking more time than usual. Addison chuckled. "Well, Brontë, I will be in the barn when you are ready."

Addison was still smiling as she tossed hay into the corner.

Brontë had to be the most stubborn woman she had ever met. Her smile wavered as she thought about the night that Brontë had been forced to stay at her cottage, how she had stubbornly refused to allow Addison to sleep in the cold back room. *If she were aware of the liberties I took...* Addison's lips tightened at the thought. The fact that Brontë had no way of knowing of her activities that night was very little comfort.

Addison tossed her pitchfork into the hay and sat down, leaning her head back against the hay. Something about Markby had nagged her father to the day he died. Addison assumed it had something to do with her mother but she could never be sure. She needed to find out to understand what this place held over him before she could leave it fully. That always been her plan. But Brontë was not something she had planned for. Ignoring the pain in her chest, she thought of the kisses that they had shared. Now it all seemed like a figment of Addison's imagination, meant only to torment and cause pain. Addison sat up, startled as she realized that she was being observed. She jumped up, took a heavy bucket from Brontë, and sat it down on the floor. "Is there something you need me to do for you, Brontë?" She gestured at the bucket curiously.

"No, it is time for me to pay up, remember?" Brontë said, her eyes refusing to meet Addison's.

Addison's chin dropped as she realized that Brontë fully intended to wash her feet.

"Do you not wish to sit down?" Brontë asked.

Addison mutely sat down on a sack of grain as Brontë knelt at her feet.

Brontë swallowed as she began to unlace Addison's heavy work boot, dropping it to the floor with a thud that made both of them jump. She concentrated on anything but the woman in front of her as she gently removed the wool sock that covered Addison's right foot. Addison, for her part, was in shock. She knew she should tell Brontë to stop, but she didn't want to, at least not yet. Brontë inhaled the sweet smell of freshly cut hay as she unlaced the second boot and allowed it to drop to the floor as well. Aware that Addison was more than likely staring down at her, Brontë didn't look up once as she slowly rolled Addison's woolen trousers up around her strong brown calves with shaky hands.

Brontë reached into the bucket, keeping her eyes focused on her task and refusing to look at the dark-haired woman above her. She squeezed the water from the cloth she had retrieved from the main house and looked down at the two surprisingly slender brown feet.

"Perhaps," Brontë cleared her throat, "perhaps you should lie back." She made the mistake of looking into Addison's heated blue eyes before looking back down at the foot in her hand. Addison decided lying back was not such a bad idea since she was feeling a little dizzy at the moment.

Addison carefully lay back and stared up at the wooden beams of the barn rafters. She wondered again if she should stop Brontë. She closed her eyes as small warm hands picked up one foot, and then a soft wet cloth caressed the top of it. Addison almost groaned as she realized that Brontë had taken the time to warm the bucket of water. She almost never indulged herself in heated water. It took too much time to heat when she could have just as easily washed with cold water and been out the door.

Brontë was having trouble breathing. It was the strangest feeling. On the one hand, she was the Lady of Markby; yet on the other, here she was servicing Addison as if she were the Lady. Brontë realized she would much rather service Addison than an ungrateful John any day. A sudden movement from Addison startled her out of her thoughts.

Brontë looked at the bluish-gray bruise that stopped just above Addison's toes wondering how she had managed to hurt herself in such an odd place. However she had done it, it was obviously very sore; she had flinched away from the light pressure that Brontë had put on it. It was no wonder she had been limping earlier.

Placing the cloth back in the bucket, she examined the bruise, running one finger over it lightly. She looked up at Addison, who seemed to be doing fine other than the rapid rise and fall of her chest.

Addison was not doing fine. She dug her fingers into the sack on which she rested and waited for the wonderful torture to end.

Brontë took a nervous breath before leaning forward and kissing the bruised foot.

A small sound escaped Addison and her knuckles turned white as her grip on the burlap tightened. She needed to stop this; it was too much. She had just opened her mouth to tell Brontë that her debt was paid when her injured foot was caressed from the heel to her toes and back again. Then small kisses were placed on her bruise and on every one of her toes.

Addison moaned again helplessly.

"Does it hurt, Addison?" Brontë asked gently.

Addison shook her head and then, realizing Brontë could not see her, she croaked out. "No, it does not hurt anymore."

"Do you like what I am doing?" Brontë asked, concerned. She could not tell whether Addison was in pain or enjoying what she was doing.

"Yes," she croaked.

Swallowing, Brontë leaned down to kiss the injured foot once again, letting her lips caress the toes before pulling away as a shiver coursed through Addison. She was now lying so still that Brontë decided to try the caress again to see if it was her imagination. This time her pink tongue, almost of its own accord, slipped out to taste Addison's skin, causing Addison to shake again violently. Brontë was enthralled.

Surely Addison was not ticklish? She stuck her tongue out and gently caressed the tops of her toes, causing another shudder and a shift in breathing that Addison could not hide.

Addison was in serious trouble. She had no idea that her body would rebel against her. She thought to close her legs, but Brontë was practically kneeling between them as she ministered to her feet.

Addison felt another flush of heat hit her center as she felt what she was sure was Brontë's tongue, caressing her toes and the tops of her feet. She was no longer able to keep herself quiet and was fast approaching the point where she would have to tell Brontë to stop or embarrass herself.

Brontë was enjoying herself now. She felt extremely powerful as the strong Addison groaned softly with each gentle caress to her feet. Just as she came to the end of her ministrations, a new idea occurred to her and she decided to give it a try. Brontë carefully put Addison's toes into her mouth, eliciting a loud moan. Addison attempted to stop the torture but was held firm. She sat up on her elbows to look down at Brontë, whose eyes were closed as she took three of her toes into her warm mouth and began to gently suck on them. Addison's eyes closed slowly and she sank back onto the hay. *This feels so good*, she thought, as Brontë increased the suction on her toes. Addison wondered briefly where she had learned how to do this before all thoughts were driven from her mind as Brontë finally began to suck her big toe, flicking her tongue between the large and middle, causing Addison to arch up off the sack.

Addison could not stop herself from whispering Brontë's name.

Brontë smiled around Addison's toes and really began to concentrate on her task. Moments later Brontë looked up from her task to find Addison writhing in pleasure.

"Brontë. Brontë, you can stop now. You are all paid up!" Addison groaned. She was a fool to think that she could let this woman do this to her and not become aroused.

Brontë considered stopping, but thought if Addison really wanted her to, she could pull her foot away at any time, so she increased the suction on the toes while using her tongue to lightly flick between each one.

"Brontë. Please stop, please." Addison sobbed brokenly,

unable to control her shaking body as it betrayed her once again. Frightened, Brontë quickly put Addison's foot down and stood up.

"Addison, what—?" Brontë was shocked to see that Addison's face was wet. She had obviously been crying and Brontë could not figure out what she had done to make her cry. She had truly believed that Addison was enjoying what she was doing.

Addison shoved her feet into her boots, unwilling to meet Brontë's eyes. Not bothering to pick up her socks, she walked out of the barn before a stunned Brontë could react.

"Addison, wait!" Brontë jumped to her feet and ran to the front door of the barn. She was just in time to see Addison, who had obviously broken into a sprint soon after leaving the barn, disappear into the trees. "Addison, forgive me."

Addison ran away from her problems, as she often did, her temples pounding as she neared her cottage. She ran until she reached her front door, which she thundered into and leaned against it as if she was being chased. She unbuttoned her white shirt and dropped it to the floor, kicked her muddied boots into a corner; her trousers soon followed.

She dropped to the cot, her eyes closed, breathing still coming in raspy gulps as she remembered the way the Lady's mouth had felt on her body and how weak her legs had felt as she had kissed her. Addison moaned as she drew her hands up to her heated breast, circling one nipple and then the other, imagining what it would feel like to have Brontë kiss her there. She moaned again as she imagined her own hands touching milk-white flesh, then trailing lightly over her stomach and hovering over the dark hot curls that hid her femininity. Her fingertips grazed the hot curls before parting the lips and rubbing her own wetness, and it was only moments before Addison's body took pity on her and she climaxed, her body lifting slightly off the bed before she collapsed.

Chapter
Fifteen

BRONTË ENTERED HER room, closing the door behind her. She sat down on the bed, her head bowed, as she thought about Addison and what had just occurred. Brontë removed her boots and curled up on her bed as hot tears coursed down her cheeks. The memory of pain, fear, and embarrassment she had seen on Addison's face made Brontë curl tighter into herself, and it was all because she had gone too far. Brontë's breath hitched in her throat as she sat up in her bed and quietly began to disrobe. This time, instead of laying the clothes out for Mary to wash, she pushed them under her bed. She was sure that Addison would not be requesting her company any time soon. The thought almost sent Brontë into another fit of tears.

"Brontë? Brontë, I know you are there; come quickly, please. I wish to speak with you," John called in his perpetually angry voice from the other room.

Brontë grabbed a handkerchief off of her writing table, wiped her face, and, after donning her night robe, hurried through the connecting door, dropping the handkerchief on the bureau as she went.

"Coming, John."

No one heard the small commotion, or the quiet weeping that followed.

"Next time I call you, you will be quick about it."

The forgotten handkerchief dropped from the bureau to the floor, the letters *A.L.* embroidered in black stark and lonely against the pure white folds.

AFTER TOSSING AND turning all night, alternately thinking about Brontë and forbidding herself to do so, Addison decided she needed to do something to take her mind off Brontë and the incident in the stables. Deciding it was time to try to talk to Doctor Thatcher, Addison got up a full two hours before she normally did and began her day.

She rushed through the chores that would not wait until she returned, trying to keep her thoughts as far from the Lady of Markby as possible, only succeeding for a few minutes before her mind strayed to Brontë's well-being.

Addison quickly finished feeding the animals and saddled Magnus for her journey to Glen Meadow. It would have to be a quick journey, as she was afraid that Wesley might question why Thomas was covering for her if something came up. She didn't worry as much about the death of her father anymore. The only people observant enough to figure it out were Cook, Brontë, and perhaps Wesley. Brontë had taken him pretty much out of the equation, as she had taken great pleasure in making sure that Wesley was kept busy about the manor house, so he had not had enough time to stick his nose where it was not wanted.

Addison arrived in Glen Meadow a little less than an hour after leaving the estate. Although she had never been there before, the people didn't seem to think twice about the fact that she was a woman on a horse, riding alone. It was odd, really; she had spent all of her life outside of Glen Grove. Most of the people at the very least knew of her and yet they all looked at her as if she were a stranger when she would pass through. Here, the people didn't know her at all and yet they rarely spared her a glance; even if they did, all she received was a vague smile or a nod.

For the first time, Addison began to believe some of the things that her father had said. Perhaps things would be different in the world outside of Markby and Glen Grove. Perhaps things would be better. Addison shrugged. Perhaps not, but it could not possibly be that much worse, could it? Her inner mind supplied that it could, especially without Brontë, but she chose to ignore it, continuing down the street toward Doctor Thatcher's house, and hopefully the answers that she needed.

Addison arrived at the well-manicured home and stood for a moment. She tied Magnus to a convenient tree and left him grazing contentedly on some grass. Nervously, she opened the gate in the white picket fence, walked up to the door and gave three light knocks.

Receiving no answer, Addison knocked again. She waited, this time a little less patiently, before knocking again. She reasoned Doctor Thatcher had to be pretty elderly at this point, because from what the clerk had said he was old twenty-two years ago. Addison was forced to knock a bit harder before the door was yanked open by an older lady dressed in a crisp floral dress.

"Why are you banging on my door?" the woman yelled.

Addison jumped as the ferocious woman looked her up and down a few times before crossing her arms and tapping her foot impatiently.

"Well, I am—"

"What? Speak up girl, I cannot hear you."

Addison cleared her throat and tried again. "I—"

"Heddie, bring me my damned lemonade, woman!" An old cranky voice hollered from the back of the home, causing Addison to jump again and Heddie to roll her eyes.

"I will bring your lemonade when I am good and ready, old man!" she screamed back, causing Addison to jump again, her eyes wide.

"Well, you might as well come in, then. What is wrong with you, you dumb or something?" Heddie was already walking away when Addison opened her mouth to reply angrily.

"No, I am not dumb. I just came here to see Doctor Thatcher." Addison shut the door behind her and followed Heddie.

Addison watched as she poured the lemonade into a glass along with something from a brown bottle. She stirred it with a spoon and then took a sip.

"Umm, perfect. This will put him down for awhile, then maybe I can get some work done around here," she told a bewildered Addison. She swept through the doorway, muttering as she went. "Well, come on girl. If you want to speak to him you better get a move on. After he drinks this he will be out until tomorrow. At least!"

"*Hedddiiiieeeee!*" old Doctor Thatcher yelled.

"I am coming, you old arse!" Heddie yelled at the top of her lungs.

"Well, hurry up, you," Doctor Thatcher's voice trailed off to a grumble just loud enough to make Addison certain he gave as good as he got. She had to walk quickly to catch up with Heddie. She was determined to get her information and get out as soon as possible; all the yelling back and forth was making her more than a little uncomfortable.

Heddie pushed open a door with her foot. The first things Addison noticed were the hundreds of books that lined the walls and the stale smell of illness that permeated the air. The room had a large canopy-styled bed in its center that left little space on either side to walk. It took Addison a moment to spot the little old man in the middle of the bed.

"You have a visitor, Thatcher," Heddie growled as she picked up the pillow that had obviously been chucked at the door.

"Who is it? One of your good-for-nothing children here to beg for money again?"

"No." Heddie looked Addison up and down. "No, she is not one of mine. Could be one of yours, though. Everyone knows what you got up to in your day." Addison flushed bright red at the implication. "Here is your lemonade." Heddie handed the feeble old man the glass and to Addison's surprise gently held his head and hand while he drank the dubious concoction.

"Ahh, now that hit the spot. Thank you, Heddie, you are a dear." Heddie growled at him once before leaving the room.

"More like a moose," he whispered to Addison conspiratorially.

"I heard that!" Heddie yelled from the other side of the door.

"Ahh, pshht." Doctor Thatcher waved at the door with both arms before turning his attention to the nervously waiting Addison. He picked up the glasses that were hanging from a gold chain around his neck and put them on before squinting at Addison again. "Well, what can I do for you, boy?"

"I-I am a girl, sir."

"I know that! What do you want, girl?"

Addison walked a bit closer, hoping that he would cease to speak so loudly if he could hear her better. "My name is Addison Le Claire and I was born in Glen Grove in December, twenty-two years ago. I do not know who my mother is or what happened to her. I was hoping you delivered me and had some information on her."

Doctor Thatcher studied Addison, his eyes seeming to swim behind the thick glasses.

Addison waited for what seemed like forever without a sound being uttered by either of them. She opened her mouth to speak, thinking he had forgotten she was there, when he finally spoke.

"I am sorry, child, but I didn't deliver any girls in Glen Grove in December of that year. I would remember, it was a long cold winter and only three babies survived. All of those were boys."

Addison's heart sank. "Are you sure, Doctor Thatcher?"

"Yes, I am very sure. What did you say your name was again?"

"Addison Le Claire."

"No, the name does not sound familiar. What is your father's name?"

"Addigo Le Claire, sir."

"No, I would remember that name, I am sure. I do not think I delivered you, child. Lots of people used midwives back then, or had an old aunt do the delivery. If that was the case, good luck finding the information. I kept meticulous records of my births, but those women were not professionals and would not have kept anything." Doctor Thatcher harrumphed with disdain and settled back against his pillows.

Shoving her hands in her pockets, Addison was prepared to thank the doctor and leave when she thought of something else.

"Doctor Thatcher, I was born at Markby Estate. Does that help at all?"

Doctor Thatcher frowned as if in deep thought. Then he yelled, "Heddie, bring my journal!"

Heddie came in a few moments later, drying her hands angrily with her apron. She walked up to one of the shelves in the room and studied it for a moment before reaching up and pulling down a brown leather volume. She sat the book on Doctor Thatcher's lap and after a roll of her eyes turned to leave again.

"Heddie, just a moment. I cannot read it and I do not want a stranger reading my journal. No offense, dear."

"None taken." Addison answered, relieved.

"Heddie, look up December 1881, under the birth records."

Heddie wordlessly did what she was told, frowning until she found the right page. Addison peered over her shoulder and shook her head. Doctor Thatcher's handwriting was worse than hers, if possible.

"I have found it, what are you looking for?"

"How many babies did I deliver?"

"Three," she answered.

"Any girls?"

"No, all boys."

Doctor Thatcher crowed with delight. "See, my mind is as sharp as when I was twenty-five years old; I remember them all!"

Addison's heart sank. "What about at Markby Estate?" she asked, grasping at straws.

Heddie frowned at the book again, as she tried to decipher the Doctor's scribbles. "No, it does not appear as if there were any born there then, but there was a boy, John Patrick Baptiste, born to Lady Elizabeth M. Baptiste in January. Does that help you at all?" Heddie asked, noting Addison's pallor.

"No, not really. I hoped that I would be able to find out what happened to my mother from Doctor Thatcher."

Addison noted that Doctor Thatcher had apparently dropped off to sleep, so she thanked Heddie and made her way to the door. She felt almost weak with disappointment.

"Are you all right?" Heddie asked.

Addison nodded and gave a Heddie a weak smile. "Yes, I am just a little disappointed. I thought he would be able to help me."

Heddie patted Addison on the back. "That is unfortunate, dear, but he was meticulous about those records. If that book says he did not deliver any girl babies at Markby Estate then you can be assured he did not. Have you tried some of the midwives in town? As I remember it, there were quite a few people that preferred to go that route back then."

"No, I had not thought about it. I hoped that Doctor Thatcher could tell me something."

"Well, dear, sometimes the road to truth is the hardest road to travel."

Addison nodded, not really hearing Heddie's remark. "I should get back to Markby before I am missed. Thank you for your time."

Addison mounted Magnus and slowly made her way back toward Markby Estate. She had never felt so alone in her life.

JOHN WAS SURPRISINGLY amicable as Brontë helped him to dress. "Did you have nightmares last night?" he asked.

"Nightmares?" Brontë repeated, as she placed his foot onto the bath chair and straightened his leg.

"Yes, I thought I heard you crying during the night."

"No, I do not think so," Brontë said.

"I felt sure that I heard you, but I could be mistaken."

Brontë didn't answer and John seemed content for once to let the matter drop.

"I was thinking. Why do you not have Thomas do some of these things for me? You are too young to be in the house all the time. I am sure you would like to get out more often."

"Oh, John, are you sure?"

"Of course I am sure, Brontë. Call Thomas, I will speak to him about it and we shall start today." Brontë was so ecstatic that she didn't notice that his smile didn't quite make it past his lips.

"I will send him right up." Brontë said excitedly and rushed out the door to find Thomas, unaware of the contemplative look John wore as he watched her leave.

All morning, Brontë had been thinking of the things she wanted to say to Addison. She was not sure if she should apologize or act like the foot bathing had never happened. Brontë was on her way to the library when she caught sight of Addison through an open window, returning to the stables on her horse. The way she slouched in the saddle made Brontë think she was either very tired or hurt.

"M'lady, Lord Baptiste wishes to see you." Brontë looked up at Thomas and then back through the window. Addison had already disappeared into the stables.

Concerned, Brontë tried to make as many trips to the kitchen that day as she could, always keeping her eye out for Addison. But either Addison had forgone her now-daily ritual of eating lunch with Cook or she had come when Brontë was helping to wash John.

John had decided to take a nap. Thomas would be sitting with him when he woke up, so Brontë was faced with the unusual situation of having extra time on her hands. With Mary's help, Brontë quickly slipped on her riding clothes. She realized with a start that she preferred the trousers to the dresses that she normally wore. She quietly left the house and headed to the barn in search of Addison. If she had not been so concerned about Addison, she might have noticed that she was being observed. As it was, she went into the barn, then the stable, looking for Addison to no avail.

Without considering that she might be unwelcome, she followed the slight trail that led to Addison's cottage. She reached the outskirts of the small clearing to the chorus of the hounds. She slowed her pace, expecting Addison to pop out of the cottage at any moment.

When Brontë reached the door with no sight of Addison, she was tempted to turn around and head for home, but instead she knocked lightly on the door. After listening for a minute, she knocked again. This time she heard a small snuffle and then a dog whining from inside.

"Perry, is that you, girl?"

Brontë decided to try the door, halfway hoping to find it locked. The door swung open easily and she entered to find the usually neat cottage in disarray and Addison apparently asleep at the table. Papers and books spread around her.

"Addison?" Brontë called to her from the open doorway. "Addison, are you ill?" Concerned, Brontë placed her hand on Addison's arm. When she still received no reaction, she put her hand on Addison's forehead and lifted her face. Addison groaned a few times and then opened her watery eyes.

"Oh, is it time for the lesson yet?" She wiped the drool from the side of her mouth.

"What lesson?" Brontë asked, confused.

"You were late so I started without you." Addison looked at the papers spread out in front of her. A puzzled frown appeared on her brow before her head fell forward and, with a loud thump, hit the table.

"Oh my goodness." Brontë tried to get Addison to wake up, but her head just seemed to loll forward every time. Frantically, Brontë looked around for a cloth that she could wet Addison's face with, and then she saw the half-empty flask. Brontë only needed to smell it once to know it was alcohol, and that Addison was inebriated.

Brontë shook Addison's shoulder but she only moaned and seemed to settle into a deeper slumber. "Addison, why would you do this?" She shook her hard enough to cause Addison's eyes to flutter briefly.

"Addison, please, we need to get you over to the bed. It is only a few steps." Addison mumbled something incoherent as Brontë finally got her to sit up. With her hand around Addison's waist, she pulled her up until she was standing. *Well, so much for a day off from nursing,* Brontë thought wryly as muscles came into play that she now used daily to take care of John. "Addison, come on. I need you to help a little, please."

"Forgive me, Brontë," Addison said thickly, as she tried to make her uncooperative feet move.

"We are going toward the bed. Only four steps. Can you do that for me?"

"Yes, Brontë." Addison nodded vigorously, trying not to look as drunk as she actually was. The four steps turned into six as Addison's steps were more careful and measured than usual, but they made it without incident. Brontë was about to breath a sigh of relief when she felt herself being pulled onto the bed with the intoxicated Addison. They landed with a grunt and then silence as Addison almost immediately blacked out.

Brontë shook her head, exasperated. "You are going to pay for this in the morning."

Removing Addison's arms from around her waist was not as easy as it sounded, but Brontë did it. Looking around the untidy cottage, Brontë went about putting things in some sort of order before she left. It took her nearly half an hour, but eventually she had everything neatly back in its place. Addison had not even stirred from her splayed position on the cot. Brontë put fresh water and food out for Perry and prepared to leave. As an afterthought, she went into the hardly used back bedroom and grabbed a blanket.

Brontë took Addison's shoes off as quickly as possible, memories of the stable incident burning in her mind. She carefully placed the blanket over Addison's broad shoulders and then, almost without thought, bent to place a kiss on the dark-haired woman's lips. Addison's eyes fluttered open, causing Brontë's stomach to flutter.

"I love you, you know," Addison said, her blue eyes focusing clearly on the green above her.

"I love you, too," Brontë answered and knew deep down in her soul that it was the right thing to say. It was the truth.

"I know that. I have always known." Addison rasped before closing her eyes in what appeared to be a peaceful sleep.

Chapter
Sixteen

THE NEXT DAY was a long and tiring one for Brontë. John was in a mood, to be sure, and found fault with everything that she did. She had managed to avoid confrontation until she had begun to help Beatrice with the linens. John said she had taken too long to respond to his call and had slapped her for it. Brontë had gone back downstairs with her eyes stinging from the brutal reprimand and hoped that Beatrice did not notice the bruise forming on her cheek. Both she and Beatrice were still somberly folding the linens when a knock sounded at the door.

Addison! Brontë made an effort to still the pounding in her chest. Since the incident in the office, the front door had been kept locked, and only she had a key to open it. Dropping the linens on a table as she passed, Brontë raced to the door, unlocked it and yanked it open. The welcoming smile spread across her lips froze.

"Good afternoon, m'lady. Is Lord Baptiste available?"

"Good afternoon, Sheriff," Brontë answered. "Please come in. I will go up and ask him." Brontë shut the door behind the sheriff and went upstairs. She dreaded speaking to John after the earlier incident. She was surprised when John greeted her cheerily, almost as if he did not remember that he had slapped her across the face as she had freed his chair from the curtains. Thomas was sitting next to the Lord; they had just finished his exercises. Meant to keep the muscles in his legs from going flaccid, they usually left him in a foul mood.

"John, the sheriff just arrived. He would like to speak with you."

"Well, send him up, Brontë."

Brontë quickly went downstairs and led the sheriff to John's room.

"M'lord, I am glad to see that you are recovered."

"I am as well as can be expected while still attached to this chair," John said.

The sheriff looked at Brontë and Thomas before saying, "Perhaps we should speak alone, m'lord?"

"Sheriff, there is no need for that. Why don't you tell us what brings you here?"

"Well, I have some good news. I have caught the person responsible for your shooting." Brontë's mouth dropped in disbelief.

"Really?" John's eyes were as wide as hers as he looked at the sheriff. Thomas continued to try to look busy as he ran a cloth over John's headboard, although his movements had slowed noticeably. "But how is that possible? I didn't know you even had any leads. Well, speak up, man, who was it?"

"Jack Timmons, m'lord."

John's face had gone completely white. "Timmons? I do not know a Jack Timmons. Why would he try to kill me?"

Brontë frowned; she barely knew the man herself. He had chopped wood for her father during the winter and her mother had complained bitterly about him being near the home because he was more often drunk than not. Brontë could remember being a girl of about eleven, hiding with her brothers behind the woodshed as Timmons sang a bawdy song about the fair ladies of London. Dirty mouth or not, she did not believe him capable of hurting anyone.

"Timmons, Sheriff? Are you sure? He does not seem the sort," Brontë said.

"Yes, I am quite sure." The sheriff looked embarrassed for a moment before admitting under his breath, "He confessed."

"He did? Good. Good. I must say it has been worrying me some," John said weakly. Brontë glanced at John; if it had been worrying him, he had made no mention of it to her.

"Seems he was poaching in your woods and was taking a shot at a buck and accidentally hit you, m'lord."

"What made him confess after all this time?" The sheriff frowned at Brontë, but before he could answer her, John interrupted.

"Well, whatever it was, I am certain the sheriff will make sure we never have to see or hear of this person again." John was looking more and more peaked by the moment.

The sheriff visibly puffed out his chest. "That shall be an easy task, m'lord, as he has already confessed."

"Sheriff, shall I see you out now?" Brontë asked.

"What?" The sheriff had been watching John with interest as well. "Oh, yes, that would be fine, thank you."

Brontë was closing John's door when he called to her. "Brontë, why do you not take some time to yourself this evening? I am sure that Thomas here can see to my needs for a while."

Still smarting from the slap across the face less than an hour before, Brontë simply nodded and closed the door quietly behind her. After showing the sheriff out and speaking to Wesley, she made sure that Beatrice had finished the linens before escaping to her room. Brontë sat down at her desk and stared out the window until she was nearly blinded by tears of boredom.

"Enough of this," she said aloud, and in moments she had gathered up her riding clothes, stuffed them into a satchel and was making her way to the stables, in the hopes of catching Addison before she went home for the evening.

Brontë was disappointed when she reached the stable and there was no sign of Addison. She was just about to leave when she heard a noise behind her. Addison came around the corner carrying the saddle that Brontë had used for her rides on Sage.

"Good afternoon, Addison." Brontë immediately felt ten times better.

"My lady." Addison's voice was deep, her eyes focused someplace to the left of Brontë.

"How are you feeling today?" Brontë suddenly felt very shy. The last time she and Addison had been in the stables together, Addison had run from her in tears.

Addison inhaled sharply and looked up at Brontë, startled. "I-I thought last night was a dream."

"No, it was no dream. But do not worry. I understand that it was the spirits talking." Brontë tried to hide her disappointment as Addison nodded her agreement gratefully and continued to look at the floor.

"My lady, I just wanted to explain why I ran away that day. I was afraid, I suppose. Hardly anyone ever..." Addison paused, unsure of exactly what they had been doing.

"Addison, we do not need to talk about it if you do not want to. In fact, why do we not act like it never even happened?"

Addison agreed, while secretly thinking she would never forget.

Brontë's throat constricted as the hopelessness of their situation began to bear down on her. Pushing away her grim thoughts, Brontë held up the bag that she had been holding.

"I thought maybe we could take Sage and Cinny out before it gets too late."

"You are not going to change in here, are you?" Addison looked around, horrified.

"Why not?" Brontë smiled; she knew she was giving Addison a hard time, but she looked so adorable right now that she could not help herself.

Weeks of fatigue vanished as the woman her mother thought of as rough looked around, mortified by the thought of Brontë disrobing in there. Brontë, for her part, had nary a qualm. After Addison helped her unbutton her dress she went into one of the stalls and, while keeping up a running conversation with Addison, quickly donned the clothing that she had grown to love.

Addison stood nervously with her back turned. When Brontë emerged fully clothed, Addison had already saddled Sage for Brontë and had a box set up so that she could mount Sage with little or no help from her.

"Are you ready?" Addison asked.

Brontë nodded, grinning. Addison was mounted in minutes and they set off on a leisurely ride along the path that they had traveled before. The conversation flowed easily from the moment they were out of view of the manor house.

"It is so strange that Timmons would be the one that shot John. He always seemed like such a nice man." Brontë frowned as she mulled over the earlier conversation with the sheriff. Addison had been as shocked as she had that the sheriff had actually found the person responsible for injuring John.

Addison looked through her eyelashes at the Lady as they approached the stable; the pleasurable ride was fast coming to an end.

"John's reaction was—well, frankly, it was odd."

"In what way, Brontë?" Addison looked at the Lady straight on for the first time that day. She suddenly leaned forward in her saddle and inhaled sharply. "My lady, what happened to your face?"

"What?" Brontë stiffened. "What is wrong with it?"

"You have a bruise! What happened? Did someone strike you?" Addison asked angrily.

"No, no, Addison. It was my own fault. I was helping John and I ended up getting in the way of a hand as he was moving from the bed to the chair." The untruth came so easily to Brontë that she felt a deep sense of shame. *Damn John for making me lie to her.*

Addison studied Brontë for a moment before sitting back in her saddle. "You should be more careful. That looks like it smarted."

"No, it was an accident. It did not hurt much."

Addison continued to look at the bruise until she was distracted by the appearance of the stables. She had been enjoying Brontë's company so much that she could not help but feel disappointed as they rode the horses through the stable doors. Addison jumped down from Cinny, once again avoiding Brontë's eyes, afraid the Lady would notice her disappointment.

"Wait, my lady. I will go get a crate so that you can get down." Addison was already jogging toward a likely box.

"Excuse me?"

Addison skidded to a stop and turned around warily, recognizing the stubborn tone of voice. "I-I...the horse is so tall. I merely

wanted to find something so that you might step down yourself."
Addison stuttered as she attempted to explain her reasoning.

"You do not think I can get down without your help?" Brontë
asked.

"Oh no, I did not mean...I think you could, I just wanted to
help you."

"You know, Addison, you should not lie to me. I always know
when you do; your eyebrow twitches when you are not telling the
truth."

Addison's hand went immediately to her eyebrow.

"It does?" she asked, experimentally wiggling the offending
eyebrow.

"Hmm."

Brontë glared at Addison and then swung her leg over the
front of her saddle, her first mistake. Addison opened her mouth to
say something, but after another glare from Brontë, she decided to
keep quiet.

Brontë swung her leg back over the saddle and sat for a second
or two. Nodding to herself, she decided on a backward shimmy
approach, and, swinging her leg over the back of the horse, she
began her slide down. A triumphant grin was already on her face as
her toes touched ground.

Addison watched, amused at the dismount technique. Though
it lacked skill, it gained points in her book for functionality. She
was prepared to accept any ribbing that the Lady chose to dole out;
then she noticed that the Lady had not moved away from the horse.
In fact, she seemed to be dangling in midair. Addison stared at the
shapely rear end as she hung suspended above the ground. Her
frown deepened as the small body seemed to tremble violently.

"My lady!" Addison rushed over and, placing her hands on
Brontë's shoulders, turned her slightly to reveal a face streaked
with tears of mirth.

Addison stepped away from Brontë, deciding that she had
gone insane. Until she noticed that the Lady's shirt had caught on
the saddle as she had shimmied down, essentially hanging her and
leaving her suspended above the stable floor.

"My God," Addison whispered, as Brontë's body swung from
side to side, as she laughed hysterically at her self-imposed predic-
ament.

"My lady, how did you..." Addison wrapped her arms around
a slender waist and lifted, attempting to release the shirt from the
saddle. Brontë, who was still laughing hysterically, was no help in
getting herself unhooked and only managed to make Addison
laugh too.

"Lady, I need you to..." Addison's voice trailed off as her smile

froze on her face. There, slightly above eye level, were two tantaliz-
ingly beautiful nipples. Addison realized dully that Brontë's
breasts had been exposed because of her precarious position, hanging by her shirt buttons. Addison slowly stood to her full height,
bringing Brontë close to her body, her eyes focused on the two perfectly proportioned breasts.

Brontë placed both hands on Addison's shoulders and looked
down at her dark-haired savior. She was about to thank her when
she noticed Addison's focused gaze. A moment of silence ensued;
both were caught up in the moment, neither wanting to break the
spell. Addison lowered the Lady's body, bringing the tempting
breasts even with her mouth. Brontë gripped Addison's shoulders
as she waited, lips wet and parted. Addison watched for any sign of
fear or displeasure; seeing none, she gave in to the power of her
desire. Closing her eyes, she took Brontë's right nipple into her
mouth and suckled it as if getting nourishment.

It happened so fast that Brontë could only open and close her
mouth once before leaning more heavily into the lips that were giving her such pleasure.

Brontë's toes curled and uncurled painfully in her riding boots
at Addison's relentless suckling, her breath coming in desperate
gasps of pleasure. A moan of protest and then a muffled gasp of
pleasure as Addison's warm mouth left one breast to give attention
to the other.

Addison's arms and shoulders were trembling now and heat
was gathering in her stomach. Brontë was uttering sounds that she
had never heard before. *My God, she thought as she suckled the succu-
lent nipples. The sound she is making is driving me crazy.* Addison
swayed as she blindly moved to where she knew freshly cut hay
had been stacked only yesterday. Sitting down with Brontë's knees
on either side of her hips, she groaned as Brontë's small hands
hooked the leather tie in her hair and pulled it loose. Her fingers
dug into Addison's scalp and pulled her even closer to her breasts,
the whole time making soft sounds which started in the back of her
throat and seemed to end in Addison's crotch.

Addison cupped the Lady's backside and squeezed it as she
had dreamed of doing from the moment she had seen the Lady in
trousers, pulling her forward until she was grinding against her.
Brontë's throaty moans grew louder by the moment, further inflam-
ing Addison.

Brontë was beyond thought or comprehension. When she had
found herself hanging from the saddle, her first thought had been
that she deserved whatever teasing she had to take at the hands of
Addison Le Claire. This was by no means abuse. The suction on
her nipples was driving Brontë mad. The first movement against

Addison's hips had been simply to try to relieve some of the pressure. The second thrust was to see if she could get the rolling waves to repeat themselves.

Addison grabbed hold of Brontë's hips; she didn't want this moment to end too soon and she could tell by the way Brontë was moving against her that the smaller woman was approaching climax. Addison quickly turned them both until she held Brontë cradled beneath her and continued to suckle her breasts relentlessly. Brontë, frustrated, now moved against Addison's stomach; not getting what she needed, she groaned angrily.

Addison shushed her and straightened, stilling her writhing hips with one hand. Staring into Brontë's green eyes, she eased her thigh up until it was pressed firmly against Brontë's heated center.

"Addison?" Brontë whispered fiercely. "Addison, please."

Addison's mouth closed over her breast again, her eyes shut tight as her heart pounded in her ears. She ran her hands down Brontë's sides as she suckled her breast. Brontë was once again groaning loudly.

Her hips moved rapidly; Addison let go of Brontë's nipple and studied the conflicting emotions of anger and need warring in her green eyes. Brontë's hips began to move faster even as her hands went to Addison's shoulders to push her away. Addison took a shuttering breath and whispered in Brontë's ear.

"Do not fight it, Brontë, let it come. It feels good, I give you my word." Almost instantly, Brontë stopped struggling against the relentless tide of pleasure that she was afraid would drown her.

Addison sensed that Brontë was close, so she increased the suction, causing Brontë to nearly buck Addison off her as she climaxed. The noises Addison was beginning to love were coming from Brontë's throat faster and at a progressively higher decibel until Addison thought she would climax herself just from hearing it. All too soon Brontë's movements stilled and all that could be heard was the heavy panting of both women.

Brontë lay wide-eyed and trembling. It now made sense. She had never understood why people went to such lengths to get this. *We did not even remove our clothes!* The thought of having Addison's lean, nude body pressed against her so intimately made Brontë flush, her body stiffening as once again she felt the addictive pull of arousal. Addison raised her head finally to look at Brontë. They stared at each other for a moment, both of them shocked by what had just occurred.

"Brontë?" Addison whispered.

"I am fi—" Brontë whispered. Her voice hitched as the part of her still pressed into Addison gave one final contraction.

"Brontë?" Addison's lips brushed Brontë's as she spoke. "May

I taste you now?" She looked up into the Lady's confused green eyes. "I want to taste what I do to you," she explained awkwardly, and then blushed furiously at having to voice her desires.

It was obvious that Brontë still didn't understand, so Addison closed her eyes and tried again. "May I show you what I would like to do? If you get uncomfortable or you want me to stop, just tell me, and I will."

Brontë nodded, still struck mute by the intensity of the pleasure that she had just experienced with Addison. Addison eased her body to the side of the smaller woman; Brontë grabbed her arm.

"I am not going anywhere, I just do not want to crush you," Addison gently brushed a wisp of hair back from Brontë's forehead. "How do you feel? We can stop if this is too much for you."

"No." She had to clear her throat because of all the vocalizing she had been doing moments before.

"Are you certain?" Addison asked, but the concerned frown had left her face and she was already grazing Brontë's stomach with her fingertips.

"Yes, I am certain."

Addison let her fingers trail to the waistband of the trousers, pausing before once again covering the smaller woman with her body and kissing her until her breathing was erratic. Addison kissed the side of Brontë's neck before revisiting her breasts, where she had to force herself to move on because she could tell by Brontë's moans that she was beginning to get aroused too quickly. Addison kissed her small belly button, her hands going to Brontë's waistband, pulling it lower so that she could get to the sensitive skin below her belly button; she was fascinated as the muscles beneath her lips tensed and flexed. Addison raised her desire-filled blue eyes to find green eyes watching her every move, arousal plainly written across her face.

"Remember if you want me to stop, tell me," Addison whispered before lowering her head to continue on her journey south.

Brontë's eyes widened, a warm rush of wetness hitting her crotch as she realized that Addison intended to pleasure her with her mouth.

"That feels so good," Brontë encouraged, brazenly, the soft kisses that were already progressing lower. She was about to say something else when the sound of someone opening the door came from the front of the stable. Hearing it a second time, Addison jumped to her feet, and, after putting a finger to her lips to shush Brontë, she started frantically tucking her shirt into her trousers. Holding up her hands in a gesture meant to tell Brontë not to worry, she walked around the four stalls that had hidden her and Lady Baptiste from view.

Addison nearly groaned when she saw the offending party. "What do you want, Victoria?" She flushed as she heard her own husky voice.

"Addison, why do you have to be so rude? I was just coming by to see if you would like to offer me one of those riding lessons that you are so fond of giving."

Addison stiffened and approached Victoria, her hands balled tightly at her sides. "What are you saying?"

Victoria placed her hands over her chest. "Why, Addison, I am not saying anything in particular. I just noticed you seem to enjoy giving riding lessons, and I thought you might enjoy giving one to me."

Addison glowered down at the annoying woman and then said as pleasantly as possible, "Sorry, Victoria, I have all I can handle at the moment. However, if I should get some free time at any point, you will be the first person I let know."

Victoria smiled, entirely unfazed by Addison's rejection to her open-ended invitation. "That is too bad. Perhaps next time?"

"There will not be a next time, Victoria. As I said before, I have more than I can handle as it is."

"What is the problem, Addison? You found someone else to bring to the stables already? Well, you cannot blame a girl for trying." Victoria smiled and, after a quick perusal of Addison's disheveled appearance and a wistful shake of her head, left the stables.

Addison waited until Victoria was some distance off, then quickly shut the doors and pulled the storm latches into place.

"Brontë, I..." Addison rounded the stalls, only to find the bed of hay empty and no sight of Brontë. Looking around anxiously, Addison finally noticed that the back door was ajar.

Running over to it, Addison pushed the door open and frantically looked around for any sign of Brontë.

"Damn you, Victoria!" She walked back into the stables, slamming the door behind her.

Chapter
Seventeen

"ADDISON, UP HERE."

Addison was cursing for all she was worth and had managed to kick just about every sack, crate, box and bundle on the floor of the barn.

"Addison, I am up here," Brontë said again as her face flushed from the filth streaming from Addison's mouth.

It finally registered in Addison's brain that her name was being called; glancing up, she could see the Lady leaning over the side of the loft, watching as she threw a very childlike temper tantrum. Their eyes locked for a moment before Brontë broke the spell by grinning.

"If you are quite done, you may help me down from here."

"Oh, oh of course. I can do that," Addison said, embarrassed. "Why did you crawl up here, anyway?" She held Brontë's hips, averting her eyes from the bottom that seemed to call to her at every turn.

"I was afraid whoever that was would try to come back here and I didn't want them to see me, so I climbed up top. Climbing up was a lot easier than climbing down." Brontë knew she was babbling, but she didn't know what to say. Her mind was finding it hard to get around what Addison and she had just done together, yet it had felt so right and so good.

Addison could not believe her luck; Brontë had not heard what Victoria had said to her. "How do you feel?" Addison asked softly.

Brontë looked up once, and then quickly away for fear of jumping into those warm caring arms and begging her to never let go.

Addison mistook the gesture for shame as opposed to the shyness that it actually was. "I know I should apologize, but I will not."

Brontë looked up as Addison's voice took on a hard edge. Brontë looked away, disappointed. Addison had her mask of indifference firmly back in place.

"I cannot." Addison's last words were more of a plea than a statement.

"Addison," Brontë started, but Addison turned away.

"Do not say it, Brontë, I know all of that. I know you are married, I know you cannot be with me. I understand all that. I tell myself that there is nothing between us, that you feel nothing more for me than you would any number of acquaintances. But there is more. You feel it too. I know you do. We belong together. So I will not apologize for kissing you or holding you, or anything else that we have done together." Addison continued to stand with her back to Brontë, waiting for the sound of Brontë leaving or denying her feelings or anything more than the bleak silence.

"I was not going to ask you to apologize, Addison, I am a part of this, too. I am not blaming you for anything. It is just that..."

Addison turned around as she heard the Lady's voice falter. "Do not cry," she said, too late, as one solitary tear escaped down Brontë's cheek. She enveloped the Lady in her arms. "I didn't mean to upset you," Addison whispered as she moved both of them to the bed of hay and pulled Brontë onto her lap, where she held her close while rocking her. "I am just so frustrated. I feel like everything in my life is a test. Like I did something wrong that I have to make up for," she explained brokenly. "I feel like I am being tested to see how or what I will do, but no one is telling me the rules, so I can never win.

"Brontë, I think about you all the time," she admitted haltingly. "I think about how hopeless it is for us to ever be together. But I miss you desperately when I cannot see you." Brontë tried to straighten up, but Addison held her crushed to her body. "Wait, let me finish," she said into her neck.

Addison spoke for what seemed like hours, but was probably only thirty minutes, about how she had felt alone most of her life. How her father, though he loved her dearly, had refused to discuss her mother with her. How she felt that he had stayed at Markby Estate solely in the hopes that she would one day return to them. And finally, how she had felt that her mother had left because of her.

"But why would she leave because of you?"

"I do not know, but according to my father, she left three days after I was born."

"Did he tell you why?"

"No, he would never say, and after asking him a few times and getting him upset, I stopped asking. I thought there would be plenty of time to find out from him, but there was not. He died and now I am alone. I do not even know her name, Brontë," Addison said flatly, as she finally loosened her arms.

"Addison?" Brontë put her hand on Addison's chin, turning it to her before she gently placed her lips over Addison's. She felt

Addison start to pull away, but she would not let her; she deepened the kiss until Addison started to relax against her. Finally she released her mouth, her thumbs gently caressing Addison's closed eyelids.

"I cherish you, Addison. You are not alone; we will work something out."

Addison smiled tremulously. "Will I see you tomorrow?"

Brontë nodded. "Yes. I will figure out a way."

Addison helped Brontë to her feet and had started to help brush the hay off her but stopped when they both flushed from arousal.

"Forgive me." Addison stepped back and ran her moist palms down the sides of her trousers.

Brontë smiled. To think Addison would be embarrassed over something so innocent after what they had done together. "I should get back to the manor before I am missed." Brontë noticed the thinly veiled disappointment and felt a small pang of helplessness that she immediately pushed away. Standing on her toes, she kissed Addison again before leaving the barn and shutting the door behind her.

Addison slumped back on the hay, her eyes closed. She felt colder than she had before she had purchased that bottle of spirits.

Addison's mouth tightened; it would always be like this between her and Brontë. Brontë would have to go back home to her husband and Addison would be left at the cottage alone. Thoughts of the cottage caused a memory to flash through Addison's head.

I love you, you know.
I love you too.
I know that. I have always known.

"She said she loves me too!" Addison said aloud. "How could I have forgotten that part? She said she loves me!" Addison jumped up and looked around for something, anything to do to keep her busy until she could see Brontë again.

Tomorrow suddenly seemed like a long way off. It took Addison a couple of minutes to right the hay they had disarranged, the sacks and bundles she had kicked when she thought that Brontë had left. Looking around the stables, she decided there was nothing more to be done there and, after shutting the doors behind her, she walked home slowly whistling a quiet melody that she had heard once when she was very, very young.

"BRONTË. BRONTË!" JOHN bellowed from the other room,

just as Brontë sat down to remove her riding boots. She had tried to be as quiet as possible when she returned to her room, but apparently John had heard her enter.

"Just a minute, John, I will be right there." Brontë hurriedly started to remove her riding clothes.

"No. Get in here now, woman. I will not tell you again!" John yelled ferociously. Brontë jumped and looked around for her sleeping gown; upon not seeing it immediately, she realized she had no choice but to open the doors that separated the two rooms to find out what John needed.

"Coming, John," she twisted the knob and walked barefoot into the her husband's suite.

"May I help you with something?"

"Of course you may, that is why I—what the devil are you wearing, Brontë?" John roared.

Brontë jumped as John's face turned a frightening red color in a matter of seconds.

"They are just trousers, John, I wear them when I walk; I can move more easily," Brontë said, afraid to look at John.

"Move more easily? More easily?" John repeated to himself. "You look like that stable girl. What is her name, Addison? You look just like her."

Brontë stiffened at John's calling Addison a stable girl, but kept her mouth shut. It would not do to arouse John's suspicions about Addison if she hoped to sneak away and see her tomorrow. So she held her tongue and asked as civilly as she could, "Is there something you needed, John?"

"Yes, my riding crop. Would you pick it up for me? I dropped it earlier, and that damn Wesley has gone somewhere." John used a riding crop to help him point and reach things that were just out of his reach.

Brontë bent and handed John the riding crop, so grateful that John seemed willing to let the subject of her attire go that she remembered too late how John had taken advantage of her in a similar situation. Before she could finish the thought, the riding crop landed across her cheek and neck, missing her eye only by chance. The fiery path of pain made Brontë's eyes smart but she was too shocked to cry as she looked into the distorted red face of her husband as he raised the riding crop to hit her again.

"I wish I had never married you. You are all the same, unnatural." His words came in a rush and spittle flew from his mouth as he rained two more blows on Brontë that she partially blocked with her arm. The third blow caused something in Brontë to snap. Never one for violence, Brontë had endured every verbal and physical blow that John had given her, never once striking back.

Her hand caught the riding crop with a solid smack. "Do not try it," she growled, her green eyes boring into John's shocked blue ones. "You will not hit me again, John Patrick Baptiste."

John's stunned look quickly turned into amused indulgence. For the first time Brontë began to wonder if the bullet had taken more then his mobility. The gamut of emotions he seemed capable of displaying in one minute was staggering. Brontë released the riding crop and stepped away from him.

He chuckled. "You do not tell me what I will and will not do, woman. You are my wife!"

"Not for much longer if you hit me again, John." Brontë said evenly.

"Ohhh, so you are starting to get a backbone, are you? Surely you didn't learn that from your little friend." John laughed gleefully. "Did she tell you how I broke my cane? No, I do not suppose she would. You know," he tapped his chin as if deep in thought. "That one likes people to think she is so strong. Perhaps she is; did you know that I slammed Father's cane down on her foot and she never even screamed? I did it so hard that it broke clear up the shaft." John cackled maniacally, as if he had heard the funniest joke on earth. His voice was cut off mid-cackle by small but strong fingers gripping his neck.

"Do not ever touch her again!" Brontë said. Her vision threatened to blur and she blinked furiously.

Tightening her grip even more, she whispered, "Do you understand me, John? You keep your hands to yourself." John tried to choke out a reply but could only manage to nod his head.

Brontë experienced a moment when she thought about not letting go of John's neck. Tears came to her eyes as she remembered Addison saying she had hurt her foot working. The thought of John purposely hurting her, just because he could, made Brontë feel ill.

John's face had turned a sickly pale by the time Brontë let go of him. Brontë's turned away from John, the hate that she now felt threatening to choke her. "You had better hope you do not need anything else tonight, because I will be damned before I help you." She slammed the door behind her, John's rusty laugh following her even through the solid oak doors.

"Brontë. Come back, let me talk to you," he called, his voice light, almost amused, as if they had had a simple lover's quarrel.

Brontë lay down on her bed fully clothed and allowed tears of hurt, anger and regret to soak her pillowcase. She should never have married John; her family should have been forced to work things out like everyone else. She had been sold—no, worse, she had given herself to a monster.

BRONTË HEARD MARY'S voice from down the hall. Opening

the door, she cautiously called to her.

"Yes, m'lady." Mary approached, but Brontë stepped back into the darkness of the bedroom and partially closed the door.

"Mary, will you tell Wesley that he needs to see to John's needs today? I am not feeling very well."

"Yes, m'lady. Should I bring your breakfast up with Lord Baptiste's?"

"Yes, that should be fine," Brontë agreed, shutting the door quickly before Mary could see the bruise on her face.

Mary walked into the kitchen to find her mother and Cook talking quietly about something. "Cook, Lady Baptiste is ill, she wishes to receive her breakfast in her bedroom."

Cook and Beatrice glanced at each other sadly before turning back to Mary. "Was she very ill? Did you see her?" Beatrice asked, careful to keep her voice neutral so as not to arouse her daughter's curiosity.

"I do not know. She didn't come out of the room. She just said to tell Wesley to care for Lord Baptiste and that she would be taking her breakfast in her room today."

"Well, I shall find Wesley," Beatrice rose tiredly to her feet, "and bring the Lady her breakfast if you will see to the Lord's."

Mary and Beatrice left and Cook turned to her pot, a frown marring her smooth forehead as she muttered under her breath. "Sins of the father."

ADDISON HAD WASHED quickly at the well and was on her way to cajole Cook into preparing a lunch for Brontë and herself. She was exiting the stables when she heard the sound of horses coming up the road. *Now, who could be dropping by unannounced in a fine carriage such as that?* Normally Wesley or one of the others would have alerted Addison to expected guests.

Addison leaned back against the wall of the building, her arms crossed and a look of annoyance on her face. She hoped that whoever it was would keep going to the manor house. She sucked air between her teeth in annoyance as the carriage headed straight toward the stables where she now stood and stopped only a few feet in front of her.

Addison watched as the impeccably dressed driver jumped down from his seat and opened the door. Addison had unconsciously already taken on a look of boredom as she waited. Her mask slipped considerably as a vaguely familiar woman stepped none too daintily from the confines of the carriage. "Heddie?" Addison breathed, shocked at the woman's finery.

Addison could not believe it; gone were the uniform and the

haggard look. Heddie looked ten years younger and the proud smile on her face told Addison that she knew how good she looked.

"You look different." Addison continued to stare rudely, her mouth slightly agape.

"Thank you, dear, this is what a little rest, lots of time and a lot of money can do for someone like me."

Addison simply nodded, curious as to what had brought Heddie here to speak to her. It was obvious she had fallen on good times.

"I wish I could have come sooner, dear, but Doctor Thatcher took very ill soon after your visit."

"Oh, no. Is he feeling better now?"

Heddie's eyes filled with tears. "No, I am afraid he passed away."

Addison was at a loss for what to say. "I had not heard of your loss, Heddie."

"I am going to stay with my boys in London. I only stayed here as long as I did because Thatcher refused to leave. He always said that this is where he wanted to die."

Addison shifted uncomfortably on her feet as Heddie got a far-off look on her face before she seemed to snap out of it. "Oh, I almost forgot the reason for my visit." Heddie reached into the carriage and pulled out two dark volumes, handing them to Addison. "I told him that I would give these to you."

Addison looked down at the books. "He wanted you to give me his journals? But, why?"

"I do not know, but he made me promise. When he started getting worse, he babbled a lot. He made me promise that I would get those to you, said he'd finally made a mistake. That there was a storm in 1881 and that you should look at 1882. He got worse after that, it was as if the fact that he thought he made some mistake hastened his death."

"But I do not understand. What does it mean?"

"I do not know, it didn't make any sense to me either. I looked at the logs for 1882; it still does not say any girl children were born here, just the boy."

Addison frowned for a minute, something tickling at the back of her mind.

"Well, I should be going. The boys will be expecting me."

Addison opened one of the volumes and stared down at the messy scrawl. "This is worse than mine." She looked up just in time to see Heddie being helped up into the carriage. "Thank you for bringing them to me, Heddie, I guess I will figure it out eventually." Addison stepped back as the carriage driver took his seat up top. Heddie leaned out of the window as the carriage began to pull away.

"If you are ever in London, look up Heddie Thatcher or her sons of Canterbury Lane."

Addison's hand froze in mid air as Heddie's words floated back to her. "Heddie Thatcher?" she breathed. *My God, but they fought like cats and dogs.* Addison remembered the look of utter sadness on Heddie's face when she said that Doctor Thatcher had died. She walked slowly into the stables and sat down on her workbench. *Heddie was married to Doctor Thatcher! I thought she was his maid, the way he treated her. Well, the way they treated each other,* she corrected. Heddie certainly gave as good as she got. And from the looks of her, Doctor Thatcher certainly seemed to have provided for her after his death. Addison placed the volumes on her workbench and left them there. She was in far to good a mood to dwell on the oddities of the old couple's relationship. Addison was certain that it was something that she would never understand.

COOK WAS STILL thinking about Lady Baptiste's situation when she was suddenly grabbed from behind in a powerful hug.

"Good morning, Cook." Addison kissed her loudly on the cheek before releasing her.

"Addison Mari Le Claire!" Cook stood with her hands on her hips, glaring at Addison.

Addison, in an attempt to mock Cook, put her hands on her hips as well. "Cook. What is your real name, anyway? You never told me." Addison slouched down in a chair at the little table and waited while Cook slapped her lightly in the back of the head with one hand and poured her a cup of tea with the other.

Addison chuckled, not expecting an answer and not receiving one. Cook was, and always would be, Cook. Addison had known her all of her life, but did not know her real name. Neither did anyone else, as far as she knew.

"Cook, have you seen Lady Baptiste today?"

"No, I have not. I do not suppose you have anything to do with that?"

"With what?" Addison knew it was not like the Lady to miss a meal.

"The Lady all of a sudden taking sick? What did you two get up to yesterday?"

Addison inhaled her tea too fast and choked as it went down the wrong pipe. Cook patted her on her back for a minute before deciding it was a lost cause and going back to stir her steaming pot.

Addison cleared her throat finally. "What do you mean, Cook?"

"I saw her leaving here yesterday in those clothes she thinks no one knows she has. I also know you two get up to more than just studying."

"We-we went riding."

"And?"

"Cook, what are you asking?" Addison sat her cup down on the table with a thump.

"Addison," Cook sighed. "I just want to know if you two had a disagreement. I know something was going on with you two a while back, I could see it in both your faces. That is why you have been around here so much. Used to be that I had to practically lay a trap to get you to come in here and talk to me. Now I am not being a busy body, I just want to know if you two quarreled yesterday."

"No, no we didn't," Addison said earnestly. "When she left to come home we made plans for today. In fact, that is why I am here; I was going to ask you to make a lunch for later with some of her favorite things in it."

"Hmm," Cook said, still not looking at Addison.

"Cook, I didn't upset her." Addison was worried now. "At least, when she left me she seemed happy. Unless..." Addison's mind started working overtime. Brontë had seemed happy. But maybe she was regretting yesterday and needed some time to think things through. "I need to speak to her." Addison got to her feet and walked toward the door.

"Addison, are you sure you want to do that?" Cook spoke without turning around as she continued to stir her pot. "You could be making things complicated for her with Lord Baptiste, and she could very well just be sick. Give her a day or two. See if she comes around."

Addison walked back into the kitchen and sank back down into the chair, a frown marring her strong features. "No, I guess not. I will wait for her to come to me."

"I am sure she will feel better by tomorrow."

Addison was wondering if her heart had betrayed her by giving itself to the Lady Baptiste. "I hope so, Cook. I truly do." Addison somberly got up from her chair and, after exchanging a hug with Cook, left to begin her day.

She pushed herself that day and the next, until it was all she could do to fall into bed fully clothed at night. Even in sleep, however, she was tormented by thoughts of Brontë. As days turned into nights she could not help but ask herself what she had done wrong, or how she could have handled the situation better. On the sixth night of no contact with Brontë, Addison's sorrow became anger. She could understand Brontë not wanting to be with her—after all, she didn't have much to offer—but she could have at least told

Addison to her face. Addison stormed out of the cottage; she was
not sure what she was going to say to Brontë, but one way or
another she was going to find out how things stood.

Before Addison knew it, she had nearly reached the manor
house. A soft female voice followed by a male voice made Addison
stop in her tracks; she stepped slightly to the right, where she knew
she would not be seen through the trees. Looking up, her face
crumpled as she saw confirmation of her worst nightmare. Brontë
sat on the lap of her husband, her blonde head resting on his shoulder. Addison's eyes watered. By the time she had angrily brushed
the tears away, Brontë had pushed John's chair into the bedroom.
Addison caught another glimpse of blond hair before the curtains
were snatched closed and Addison was left in utter darkness.

Chapter
Eighteen

BRONTË ENTERED THE kitchen with little of her usual cheer, sitting down unknowingly in the chair that Addison usually took. She nervously rubbed her hand on the smooth tabletop, waiting for Cook to speak. After spending the last few days confined to her room, she had felt she had no choice but to rejoin the land of the living. Her bruises had faded enough that it would be hard to pinpoint them, even under the most detailed scrutiny.

Realizing that Cook would not be making things easy on her, Brontë cleared her throat.

Cook pretended to have just noticed her sitting there. "Oh, good day, Lady Baptiste, I didn't notice you walk in," she lied sweetly.

"Good day, Cook," Brontë returned with a smile that didn't quite reach her eyes. Brontë endured another long silence in which Cook seemed quite content to stir her pot without saying another word.

"Have you seen Addison today?" Brontë finally could not help but ask.

"No, not today, though I am sure she will be along shortly. She has been here daily, asking after you."

Brontë continued to trace a nonexistent pattern on the table. "How is she?" she asked, so quietly that if Cook had not been waiting for the question she would have missed it.

"Do you really want to know, m'lady?" Cook stopped stirring the plain water in her pot. It was a technique that she often used when troubled people came into her kitchen. They seemed to get their feelings out easier if they weren't being stared at, so Cook stirred whether she had something in the pot or not.

"I really want to know, Cook."

"She is feeling, and looking, like she's just been kicked in the stomach and abandoned," Cook answered, sitting down at the table.

"I didn't," Brontë felt tears welling up and turned her eyes away. "I didn't abandon her, Cook. I shall explain it to her. I am sure she will understand."

"Will she?" Cook asked. "I am not so sure. I have known Addison all of her life, m'lady, and if there is one thing that I know about her, it is that when she gives her heart, it is not on a whim. She does not take kindly to being hurt. She does not take kindly to it at all."

Brontë nodded. "I know. I will just have to try to make her understand."

Cook sighed and looked at the Lady Brontë, thinking how young she looked, and how sad. "May I make a suggestion, m'lady?"

Brontë nodded, eager for any insights that Cook might have.

"Tell her the truth." Cook looked Brontë in the eye as she spoke.

"What do you mean, Cook? Of course I will tell her the truth. I have no reason to lie."

"M'lady, I have been on this earth a lot longer than you might think. I have gone through a lot; I have done things that I still struggle with. I see how you two look at each other. I know love when I see it. Some people might not think it is right, but I do not think love that deep could ever be wrong."

Brontë inhaled, her eyes wide. "I do not know what to say."

"You do not have to say anything. Your face says it all. Just the same as hers did when she asked how you were. But she is awfully hurt, m'lady. She does not understand how you would have feelings for her and then just not see her anymore."

"I had to stay away from her, Cook. I could not let her..." Brontë threw her hands up, once again frustrated at not being able to explain her actions.

Cook watched the play of emotions on Brontë's face for a moment. "He hits you, and you were hiding it from the one person that would dare to question a fall or one too many accidents."

Brontë tried to deny it, but her face crumpled and before she knew it, she was pressing it into Cook's soft bosom as she cried her heart out. "My goodness," she laughed shyly after she had managed to calm down a bit. "I thought I was all cried out, but it looks like I still had some left."

Cook handed her a handkerchief. "Well, what are you going to do, m'lady? Addison does not deserve to be hurt."

"I do not want to hurt her, Cook. I-I do love her."

"Then tell her the truth." Cook reached across the table with an extra handkerchief to help Brontë dry her wet cheeks.

"I am just so afraid that she will do something foolish, like go after him."

Cook chuckled. "That one does have a bit of a temper. You will just have to trust her, I am afraid, m'lady. But I think you should tell her the truth. She may surprise you." With those final thoughts, she got up from the table and returned to her pot of steaming water, leaving Brontë to think about what she had just said. Cook slowly stirred her pot, her mind regressing to a time long ago when she had had a similar conversation with another unhappy Lady. She smiled sadly and thought, *Perhaps these two will turn out differently.*

ADDISON TRIED TO do her work, but to no avail. Try as she might, she could not get the vision of Brontë sitting on John's lap out of her mind. When the curtains had been pulled, Addison had run sobbing back to her cottage where she had sat motionless in a chair, staring into the fire as it slowly died. Perry had sat next to her through the night, looking at her with soulful eyes. "So this is what a broken heart feels like, Perry," she had said to her companion as she gently stroked between her ears. "I thought it would hurt, but it is not that bad," she told Perry. "I hardly feel anything at all."

Addison was dressed and heading for the stables long before the sun rose. Pitchfork in hand, she stood staring at the bed of hay where she had held the Lady in her arms, where she had poured her heart out to her, and where she had cried with frustration over her.

Addison dropped the pitchfork, and without a backward glance, walked out of the stable. It was time to leave this place, before it killed her.

She went through the cottage packing her few meager belongings. *I will give the portraits to Beatrice and Mary since they like them so much.* She had nearly finished packing when she came to her father's old trunk. Addison had always respected her father's privacy, as he had hers.

She really wanted something to remember him by; she opened the trunk in the hopes of finding some memento to take with her. The trunk contained a few coins and some small books. Also, oddly enough, a lock of curly blond hair tied with a faded red ribbon. Addison had just pulled out the lock of hair when there was a knock at the door.

Heart pounding, Addison walked to the door, trying hard not to wish that it was Brontë, but failing miserably. Addison swung the door open expectantly. "What do you want, Victoria?" Addison asked, exasperated, as she looked the young blonde maid up and down.

"Now is that anyway to treat a visitor, Addison? Are you not going to ask me in?" Victoria smirked as she flounced through the door, looking around the neat little cottage before sniffing disdainfully and turning to Addison.

"Why are you here, Victoria? And do not say for a visit, because you never come out here."

"Well, there seems to be a bit more activity around here lately, and I wanted to see what I was missing."

Addison gritted her teeth. "There is nothing for you here, Victoria. Stop your incessant teasing and go on back to the manor house."

"Addison, why do you have to be so mean? I am here to help you." She stepped closer, swinging her little carrying bag in tight little circles, as she tried to look put out by Addison's comment.

Addison eyed her suspiciously. She wanted very much to tell Victoria to just leave, but she had to admit, her curiosity was piqued.

"Well," Victoria moved a little closer until she was standing directly in front of Addison, "I see what Little Miss Priss is doing to you. I see how your hands shake whenever you are around her."

Addison gnashed her teeth and opened her mouth to tell her to leave.

"I would never do that to you, Addison. I can help you get over this infatuation with Lady Do-Gooder if you would only let me."

Addison felt the shameful well of desire as it settled in her lower belly. Victoria was right, was she not? It was not as though Brontë had even acknowledged what had happened in the barn. The previous time with Victoria had been a release, nothing more. *Perhaps I will be able to think straight afterward.*

"Let me love you, Addison," Victoria said softly. Setting her bag on the table behind Addison, and placing a hand on Addison's chest, she pushed her against the table until she was half sitting, half leaning on it.

As Victoria's hands began to sneak under the wool sweater that Addison wore, Addison breathed a shuddering sigh and closed her eyes, trying to pretend that Brontë was the one caressing her stomach and unbuttoning her shirt, Brontë's fingers the ones slipping under the wrapped cloth that covered her breasts. Addison moaned as experienced hands caressed her nipples.

"Victoria," Addison gasped, "you need to stop."

"Addison, let me taste you. Let me touch you like you want her to. I know what you want. I can see it in your eyes every time you look at her. Even when you are running away, I can see how much you want to be with her. But she does not understand people like you and me, and she never will. Let me touch you this time. Let me touch you like she never would."

Victoria opened Addison's shirt and leaned heavily against her. The muscles in Addison's stomach quivered as Victoria's cool lips kissed her neck and began to work their way downward.

Addison tried to imagine Brontë kissing her like this, taking her in this way and, for a moment, white-hot desire flared deep in her stomach as slender fingers began to work their way underneath the waistband of her trousers.

"Oh, God, I want—" Addison's voice caught in her throat with a hitch as she almost said out loud something she had yet to fully admit to herself. She wanted only Brontë, with a passion that she could not control. Eyes still closed, she thought of the Lady's voice, the warmth that she felt when the Lady touched her, the way she smiled at her when she read a word or a phrase correctly by sounding it out.

"Mmm, Addison, you really want me, do you not?" Victoria's question penetrated Addison's brain like a sword, viciously separating the fantasy from the reality and leaving Addison wanting.

No, Addison thought, I do not want you, Victoria. I never have. I only want her. And if she will not have me, then no one else will, either. Eyes still closed, Addison gripped the small shoulders of the woman now kneeling in front of her. It was time to stop this; it had already gone too far.

"Addison!"

Addison froze, her hands still gripping Victoria's thin shoulders. *My God, no, please do not sound like her. I cannot take much more of this, damn it.* Slowly, Addison became aware of the tension in the thin shoulders that she gripped.

"Addison?" Brontë stood in the open doorway, her eyes going from Victoria to Addison. Comprehension dawned and her hand went to the wall to steady herself.

Addison turned away. She could not bear to look at her anymore, she was so ashamed of herself for what she had almost allowed to happen.

Victoria stumbled to her feet. Brontë fixed now-cool eyes upon her. "I want you to go home, Victoria. I expect to see you in John's office bright and early tomorrow, do you understand?"

Victoria nodded and squeezed past Brontë without looking back; she hurried down the path and away from the cottage as fast as her feet could carry her.

Addison still could not bring herself to look at Brontë. How could she have allowed it to get so out of hand?

Brontë's lips trembled as her eyes begged Addison silently for some sort of explanation. Her hurt was quickly replaced by confusion, which was soon replaced with molten anger.

"It seems I unwittingly interrupted your little get-together with Victoria. I had some time and I thought I would see if we could go riding." Brontë's voice sounded bitter, even to her own ears.

Addison reacted the way she always did when she felt backed into a corner; she got angry. "Well, it was kind of you to find time for me in your busy life."

"What are you implying?" Brontë walked heedlessly into the cottage, not bothering to close the door behind her.

"I am not implying anything." Addison turned away from her, her heart beating an agitated staccato inside her chest.

"I should never have come," Brontë said, but she didn't leave. She just glared impotently at Addison's back. She felt the unfamiliar need to hurt Addison the way that she was now hurting. "What is wrong with you anyway, Addison?" she asked cruelly as she walked closer. "Is it so hard for you to control yourself that you have to go to Victoria to fulfill your needs?"

Addison turned around quickly. "Yes, perhaps it is. Victoria has always been very accommodating in that area."

"What do you mean, *always* been accommodating?" Brontë's eyes widened as it dawned on her that this was not the first time that Addison and Victoria had been together.

"You heard her back on the stairs that day. Did you think she was just talking, *my lady*? She was speaking from experience. At least she admits that she wants me, unlike you, who is happy to stay in a loveless marriage instead of admitting some truths to yourself."

"Truths? What truths?"

"The truth is you want me as much as I want you."

"Why would I want you, Addison? I am not like you or Victoria. I can handle my own needs, and for those needs that I cannot handle myself, I have a husband who is perfectly capable, contrary to popular belief, of taking care of them for me." Never had dishonesty come so easily to Brontë.

"You are lying," Addison growled, even as her heart shattered into a thousand shards.

"I am not the one lying, Addison. You are. You are the one lying; to yourself, not me."

Addison snarled as Brontë turned to leave. *"Your lord* could never hope to pleasure you the way that I could have." Addison grabbed Brontë's wrist and, in an effort to hurt Brontë the way she had been hurt, she added, "Just ask Victoria. She came back for more, so it must have been pleasurable."

The feral and lecherous look that crossed Addison's face at that moment was the last straw. Throwing all caution aside, Brontë reacted in a way that would shock her later, upon retrospect. Her hand shot out and connected firmly with Addison's jaw, sending her head snapping to the left. Addison blinked back tears of shock.

"You and Victoria deserve each other," she growled through lips that almost refused to move. "You are both no better than animals rutting around in the forest." Brontë angrily spun on her heels and left Addison to watch as she ran recklessly down the dark path toward the main house.

Pain, frustration, and anger warred within Addison as she watched the Lady disappear farther and farther down the path. Soon she would be completely out of sight, behind the walls of the main house with her bastard of a husband. Addison's hand went to her chest as a sharp pain coursed through her, settling like a cloak over her heart. She nearly stumbled, blinded by her anger.

She had allowed herself to trust someone. But now the dream of having a more important role in Brontë's life had disintegrated. It was a lie. Everything she thought was real had been based on lies. Her mouth stretched into a toothy smile that held no mirth. No, not everything was a lie. The Way Brontë reacted to her touch and her kisses, that was real. Whether she admitted it or not it was real. And she would admit it.

She started up the path and in no time, Brontë was in her sights. Through the gloom of the evening, Addison could make out the outline of the main house. Picking up speed, she intercepted Brontë in seconds. Silently, she took one more loping stride before grabbing Brontë tightly and pulling her close to her body.

"Not a word, my lady," Addison whispered, as she held the smaller woman against her with one strong arm, and held her mouth closed with the other. "Was it fun tormenting me, my lady?" She asked angrily as she walked, carrying the futilely struggling Brontë. "Did you both laugh at me every night as you gave him what I wanted?" The question was a hot whisper in Brontë's ear.

Brontë frantically shook her head, tears streaming down her face as she tried to kick back at Addison. But Addison only tightened her hold.

"It was all a lie, was it not, Lady Baptiste? You never felt anything for me at all." Addison's voice had gotten lower and lower as her frustration and resentment combined in a volatile mix of passions. She easily carried Brontë another few feet before putting her down on the very log that she herself had sat on to watch Brontë marry Lord John.

"You want to laugh at me, my lady? That is fine, I do not mind. Everyone laughs at me." She held Brontë pinned against her body. Brontë bit down on Addison's hand, making her inhale sharply and pull the blonde head that she held back, so that she was staring into angry, watery green eyes. "Do not do that again or I will bite you back," she said.

Brontë closed her eyes and attempted to turn away, only to have Addison hold her head firm so that she was forced to either leave her eyes closed or look at Addison.

Addison loosened her grip on Brontë's mouth so that the Lady was able to sit up straight, though Addison still had her firmly around the waist. "Look up there." She spoke so softly that Brontë could barely hear it over the sound of her own harsh breathing.

Brontë looked up and was shocked to see that Addison had brought her to an area of the property that was almost completely covered in trees. However, she could clearly see John's balcony as well as the Lord himself, who was staring into the exact spot that she and Addison now stood. Brontë froze.

"What is the matter, my lady? Afraid that your loving husband would be angry if he learned that you were out this late? What do you think he would say if he knew you came out to see me often?"

Brontë shook her head angrily.

"No?" Addison taunted. "You think he would not care that you spent the night with the likes of me while he lay practically on his death bed? Do you think he would believe that I didn't touch you while we lay together?"

Brontë held herself stiffly, telling herself that she would not give Addison the pleasure of seeing her struggle.

"What do you think he would say if he knew that I did touch you? I touched you while you slept." Addison's body shook with anger as she admitted the private shame. "I could not help myself. You were right, I am no better than an animal, just like Victoria. But at least I do not deny what I am." Her hot raspy breath caressed Brontë's ear as she spoke.

"Look at him, my lady," she whispered into Brontë's ear, forcing her head up so that she could see the stony face of the Lord of Markby. "What do you think he would do if he saw you down here? If he knew that you let me touch and kiss you in the stables?"

Addison's mouth was pressed against Brontë's ear now, as they both trembled with anger and something else that was on the one hand entirely different, but on the other, not so different at all.

"How did it feel?" Addison whispered into Brontë's ear, "To know that you left me hurting every night? Did it feel good to you, Brontë? Did you enjoy going back to your big home and allowing your husband to touch you as I could not? Did you tell him when you made me cry?" Her voice was so low now that Brontë could barely hear her, even though her lips were still pressed firmly into her ear.

Tears mingled with Addison's perspiration as images of Brontë lying willingly with Lord John filtered through her subconscious, sending pain shooting through her core, a sob escaping her unwilling lips.

Brontë froze as her anger at finding Addison entwined with Victoria began to fade and she realized how her denial of her feelings was hurting the strong woman behind her. She tried to speak Addison's name, but the hand over her mouth tightened and she was pulled back against Addison's body again.

"Do not say a word. Do you hear me? I should have taken you in the stables when I had had the chance. Would you have told him that, my lady?"

Brontë tried to speak once again, but it only seemed to make Addison angrier, so she just shook her head resignedly.

"No? I do not suppose you would have, would you? You would have had to tell him how wet I made you then, would you not?" Addison was getting angrier by the minute as she thought of her many sleepless nights and how hard it had been to back away from the Lady that day. "I could have had you that day. I could have taken you as many times as I wanted and you would have let me."

Brontë did not move or respond, save for the tears that flowed down her cheeks and over the hand that was clamped over her mouth. There was nothing she could say; it was the truth. She had wanted the angry woman behind her from the very beginning, though she hadn't known herself what she had desired.

Addison wished she could hold Brontë and apologize for almost giving in to Victoria. She pushed those thoughts aside as she looked up into the far-off gaze of Lord Baptiste. His mere presence on the balcony served to infuriate her, as she remembered how she had watched Brontë wheel John back into the room and close the curtains, leaving Addison to her own nightmarish thoughts of what the Lord was doing with the woman she loved. *Loved?* Addison's lip curled into a snarl. *It was a lie, all of it.*

Addison began to pull at the shirt tucked into the overly large waistband of the riding trousers that Brontë wore. Her hand caressed the flat planes of Brontë's stomach before withdrawing, leaving Brontë stunned in its wake.

"Do not move, or your husband is going to do more than hear about what I can do to you. Do you understand?" Her voice was an angry purr in Brontë's ear.

Brontë nodded, her breath catching in her throat as she wondered what Addison planned. Addison's right hand was only gone for a moment before it returned, long fingers caressing Brontë's stomach, leaving a trail of raised flesh, before going straight to her breasts.

Brontë's knees buckled and she went to get off of the log, but Addison held her firmly in place, whispering in her ear, "No! You get down when I tell you that you can. Do you understand me?" Brontë nodded, her breath coming in gasps as the long fingers captured her nipples once again.

"Did you tell your husband how you tremble when I touch you? Did you tell him that you respond to me even in your sleep, your nipples hardening and aching because they want me to touch them?"

Brontë's breathing was becoming labored as chills shot up and down her neck, the warmth of Addison's lips and hot breath dueling with the chill in the night air. The dark night was rent with the sound of cloth being ripped as Addison tore the shirt open with one hand, leaving Brontë's breasts and stomach exposed.

Up above, John looked directly into the woods where they were, causing Brontë to freeze for fear that he would see them.

Addison, however, was past caring. Her mouth closed over the small vein that pulsed rapidly on the side of Brontë's neck as she gently squeezed and teased the Lady's breasts, systematically warming them with her hands and leaving one or the other to harden in the night air.

"Does he make you shiver like this, my lady?" Addison asked, as her fingers slipped past the waistband of the trousers and, for the first time, caressed soft curls. Addison closed her eyes, unbeknownst to Brontë, whose eyes were still riveted on John as he slowly leaned back in his chair, his unsuspecting gaze still directed into the forest.

Addison's hand unbuttoned the trousers that Brontë wore and before Brontë could utter a protest, she was picked up and sat back down, leaving her in boots and an open silk shirt, seemingly in full view of her husband.

Underneath Addison's hand, Brontë opened her mouth to protest.

"No, Brontë, not a word. You want this as much as I do. It is time for you to be honest with yourself." Addison's voice had lost most of its anger and her grip on Brontë's face loosened. "I am going to let go of your mouth now," she said. "Do not make a sound, do you hear me?"

Brontë nodded as Addison's hand eased its pressure and slid gently down Brontë's throat. Addison pulled the blonde head back as she whispered into Brontë's ear, triumphantly. "I may be an animal, but you are no better. Are you?" And with that, her large hands pulled the smaller body back.

Brontë jerked in shock as her backside came into contact with

Addison's womanhood. Unbidden, the memory of that dark thatch of moist curls peaking through open trousers sprung to Brontë's mind, and she inhaled sharply, as if the air had been knocked from her by some unseen specter.

Addison, misunderstanding the action, pulled Brontë more tightly against her and whispered hotly into her ear, "If you want me to stop, ask me to stop. Tell me that you do not want me, and I will stop this right now." Her hands were gliding down Brontë's stomach as she spoke. Brontë blinked once in shock and a second time in passion as her tormentor continued to whisper into her ear. She closed her eyes, but snapped them open instantly when a hot voice ordered her to.

"Look at him, damn it. Does he make you feel like this?" Brontë jumped again as a warm hand grazed the hair that covered her womanhood. "Did you let him touch you like this after you saw me, Brontë? Did he feel how hot and wet you were from me after your *riding lessons*?" Addison used her hand to part Brontë's bare legs. She raked gently through the golden curls before allowing one of her fingers to trail lower.

Brontë jumped once again, violently, at the first touch of Addison's finger as it glided over her aroused clitoris, past her entrance, then back up over her clitoris, coating the long digit with the copious evidence of Brontë's need.

Addison's throat hitched and she used the hand between Brontë's wet lips to pull her hips back against her. The last time she had been in a similar position with Brontë had been nothing compared to this.

Brontë's soft skin was now nestled firmly against Addison's. The longer she held this woman in her arms, the more engorged Addison's clitoris seemed to get. Addison groaned under her breath and parted her own legs a bit before pulling Brontë more tightly against her. The fingers cupping Brontë's sex began to move slowly. Moisture allowed her to move easily between Brontë's outer lips, causing her to inhale deeply and throw her head back.

"Shh," Addison whispered, her voice trembling, as she said, not unkindly, into Brontë's ear, "Feel good?"

Brontë swallowed and nodded, her eyes closed, as Addison continued to use her own wetness to increase her pleasure.

Addison moved her arm and wrapped it around Brontë's waist as she held the shorter woman steady on the log that brought her even with Addison's six-foot frame.

A small murmured moan escaped Brontë's throat and Addison slowed her pace, whispering, "Not yet, my lady. I want this to last." The long digits continued their pleasurable stroking while Addison ground her now fully engorged clitoris against Brontë's bottom.

Addison felt a flood of warmth and Brontë let out another soft whimper. Addison's fingers glided tortuously over Brontë's clitoris once more before pausing at the opening to Brontë's center.

Brontë stiffened as she waited for the expected pain. What she felt was a slight discomfort that was so far from pain that she fought down the urge to sigh in relief.

"Relax, my lady. You need to relax." Addison's voice sounded so loving, so caring, that Brontë was able to close her eyes and imagine that the woman taking her now was actually making love to her.

Addison spread her legs on either side of Brontë and braced herself. Using her upper torso, she bent forward slightly, forcing Brontë to do the same, pressing her aching clitoris against the Lady's firm bottom. Addison was only able to partially stifle her groan in the moist shirt that now hung limply over Brontë's back.

She began to move her long digit in and out of Brontë's core as she moved her mound against the Lady's backside. Brontë groaned from the feel of the two sensations; her head swam with the pleasure brought on by both the long finger inside of her and the feel of the hot crisp curls and the small, aroused nodule creating friction against her from behind.

Addison moaned again, this time not caring who might hear, as another wave of warmth coated her finger, allowing her to move more firmly into Brontë without the fear of hurting her.

Brontë had managed to work one arm free of Addison's and was using it to press Addison's hand more firmly into herself. Her eyes were completely closed as she imagined the passionate expression on the woman's face behind her.

A short, high whimper escaped from deep within Addison's throat before she cut it off, but not before the delirious Lady that she held in her arms heard it. Another wave of warmth passed over Addison's finger and she bit down hard on her lower lip to keep from crying out in response. Addison was trembling with her effort not to release. Remembering how drained she had felt after her last two encounters with Brontë, she wanted to make sure to give her as much pleasure as she could before she released herself.

Addison's legs were trembling with the effort it took to hold herself and the nearly delirious Brontë upright. Her whole hand now almost fully covered with evidence of the need that she feared Brontë would never admit to.

She smoothly entered Brontë with another finger, causing the smaller woman to nearly double over before Addison weakly pulled her up into the half crouch that they had adopted. As she increased the speed of her movements against the Lady she held in her arms, a sound much like a cough escaped Brontë's throat, but she and Addison were too far gone in the throes of passion to care whether they were being heard.

Brontë was now gripping the back of the hand buried between her legs. She pushed and pulled firmly to make Addison adopt a more forceful pattern. The sounds of flesh gliding into wet flesh could be heard as Brontë closed her eyes against the onslaught of sensation. Addison was now practically lifting Brontë with the force of her thrusts, each motion smashing Brontë's backside into her eager mound. With one final thrust Addison brought Brontë's body rigidly against hers.

"Do not cry out," Addison whispered gently just as she felt Brontë's body constrict around her two fingers.

Brontë released her death grip on Addison's wrists, covering her mouth to keep from screaming as her body shuddered. The smell of her own sex almost made her cry out again before she clamped her mouth closed and fell forward.

Behind her, Addison was not as successful in keeping quiet. The small, high whimpers, so unlike her normal speaking voice, came at regular intervals. Brontë's backside was now coated almost completely with Addison's essence. The air around them was thick with the smell of their coupling. Addison held the smaller woman in her arms as she moved her aching mound into the heated flesh that had tormented her for so long.

The dam that had been holding back all of the emotions that she had for this woman broke and she sobbed brokenly into Brontë's back as she murmured her name over and over again, valiantly struggling against the flood that threatened to pull her under.

Brontë's small hands weakly grasped Addison's forearm. Addison's other hand lay flat against Brontë's cooling curls, pressing her firmly back against Addison's throbbing clitoris. "Brontë," she moaned as she came. "Brontë, oh, please, Brontë." The last whisper seemed to be dragged forcefully out of her unwilling throat.

Chapter
Nineteen

BRONTË SLOWLY STRAIGHTENED, her eyes going fearfully to the balcony above. To her surprise John was not there, and the double doors that led to his bedroom were shut. Brontë had just opened her mouth to beg Addison to listen to her, when she was tightly grabbed from behind. She started to struggle as a hand was placed over her mouth and she was lifted.

"Shh, someone is out here!" Addison said into Brontë's ear. She crouched down behind a tree with her arms wrapped tightly around Brontë.

Brontë peered through the darkness, but could not see ten feet in front of her face. Without the meager light from John's room, the forest surrounding her was nearly pitch black. Brontë opened her mouth to whisper to Addison that she didn't think anyone was there, then she heard the telltale crack of a twig. Brontë shivered, and Addison pulled her back against the natural furnace that was her body.

"Listen to me, damn it. I want to know why that drunk confessed. I tried to get it out of that idiot Baptiste. I got all dressed up and everything, and he could not even perform." The voice sounded disgusted, then amused. "But there is more going on here than Baptiste is telling us, and I want a piece of it. No, listen, I am not going to discuss this out here. You get over to town. Talk to the sheriff and find out what is going on."

Brontë let out her breath in a sigh of relief as the footsteps receded and finally disappeared.

"Wait here," Addison whispered and was gone before Brontë could protest.

Brontë waited, shivering, her thoughts a jumbled mass of feelings over what had just happened moments before. She had no idea what she would say to Addison, but she felt she owed the other woman something. She nearly cried out when Addison's warm hand touched her arm.

"It is only me," she said flatly. "They are gone. Here are your clothes."

Brontë silently took her clothing, still unsure of what to say to Addison after what had just happened between them.

"Addison, that sounded like Victoria," Brontë volunteered hesitantly.

"I thought so, too," Addison said shortly. Addison suddenly went completely still as the overheard conversation played itself out in her head.

'I got dressed up and that idiot Baptiste could not perform.' Addison was nearly knocked down by the next thought that filtered through her frozen brain: *It was Victoria, not Brontë, who had been on the balcony with John.*

Addison sucked in her breath, horrified. "Oh, God, no!" she exclaimed in a weak whisper and dropped to her knees.

"Addison!" Brontë whispered, reaching out frantically.

"Oh, no," Addison whispered again, brokenly.

Brontë's hand finally grazed Addison's hair and face, trailing down to the stiff shoulders. "Addison, you are scaring me. What is wrong? Please, are you hurt?" Brontë was nearly in tears as Addison rigidly knelt in front of her, breathing shallow.

"What have I done?" she whispered.

"Addison?" Brontë pulled the kneeling woman to her and was immediately held in a vice-like grip around her waist. Addison buried her face in Brontë's stomach.

"It was Victoria!" she said.

Brontë stiffened. She did not understand what Addison was saying, but she was positive that if Victoria was involved it had to be something bad. "Addison, please tell me what is going on; you are scaring me."

"I saw you on the balcony with Lord Baptiste, laughing and kissing him. I thought you had lied to me about what you felt, that you were playing some twisted game. I was so angry, so hurt."

"Addison, I never—" Brontë was so shocked that her voice broke. "That was not me. I never lied to you."

"I know." Addison buried her face in Brontë's stomach again. Brontë could feel the warm wetness from the silent tears that Addison was shedding. "I was so angry that I could not see straight. I thought it had been a game to you."

"No, it never was." Brontë held Addison tighter as the silent sobs racked her body. She had made a mistake in not confiding in Addison. Because of it, Addison was hurting now.

Addison forced herself to her feet. She had already shed more tears in the last few weeks than she had in her entire adult life. "Brontë." Her voice sounded dead to her own ears. "Please forgive me. I do not know what you want to do about this, but I am willing to do..." Addison's voice caught and she didn't try to finish.

"Addison, there is nothing to forgive." Brontë wanted to comfort Addison but she was not sure how she could. Addison had already condemned herself.

Addison took a deep breath and let it out. Brontë reached out and touched Addison's arm. "You should go home," Addison said, even as she covered the smaller hand with her own.

"What about you, Addison? I do not want you to be alone."

"I am fine, Brontë." Addison shook her head, unable to believe that Brontë was thinking about her after what she had done. "I want to make sure you get back in the house."

"No, I want to go with you," Brontë said determinedly.

"Why?" The pain in her voice was so tangible that it caused Brontë to blink back her own tears.

"Because you are hurting and I am partially responsible. I want to be with you, Addison. No matter what you thought, I am not ashamed of loving you."

"I should have known it was not you," Addison said, her misery cutting through the darkness.

"How would you know? We never talk about it. We just circle each other warily and try not to scare the other person with our feelings. I do not want to do that anymore. I take full responsibility for all of this. I have let other people rule my life for too long. I should have come to you earlier, but I needed to think things through. I spoke with Cook, and she made me see how unfair I was being to you. I decided to come and talk to you about it. So you see, Addison, I am just as much to blame as you are."

Addison leaned back with her eyes closed. "I should have trusted that you would not do that to me. How can you forgive me after what I just did to you?" she asked miserably.

"Because I love you. And I enjoyed it." Brontë was happy for the darkness that hid her heated face.

"You did?" Addison asked, in need of reassurance.

"Yes, I did. Very much." Brontë reached out her hand seeking and then brushing across Addison's damp cheek.

"I have been thinking about you all week. Missing you. I thought you regretted what we did. And when I saw you, her, all kinds of things went through my mind. I thought that you were playing with me, that you both were laughing at me. Oh, God, Brontë, what have I done?" Addison silently shook as she tried to keep herself from sobbing aloud. Her shoulders were suddenly grabbed as she was pulled into a surprisingly strong grasp.

"Nothing we both didn't already want," she said fiercely. "I could have asked you to stop, but I did not because I wanted you. I still want you. Please do not cry, Addison." Brontë's stint as the strong one ended as she too felt her throat close up, feeling Addison's anguish.

"But I didn't want it to be like that. I wanted it to be..." Addison paused, at a loss for words.

"To be what?" Brontë asked, as she reached out in the darkness for the dark-haired keeper of her soul.

"I wanted it to be more loving." Addison stumbled as she tried to explain how she had always envisioned herself loving Brontë. "I wish I could take it back, Brontë. I wish I could take it back," she said, her voice sounding so young it broke Brontë's heart.

"Come back to the cottage, Addison," Brontë ordered as she brushed her tears away. "It is getting cold."

Addison stood up and Brontë placed her arms around Addison's waist, while Addison leaned heavily on her as if too weak to even walk on her own. They silently walked back to Addison's cottage, each lost in her own thoughts.

Brontë looked around the cottage for a minute, noticing the satchels sitting in the corner and the fact that the place no longer had Addison's paintings hanging from every wall and realization dawned. "You were going to leave?"

Addison looked away before nodding her ascent.

"Without speaking to me first?" Brontë could not believe the amount of pain she was feeling.

"I could not take the thought of you with him, Brontë."

"But what about your mother? I thought you were staying to find out information on her whereabouts."

"I do not know. I think I am going to let that dream go. I have been here all my life. If she wanted me she could have come here to find me. I am not even sure if she is alive anymore."

"Addison, look at me." Brontë pulled Addison's chin upward, her breath almost catching in her throat as she looked into the most desolate sea of blue. "I want you. I want you with all my heart. I do not want you to leave, Addison. I would be lost without you." Brontë held the crumpling face in her hands for a moment before tenderly covering Addison's mouth with her own. She nuzzled at Addison's lips before Addison weakly gave her access. Brontë explored Addison's sweetness like a bee in a field of flowers, tasting and exploring until she was familiar with every crevice; until she was certain that she was as familiar with Addison's mouth as she was her own.

Brontë placed her knee on the cot and pressed Addison back until she was lying half on the cot and half off. "I want to touch you like you touched me."

Addison's eyes grew wide as she thought of the Lady touching her. Even in her dreams, she had always thought it would be her touching Brontë, not the other way around.

"Your shoulders are so strong, Addison. I often wondered what they looked like under your shirt. May I take it off?" Brontë asked, lightly kissing Addison's neck.

Addison nodded, unsure of how far the Lady intended to go.

The aroused vibration coursing through Addison's body was enough to make Brontë determined to continue. She kissed Addison as her right hand unbuttoned the work shirt. She snaked her hand under the wrapping that Addison wore daily until she touched the soft mounds of her breasts. The contrast between the hard body beneath her and the soft breasts under her hand caused Brontë to groan softly in Addison's ear. She was finally able to push Addison's shirt off and had free reign with her breasts. She caressed her nipples until they were both hard pebbles under her fingers. Remembering how Addison had suckled her own breasts in the stables, she scooted down until her mouth was level with Addison's dark brown nipples. Sticking her tongue out as she had with Addison's feet, she tentatively tasted the tip of Addison's nipple, causing Addison's body to jerk in reaction. Feeling a powerful trail of arousal course through her body, Brontë licked the hard nipple again, this time circling it slowly before taking it into her mouth while continuing to caress it with her tongue.

Addison gripped Brontë's back, pulling her closer, and closed her eyes. Her hips were unconsciously moving as she sought relief from the building pressure. Brontë decided she was paying entirely too much attention to Addison's right breast; gently pushing them both together, she began to lick and suck them both slowly.

Addison dreamily realized that Brontë made love like she ate, slowly, savoring every bit. In theory, it was a wonderful idea; in truth, it was driving Addison crazy.

"Brontë," Addison breathed. "You. Uh."

Brontë stopped, looking up at Addison's feverish eyes. "You do not like what I am doing?" she asked innocently.

"No, I—no, I like what you are doing. Please do not stop."

"I will not stop." Brontë happily went back to her slow torturous tasting of Addison's body, unbeknownst to Addison, with a delighted smile on her face. Brontë finally tired of only tormenting Addison's breasts and started kissing down Addison's stomach, her hands unbuttoning Addison's trousers as she went. She remembered how pleasurable it had been to have Addison's lips on her body. Addison had asked if she could taste her. Her eyes had promised pleasures that she had been unable to fulfill due to an untimely interruption. There would be no one to interrupt tonight. But it would be Brontë that would have the pleasure. Addison's eyes were wide in the dim light of the fire. Brontë tugged on Addison's trousers as she made to disrobe her lover.

Addison immediately rushed to help, shucking her shoes and trousers all in seconds. Brontë was grinning now and even in the darkness, she could see Addison's embarrassed smile as she settled back down on the cot. Brontë's eyes caressed Addison's flat stomach and slender waist before lingering on the dark curls that she loved so much and then traveling down the long dark legs as well.

"Do you know how beautiful you are, Addison?" Brontë whispered as she stood, undressing quickly so that she could get back to ravishing Addison's body.

Brontë had half of her own shirt open when she focused in on the ragged breathing coming from the cot. Brontë could barely see Addison, but Addison could apparently see her just fine and was enjoying the show. Brontë slowed her pace, having started to enjoy herself. She nearly laughed aloud when she finally let her shirt drop to the floor and Addison sucked in a hard breath and swallowed. Brontë kept her head lowered so Addison would not see her grin. She turned around, kicking her boots off as she went, and finally allowed her trousers to drop to the floor. Brontë paused for a second, a frown slowly appearing on her forehead, as she got no reaction from Addison. She had concluded that Addison had a thing for her bottom and thought that she might enjoy looking at it, but now she was wondering if she had been wrong. *Addison hasn't even...*

"Oh God, Brontë..."

Ahh, there it is. Arousal permeated Addison's voice and the air between them fairly sizzled with the force of Addison's arousal. "Please, come to bed," she begged.

Brontë slowly slid into bed as Addison settled both her hands on her bottom. "Addison, can I continue what I was doing? I was enjoying myself."

"Yes, please," Addison said.

Addison closed her eyes as Brontë slid lower and lower. Addison's mind was already painting the tantalizing image of Brontë kissing even lower. Addison's eyes shot open as Brontë whispered, "Addison, is this what you want me to do?"

"Only if you want, my love," Addison croaked, and then prayed with all she had in her that Brontë would continue. Addison jumped as the warm lips pressed against her twice before Brontë's tongue came out to gently explore her. Brontë watched as Addison opened to her like the petals of a rose; she lowered her head again.

Addison was breathing hard, she could not believe that Brontë was doing this to her. No one else ever had, discounting Victoria's aborted attempt; these were untested waters for Addison. To be on the receiving end of something like this had always been a fantasy.

Brontë's tongue continued to explore Addison, taking slow,

soft strokes of her warm moist center and the bundle of nerves that was practically throbbing under her tongue.

"Brontë. Brontë, please!" Addison lifted her hips, trying to get closer to Brontë, but Brontë grabbed her hips and held them firmly in place on the cot.

"Feel good?" Brontë gently teased Addison as she had done to her. Addison's answer was a groan as she tried to press closer to Brontë's mouth, but was not allowed to.

"Brontë, I am going to..." Addison's fingers dug into the sheets beneath her.

Brontë felt the orgasm coming before Addison knew what hit her; she was prepared when Addison's body, of its own accord, jerked upwards, only to be grabbed and anchored to the cot by Brontë's small hands.

Brontë wanted to feel Addison as she had felt her, so she quickly moved up Addison's body, her hand going to Addison's dark curls. Where her mouth had been soft and gentle, her fingers were strong and firm. A scream of pleasure ripped from Addison's mouth, only to be immediately muffled by Brontë. Brontë inserted two fingers into Addison the same way Addison had done to her and swallowed up more of Addison's scream of pleasure until it was but a muffled whimper.

ADDISON WATCHED BRONTË'S breasts rise and fall as she slept. She could not believe that Brontë was here with her. Drawing her finger down the pale arm lightly, Addison watched the flesh pucker.

"Good morning." Brontë's sleepy voice made Addison look up, embarrassed at being caught staring.

"Good morning," she said, returning Brontë's smile. Leaning in, she gave Brontë a sweet kiss before snuggling closer to her and sighing regretfully. "You know, the sun will be up soon. I should probably get you back before you are missed."

Brontë sobered quickly, her mind on the altercation with John and the comments made by Victoria. "Addison, what do you suppose is going on? It just all seems so strange. Why would Victoria be out in the middle of the night talking to someone about John, and what information would she be trying to seduce John to get?"

Addison frowned, deep in thought. "I do not know, Brontë. But all this strangeness started right after you married him."

Brontë laughed. "Well, that is reassuring."

Addison chuckled and pulled her closer. "No, what I should have said was I never could understand why Victoria was still around. But I never really thought about it that much. She honestly does not do anything here, yet they do not fire her. I figured she was sleeping with Lord Baptiste, so I didn't think much of it." Addison took a quick look from under her lashes at Brontë to see how she reacted to the news.

Brontë snuggled deeper into the crook of Addison's arm, totally uninterested in who slept with John as long as it didn't have to be her. "Do I have to go back there?"

"Hmm, yes, they would probably wonder if you didn't show up, you know."

Brontë sighed, but made no effort to move from the small but comfortable bed.

"My lady, let's get you up. Besides, since I will be staying, it looks like I have work to do."

"Mm-hmm, give me a few minutes," Brontë mumbled. Addison smiled and squeezed the smaller woman's body closer to her, and decided a few minutes would not hurt. "Addison?" Brontë mumbled. "Why do you call me 'my lady'?" she asked, already half asleep.

"Hmm?" Addison paused, her fingers still buried in Brontë's soft curling hair. "Is that not what I am supposed to call you, my lady?" she asked teasingly, as she caressed the soft skin of Brontë's back and tried to ignore the heat gathering in her nether regions.

"Hmm? Yes. No. What I mean is, the others call me m'lady or milady. But you've always called me *my lady*. I didn't really think about it before, but you call John milord, when you call him anything."

"I never thought about it before, Brontë, but I guess from the moment I saw you, I felt something. At first I thought it was a need for friendship, since it gets lonely here sometimes, but it changed fairly quickly. I think, deep in my heart, I always hoped you would be mine," Addison admitted and shyly peaked down to see what the Lady's reaction would be. But Brontë had already dozed off. "I love you," she whispered and joined her Lady in the realm of dreams.

A FULL HOUR later, Addison reluctantly opened her eyes. She had always been a fitful sleeper, surviving on less than four hours a night. But sleeping with Brontë had been so relaxing that she had not been able to resist the nap.

"Brontë?" Addison gently shook Brontë's shoulder and was rewarded with a growl.

"Stop it, Crumpet, this is my bed."

Amused, Addison shook Brontë once more.

"What, what, what?" Brontë sat up, her hair standing on end, looking rather put out at being awakened. Addison thought she looked darling. Brontë glared into the most beautiful blue eyes she had ever seen.

"You are beautiful," she said and watched as a dark red started at Addison's neck and then traveled up her cheeks to her forehead. "Simply breathtaking," Brontë finished, now fully awake.

"Thank you, but I am too tall to be beautiful," Addison said, as she got out of bed totally uninhibited in her nudity. Brontë took it all in as she too got up, clutching the sheet to her small frame.

"Who told you you were too tall to be beautiful?"

Addison shrugged, grabbing her pullover and throwing on her trousers. She would have to come back and bathe later. "I just always knew. When I would go into town with my father, I would hear people whispering about how tall I was." Addison watched Brontë struggle into her clothes, wondering if there would ever be a time when she didn't lose her breath when looking at that round bottom. *Death*, her mind supplied, and she nodded; that worked fine for her.

"Ready?"

"Yes, I am ready." Brontë replied, her tone grave.

They left a happily snoring Perry and the warmth of the cottage and entered the crisp morning air.

"Cold?" Addison asked as Brontë hugged herself as she walked.

"No, not really. I was trying to think of a way to avoid going back there."

Addison stopped and looked over at Brontë. "Come here," she said, and pulled Brontë to her, holding her close. "If he so much as raises an eyebrow your way, come find me. Do you understand?"

Brontë nodded, the lump in her throat growing even larger. "I do not want to leave you. We have only just found each other."

"You are not leaving me, my love. I will be on the grounds all day. I can stop by to see you later if you want me to, or perhaps if you get some time, maybe you can come to the cottage. I have been working on the lessons on my own, I would like to show you where I am with them."

"I would love to see how much progress you've made on your own." Brontë tried to fight down the feeling of foreboding.

Addison kissed her gently, holding her as close as she could. "We will figure out a way," she whispered.

Brontë kissed her back hard before running into the manor house and closing the door behind her.

Chapter
Twenty

ADDISON WORKED LIKE a madwoman all morning. She had hoped to finish up early enough to convince Brontë to join her for lunch. With Thomas helping out more with many of the chores around the estate, Addison found that she often had extra time on her hands. Addison whistled happily as she picked up Brontë's saddle, intending to clean it and repair a small torn area that she had noticed the last time they were out.

Perry, it seemed, had caught Addison's high spirits. After Addison returned home to bathe, Perry had followed her out the door and down the road to the stables, something she had not felt well enough to do in months. "Well, Perry, it is certainly nice to have company. Although you will have to excuse me if I prefer Brontë's company to yours." She looked down at Perry for a moment, waiting for an answer. When she got none, she shrugged and continued with her whistling.

"Come, Perry, I need to take this over to the barn where my tools are. You coming?" Perry who was steadfastly ignoring Addison, was settled down in some hay with her eyes closed.

"Aww, come now, Perry, I was teasing." Perry opened one eye, looked at Addison, and promptly closed it again. Addison smacked her lips in mock disgust and left Perry to stew in her own juices.

"Women," she grumbled under her breath and grinned, thankful that there were no women around to hear her. She had just rounded a corner of the barn when she noticed Thomas bringing the carriage around to the front of the manor house. It was somewhat unusual for Thomas to drive and not her, but Addison shrugged it off. After all, contrary to what Wesley believed, Thomas had been hired to drive the carriage, not polish the silverware. She was about to turn away when she saw Victoria bustle out of the front door and climb into the carriage. Thomas drove off quickly, leaving a gaping Addison to watch after them.

Now *that* was unusual. None of the other servants ever used that carriage, to her knowledge. There was a smaller carriage for running errands, or they just walked. Suspicious, Addison decided to investigate. She ran into the stable, quickly saddled Magnus, and then rode off like her tail was on fire.

Addison spotted the estate carriage heading in her direction just as she reached Glen Grove. She hurriedly guided Magnus down a side street and watched as Thomas drove by. It took her a moment to find Victoria, but once she did, it was fairly easy to keep track of her.

Staying unnoticed in town was harder than Addison thought it would be. It was not as though women of her stature walked around Glen Grove often, particularly not ones dressed like men. Addison avoided the place like the plague when she could. She tilted her hat down on her head as she watched Victoria stomp into yet another store and buy yet another yard of cloth, more ribbon and a fourth bag of sweets.

Addison shook her head. *Where is she getting the money for these things?* She watched as Victoria gave a young boy of about fourteen a coin to carry her packages for her.

She is throwing money around like she is made of it. I suppose I should not have felt bad about the raise after all. It looks like Victoria is making a lot more than I ever did. Addison straightened and started walking as fast as she could without bringing attention to herself.

Inevitably Addison's thoughts turned to Brontë. The thought of her name brought a smile to Addison's face. Dreamily, she began thinking of the wonderful things the Lady had done to her. No one else had ever made her feel so satisfied. Addison was so deep in thought that she almost missed seeing Victoria impatiently snatch her packages from the boy carrying them and dropping another coin on the ground before she stomped into a shabby nondescript house.

"You there, boy," Addison called quietly to the angry young man as he spouted obscenities at the oblivious and uncaring Victoria.

The boy came over to Addison, warily taking in her clothing. To Addison's amusement the dirty young man seemed to find her lacking in some way and he took a step back.

"What do you want?"

"I have another one just like the one she just tossed on the ground if you care to talk."

The boy looked at Addison's clothing again. "As long as it is just talk," he said sullenly.

Addison stared at him, wide-eyed, and then crowed with laughter after realizing he thought she might proposition him for sex. "I just want to talk, and besides, you would have had an impossible act to follow."

The boy screwed up his face, thinking he had been insulted.

"So, what do you want?" he asked gruffly, his pride hurt, though he could not have said why.

"Well, first of all, what did she buy?" The boy confirmed what Addison already knew. Victoria had gone on a spending spree that would put the most qualified of ladies to shame.

Addison was still wondering how Victoria had come across so much money when the boy, annoyed by this time, sighed. "She does that almost twice a month. Goes into town, buys a bunch of stuff and has me lug the stuff all the way here and drops the money on the ground like I am some beggar that she could not bear to touch. She will not even give any of the blokes down at the store the time of day anymore now that she has that rich benefactor."

"What rich benefactor?" Addison's thoughts immediately went to Lord Baptiste.

"I do not know who the bloke is, but that is what we all figured since she is spending so much money and has her nose in the air so much."

"And you say she does all this spending twice a month?"

"Just about." The boy rubbed a dirty hand across a nose badly in need of a kerchief and eyed Addison expectantly.

"Here is your money." Addison dropped the coin in his hand, but just as he was about to close his finger around the coin she snatched it back.

The boy opened his grubby hand and looked up at Addison with new respect. "Here now, tell us how you did that?"

"Hmm, it is a secret." Addison grinned. "Does she ever say anything around town about Markby or anything that is going on up there?"

The boy honestly seemed to think about it before he answered. "No, the only thing is the money she has. We just figured she was his wh-oh excuse me, uh, we figured she had some arrangement with the Lord of Markby."

Addison fought down an irrational flood of anger as she wondered how anyone could willingly take Victoria over Brontë. Absently she handed the boy the coin and turned to go, her mind mulling over the possible scenarios and still coming up blank.

"Wait, there is one other thing, it might be worth something to you," the boy said, his eyes darting to Addison's pockets. Addison dug in her pocket and flipped him a coin, which he promptly caught with one hand; he looked at it askance. "This is it?"

"I already gave you money. Now speak up or you will find my boot in your backside," Addison growled.

"Perhaps I am the first to inform you that belligerence is not attractive in a woman?" Addison took a menacing step forward, causing him to hold up his hands and start talking quickly. "My friend Dorian and me were out by the bridge Sunday before last, um, fishing. We see her coming up the road from Markby with a big sack. It is so big she is practically dragging it with her. The whole time she is cursing her fool head off. So, just as she reached where we were, the bag breaks. Well, she starts kicking at it, and stomps off, cursing for all she was worth. Well, me and Dorian go over and take a look. She just left it there, so's finders keepers," he said, looking at Addison for approval. Addison nodded her head and he went on eagerly. "Well we get to the stuff, and it is food!"

"Food?"

"Food. She had enough food in that bag to feed a caravan of gypsies," the boy said excitedly. Addison frowned; times were hard for most people in town so she could see how this sort of thing would stick in the mind of the excited youngster.

"Me and Dorian split it all up and we were able to feed both of our families for four days each. And you know what is odd? I do not think she ever came back to get the food. We hid in the trees to see if she would call the sheriff or something 'cause we took the food, but no one ever came."

Addison mulled the information over in her head. *So Victoria is probably stealing food from Markby. But why?* It made no sense.

"Well, I would love to sit a spell longer, but I have a card game that I am late for." The boy shook his coins and with a grin and a flip of his hand, left Addison to her thoughts.

AFTER RUBBING MAGNUS down and giving him an apple as an apology for riding him so hard, Addison once again found herself thinking of Brontë. She was curious as to Brontë's thoughts on Victoria's spending habits and the mystery of the food she was apparently stealing. After completing the same needless task twice, Addison gave up and headed towards the kitchen. Perhaps if she were lucky she would find Brontë there. Perry, who was no fool, decided to forgive Addison just this once as the nice-smelling woman in the big house usually had something tasty, like a big meaty bone, to give her.

Addison quietly snuck up behind Cook, engulfed her in a tight hug and gave her a loud kiss on the cheek before letting the sputtering woman go. "Afternoon, Cook."

"Addison Mari Le Claire!"

"Cook, what is your real name, anyway?" Addison asked with a grin.

Cook harrumphed and turned her back to Addison to hide the large grin that spread across her face at the young woman's antics.

"Aww, come now, Cook. I was just teasing. Now give us some

sweetness, let's make up." Addison tried to hug Cook again, but Cook shrugged out of her playful arms and shook her finger at Addison.

"Now you stop that. That is all I need is for Lady Baptiste to come strolling in here for her snack and find you pawing on me like that."

"Ahh," Addison pishaw'd, "she would not mind at all, Cook." They grinned at each other for a moment.

Cook sniffed as she continued to stir her pot. "You could be right, she might understand. Goodness knows how you could help yourself, me being so irresistible and all." Cook cackled at her own joke, Addison joining in.

"Cook, I really wanted to thank you for telling Brontë that she should come talk to me," Addison said, still grinning at Cook's humor.

"Ahh, good," Cook said. "She finally told you, did she?"

"Yes, she did." Addison slouched into a chair, grabbed a biscuit from the plate on the table and absently munched on it as she thought about Brontë.

Cook turned her back to Addison. "It was so hard for her to tell you, Addison." The happy grin that had formed on Addison's lips began to fade as she watched Cook's shoulders slump. "Did you know that I was married once?"

"No. I didn't know that. You never really talk about yourself."

"Yes, I was married when I came to work at Markby. The young Lord's mother noticed when I would come in with bruises and she would beg me to let her help me, but I refused. Thought I could change him, make the drinking stop. Finally, it got to be too much and I asked the Lady for her help." Cook stopped stirring her pot for a minute and looked up deep in thought. "And you know, she gave me a home here with no thoughts of it. It was just that easy. 'Here is your room,' she said. I have been here ever since."

"She sounds like she was a wonderful woman," Addison commented quietly, wondering why, after all these years, Cook suddenly felt it necessary to talk about herself.

"She was," Cook said, dropping her spoon on the stove. "That is why I do not understand how her son could come out like he has."

Addison almost asked like what, but stilled her tongue. Cook was so deep in her own memories that she didn't notice Addison's normally bronzed skin as it paled. *Nooo!* her mind screamed, but the puzzle pieces slowly fell into place. Brontë's avoidance of her had been not because she was afraid of her love for Addison, nor was it out of a need to think. It had been an attempt to hide her bruises. Bruises that the Lord had placed on her.

"I always wondered, if she had stayed, would he have come out..." Cook turned to continue speaking to Addison, but her chair stood empty. The only evidence that she had been there was its position in the middle of the floor. Just then, Thomas walked in carrying wood for the stove. Cook rushed over to supervise the unloading into the special wood box near the stove, temporarily forgetting her conversation with Addison.

Tears of rage and pain blinded Addison as she ran up the stairs and down the hall. Somehow, she knew exactly where Brontë would be. She burst into the library and closed the door behind her, eyes scanning the dimly lit room frantically.

"Addison?"

Addison had almost missed Brontë's small form curled up on the couch under an afghan, obviously napping. "Please, tell me that she was mistaken. Tell me that he didn't hurt you." Addison's voice was deathly calm as she spoke. Her face was hidden completely in shadow as she leaned against the double doors, her fists balled at her sides.

"Addison, what are you talking about?" Brontë could see Addison's knuckles clench tighter as she bit out the next words. She pushed the afghan off her shoulders and struggled to her feet.

"He hurt you, and you didn't tell me."

"He hurt you, too." Brontë sobbed, afraid that Addison would not understand. "Why didn't you tell me what he did to you? You led me to believe that you hurt your foot working."

Addison stepped forward, her face a mask of rage as she approached Brontë. "That was different. He was trying to intimidate me and I refused to back down. I should have seen it coming, but I didn't. You are his wife. He should...he had no right to put his hands on you."

Addison was not only mad at John, but at herself, as well. As much as she tried to remember what Brontë had said, she still felt guilt about how she had taken her so roughly. Now, knowing that Lord Baptiste mistreated Brontë made her livid, and she was hard pressed not to track him down and hurt him in return.

Brontë took a step back, aware that the anger was not directed toward her, but still not used to seeing this side of Addison. Even the night before, her anger had been obviously driven by pain.

Addison noticed the movement, though, and instantly took a step back. "Oh my God, Brontë. Do not be afraid. I was not mad at you," she said, frustrated, as she rubbed her hands against her trousers. She sat down heavily on the couch, her hands gripping her head. "Brontë, I do not think I can stay here anymore," she said, not looking up. "I cannot stay here and watch him treat you worse than a servant." She looked up then and said, "If he were to hurt you again, I would not be able to stop myself. Do you understand?"

"Yes," Brontë answered, trying hard to blink away the tears. "Where will you go?"

"Paris first, then, I do not know. I want to travel and see different people and things. I have been here all my life. I think traveling will help with my art tremendously."

Brontë's heart tried to leap through her throat as she realized that the only person she ever loved, or would ever love, was leaving her.

"Brontë, I do not have anything..."

"I understand," Brontë said.

"You do?" Addison said, twisting her hands between her legs. Not looking up at Brontë.

"Yes, I do." Brontë looked away as tears rolled freely down her cheeks. "Will you," she tried to laugh, but the sound refused to leave her throat. "This is hard. Will you write me? As best you can?"

With an almost audible click, Addison's heart broke completely in two. "Yes." Addison felt, rather than saw, Brontë get up and move to stare out of the dark library window.

"Will you ever come back?" Brontë asked as the tears continued to course down her face. They seemed to pool in her throat, threatening to strangle her at any moment. Part of Addison wanted to run from this place of pain and into the woods where she could lick her wounds in peace, but the other part, the part that loved Brontë more than life itself, wanted to fight for the love that they could have had together.

Addison walked up behind Brontë. Noting the hands wrapped protectively around herself, Addison reached out, wanting to console her, but stopped. What could she say when she, herself, hurt so much she could barely speak? "I will come by tomorrow to say goodbye," she choked out and, almost at a run, moved quickly toward the door. She was almost out of it when she heard the most gut-wrenching sound she had ever heard.

Brontë was leaning forward, her head pressed against the windowpane, her back shaking with the force of her sobbing. Addison shut the door and engulfed Brontë from behind, pulling her back against her chest, and closing her eyes against her own tears. "Do not cry."

Addison held Brontë to her, crushing her chest into her back and kissing her temples, her cheeks and finally her tear-covered lips. Addison moaned as Brontë's mouth continued to quiver beneath hers as they tried to comfort each other.

"Please, do not leave me." Brontë sobbed. "Let me come with

you." Addison froze, stunned by Brontë's words. Brontë began to sob harder as she perceived Addison's sudden quiet as a refusal. "Please, Addison. I can work while you paint. You will not have to worry about providing for us. I will take care of us both."

Addison was so stunned that all she could blurt out was, "I-I would not ask you to do that."

Brontë's back began to shake even harder as she closed her eyes against the onslaught of pain coursing through her chest.

"No, Brontë, do not cry," Addison pleaded and turned Brontë around to finally face her own tear-stained face. Addison wiped away Brontë's tears with her thumbs and cupped both sides of her face to make sure that she looked into her eyes. "What I was trying to say is that I am strong, I can work two jobs and paint if I have to. I do not need you to take care of us," she said, trying to coax a smile out of Brontë.

Brontë smiled back at her as the pressure on both of their hearts seem to ease simultaneously. "Then I may come with you?"

"Yes, of course, you may. That is what I wanted from the beginning, but when you said that you understood and asked if I would try to write, I thought...you didn't want to come with me." Addison continued to caress Brontë's face with her thumbs. "I give you my word. You will never want for anything. I will do whatever I need to do to take care of you if you will just..." Brontë cupped Addison's cheeks, mimicking Addison's own soothing gesture.

"Shh, we will take care of each other," she said before bringing Addison's head forward and kissing her gently first on one eye and then the other. Addison took one body-shuddering sigh and felt as if the weight of the world was lifted off her shoulders.

"I love you, Addison Mari Le Claire."

"And I love you, Brontë, with all my heart," Addison said, as if she was taking a vow. And in a sense, she had been, she thought to herself much later.

"Would you hold me? Please?"

Addison broke the kiss, breathing heavily. "Here? What if someone comes in?" She looked around the library as if to make her point.

"Mary is the only one that knows I come here and she would not disturb us." Brontë's hands went to the tie that held Addison's hair back and tugged it loose. As her hair fell forward, Brontë sank her fingers in it and began massaging Addison's scalp. Addison closed her eyes as the flesh raised on her neck and arms. She could not help but moan in pleasure as Brontë gently massaged her scalp before pulling her in to a deep, soul-searing kiss.

"You should stop, if we are to just hold each other," Addison teased, hoping to get a smile out of the still-pale Brontë. She received the smile she was seeking and more in a sweet kiss that soothed her heart of the ache that still lingered from the thought of a life without Brontë.

Addison began the task of lovingly disrobing her Lady. She unbuttoned Brontë's dress, stopping long enough to kiss the beckoning creamy skin of Brontë's neck before returning to her task. Brontë was concentrating on the buttons of Addison's shirt. Soon they were both nude and Addison saw Brontë for the first time without a shirt or blanket of darkness obscuring her body.

"You are so beautiful, my lady," she whispered appreciatively, before holding out her hand toward Brontë. She flushed as her voice came out in a croak, her throat deciding to take its revenge for all of the crying it had been forced to do. She met Brontë's eyes and smiled.

"Let's hope this will be the last time we cry over each other." She tugged Brontë closer before settling back on the couch and pulling Brontë down on top of her. Addison pulled the afghan over both of them and rubbed Brontë's back until the muscles there finally loosened. Addison sighed.

"I never thought that I would ever hold you as I am now. I dreamed of it, and even in the dream I knew it could not be true," Addison said, her eyes closed.

"Why could it not be true?" Brontë asked.

"Because I never thought you would give up all this for me." Addison looked down at the head tucked under her chin. Brontë's breathing had evened out and Addison thought she had fallen asleep.

"I have given up nothing. I feel like I have gained so much. I never wanted material things, Addison, just the kind of love that you read about. I believed I had no chance of that when I married John. But if I had not come here I would have never met you."

Addison tightened her arms around Brontë, then abruptly released her for fear that she held her too firmly. "This feels so good," she said, wiggling a bit. Brontë gave a shuddering sigh as Addison caressed her back under the afghan, soothing both of them. With a contented smile on her lips, Brontë finally fell into an exhausted sleep.

Addison stayed awake for as long as she could, listening to Brontë's even breathing and reveling in the feel of just holding her. Addison finally allowed sleep to overcome her. *I will never have to say goodbye to her again.*

Chapter
Twenty-one

ADDISON WAS NEVER quite sure what caused her to awaken when she had. She had barely opened her eyes when she saw the dark object descending fast toward her and Brontë. She was able to block a blow with her forearm, but not fast enough to keep Brontë from being snatched from her arms.

"Get up, you filthy whore!"

Addison leapt nude from the couch, her fists raised to fight off their attackers.

"I would not do that if I were you, Addison." Brontë froze, the afghan clutched tightly to her chest, as Thomas pointed one of a dueling pistol at her temple.

"Thomas, let her go," Addison ordered, her voice laced with fear and anger. Her fists clenched and unclenched as Brontë's eyes begged for her help.

"I have two shots, Addison." Thomas gestured down to the other pistol shoved into the waistband of his trousers. His normally pleasant features were twisted into an angry mask of hatred as he spoke. "She can have hers right now if you like."

Addison backed away, trying to make eye contact with the terrified Brontë. "What is this about, Thomas? I have never harmed you."

"Well, this is actually about a lot of things." John spoke from a corner of the room shrouded in shadow. Up until that moment neither Brontë nor Addison had realized he was there.

"Good morning, wife." John greeted Brontë quite pleasantly before turning to Addison, his hands folded neatly on his lap.

"And you, Addison, how did you sleep? I hope the couch was not too lumpy for you. I would ask Brontë, but she was apparently astride you the whole time."

Brontë managed to speak then. "John, let's stop this now. This is not her fault. Please, just let her go. She was just here to say goodbye. She is leaving tomorrow. Your quarrel is with me." Brontë continued to struggle against Thomas. Addison never removed her eyes from John, but she heard every word that Brontë had said.

"She is leaving here with me," Addison said. "She does not love you, and from what I can see, you never loved her, so why are you doing this?"

"You think this is about her?" John threw back his head uproariously. "It was never about her, Addison. It was always about you."

"What are you talking about?" Thomas laughed at Brontë's fruitless struggle to hang on to the afghan that was barely managing to preserve her modesty. "Let her go, damn it!" Addison thundered.

John turned to Thomas. "Let her go, but keep her over there. If she moves, shoot her, and then shoot the big one next."

"John. John, listen to me, please. I can explain," Brontë called out as Thomas released her.

"Explain what?" John bellowed. "Explain how you ended up lying on top of this, this woman? Is that what you want to explain, Brontë? Well, save your energy because quite frankly, I could care less who you choose to bed."

"If you do not care, why are you here?"

"All in good time, dear Addison." John tapped the side of his face with his riding crop as he looked Addison up and down. "You know, it is too bad you are sick, because you are not half bad under those men's clothes you wear."

Brontë hissed under her breath and glared at John.

Addison ignored the comment, having heard similar ones all her life. "If you do not care about Brontë, what do you want from her? Why not let her go?"

"Her?" John smirked. "Well, she just happened to be in the wrong place at the wrong time. I have been planning on coming after you for quite some time now. Speaking of which, I was saddened to hear about Addigo."

"What do you know of my father?" Addison asked hoarsely.

"Well, everyone here knows he is dead. Thomas followed you to his grave. Last week, was it not, Thomas?" Thomas nodded and continued to eye Addison.

"What does my father have to do with anything?" Addison asked, still trying to find some common ground as she racked her brain for a way out of this, if not for both of them, then at least for Brontë.

"He has everything to do with this!" John suddenly screamed so loudly that everyone in the room jumped, including Thomas. "This is all his fault." John swung the riding crop wildly as he spoke, spittle flying from his mouth.

"What are you talking about? My father had nothing to do

with you. He warned me away from you and your father."

"Oh he did, did he?" John laughed again. "Well, maybe I shall have to rethink my opinion of old Addigo Le Claire. Perhaps he was not as dumb as he appeared."

Addison stiffened. "I will not ask you again. What do you want?"

"Did you hear that, Thomas? Giving orders like the Lady she is. What do you think of that, Brontë? Hmm? Good old Addison here is actually more of a Lady than you are. Who'd ever believe that?" John cackled to himself, tapping the riding crop against his temple as he spoke.

"John, stop this. This is utter madness. Please have Thomas put the gun down and we can talk like civilized adults," Brontë said.

"Shut up!" John shouted and Addison clenched her fists in frustration. Thomas continued to watch her warily, not saying a word. "You want to know what this is all about, do you, Addison? Well that should be fairly easy. Let's see, where shall I begin, hmm? Ahh, yes, you asked about how Addigo fit into this little soirée we are having? Well, I guess, let me see, about twenty-two years ago, give or take nine months, my mother fell in love with your father and after a little slap and tickle, found herself very pregnant."

Addison sucked in a breath as John's words sank in.

"Hmm, I anticipated that you would be more surprised, sister." John seemed disappointed by Addison's minimal response.

"No. I always felt that he was waiting for my mother to come back. It was the only explanation as to why my father would stay here and work for such poor wages. I had no idea that it was Lady Baptiste that he waited for."

"Waiting for her to come back? Waiting for her to come back?" John laughed, the riding crop hitting the side of his head with increasing force. "Oh no, Addison. Mother dearest is never coming back. In fact, I have known since I was ten years old that she was dead."

Addison felt a sharp pain in her heart as she realized, with those few words, that her quest was, once and for all, over.

"How do you know?" She was unwilling to believe John, though she sensed in her heart that it was true.

"Addison." Brontë moved to comfort her, but was stopped by a bellow from John.

"Do not move, Brontë. Thomas, if she moves you may shoot her." Thomas nodded, this time with a smirk, as he raised the dueling pistol a bit higher.

"How do you know she is dead?" Addison asked again. She would deal with the pain later. For now, she would only think of Brontë's safety.

"I overheard him talking to Victoria's mother. Another whore. Seems Markby was the place where they all resided back then, eh, Thomas? Seems old Lord John had a regular old bordello going on here. You see, he killed our dear mother in a fit of rage."

Addison choked on the bile that rose in her throat as she looked at the impassive face of the man claiming to be her brother, as he talked about their mother's murder. Her heart ached for a woman she had never known.

"He would have gotten away with it, too, but he made the mistake of recruiting Victoria's hag of a mother to help him do his dirty work. Is it not ironic that we are all here under such similar conditions?" John sighed and looked at Brontë, Addison and Thomas like they were his long lost comrades.

In that moment, Addison was able to make eye contact with Brontë. She would have to make a move soon. John had obviously lost all semblance of sanity and unless she did something soon, both she and Brontë would lose their lives.

"Would you like to know how my father told me it happened?" His voice had taken on an almost childlike glee. "He said that our mother came and told him that she did not love him, and that she would be leaving the next day. Is that not some coincidence?" He looked at Brontë then, a large smile deforming his features until he truly looked like a madman. "That was what you were going to do as well, was it not, Brontë? That the same situation would repeat itself, twenty-two years later!" He looked around at everyone as if to get his or her opinions. By this time, even Thomas was getting nervous.

Brontë decided to try to reason with John again. "John, please, can we not discuss this?"

John looked at her for a moment, his brow furrowed, as he appeared to seriously give Brontë's request some serious thought. "No, Brontë, I do not believe we have anything to talk about. You will die, just like this one will in a few moments." He pointed his riding crop at Addison.

"Unless..." he brightened. "You would not by chance be pregnant, would you? Would not the irony of that just be amazing?" Addison went rigid as her eyes went to Brontë's. "Had you forgotten, sister dear? I was there first." John's grin was wide and proud as he went for Addison's jugular verbally and got the desired effect. Addison leapt on him, her fist raised to pound the maniacal grin from his face forever, when she heard the cocking of one of the dueling pistols behind her.

"Move away from him or she dies."

Addison looked up in time to see Brontë standing with Thomas's arm wrapped around her throat. One hand clutched fiercely at the afghan while the other gripped, claw-like, Thomas's forearm.

Addison quickly released John and backed away from him, her hands up in the air, and her eyes never leaving Brontë and Thomas. "Let her go. Now," she said.

"Let her go, Thomas," John ordered. Brontë sank to the floor in relief, her fear making her tremble uncontrollably.

"Now, where was I?" John said to himself as he massaged the circulation back into his neck. "Oh yes, Elizabeth. That was her name, did you know that, Addison?"

He waited for her to answer and when she didn't, he went on as if he did not have a care in the world. "As I was saying, apparently what Lord John didn't know was that there were twins born that night. He firmly believed that I was his son until his death. It seems our mother, with a little help from Cook, managed to smuggle you out of the house right after you were born. You were the spitting image of Addigo, I am sure they didn't want old Lord John to be suspicious. I was lighter so they probably thought Lord John would not be suspicious.

"They even went so far as to lie to the doctor about my birth date. You see, from what I could ascertain, there was a storm that kept my father away for days. Long enough for you and me to be born, and you to be smuggled out of the house. Cook was our mother's confidante and the only person in the room when she gave birth to us, so I assume she is the one who smuggled you out and told Doctor Thatcher that I was born days after I really was. She will have to be dealt with as well," John said thoughtfully before shaking his head and returning to his story. "According to the records, I am exactly nine days younger than you and born in January, but in truth we are twins, born on the same day. You barely an hour before me."

Brontë gasped. Two more unlikely siblings she had never met. But twins?

"Yes Brontë, amazing, is it not?" John said as if reading her thoughts.

"But why, John?" Brontë asked the question that Addison herself was now thinking. "Why are you coming after Addison? She had nothing to do with any of that. Why are you taking out your revenge on her?"

"Revenge? Who said anything about revenge, Brontë?" John laughed. "This is about money."

Addison looked at him incredulously. "Money? Are you completely daft? My father had no money! I have nothing."

"Of course he had no money," John said, brushing aside the comment with a disdainful swish of his riding crop. "Perhaps I could continue my story, unless you two are in a hurry to take this up with both my fathers in heaven or hell, wherever you should end up? No?" John didn't wait for an answer. "I didn't think so."

"You see, it all started when I was shot. As I lay there recovering, I started to wonder who would want to kill me. I came up with only one likely suspect. So I instructed Wesley to start doing some research on Addison here."

Brontë gasped. Addison turned to Brontë to deny any wrongdoing, but Brontë had already risen angrily to her feet, ignoring Thomas completely. "John, Addison had nothing to do with your shooting. She would never hurt anyone in such a cowardly way! Not even you."

Had their situation not been so dire, Addison felt like she would have kissed her. The pride and trust that she felt toward Addison was readily apparent in those few words. *I must get her out of this, even if I have to lose my life to do so.* Determined, Addison listened with one ear as John plowed on with his story. The minute Thomas let down his guard, Addison was determined to make her move.

"You see, dear sister, you may not know this, but the world revolves around money." John whipped his riding crop in a circular motion. "Everything is about money, and this situation is no different. You would not know because you have never had any. You see, the old Lord's downfall was money. He wanted to keep his, so he killed Elizabeth and hid her body under the barn." Brontë and Addison gasped, horrified.

"That is correct," John continued gleefully. "Right where Addigo had to work every day, and the one place he would never look. You see, old Lord John paid Victoria's mother, Calliope, to lie and tell the sheriff that she had seen his wife leave the estate with some strange man. What he didn't count on was the fact that Victoria's mother had tried unsuccessfully to blackmail Elizabeth for money. You caught Thomas here searching the study for the letter that Calliope wrote. Our mother, it seems, had more backbone than the old Lord and had attempted to burn the letter. Lord John found the unburned half of it soon after he murdered her, and kept it for some reason. Of course when Calliope found out that her potential meal ticket was gone, she made Father her new one, and hence has never worked a day in her life again. Not bad for telling one lie, would you not agree? All Lord Senior had to do was keep her lazy family in food and clothing for the rest of their lives. The only thing they had to do was send one of the brood over to make sure that their interests were being looked after."

"So that is the reason Victoria gets paid so much more than the others?" Brontë surmised.

"And why she took large amounts of food home?" Addison

asked, only half listening to the story. For the most part, she no longer cared who did what, her only concern was Brontë.

Brontë, noticing Addison's quick looks at Thomas, decided to help as best she could by taking the attention of Thomas and John off Addison as much as possible.

"Yes, that is the reason I continued to pay the blackmail. Because I needed Victoria's help, although she has no idea about Addison's relationship to me or she would probably have upped the blackmail amount."

"So that explains Victoria's involvement in all this, but what of Thomas here?" Brontë asked.

"Ahh, now that is an interesting piece of information. You see, Victoria is to be thanked for finding our Thomas here. They apparently met when Thomas was in his cups and bragging about how he is the son of Lord John Baptiste and therefore should rightfully receive his inheritance!"

"Inheritance, what inheritance?" Brontë asked, truly confused now. "Thomas is Lord Senior's son? How is that possible?"

"Brontë, has your memory failed you of our wedding night? Lord John was more unfaithful than Elizabeth and had already had numerous affairs before Elizabeth took up with Addigo. One was with a young woman over in Glen Meadow, but when the young lady told him of her condition, he of course denied parentage of the child and left her."

"But how do you know he is really Lord Senior's child?"

"You know, Thomas, my wife has a point. How *do* we know that you are Lord Senior's illegitimate offspring?"

Thomas angrily glanced at John before returning his eyes quickly to Addison. "My mother told me I was, and she never lied to me."

John threw his head back. "Is that all the proof you have?" he asked amusedly. "Oh, good God, man, have you not been listening? I am sure my dear sister will agree with me when I say mothers lie all the time. Why, my very own mother was going to leave me with a man not my father and yet she took her." John pointed with his chin. "Even gave her her name. How is that for a caring mother?"

"What are you talking about? My name is Addison, not Elizabeth," Addison said angrily.

"I know what your name is!" John screamed. "I have hated you and that name since I was ten years old, Addison Mari Le Claire. She gave you her middle name and used Addigo's first. Madison and Addigo make Addison. She named me John, after a man who was not even my real father, a coward who allowed himself to be blackmailed by women. A man that lived his life in fear, because he left loose ends.

"Most of the money for Markby is in trust to be received on our twenty-third birthday. You do not deserve any part of that inheritance. I earned it, you didn't. I am a Baptiste and you are a Le Claire. When those papers are opened on our birthday, they will name both of us as the owners of Markby Estate. The only problem is, there will be no you."

Brontë, who had been listening to John's ranting, suddenly began to clearly see the chain of events that led to the murder of Addison's mother so many years ago, but something still didn't add up. Then it dawned on her, a discrepancy in John's crazed ranting. "John, you said that you and Addison would be named as the owners of Markby Estate?" The smile that had been on John's face since this had begun faded as he looked quickly at Thomas and back to Brontë.

"Yes, that is correct, woman. Are you suddenly hard of hearing?"

"No, it just does not make sense. Why would Addison receive money in this trust?" A persistent memory teased the very back of Brontë's mind. A memory so small, so insignificant, that she almost pushed it away. Almost.

'Lady Elizabeth...I cannot read it, it is too tarnished.'
'Oh yes, m'lady, now I remember. That is the Lady Elizabeth Markby, Lord Baptiste's mother.'

John realizing that his secret had been uncovered, shrugged. "Kill her, Thomas." He spoke with a deathly calm voice. "I am tired of looking at her."

Thomas raised the pistol as Addison shouted, "No!"

"Thomas, you must listen to me, he lied to you. He lied to you about the money." Thomas paused for a moment, looking into Brontë's desperate green eyes. "He never intended to give you any of the money, Thomas. He was going to blame you for everything."

"Kill her now, Thomas," John ordered imperiously.

"No!" Addison looked around desperately for a weapon, something to throw at Thomas.

Thomas raised the pistol to Brontë's head and Brontë closed her eyes, speaking quickly. "Thomas, listen to me, please. It occurred to me as he was speaking that he could not possibly get away with all of our deaths. Unless he had a scapegoat. That scapegoat is you, Thomas. He plans to blame it all on you!"

"I do not care what he does. I am going to get out of here as soon as I get my money next week," Thomas growled.

"Do you not see, Thomas? There will not be any money, at least not for you. He never had any intentions of sharing it."

"Well, if he does not, I will just go to that lawyer in Glen Meadow and tell him who I am!" Thomas said, his attention fully on Brontë now. Unseen by either, Addison took a step forward.

"Thomas, you do not understand," Brontë pleaded as tears flowed down her cheeks for this young man who had obviously been ruined by his parents' infidelities, just as John had. Addison thankfully had been spared that. Brontë only hoped that she would get another chance to appreciate the beautiful person that Addison was. Taking a deep breath she said steadily, "You will receive nothing. The money was never Lord Senior's!"

The deathly calm in the room was suddenly broken by a loud shrieking laugh from John. "Excellent, Brontë! Who would have thought that you would figure out my little secret?" He grinned.

"What are you both talking about?" Thomas took a step away from Brontë so that he could keep both Brontë and John in his sights. Addison could have screamed in frustration; she had just been about to jump on Thomas when John had spoken.

"Go on, Brontë, tell him how brilliant I am," said John with his fingers steepled under his chin, rocking back and forth in his excitement, a little smile playing across his lips.

"Thomas, think about it. Why would Addison be named as an inheritor? Lord Senior's name is Baptiste, not Markby. He certainly would not have left money to the offspring of his wife and the caretaker. The money was never his to give. It belonged to Lady Elizabeth Madison Markby. Therefore, Lord Senior's illegitimate son would have no right to Markby money."

The air suddenly left Addison's chest as Brontë's words sank into her brain.

"Your father, Lord John Baptiste, married Lady Elizabeth Markby for money. They had no more love for each other than John and I had. It was probably a marriage of convenience. I wouldn't be surprised to learn that Lady Elizabeth Madison Markby was already pregnant when she married Lord John Baptiste.

"Perhaps it was pressures from her family, I do not think we will ever know why." Brontë looked at Addison. "She loved Addigo, but was not strong enough to give everything up, at least, not then." Brontë smiled sadly. Had she made the same mistake? Would it now cost both her and Addison their lives? "Lord Senior had the upbringing, the title; he was acceptable, so she married him to keep up appearances. He killed Elizabeth, because to let her leave would mean to give up any hopes he had of getting his hands on the Markby fortune."

"Most excellent! Brontë, I must say that I am truly impressed!" John clapped his hands delicately above his ear. "Forgive me, Thomas, I didn't want you to find out this way. It was my full intention to make good on our agreement once these two and Cook were disposed of."

Thomas looked at John uncertainly for a moment and raised his gun again. Addison prepared to leap at him when Brontë shouted, "Thomas, do not believe him, he is lying. I can prove it to you. Do you remember how he looked when the sheriff said that Jack Timmons confessed?"

Thomas squinted his eyes, trying to see where Brontë was going with the question. After a second or two, he nodded his head.

"Do you remember John's reaction to the news?"

"Yes, he was shocked. So were you," Thomas said defensively.

"I was shocked because I could not believe that the Jack Timmons I remember would do such a thing."

"Yes, well, shows what you know. Victoria had me go down to the jail. I have a friend down there and he let me speak to him. He shot him just as the sheriff said, he said it was an accident and he was drunk and hungry. Thought it was a deer," Thomas said. Gone was the gracious servant of days before.

"Thomas, think about John's reaction to the news. Was he shocked like me, or was he disappointed, almost like it ruined some plan?" Thomas seemed to think about it for a moment.

"Perhaps he was," he said, watching the amazingly calm John out of the corner of his eye.

"Thomas, he intended to frame you for shooting him, then killing Addison, Cook and me. His intention was to make you think that you stood to gain from this arrangement. Then he could kill you somehow, and make it look like he was protecting himself against a madman who was threatening his life. He would get rid of all the loose ends, you, Addison and Cook all in one fell swoop. As he said, I was in the wrong place at the wrong time, so I became a part of the plan, too, when I fell in love with Addison."

"You fell—you fell in love with Addison?" John laughed. "Oh my, oh my, that is the funniest thing I have ever heard. You love her, do you? Well, is that not just rich? And what of you, dear sister? Do you love her too? And what if she is pregnant with my child, what would you have done then? It would obviously have been mine as," John made a show of looking Addison's nude body over thoroughly, "I do not see the equipment to make babies, although, one can never be sure." John laughed uproariously again as Addison squeezed her fist until her knuckles paled from lack of circulation.

"Shut up!" Thomas screamed; the hand not holding the pistol went to cover one of his ears as the hand with the gun pointed towards John. "You shut up right now," he ordered shakily. "You lied to me."

"Yes, I did," John admitted. "It was for your own good. What she said about framing you for the murders, though, that part is not true. I have every intention of giving you half the money. Why, I already think of you as a brother."

"I do not believe you," Thomas said sadly. The gun started to shake, and his body appeared to shrink under the pressure.

John noticed the tremor and, in true Baptiste form, went for the jugular. "You are weak even for a Baptiste, Thomas. You should have killed them both already; we would be done with this."

"Shut up!" Thomas screamed, his face red as tears streamed from his eyes.

"You have let a woman talk you out of your fortune, just like your supposed father. You are no brother of mine." John's voice had taken on the taunting cadence of a child or a lunatic.

"Shut up, shut up," Thomas screamed again.

John put the final nail in the coffin. "Lord Senior would have been ashamed to call you his son." The loud report from the dueling pistol deafened Addison as the ball from the pistol hit John squarely in the forehead, killing him instantly and throwing his body backward in his chair. Addison saw Brontë dive safely behind the couch before she too sought cover as Thomas quickly dropped the spent pistol and retrieved the one in his waistband.

The library was filled with the sounds of desperate sobs as Thomas realized his dream was lost to him.

A loud hammering on the door caused him to cease his sobbing for a moment and Wesley's worried voice could be heard through the door. "Lady Baptiste! Are you in there? Are you hurt? We thought we heard a shot."

The library was deathly quiet as Addison tried to figure out a way to make sure that Brontë was not in any danger.

"Get out here," Thomas growled and Brontë gave a short scream as he pulled her up from behind the couch. "Addison, I want to see you now or she gets a bullet in the head."

Addison quickly stuck her hand up from behind the chair that she had taken cover behind and said, "I am here, Thomas. Do not hurt her."

"Good." He sniffed. "You listen to me, now. All my life my mother told me that money was mine. That Lord John was my father. The way I figure it, I deserve that money just as much as you, if not more," he reasoned badly.

Addison nodded her head. "Of course, Thomas." She started to lower her hands, relieved. Money meant nothing if she could have Brontë back safe and sound.

"Get your hands up where I can see them, right now or she dies!" Thomas screamed. Addison hurriedly put her hands back up as Thomas tightened his hold on Brontë.

"You so much as move and I am going shoot her right where she stands. Do you understand?"

"Yes, Thomas, I understand. I will not move." Addison was truly afraid. She was too far away from Thomas to make a run at him without possibly getting Brontë hurt.

Thomas pushed Brontë forward. "Get some clothes on, you are coming with me."

"Thomas, where are you taking her?" Addison was unable to keep the fear from creeping into her voice.

"Do not worry. I am not going to hurt her. I just want what is rightfully mine, and then you can have her back."

Addison's heart started beating heavily in her chest. "Thomas, why do you not take me instead? You may not believe me, but I am on your side. I was raised without any money either. I didn't know about this money until just now. I would be more than happy to give it to you."

"Why would you do that?"

"Because I love her and I do not miss what I never had."

Thomas seemed to think about it for a moment and then shook his head. "No, I do not think so. I would have to watch you all the time. If I am going to have a captive for a week, then I would rather it be her than you. You hurry up!" Thomas swung the gun toward Brontë just as a loud crash from outside caused the doors to the library to shudder.

Thomas swung around and aimed his gun at Addison. "You tricked me, you lying bitch," he yelled and took aim at Addison's head.

"Addison!" Brontë screamed just as the doors to the library flew open. She hurled herself at Thomas. Her only thought was of protecting Addison. The burning sensation that hit her head and Addison's anguished scream told her that she had been at least partially successful. Another loud report and then all Brontë heard was Addison's soft sobs as she was cradled in her arms.

"Addison. Thomas?"

"Oh, God. Shh, do not talk. He cannot hurt us now, Wesley shot him." Addison sobbed as she placed her hands over the stream of blood pouring from the side of Brontë's head.

"Were you hurt?" Brontë asked as she noticed all the blood on Addison's bare chest.

"No, Brontë. Please do not talk, sweetheart. It is not my blood."

"Good," Brontë said feeling sleepy. "I had this feeling something bad was going to happen when I left you yesterday morning. I just didn't know it was going to be this bad." She tried to laugh.

"Oh please, Brontë. The doctor is on his way. Please do not talk anymore." Addison was openly sobbing now.

"Addison, promise me that you will go to Paris, and all those places you want to go. No matter what happens."

"You have my word, Brontë. We will go together, my love."

Brontë smiled. "I would love to go with you," she whispered, the smile turning dreamy as she closed her eyes.

Wesley's voice spoke urgently from behind Addison.

"Oh God, Brontë. We do not think you are supposed to go to sleep! Please do not go to sleep. I need you." Addison curled around Brontë's body as Brontë's eyes slid shut. "Do not go to sleep, Brontë. Do not go to sleep," she sobbed.

"Forgive me Addison, I..." Brontë tried with everything she had, but the darkness beckoned her and the pain was becoming too great. After one final valiant struggle to keep her eyelids open, she lowered them. Her last thought before falling into darkness was a wish that Addison Mari Le Claire one day be as happy as she had made her.

ADDISON HELD THE tool tightly in her hand as she made one last final tap that sent a stone piece flying into the air. She traced the crooked lettering lovingly with her finger before picking up the shovel and continuing to fill the hole in the rain moistened earth.

"I am sorry about the headstone. I think that I did better with yours than I did with Papa's, but it is not the best. I want you to know that I will be fine, and that I know that you loved me. I want you to know that I understand that you gave your life for mine and for that I will be eternally grateful. I just wish..." Addison's voice caught in a sob. She finally regained her composure as she went back to filling the hole around the headstone.

"Papa, I know you will take good care of her. I will come back one day to visit you both. I give you my word, but I have a promise to keep to both you and Brontë. It is time for me to go to Paris." Addison kneeled in front of the two graves and laid flowers on each before kissing the crudely, but lovingly, carved headstones. "Take care of each other until we meet on the other side. I will always carry you both in my heart." Addison stood to her full height, picked up her hat and pushed it firmly down on her head. She took one final look at the headstones, a soft smile on her face.

"Everything all right, my love?" Brontë asked as she placed a hand on the small of Addison's back. Addison put her arm around Brontë's shoulders and they looked at the two headstones nestled together in the beautiful clearing.

Elizabeth Madison Markby and Addigo Le Claire were finally

together in death, if not in life.

"Everything is fine, sweetheart. How is your head?" Addison gently stroked the red scar with her thumb.

"It is fine. I just wish he had not hacked my hair like that. It was only a little scratch," Brontë said, a tad grumpily.

Addison shuddered. "It was a bit more than that. You should have seen all of the blood, Brontë. I thought for sure we were going to lose you."

Brontë hugged Addison around the waist. "I am fine, Addison, and aside from a rather short haircut, I feel the same. Like it never happened."

"Are you sure you are up to this now? We can wait a bit longer; there is no rush."

"I am ready," Brontë said, the excitement showing in her voice.

Addison leaned down and kissed Brontë's lips before turning her toward the path back to Markby. She looked back once at the graves as they faded from view, then once again as they passed the cottage that she had shared for so many years with her father. Addison turned forward, a happy grin spread over her face.

Cook, Wesley, Mary, Beatrice and Perry waited at the entry to Markby Estate, all looking very forlorn. "Why do you have to leave so early in the morning? You have hardly had a proper breakfast, m'lady. It is not even sunup," Beatrice said.

"Now, Beatrice, we have been through this before. First, my name is Addison, and second, we want to avoid the town people. They are all still very curious after the goings on and we would like to leave quietly. Especially after the paper printed the information about Victoria and her mother." Addison looked up guardedly, trying to gauge Brontë's reaction to Victoria's name being mentioned. Brontë had had a hard time with the fact that, because no one had any proof of Victoria's or her mother's crimes, there could be no charges filed against them.

Victoria and her family were free to live out their lives. Brontë was still livid over that fact. Addison told her not to worry. A woman used to little or no work, as was Victoria, could not last very long in Glen Grove.

Addison picked up two satchels and handed the lighter of the two to Brontë, frowning as she put the heavier one on her back. Stopping in front of Wesley first, she looked him straight in the eye. "Try not to be so overbearing?"

"Yes, m'la-Addison." Addison tapped him on the shoulder approvingly and bent to rub Perry's head.

"Addison, I would like to apolo—"

Addison looked up sharply from her squatted position next to Perry and spoke quietly so that only Wesley could hear. "She is all I have, Wesley," she glanced at Brontë who was in a death clutch with Beatrice and Mary. "I do not think I could go on living without her. You and Perry saved her life. You have nothing to apologize for." Perry had barked and scratched at Wesley's door until he and Cook had come out to see what the ruckus was about. After hearing part of the conversation coming from the library, Wesley had grabbed Lord Senior's hunting rifle, broken through the door and shot Thomas. Surprisingly, Thomas hadn't died. He had yet to wake, however, and when he did he would find himself in prison for murder and horribly disfigured from the gunshot wound to his face.

After saying a heartfelt goodbye to Beatrice and Mary, Addison ambled over to the woman she had known all of her life.

Cook stood near tears. "Addison, I just want to say..."

"Cook, I understand. They asked you not to tell me. You made a promise. You kept that promise. I was happy with my father. Nothing you could have told me would have made me any happier except for perhaps that my mother loved me, and I know that now. Neither of you knew that my mother had been dead for all these years. Please do not let me leave without a smile and some sweetness." Addison grinned, trying to get Cook to smile.

Cook pulled her into a tight hug and whispered into her ear. "It is Homazella."

"What?" Addison leaned back from the embrace and peered at Cook, one brow raised.

"My name." Cook whispered, embarrassed.

"Good God," Addison whispered. "That is worse than Bonnaella."

Cook nodded again, smiling as she felt the warm camaraderie that she had thought she had lost on that fateful night over a month ago.

"Stop hogging the sweetness, Addison." Brontë elbowed her way in and practically dove into Cook's arms. Much to Addison's great amusement, the both of them burst into tears simultaneously. Addison finally pried the two apart and after more goodbyes and hugs to Perry, with assurances that both she and Brontë would write, she grabbed Brontë's hand and off they went.

"You think they will be back?" Wesley asked, as he casually wiped a tear from one corner of his eye.

"They will come back," Cook said with certainty. "Despite everything, Markby is their home."

Addison watched Brontë out of the corner of her eye. Brontë could be stubborn when she wanted to. She wanted to make sure she was not in any pain or tired. "Are you sure that you are up to walking into town?" she asked Brontë, who was still sniffling and looking back periodically.

"Yes, it will give us a chance to see everything one last time before we leave."

"What is in this satchel? It seems very heavy." Addison squirmed as she heard a hollow wooden sound.

Brontë looked down at the ground. "It is something that was delivered to the house. I thought it would be nice to have something special with us on our first night in Paris."

Addison frowned and then shrugged. She would find out what this special something was soon enough, she supposed.

"We'll be back, Brontë. You have my word," she said quietly, misreading the stifled chuckle from beneath Brontë's new hat as a sob.

"I am not worried, Addison. I could be happy anywhere so long as I am with you."

Addison smiled down at Brontë, tweaking the hat so similar to her own, but in much better condition. Grabbing Brontë's hand again as they walked, she started to whistle.

Brontë sighed happily and squeezed Addison's hand. She would miss the sunrises here most of all.

Addison smiled down at her knowingly. "Hmm. You know, with those clothes and that haircut, you look like..."

"Do not even *think* of saying I look like a boy." Brontë grinned up at Addison, not in the least bit bothered.

Addison gently tugged Brontë forward and took a long look at the back of her trousers.

"With that arse? Not likely!"

Brontë stopped, her mouth hanging open in astonishment before she screamed with laughter. Addison could not help but join in. They both were wiping tears from their eyes as they resumed their journey hand in hand.

"What are you going to tell people?" Brontë asked quietly, a contented smile still on her face.

"About what, love?" Addison kissed the small hand that she held, her eyes fixed on the skyline in front of them.

"About us. People are sure to wonder who we are, two women, traveling alone." Brontë gazed up at her dark-haired companion. "Will you tell them that you are Addison Mari Le Claire, the Lady of Markby Estate?"

Addison looked down at Brontë suspiciously for a moment, surprised by the gravity of the question, then shook her head and chuckled a little. "No, I think I will tell them I am Addison Mari Le Claire, the caretaker's daughter."

Brontë squeezed Addison's hand as she blinked back tears of pride.

"Ahh, come on, leaky eyes. Be happy, my love. We are together for as long as you want me."

Brontë looked up at Addison and slowed her walk. "Then that will be for a long time indeed." They smiled at each other and continued their walk simply enjoying each other in companionable silence.

"What will you tell them about me, then?" Brontë asked curiously.

"What do you mean, Brontë?"

"Who will you say I am? I probably cannot pass for your sister."

"Oh, that is easy; you are my servant, of course," Addison said, and after a quick slap to Brontë's arse, she took off running up the trail. Brontë shook her head and watched the tall figure lope up the trail, unknowingly carrying Brontë's instrument of revenge tucked firmly in her satchel. Brontë took one final look back in the direction of Markby Estate and, with a final bittersweet smile, ran to catch up to her Lady.

The End

Also by Gabrielle Goldsby
a book from
Regal Crest Enterprises, LLC

Wall of Silence

It was supposed to be an average bust. Minimal backup. Minimal trouble. But everyone has their limit and Foster Everett has just reached hers.

In a blinding rage Foster makes the first mistake that she can't talk her way out of. A cover-up ensues, and Foster's guilt is left to fester. Ultimately, the death of a close friend proves to be her undoing and Foster begins numbing herself at a neighborhood bar. There she meets 26-year-old Riley Medeiros, the one person strong enough to see Foster's painful secrets and not turn away. And when Foster is forced to run, it's Riley who offers her sanctuary. A small cabin on the California coast becomes Foster's safe haven, and it is there that she begins to get to know the extraordinary woman that is Riley Medeiros. But, like all secrets, Foster's will come back to haunt her. And like even the most carefully built walls, the ones surrounding Foster will eventually crumble and she will find that not all secrets are what they seem.

ISBN 1-932300-01-5

Gabrielle Goldsby resides in the Pacific Northwest with her partner of five years. Though *Wall of Silence* was her first published novel, it was written well after the completion of *The Caretaker's Daughter*. She is currently hard at work on a new novel.

Printed in the United States
22265LVS00002B/210